April 28, 1995

Dear Jackie & Ste...
    I hope you enjoy
their stories, but now that
you're _ten_ perhaps you'd have
more fun writing your _own_.
    Congratulations
        and
    Love,
            Ann

PENGUIN BOOKS

THE LITERARY LOVER

Larry Dark is the editor of *The Literary Ghost* and *Literary Outtakes*. He lives in New York City with his wife, the writer Alice Elliott Dark, and their son.

THE
LITERARY
LOVER

Great Contemporary Stories of
Passion and Romance

EDITED AND WITH AN
INTRODUCTION BY

LARRY DARK

PENGUIN BOOKS

PENGUIN BOOKS
Published by the Penguin Group
Penguin Books USA Inc., 375 Hudson Street,
New York, New York 10014, U.S.A.
Penguin Books Ltd, 27 Wrights Lane, London W8 5TZ, England
Penguin Books Australia Ltd, Ringwood, Victoria, Australia
Penguin Books Canada Ltd, 10 Alcorn Avenue, Toronto, Ontario, Canada M4V 3B2
Penguin Books (N.Z.) Ltd, 182–190 Wairau Road, Auckland 10, New Zealand

Penguin Books Ltd, Registered Offices: Harmondsworth, Middlesex, England

First published in the United States of America by Viking Penguin,
a division of Penguin Books USA Inc., 1993
Published in Penguin Books 1994

10 9 8 7 6 5 4 3 2

ISBN 0-670-84580-9 (hc.)
ISBN 0 14 01.7164 9 (pbk.)
(CIP data available)

Printed in the United States of America
Set in Granjon
Designed by Ann Gold

For Ali—
friend, colleague, partner, and more

Contents

Introduction

by Larry Dark

A man and a woman, lovers, are walking down a city street at night. She complains that her underpants are riding up. He reaches up under her skirt and pulls them down. She shivers, then steps to the side, leaving her underpants lying on the sidewalk. He picks them up and slips them into his coat pocket. Later, he reflects on this as a pivotal incident in their relationship:

> He had loved that shiver, that spasm she could not control; for love must attach to what we cannot help —the involuntary, the telltale, the fatal. Otherwise, the reasonableness and the mercy that would make our lives decent and orderly would overpower love, crush it, root it out, tumble it away like a striped tent pegged in sand.

This scene, and the accompanying insight, are from John Updike's "Love Song, for a Moog Synthesizer." It is significant that the word "synthesizer" appears in the title because lasting relationships often result from the synthesis of the opposing attributes mentioned in this passage. After all, what is falling in love but succumbing to the involuntary, telltale, fatal aspects of another person? Yet for love to be real, to be more than an obsession, we must also bring to bear the qualities of reasonableness, mercy, decency, and orderliness.

To extend Updike's metaphor, if love is the striped tent, then each story in *The Literary Lover* presents circumstances that test the pegs securing it—how deeply they have been driven in, and how firm is the ground that holds them. The teenaged couple in Rachel Ingalls's "Faces of Madness," for instance, are undone by an accidental pregnancy and parents hostile to their relationship. A lack of decency and mercy prevents their love from taking hold. The husband and wife in Richard Bausch's "Letter to the Lady of the House" must find new ways to remain interested in one another after nearly fifty years of marriage. The ground has been weakened by too much orderliness and reasonableness.

These two sets of couples, from the first and last stories in the anthology, are the oldest and youngest found in *The Literary Lover*. Age was an obvious criterion for putting the stories in order, but it also allowed for an evolving consciousness of love with all of its heartache and heartbreak, intense pleasure and deep disappointment. The youngest lovers are teenagers and, as might be expected, innocents. The high-school-aged protagonist of Steven Millhauser's "The Sledding Party," for instance, is deeply shaken by an unexpected declaration of love from a boy she thought was just a friend. The older lovers are more experienced and usually wiser for it, though not necessarily any happier. The stories with more mature characters allow readers insight into a subject rarely taken up in popular culture—passionate, romantic love between older men and women. In addition to the septuagenarian husband in Richard Bausch's "Letter to the Lady of the House," we encounter, in "Instruments of Seduction" by Norman Rush, a woman of nearly fifty who has mastered the art of seducing men using guile rather than beauty and who has succeeded in taking more than three hundred lovers without arousing her husband's suspicion.

"Instruments of Seduction" ends with a lovers' embrace, but many of the stories in *The Literary Lover* go further, presenting unapologetically frank and vivid descriptions of lovemaking. What distinguishes these passages from pornography is that skillful literary writers use sexual description to advance plot and to define character, rather than

merely to titillate the reader. The erotic "Jewel of the Moon" by William
Kotzwinkle tells of the teasingly slow consummation of a marriage and
of how a clever husband creates desire in his young bride. In contrast,
the frenzied, almost comical efforts of the male protagonist of Harold
Brodkey's "Innocence" to bring his lover to orgasm have more to do
with his overreaching ambition and eagerness for attention than they
do with his lover's needs and desires.

Joyce Carol Oates uses explicit sexual description brilliantly to il-
lustrate her adulterous heroine's predicament in "Morning." A turning
point in the story occurs when Lydia meets her married lover in a motel
room just before he is due to go off on vacation with his wife and
children. After waking from an overlong, post-coital nap, Lydia tele-
phones her husband to tell him she will be late for a social engagement.
He senses something is wrong. While Lydia tries to reassure him, her
lover begins to fondle her. She continues to converse with her husband
even while succumbing to her lover's advances, eventually dropping the
telephone receiver (and her marriage) to the floor. Through Oates's
frank description, Lydia's emotional dilemma is made physical, her
duplicity literal, as she experiences the simultaneous pulls of a lover
and a husband.

Quite a few stories in *The Literary Lover* concern adulterous relationships, but not because the writers are advocating promiscuity. Conflict is essential to literary fiction and adultery is a rich literary subject
because it presents the double conflict of a test to an existing relationship
and the challenge of a new one. The arc of a love affair is also better
suited to the length and structure of a short story than is a lifelong
relationship with its many ups and downs and uneventful stretches. In
the stories found in *The Literary Lover*, as in life, the motivations of
men and women entering into adulterous relationships are diverse,
ranging from the misery of a bad marriage to indifference born of
boredom. In David Leavitt's "Houses," for instance, a real estate agent
leaves his wife for a man and is faced not only with choosing between
a wife and a lover but also between two conflicting ways of life. At the
other extreme, the strong-willed, independent poet in Alice Walker's
"The Lover" has an affair simply for the pleasure and adventure it
affords her, with no intention of ending her comfortable marriage.

The tensions of married life, of fulfilling the sometimes conflicting roles of lover and partner, is the subject of several stories. In Maria Thomas's "Come to Africa and Save Your Marriage," dual infidelities under trying circumstances bring a marriage to the verge of destruction. In Ward Just's "Costa Brava, 1959," a young couple takes a European vacation after the wife suffers a miscarriage. In the unfamiliar, neutral setting of coastal Spain they each contemplate the strangeness of sharing a life with another person. Able for the first time to see each other clearly, the young husband and wife begin to take steps toward sharing their grief and salvaging their marriage.

One of the most difficult aspects of love is that it involves two people, each with his or her own hopes, expectations, and desires. To idealize or demonize others, to burden them with our preconceived notions and false expectations, is to objectify them—that is, to treat them like objects rather than as autonomous persons. Such an attitude is difficult to avoid because we bring such high hopes and demands to all relationships, especially romantic ones. Objectification, a recurring theme in *The Literary Lover*, can present a nearly insurmountable obstacle to achieving true intimacy. In Edna O'Brien's "The Love Object," the protagonist objectifies her married lover to protect herself from being hurt, but in the end she falls prey to her own warped view. An aging London impresario, in Doris Lessing's "The Habit of Loving," fails at his last stab at a satisfying relationship because of his overpowering need for the feeling of being in love, an impulse which makes him incapable of honestly appraising his young wife.

Not every story in *The Literary Lover* is about marriage or adultery, innocence or objectification, and none is about these themes alone. What led me to choose these twenty stories is the clarity and truthfulness of each writer's vision and the original way each treats the subject of romantic love. While instances of passion and romance make for good love stories, it is moments of reflection and deep insight into specific characters and situations that make them literary. Extending John Updike's metaphor further, the power of a good short story ultimately resides in the ability of the writer to open him- or herself up to the involuntary, the telltale, and the fatal, and to temper these impulses through the reasonableness of narrative and the mercy of words.

*The
Literary
Lover*

Rachel Ingalls

Faces of
MADNESS

Four other boys in William's class shared his name. At home he was Will. At school someone else was called Will; two were Bill and one went under a middle name. Only William was given the full, formal version.

His family had money. They owned a large house in town and a summer place at the beach. He was closer to his cousins—until they moved away—than to any of the boys and girls in his class. Everyone liked him, but he had no special companions. He had pets: as a child he'd kept mice, frogs, goldfish, and a dog his parents had bought for him when he was two. The dog lived to be almost thirteen and died of kidney disease. After that, William didn't want another pet. His energy went into the car he was learning to drive.

When he wasn't out on the road, he'd spend his time playing phonograph records. He had hundreds, most of them highlights from Italian operas. He got interested in opera by listening to the radio. He liked the tunes. For years he knew nothing about the stories that were meant to accompany the music—in fact, he had no idea that the songs were intended to be played in any definite order. Later he studied the stories from booklets that came with his boxed sets. He knew the characters' names; he was familiar with their lives. The young men who sang the heroes' parts were soldiers and scholars, dukes and princes. Sometimes they were in disguise: that was the way life was then, apparently. And they loved. That hadn't changed. They were like real people to him. They were like himself. Of course, they were also melodramatic and silly, but however inane the people and the plot, the music always won out. The music persuaded him so far that he even began to like the faults as well as the virtues of opera. He was captivated by the ludicrous misunderstandings, the eccentric motives and contrived emotions, the coincidences that could never happen.

He also understood that sometimes the kind of voice a composer was writing for would determine the style of the music. In quite a few of these operas, for instance, there was a mad scene. When a coloratura soprano was in the cast, you could be fairly sure that before the last act she'd be crazy, although still able to hit a high E. Almost always, the reason for her mental collapse was desertion or betrayal by her lover, whose cloak she would press to her heart as she trilled away at the high bits. The traditions of stage madness demanded that the more crazed a girl became, the higher she sang. Purity of tone would indicate the intensity of her love and pain. Another custom governed the color of her dress: it had to be white, and of a simple, shiftlike design. You were supposed to think it was her nightgown, and that she'd be too distracted to want to change her clothes, or perhaps to remember how to. Occasionally, the nightdress resembled some sort of tattered bridal garment she'd put on, under the impression that the hero would call for her in just a minute, to take her to church and make her his wife. Her complaint might not have been insanity as the twentieth century knew it, but more a kind of madness peculiar to the dictates of Romanticism.

As his knowledge and appreciation grew, William longed for the world the operas described: the emotions of other people, given to him by the music; the place where grand events took place, usually in the distant past or at the time when the music had been composed. That

time, too, was gone. But all times in opera were equal; fictional and
historical past occupied the same world. It was the world where William
wanted to live. The time of Romance seemed more real to him than
Korea, the Second World War, the Depression, the First World War,
the Founding Fathers, and all the rest of it. A century or so made no
difference to him, nor did the setting. People still felt the same, no
matter where they were; love, hate, jealousy, the urge to kill, to die, to
sacrifice, to capture beauty: emotions didn't change. But a small American town in 1958 wasn't an ideal stage on which to express emotion.
You could get into trouble just trying to park at the side of the road
with a girl.

He'd been out in his new car one night, with a girl from the class
above his, when a policeman sneaked up and shone a flashlight at them
through the window. William came home raving, asking his parents
what kind of man would take a job like that—what kind of pervert?
His father laughed. William said, "Somebody old and ugly and envious;
some slob that hates anyone young. He wanted to see my license and
know all about the car and—I bet he wasn't even on duty. He was
probably one of those peeping toms. I'm going to report him."

"Don't do that," his father told him. "He can say he was checking
the car. To see if it was stolen, or if you'd had the brakes tested. Anything
like that."

"He wasn't checking the car. He was checking on us, to see if we
were making out."

"They just have to make sure you're not doing anything wrong,"
his mother said.

William thought he was going to choke. He threw out his arms
and stamped on the floor. "Wrong?" he said. "Jesus Christ!"

"Will, I don't want to have to keep asking you to watch your
language."

He marched up to the sideboard, back to the table, and out of the
room. His father called after him, "That'll teach you to park a little
farther out of town."

He went down to the basement room his parents had let him make
into a music studio. He put a record on the turntable. His anger and
frustration flooded away on a tide of music. The violence, intimacy,

and commitment of the emotions operas dealt with, the exaltation they allowed you: it was all wonderful. Small towns in America didn't leave any margin for that kind of uplifting experience. They didn't even let you try it out in your own car.

He was in his third year of high school when he started going out with Jean. She was two years younger than he was. His mother didn't approve of that. She didn't trust Jean's parents either, who were ordinary people no one had ever heard of. She had sound instincts about that sort of thing; his father thought so, at any rate. Once William knew what his parents' attitude was going to be, he spent a lot of time going out with other people in his class. And he met Jean in secret.

Secrecy speeded up the affair, as did the knowledge that there were hindrances set against them. They met and embraced in an isolation as charged with expectancy as any midnight assignation between soprano and tenor. All they needed to heighten their passion was an appreciation of danger. But the dangers were so obvious that they overlooked them.

Their conversation was all of abstract things. First of all, they agreed on how wrong most people—especially the older generation—were about everything. Then they talked about love and about art. And poetry. They both wrote poems; they had written poetry long before they had anyone to write it to.

He'd have liked to listen to his records with her, but she was shy about coming to the house. She knew his parents still thought she wasn't the kind of girl he should be seeing. He had a car and good clothes and enough money to take a girl out dancing, to the movies, to restaurants. That should have been in his favor. What it actually meant was that Jean's parents suspected him of being unreliable: financial freedom leads to other freedoms.

They made love outdoors at night and then in the daytime too. As his father advised, William parked the car far enough away from the center of town not to attract attention. The fact that neither of them had sisters or brothers made it easy to keep their secret, although later it would mean that they'd have no allies against their parents' generation. And at school they hadn't found anyone to take the place of brothers and sisters. It seemed that all their lives they had been waiting for each other. William had his gang of pals, none of them very important to him. Jean was temporarily without anyone she wanted to confide in. She'd had two best friends, but both of them had left school. Her best friend had moved to another town the year before. William had taken the place of best friend.

They wrote poems to each other, and also letters. Sometimes they'd mail their poems, sometimes one of them would just slip a piece of paper to the other between classes. To exchange a look among a group of people, to brush by each other so that their hands touched, set them alight: to know, when nobody else knew.

They lost interest in schoolwork. When they weren't falling asleep over their books during the day, they'd want to laugh and joke. They liked sneaking into the back row of movie theaters to watch B features while they fed each other popcorn and tried to see how much they could do with each other before anyone noticed.

At night he'd stand outside her house while she shinnied down the tree that grew in front of her bedroom window. Later on, he'd take up his post again as she climbed back. They blew kisses to each other. He'd take long walks or drive around for a while before returning to his parents' house. When he got back, he'd turn the volume down on the phonograph and play his records. He'd sink into the harmony— his breathing, his skin, his whole body aligned to the sound of passion in the voices: the delicious pain of love, the beauty, the intensity. To be able to sing like that, he thought, would be like being able to fly. And now that he was a lover himself, he understood: that was what it was all about—desire and suffering, betrayal and madness, reconciliation, the joy of being united in love.

Long ago, opera had taken the place of a friend. Now that he had someone of his own, he hadn't lost the affection for it, but its use had changed. It supplemented his life, where before it had been a substitute. Jean had become his life.

Eventually, after several months, Jean got pregnant. She didn't tell anyone. Even though her period had never come late before, she hoped and expected and prayed that it was late just this once, and it would come at any moment. When it was three weeks late, she still hoped, doggedly and miserably. She threw up twice—once after she'd been drinking, so that didn't count. Her breasts began to hurt. But she told herself that if something had gone wrong with her period, she'd probably feel strange symptoms anyway.

Eleven days after she'd missed the second period, she told William she thought she might be pregnant. She might be; in fact, she was sure now: she was. She'd have to have an abortion straightaway. How could she get one—what could they do?

William was so amazed that for a while he could only say, "It's all right." Then he told her he blamed himself for not trying to be more careful. He wasn't the one who'd get stuck, so he hadn't worried. He should have thought about her. Now that it had happened, he said, he wanted her to have the baby. It was his; he was proud of that. And it was natural. To do anything against that, he figured, would be somehow wrong. He was stunned by the idea of a new life that the two of them had made together. "Because we loved each other," he said. The only reason why she didn't want to have it was that all the people in town were such hypocrites: wasn't it? She was afraid that they'd take it out on her, start talking about morality, and do a lot of preaching at her. But everything was going to be all right. He wouldn't let them.

It wasn't going to be easy. He could imagine how bad things would be for her. Unless she got married. Everybody knew what became of girls who got pregnant: everyone talked about them and the girls went away forever, or they came back later and no one talked about where they'd been. They were like women who had died.

If she got married, then it would be all right. She would escape from her parents, who were wrong about everything anyhow, and she'd be with William. He won her over. She'd do anything for him. He'd tell his parents. They wouldn't be able to fight it; they'd have to let him marry her in one of those states where the age limit was lower. And if his father and mother accepted that, the rest of the town would, too.

He talked to her parents. They were impressed by him and by his family. "As far as I'm concerned," he said, "we're married." But Jean's mother thought, despite everything, it was a terrible shame—the ruin of at least two lives—for a girl to have a baby at such a young age: she'd be only just sixteen when it was born. And Jean's father got to

thinking there should be some legal safeguard for his daughter, so that
in three or four years' time, or even ten, she and the child would be
provided for. Young men sometimes changed their minds.

"I'll see to all that," William said. He was still only seventeen. He
wouldn't be eighteen till the spring. He hadn't told his own parents
anything yet. Knowing them and their views about who was or wasn't
worthwhile, he'd prejudged their reactions and chosen, for the moment,
not to speak out. In any case, he'd wanted to be with Jean when she
had to face her mother and father. The money he'd have when he was
eighteen would not be much, but it would be enough to start out on.
If he had to, he could handle everything all by himself, though he'd
rather have his parents' help. He'd rather have them understand, too.

He was still mulling over the wording of the speech that would
overwhelm his parents when he was beaten to the punch by Jean's
father.

Her father had first of all let his daughter know what he thought
of her. "This is all the thanks we get," he'd said. His wife backed him
up. Jean ran upstairs, crying, and slammed her door, leaving her parents
to talk about what should be done.

Her father decided there ought to be a discussion between all four
parents on the matter of financial arrangements. He telephoned William's father. He assumed that the man knew what was going on.

Jean's father talked to William's father for twelve minutes. He
brought up the subjects of rent, food, clothes, the price of baby carriages,
hospitals, and so on.

William's father didn't say much, except that he'd remember all
the points raised: he'd have to go over them with his wife before he
could say anything definite. He left the office immediately. He went
into conference at home with his wife. Together they greeted William
on his return from school.

He opened his heart to them. They closed theirs to him. They told
him that he had no idea how difficult it could be for a young couple
with a baby—especially hard for a girl, who would have to become a
mother before learning how to be a wife.

"We know that already," William said. "What it means to be man
and wife. We don't need a piece of paper."

"Without the piece of paper, and without being the right age, the child may not be legally yours," his father told him. "Or hers."

"That can't be true."

"She's still considered to be under the care of her parents. And now her father's trying to get money out of us. He called me up at the office, started talking about hospital bills and the price of maternity clothes and everything. He seemed to think I knew all about it."

William was sorry about that, he said; he'd been racking his brains, wondering how to tell them: he'd known from the beginning that they didn't like Jean.

His parents denied it; they had nothing against the girl. Of course not. But as things stood now . . . well, there were so many difficulties.

If they wanted to, his father told him, her parents could get really nasty. She was still a minor. If William were one year older, they could charge him with rape on the mere fact of her age, and send him to jail. Even as it was, they could put her into some kind of reform school until she was eighteen. For immorality.

"That's crazy," William said. "And disgusting."

"Could you support a wife and child right now?"

"Yes," William said, wanting to win the argument.

His father didn't tell him he was wrong. He simply pointed out how hard it would be, and added that the kind of salary and career available to a college graduate was a lot better than what a man could hope to work up to after five years of living from hand to mouth. William thought that over. He saw that he'd have to have his parents' help. He knew he'd be able to count on them as long as he fell in with most of their advice.

He began to believe he might have been wrong about the way he'd handled the talk with Jean's parents. If that was the line they were going to take, they weren't worth considering, but naturally Jean would want to think there was an excuse for them. He also felt ashamed of not having trusted his own parents, who both appeared so reasonable, and so worried; they weren't angry at all.

His parents worked on him, in perfect counterpoint, until he agreed that he wouldn't see Jean for two weeks. It was an unsettling time for everybody, they said. Two weeks would be enough of a breathing space to get everything straightened out. They asked him not to telephone Jean during that period; they wanted a free hand. They didn't put a ban on letters, since his mother had long ago searched his room and found the letters Jean had written to him. Nowhere in them had there been a hint of the pregnancy, but in one letter Jean had written something about the ornamental stone jar in which the two of them had started to hide their more fervent correspondence: the jar stood at a corner of the crumbling terrace wall that bounded three sides of the old Sumner house. The house had been shut up for years. Weeks before she could have known that the letters would make any difference to her life, William's mother knew the look of Jean's handwriting. She knew it nearly as well as she knew her son's.

William wrote a letter to Jean. In it he told her about the talk he'd had with his parents. Things would turn out all right—there was nothing any parent could do to keep them apart for long, but he didn't want her to imagine he'd stop thinking about her if they just didn't see each other for a few days. They were always going to be together in their thoughts. And he hoped she'd stay certain; even though they were close in spirit, he was a little afraid of her parents' influence. He was especially worried that she might be persuaded to think everything he and she had done together was bad.

He put the letter inside the terrace urn. His mother retrieved it. She then made a surprisingly good forgery of Jean's handwriting on paper she had bought that day. Each pale-pink sheet was printed at the upper-left-hand corner with a picture of forget-me-nots tied up in blue ribbon. The paper had been a lucky find: she'd bought a whole box; it was the same kind Jean wrote her letters on. William would never suspect his mother of using such paper.

The forged letter asked why his parents couldn't help out with the money, because her father was getting really mad about it, and actually, she was beginning to wonder, too; after all, he wasn't the one who was going to have the baby. Anyway, her father had told her that William's father had said something about her, something kind of insulting, so she realized that William had been *discussing her with his parents.* She thought that was a pretty cheap thing to do; in fact, it was measly.

William's mother was proud of her letter. She thought she'd hit the tone, the phrasing, and the slang just right. Her pleasure was malicious, but her purpose wasn't. She believed that William had been maneuvered into fatherhood by a girl from a family of no background; and that if events were allowed to take their course, he'd hate the girl in a few years. It would be better to break up the affair now.

His father, too, was ready to protect William. He'd run across men like Jean's father before. He telephoned back and laid it on the line: he and his wife had no responsibility toward a girl who said she was pregnant by their son. Attempts to extort money out of their family—phoning him at his office, yes—could end in criminal prosecution. Naturally, Jean's father was free to try to prove that some compensation was owed. But if there was to be a legal battle, money would win it in the end.

Jean's father felt a deep sense of unfairness and injury after the phone call; he felt it more and more as he continued to brood about it. Every time you tried to make excuses for people like that, he thought, they turned around and ran true to type. They had no respect for other families. They considered themselves better than other people. He couldn't quite bring himself to face the fact that it had been a disastrous move to raise the question of money, and that by doing so he had probably wrecked his daughter's hopes of marriage. He'd never really had anything against William, only against the double sin of sexual trespass and pregnancy. But he'd been intimidated. He didn't like the idea that somebody in his family could end up in a law court. They'd always been law-abiding—all of them.

He told his wife that it wasn't going to be the way they'd hoped; they couldn't expect any help from the boy's parents. They'd have to start thinking about those doctor and hospital bills, not to mention the embarrassment of having to go on living in the town afterward. Jean's mother got scared. She had never done anything underhanded or shameful; she'd worked hard and made a good home for her family. And if Jean didn't get married now, it would be her parents' lives that would be destroyed, not hers.

She had a little talk with her daughter. She told her that no matter how things went, Jean wasn't to worry: it still wasn't too late to do something about it.

Jean pretended to be reassured. She wrote a long letter to William, asking him what was going on at his house, and telling him that her mother had changed, and wanted her to get rid of the baby. She had to talk to him, she said.

She ran to the Sumner house, to the urn on the terrace. She left her note and hurried away with the letter she'd found addressed to her in an excellent facsimile of William's handwriting.

His mother saw her come and go. And she picked up the letter meant for William. If she or her husband had stopped to think, they might have said to themselves that many boys and young men will sleep with the wrong kind of girl because there's nobody else around, but that this affair wasn't like that: the two were in love. Traditionally, that was supposed to make all irregularities acceptable. Therefore, if the parents disapproved so violently, it might be because they actually wished to discourage the young from loving.

William's mother realized that she could keep up the letter game for only so long. It would be stupid to assume that one of them wouldn't catch her at her substitution; or that they wouldn't come across her while trying—in spite of their promises, and against their parents' wishes—to meet each other. Nor did she look forward to having her husband discover the exact extent of her interference. She could justify her actions if she had to: a mother has excuses not available to other people. But she'd rather not have to. All she had said in the beginning was that she was going to read the letters, in order to figure out the right way to approach William: as long as she was free to act on her own, everything would be fine. Of course, if her husband wanted to read their letters himself . . . no, he'd said; he didn't think it was necessary to read anyone's letters, but he'd leave the matter to her.

She was excited, frightened, and should have been worried about her rapid heartbeat. The thrill of participating in William's drama, of saving her son from making a mess of his life, kept her at fever pitch. She was happy. She'd never had a real romance herself: the secret, stealthy, illicit going back and back again to temptation. She was having her romance now, fired by the heroic part she was playing—a woman rescuing her innocent son from ruin. She didn't blame the girl especially; it was just that a girl like Jean wasn't good enough. Girls like that wanted to get married. It didn't usually matter who was picked out to marry them. Jean would have to release her hold on William and find someone else.

Jean took her letter home and read it. She cried over it. Everything was going wrong: he was changing. If she could see him and try to talk to him, she wouldn't know what to say. His letter almost sounded as if he didn't love her anymore. But that couldn't be true.

Her mother made an excuse to the school, to keep Jean at home for a while. She thought her daughter needed time to think. Besides, Jean was looking so unhappy that her classmates might start to ask her questions; or she might just decide, out of a need to feel comforted, to talk to someone herself. Then, later, if she had to be sent away, everyone would know why. That wouldn't do. And William was there at school, too. Although he wouldn't be able to see Jean without cutting classes, he was there. He might wait around for her in the morning, or later in the afternoon.

At the same time, William's mother asked her husband to arrange for their son to take a break from school. She wanted to make sure that William and Jean didn't get a chance to plan anything on their own. She made the first suggestion herself: that William might like a change of scene for a short while, to get things clear in his mind; how about a trip somewhere nice for a couple of weeks? Nassau, perhaps; with his uncle Bertram. William said no. He couldn't leave now. As soon as the time limit was up, he'd get together with Jean. He already wished he hadn't given his word.

He couldn't bear the thought that Jean had lost faith in him. He broke his promise to his parents and went over to her house at night. He stood under her window, where the light was out. He threw small stones up at the panes. If he'd had a long black cloak, he'd have felt safely disguised: covered by darkness, the lover's friend. On the other hand, it would have made throwing the stones even more difficult. It was impossible to hit anything in the dark. He might actually break the glass if he wasn't careful. He began to get mad enough to risk it. Her light went on. Then other lights came on, too, one near her window and another downstairs; her parents had heard. He retreated. Maybe she hadn't realized he'd been there.

He looked for her at school. He asked one of the girls in her class: where was she? "She's sick," the girl told him. But it wasn't anything serious, she said. Just a bad cold.

He stopped playing his records so often. He couldn't concentrate on them. The most beautiful parts upset him, and everything in between made him impatient. He wrote a letter to Jean, though he knew she wouldn't be able to get it till she was better. He worried about her. She shouldn't be sick if she was carrying a child. He put his letter in the urn and took out the one that was waiting there for him.

His father had a long talk with him about money and compensation, college and law school. William was so distracted he could barely understand what was being said to him. The letter he had just read, and that he believed to be from Jean, told him in plain terms how little she thought of his conduct, said there were others who wouldn't have treated her so badly, talked about his petty-mindedness on the subject of money, sneered at his mother's fur coat, claimed she could sue him, and complained that he'd talked her into keeping the baby: now she was stuck with it while he was free as a bird.

His mother was just in time to intercept his desperate answer. In its place she put a letter containing a key to a box at the post office. The letter said that William was afraid he might be followed or sent away, so it was safer to use the post office.

From then on, it was easy to deceive the young couple without danger. William protested when he was sent to the Caribbean, but he gave in; the fight was going out of him. He, too, had been given a key, to a post office box with a different number. His mother was therefore able to make her exchanges without fear that a letter would slip through. She could also use William's stamped and canceled envelopes sent genuinely from the West Indies; a single numeral altered the box number. And she brought the affair to an end quickly. She sent Jean a letter that described William going to a party given by friends of his parents. These friends had a daughter he'd met years ago, when they were children. He couldn't believe now, the letter said, how much they had in common. Although he'd always be fond of Jean, he thought they'd better both admit everything between them had been a big mistake. He felt pretty upset, but he had to be honest and say he wanted to do lots of things in life—starting with college and law school—that wouldn't be possible with a wife and child. He'd come to believe, from hearing some interesting theories on the subject recently, that it was better in every way not to start having children till you were about twenty-eight. He did realize, naturally, that in a certain sense he was to blame. But she couldn't deny that she'd said yes in the first place, and nice girls didn't—he knew that now: they just had strong principles about the right way to behave in life. You had to have those high standards in order to become a mature human being. Of course he still liked her, but he thought she'd better take her parents' advice, except not about trying to get any money out of his father, because that could land them in a lot of trouble, she'd better believe that.

The letter ended, *So I guess this is goodbye.*

Jean wrote back. She pleaded with him. She knew he couldn't have meant to send her a letter like that. She asked him to read it over, and to think about what he felt, and to try to remember the way he'd known her. She enclosed his letter. She said she loved him; she'd wait for an answer.

He didn't answer. He hadn't seen her letter. She wrote again, almost immediately, telling him that her parents were taking her out of school for the rest of the year and sending her to live with her maiden aunt in the next state. She was going to have the baby there. She gave him the address and begged him to help her: if he didn't help, they could take the baby away from her as soon as it was born. That was what they wanted—for the baby to be adopted by somebody, so then nobody would know she'd had an illegitimate child.

William still knew nothing. His mother had written him a masterpiece of a letter, filled with accusations, silliness, and platitudes. It also compared parents, saying that her father had worked all his life, which was more than you could say for his father, who spent all his time swindling people and called it big business; she didn't know why he was so stingy, either. William was going to be just the same when he grew up, which would probably be never. And she was taking her parents' advice, by the way, and having an operation, because she didn't want to have anything more to do with him: she was hoping to get a steady job someday and meet a real man, and she was staying away from home for good, so he didn't need to write any more dumb letters to her.

A key was enclosed. His mother had had duplicates made. She hadn't worked out the details of her scheme at the beginning, but everything had seemed to go very well. She stopped writing any letters herself. She merely collected and read theirs. At any moment she expected to find that William had written to Jean's parents—that would have spoiled everything: but he'd lost his trust in them. He stopped sending letters. He'd come to the conclusion, suddenly, that it was over between him and Jean. He hadn't done anything, or been able to do anything, to make a difference. She had changed; she was sorry about what had happened. She hadn't loved him, after all.

His uncle Bertram said over the phone that William was desolate: he swam, and he went out in the boat with the rest of the gang, but he was so unhappy it was pitiful to see. And he'd gotten drunk one night and passed out cold. "He's getting over it," his father said.

When William returned to town and to school, Jean had gone. He finished his school year. His mother continued to collect the letters Jean was sending to the post office. At last a letter arrived that was much shorter than the others: it said simply that she loved him but she couldn't go on—she knew they were going to take the baby away, and she was tired of everything anyway. She'd decided to kill herself.

His mother didn't believe it. Girls tried that kind of threat all the time. She put the letter with the rest of them. She kept a regular check on the mailbox. Week after week there was nothing. Nothing for months. If Jean had killed herself, if she'd died—what could anyone do? It would be too late to go back. Long ago, it was too late. But there was no question of suicide; that couldn't be. Obviously the girl had just given up, finally. There was no reason to wait for more letters. The keys could be turned in at the post office.

William did well at school. He drank at parties, but he stayed away from drugs like Benzedrine and Dexedrine, which had begun to make an impression on the college campuses of nearby states. He started to go around with a girl from his own graduating class, and then went out with her friend. He slept with both of them. He had fun. He didn't intend to get serious again. He began to feel better and to think of Jean with a sense of disappointment and revulsion. She had let him down. It seemed to him that all women would act the same way in the end. They didn't want love. Their sights were fixed on other things: safety, pride, interior decorating. He saw Jean's mother in town one day. They both turned away at the same time, instantly, as soon as they recognized each other.

He went away to college, where he also did well. And to law school. He came back briefly for his father's funeral and then, after he'd started work with a law firm, to visit his mother. She'd had a heart attack. She was only fifty-seven. William was horrified by the injustice of her illness. Because his father had been so much older, that death had seemed to come at a reasonable age. She was too young. He knew she still had hopes that he'd marry one of the girls she'd introduced him to. He hadn't come home so often as she'd have liked, either. He had been thoughtless. He'd neglected her.

She had a series of slight attacks and then the massive failure that carried her off. William phoned every relative he could think of. He asked them all to come to the funeral: stay at the house, be with him. He had nobody now. When the funeral was over, he sat downstairs with Uncle Bertram and his cousins from Kentucky. He thanked them for coming. They spent a long and raucous night reminiscing, but they were gone the next day.

Later there were the clothes to give away, the accounts to put in order, the question of what to do with the house when he was away —whether to sell it, or rent it, or leave it standing empty. There was a lot of junk to sort through. And his mother hadn't thrown out any of his father's clothes; she'd just left everything of his the way it had been.

William took a bottle of whiskey upstairs with him. He plugged in his father's portable phonograph and turned it on in the empty house. He put the volume way up. He played Verdi. He started with his father's study, moved to the attic and then to his mother's room. He was glad he was alone. He could cry without restraint.

He stuffed his parents' clothes into suitcases, laundry bags, and cardboard boxes. He threw combs and brushes and shoes after them.

He opened drawers containing half-used lipsticks and unopened perfume bottles. He discovered all his old school reports back to when he
was six years old. And he found the box that held the pink-flowered
notepaper, the sheets covered with repeated phrases scribbled as practice
for the final draft. He saw the originals in his mother's handwriting,
the bundle of letters he'd written himself, and the ones from Jean: all
of them. He went out of his mind.

He smashed the empty whiskey bottle, the mirrors, the windows,
the phonograph. His hands were cut and bleeding. He threw the un-
breakable records out of the windows and snapped the others over his
knee: all his precious collection of 78s. He picked up the chairs and
banged them down on the tables, threw vases against the walls. He
screamed unceasingly, like a monkey in the forest. He slashed all the
paintings in the house, even the ones he had known from his childhood
and had loved most—the portrait of his grandparents as children, the
view of the summer house from the bay. He tore up all the photographs
of himself and his parents, set fire to the Anatolian rug, and walked
out of the room while it was still smoldering. He took his father's bird
guns from their cases, loaded them up, and began to shoot into the
walls, sideboards, ceilings, stairs. After a while, people out in the street
called the police, who came and broke down the back door. They got
a doctor to give William an injection. He spent a couple of days asleep.

When he woke up, he didn't realize where he was. A private nurse
had been left with him. She fed him some soup and said, "You feeling
better now?" She made it plain that she expected him to answer yes.

"It was the shock," he said.

"That's right. You take it easy," she told him.

He took it easy. He began to think. He thought for the first time
in years about Jean; about how he and she had been tricked, treated
with contempt; and how his parents' hatred—especially his mother's
—had not been satisfied by merely frustrating his hopes and plans: they
had had to destroy his chance of any kind of love for the rest of his
life. Jean's chance, too. What had happened to Jean?

As soon as he was on his feet, he went to her parents' house. They
were there but they wouldn't let him in. To begin with, they wouldn't

even answer the door. His shouts and sobs convinced them that it would be better to talk him into being quiet than to have the neighbors hearing that old story dragged up again.

Her father opened the door a crack. The safety chain—a recent installment—prevented entry. "We don't want you here," he said. "Go away."

William started to explain—fast, gasping, and doing his best not to yell—that his mother had written forgeries to Jean and to him, too: she'd lied to both of them and now he had to find Jean, to ask her to forgive him, and to make it up to her.

Her father said, "We don't know where she is. That's the truth. And it's on account of you. She was staying with her aunt and she was fine, almost six months to—you know. She couldn't stand the shame. She took some kind of poison."

William stopped breathing for a moment.

"She nearly died," her father said.

"But she didn't?"

"They had three doctors working on her for twenty-four hours. They couldn't save the baby: nobody in the family wasted any tears over that. They only just pulled her through. Soon as she was getting better, she ran off. Her aunt says she told Jeannie she'd better behave herself from now on, seeing as how what she did is a crime you can get put in jail for; and she would be, if anybody wanted to arrest her for it. It would be murder. I guess she took it the wrong way, got scared the police were going to come after her. That woman never treated her too kindly, from what I can make out."

"Where is she?" William asked.

"Like I told you, we don't know. We haven't heard from her since that day. We haven't heard anything about her at all. All we know is, her aunt said her mind was a little unhinged from the time she took that poison. I reckon you'd better forget about her. That's what we had to do. It's like she was dead."

William was about to ask some more questions, when Jean's mother called out from the hallway. "What are you telling him? Don't you say anything to him." She sounded drunk. She raised her voice and

screeched, "You get away from us. Haven't you caused enough trouble?
Go on, go away!" William turned and ran down the street.

He believed what her father had told him. He went back to his
parents' house. All night long he howled and wept. He cursed his
mother, he called on Jean, talking to her, explaining. He beat his head
against the walls. He slept.

When he woke, his madness had developed into quiet conviction.
He was no longer violent; the thought just kept repeating itself in his
mind: that Jean was somewhere waiting for him, and that he had to
find her. He'd find her if he had to search the world over. He had
plenty of money: he could spend his life on it.

He got into his car and drove to the capital, where he hired a firm
of private detectives. There were several clues, he told them: the hospital
she'd been admitted to would have her name and address in its files.
It would be in the same state where the aunt lived. He could let them
have the aunt's address, but he didn't want them to go near her. They
should concentrate on the medical register; there might even be a record
of fingerprints.

He gave the agency approximate dates. Nothing could be learned
from her parents, he said. It would be better not to disturb them: they
might decide to get in touch with the aunt or somebody, and everyone
would clam up. And maybe if the detectives got close to Jean or anyone
who knew where she was, they ought to say they were looking for her
because of a case that concerned distant relatives. They could pretend
it had something to do with a legacy.

He couldn't understand why her mother and father hadn't tried to
find her. Even though they wouldn't have had the money for detectives,
they could have tried the police. It seemed to him that if you looked
at the whole story, right through to where it stood at the moment, her
parents hadn't behaved any better than his—maybe even worse, because
Jean was their own child, whereas to his mother she'd been an outsider.

His detectives also had the clue of Jean's illness—her reported illness,
anyway, which meant that she could have been in hospitals afterward.
Her father had specifically cited mental instability, so the investigation
could start there, with a check on all the public asylums and private

clinics in the general area. She might have changed her name; the detectives should concentrate on anyone who was the right age. He had photographs but he knew, as the agency men undoubtedly did, too, that people sometimes changed radically in a short space of time, especially if they'd been sick. The expression of the face, the look in the eyes, could become like those of another person. A gain or loss in weight could also make someone unrecognizable. Thirty-five pounds either way was a better disguise than a wig and glasses.

William said, "I guess maybe the thing for you to do is to go through all those places, get the possible names, and then, if you think you're on the right track, I should go see for myself."

One of the partners in the firm, a Mr. McAndrew, presented William with a businesslike sheet of facts and figures, plus an estimate of costs. "Those are the short-term calculations," he explained. "This could take a long time. But if it does, our charges would drop significantly. We believe in keeping our customers happy."

William said that all sounded fine. He hoped they'd phone soon, because he was eager for news. He got up from his chair jerkily and lurched toward the door. Ever since he found the letters, his movements had become slightly uncoordinated. And he'd fallen into the habit of looking off into space, as if searching or remembering. Mr. McAndrew might have considered William a fit subject for the clinics himself, if the princely retainer he'd pushed across the desk top hadn't proclaimed his sanity.

Weeks went by. William kept himself busy with the house. He couldn't decide whether or not to sell it. He took a leave of absence from the office. His hands healed. He hired painters to clean up the house, inside and out. And he got other workmen in to repair the damage he'd done.

Mr. McAndrew found four patients in public wards whom he described as "possible suspects." Two of them were in the same hospital. If William wanted to go look for himself, one of their operatives could take him along. William said yes, he'd like that.

The detective called early. He was driving a company car. He was young, about thirty—only a couple of years older than William. He looked tough enough to deal with the rougher side of detective work, if he had to. He introduced himself as Harvey Corelli.

"Like the tenor?" William asked. "Franco Corelli?"

"Don't know him. Call me Harvey, okay?"

"Sure. I'm Bill."

"Yeah, but you're the client. You're supposed to be Mister."

"If I call you Harvey, you call me Bill," William said. People had started to call him Bill as soon as he got to college.

"Right," Harvey said. "That suits me fine." He'd noticed the sudden far-off look his boss had mentioned. He got behind the wheel.

On that first trip, they spent a week going from one hospital to another. Harvey handled the receptionists and doctors; William took a quick look at the patient and shook his head. Sometimes it was enough just to have her pointed out in the distance.

Two weeks later they started out on a second trip. They visited three institutions, all no good. While they were still traveling, Mc-Andrew came up with some more names. Harvey passed on the information after he'd made his routine call to check in. "You want to leave them till another time?" he asked.

William said no—he'd rather keep going, and follow up as many leads as possible. They could stay in motels and go down the whole list in a few days, unless Harvey had another case he was working on.

"Only this one at the moment," Harvey said. One, to his mind, was usually one too many. He had always found it less easy to sympathize with his clients than with the people who had run out on them, cheated them, or otherwise let them have what they deserved. William was no exception to that rule, but he seemed like such an idiot that he actually had possibilities. Harvey knew the area. He could speed up the chase or slow it down. He figured that he could spin it out for a long time; he could be collecting a salary practically forever, if he played his hand right. He didn't like taking orders from McAndrew. He'd been bawled out in front of other people once: he hadn't appreciated that. He wasn't going to forget it. William, he thought, could turn out to be a pretty good meal ticket; he wasn't up to much in the way of fun, but Harvey knew the ropes: he'd get William interested somehow. It might be a good idea for all concerned to give old William something to think about besides his quest for the holy bride. There were a lot of moneybags in the family vault; Harvey could think of several uses for them.

William was lonely, so it wasn't hard, despite his mania, or obsession, or—as he preferred to think of it—love. One evening Harvey suggested that they call up a couple of girls: he knew one or two in the neighborhood. William said no, he didn't feel like it.

"Do you carry on like this all the time?" Harvey asked.

"Carry on?"

" 'No, thanks, I don't feel like it.' "

"Well, I don't."

"Never?"

"I've got other things on my mind."

"Mind isn't what I'm talking about, Bill. Come on." He called up a woman he knew. He poured William a few drinks. When the woman arrived, she dropped her coat on the bed and said, "Hey Harv, just like old times." She then whipped off her dress and underclothes. William jumped to his feet. He intended to go to his own room, but he was too drunk. He fell over the corner of the bed. Harvey picked him up and slung him on top of the bedspread. The woman threw her arm over him. His buttons were being undone, his belt was being unbuckled. He heard Harvey going out of the room.

In the morning the woman was gone. Harvey knocked on the door. He dragged William into the bathroom and gave him two Alka-Seltzers. He said, "Now you've got the hang of it, you won't have to get so plastered. Next time, we'll have a party."

"I feel god-awful," William muttered. He had such a headache that he had to wear a pair of sunglasses all day, except for the moments when he looked at the hospital patients who might have been Jean but weren't.

They kept traveling for another week. William talked to Harvey about his story. He explained why it was so important to find Jean. Harvey didn't seem to think the story was anything special. He said it was a tough break, but it happened all the time. "You got to move on in life," he told William. "You got to move forward."

William was sorry he'd said anything. That was another thing

loneliness did to people—they'd spill out all the most secret, private
details of their lives to complete strangers: they'd get drunk and try to
obliterate themselves for a time, to get rid of the past and of themselves
too, by transforming everything into talk. You could always change
events by describing the truth another way, remembering it differently.
It was a method of controlling your life, of understanding it.

Harvey, in his turn, talked. He had dozens of schemes for becoming
famous, making money, cornering the market on something nobody
else had thought of. He had ideas about travel, international finance,
import-export. He wanted to buy a boat someday and trade between
Florida and the islands, like everybody else: that was where the big
money was.

William nodded and said, "Yes, I see," and, "That's interesting."
He was looking into the distance again. Harvey phoned two girls. He
wanted an evening where he'd trade girls with William; after they'd
tried out their own, they'd swap. William said all right: he didn't mind.

Harvey wondered how far he could push William. He'd gotten him
in with the girls; the next step could be a couple of other, more expensive
habits. He didn't want to take things too fast. William looked ready to
crack. Harvey thought hard about how to get him lined up just right.

Before he could do anything, they came to a sanatorium called
Green Mansions. It wasn't green and it didn't look like a mansion: it
was a three-story brick and concrete building that lacked the architectural charm of some of the older asylums. It was privately run.

There were three candidates for inspection—young women of the
right age. Harvey saw at a glance that none of the three would fit the
photographs. The women were seated around a table at the far end of
a large hall that—on the evidence of the drawings, announcements,
and other pieces of paper tacked to the walls—was the patients' recreation room. It was the room where they'd be taught gymnastic ex-
ercises and would take part in dances. Scuffed linoleum covered the
floor. There was a piano in one of the corners. The lid was down over
the keyboard. In a place like that, it would have to be locked, too.

Right at the back, a line of folding chairs ran around three sides
of the room. Patients and possibly nurses sat together in groups. There
were no white uniforms. Many people were sitting quietly on their

own, or standing. One man who tried to sit on the floor was immediately pulled to his feet by two other men: he didn't appear to be pleading for attention—it was as if he'd temporarily forgotten that people were supposed to sit on chairs instead.

A doctor led the way across the room. William followed, keeping pace with Harvey. When they were still several yards away from the three women, William said, "No," in a low voice. "I don't think so."

"Well, why don't we sit down?" the doctor suggested. "I can tell you something about the work we do here."

Harvey made a face at William. He saw the propaganda coming: *Our worthy cause, insufficient funds, these unfortunate people.* William ignored him. He told the doctor he'd be interested to hear what he had to say. Even if Jean wasn't at Green Mansions, she might be in a similar institution; he wanted to know about anything that could have a bearing on her life.

They sat. Harvey longed for a cigarette. Signs on the walls told him he couldn't have one. More than any of the hospitals and rest homes they'd seen, Green Mansions reminded him of a school he'd been sent to once. He'd stayed for a year, hating every minute. It was a school where they were supposed to straighten you out.

The doctor talked about state funds, federal grants, and private subsidies. William nodded and looked out into the center of the floor. It was surprising how many people were just standing there, not talking to anyone—just standing alone, looking like machines that had been switched off: nothing registered on their faces. "Do you use drugs?" he asked.

"In the case of a violent patient it's sometimes advisable," the doctor answered.

"But not regular doses as a matter of policy?"

"No, of course not."

Harvey turned his head to look at the doctor. Naturally they'd give drugs as a routine. It would make all the supervisory work easier. He was pretty certain that all those places did. If you weren't loony when you went in, they'd soon mess you up enough to pass for crazy.

William wasn't looking at the doctor. He was staring at one of the

patients standing alone in the middle of the floor: a girl with straight,
orange-blond hair and a pale face that had a sweet, absentminded look.
"Jean," he whispered suddenly. He grabbed Harvey's arm. "There," he
said. "It's her."

"It doesn't look like her," Harvey said.

"It's Jean."

"Doctor, who's the thin girl with the long hair?" Harvey asked.

"That's Coralee. She's been here eighteen months now. She'd be
about five years younger than the girl you're looking for."

"That's my girl," William said.

"Her parents—"

Harvey said, "She doesn't look like the photographs, Bill."

"Well, she's changed. It's been years since those pictures were taken.
And as for her name being different, I'd expected that."

"Oh?" the doctor said.

Harvey put his hand on William's shoulder and told him they'd
better talk things over. William agreed. He'd found Jean. Nothing else
mattered.

He'd known that when, at last, they found each other, the healing
power of love ought to cure her, although in an opera the heroine
usually died at the moment of reuniting, having undergone too much.
This was real life. Jean might never recover her reason, but they could
live together as man and wife and be happy. He accepted the fact that
she'd been committed under a different name and by people who
claimed to be her relatives: naturally, if she were afraid of being sent
to jail, she'd have made up a new name for herself. She might even
have found a new home for a while. He was willing to marry her under
any name at all.

While Harvey wrote down notes about the circumstances of her
admission, William put questions about getting her out. He wanted to
know what objections there might be from the authorities as well as
from her family. He was hoping that both could be bought off: the
clinic with money and proof of good intentions, the family with belief
in his love.

Her parents—the doctor said—seeing that she seldom recognized them, found it too painful to continue their visits. They got into financial difficulties, stopped paying for her upkeep, and moved away. Coralee was to enter a state asylum at month's end.

"I know this story may sound unbelievable," William said, "but to me everything makes sense now that we're together again. I'd be glad to pay whatever Coralee owes the clinic." He spoke for a long time. He was persuasive, partly because the doctor and his staff wanted to be persuaded, but also because his need inspired him. As he dug deeper into his fantasy, until he finally merged with it, his outer actions began to appear more normal and relaxed.

"I knew her before," he said, "and lost her. But I've been looking for her. And now I've found her, I want to take care of her."

The doctor was impressed by William's story, his future plans, his wealth, and his ability to treat a madwoman with kindness for the rest of his life. He didn't consider the possibility that William himself was crazed. He promised to do what he could, and to meet again the next day. He introduced William to Coralee before escorting him and Harvey out of the sanatorium.

William took her hand in his. Her eyes moved back to the world where she was standing and where he stood, his hand touching hers. Her smile reflected the one he showed her. He told her his name, and said that he was going to see her the next day: she might not remember, but he had known her a long time ago. He'd loved her. He'd been looking for her, to rescue her, and he wanted to make her happy.

He talked to her slowly and clearly. For the first time in days, she spoke. Her voice was feeble from lack of use. Later it would turn out that part of her disability was caused by deafness, for which she'd never been tested.

"Oh," she said. "I don't remember."

"That's all right," he told her. "We'll get to know each other again from the beginning. We'll have a nice time."

She smiled again. He let go of her hand. She looked after him as he walked to the door. He turned and waved. She came forward.

She walked up to him and put her hands on his jacket. "What did you say your name was?" she asked.

"William," he told her again. "Will."

The doctor was astounded. She'd never acted that way before.

She said, "You come back soon, Will."

"Tomorrow," he promised.

As soon as they were in the car again, Harvey said, "Listen, Bill, it isn't the same one."

"This is the happiest day of my life, Harvey. There's only going to be one happier one, and that's when Jean and I get married."

"She doesn't look anything like the pictures."

William smiled. He'd stopped staring strangely or seeming to go off into another dimension. Still smiling, he said, "Her sufferings have changed her."

"I just—you ought to think it over. You could be making a big mistake."

"The mistake I made was to let you talk me into going with whores."

"You liked it fine at the time."

"I was so lonely, I couldn't stand it. Now I've found her, I'm never going to be lonely again."

"Are you sure she's the same one?"

"I'm positive. She couldn't be anyone else."

"But she is somebody else. Even if she wasn't goofy, she just isn't the right girl. Different age, different name—she's got a whole different face, man."

"Unhappiness can practically destroy people. You don't know."

"It can also prevent them from seeing what's right in front of them. I can't let you do it. Just think—maybe the real girl is somewhere waiting for you. She'd have to wait forever, if you tie yourself up with this one."

"I know you're worried," William told him. "I don't believe you're just thinking about the money and the case coming to an end."

"What's that?"

"No. I know what worries you. It's love. It makes you uncomfortable. It isn't what you're used to. You see it, and you get scared."

"Don't give me that horseshit."

"Harvey, one day it's going to happen to you. Listen—one day you're going to find the right one: the only one for you. And then you'll be happy. Like me."

"Christ," Harvey muttered. He didn't trust himself to say anything more without losing his temper. He couldn't believe that William had ducked out from under so neatly, taken the first opportunity he saw to escape: in the company of some jerk girl with a dopey smile, who wasn't even the one he'd been looking for.

William got on the telephone at the motel. He arranged through his lawyers to have people waiting for him at the house. He said that calls would be coming in soon, asking questions about him, but that everything would be all right.

And it was all right. Good credentials, his family's name, the record of their holdings, their history in the town they'd lived in for four generations, guaranteed William's fitness to remove a patient from Green Mansions. His money ensured speed.

The girl didn't mind. She'd taken a liking to William. When he spoke, she leaned into his face. He held her lightly by the hand and— once they were away from the clinic—by the arm. The drive home was made in almost total silence. At the house William helped her out of the car. He said, "This is where I live, Coralee. I hope you'll be happy here."

She looked pleased. She seemed to be taking in what was happening. "Big house," she said. William handed her over to the maid, house-keeper, and cook he'd hired. That evening he asked her if she'd marry him. She said yes. In the morning he made plans for the wedding. He also asked a doctor to come on a house call to have a look at Coralee.

He phoned the detective agency and he went there, arriving as Harvey was coming off work for his lunch hour. Harvey had registered a formal, written protest against the ending of the case. If anything went wrong with William's choice, Harvey wasn't going to be held responsible. Mr. McAndrew had taken the matter calmly; he'd been content with a quick result, a large fee, and a satisfied client who admitted to overriding the objections of the agency.

"You're really going through with it?" Harvey asked.

William beamed. "She's accepted me," he said. "She likes it here."

"I bet she does. It's better than that place she was in."

"I'm giving you a bonus. That's what I'd do anyway. But I also just wanted to say I appreciate the hard work you put in on the case, even when you didn't believe we were going to get anywhere. Well, you know what it's meant to me. It's saved my life. I want to thank you." He handed over two checks, one for the firm and one made out to Harvey by name. They shook hands. William walked to the door, went down the steps, and got back into his car.

Harvey looked at the amount on his check. He thought about William and his search, the girl he'd discovered, and the life they'd have. They were both crazy, so what did it matter? And why should he be thinking about them? They might make out fine. There was no reason to feel that what had happened was so terrible. And the check was for a lot, so what the hell?

Plans for the wedding went forward. Coralee had doctors' appointments to go to. William was told that she could live a normal life, but her mind would probably never develop. Everything had been left for too long. She didn't appear to have any mental illnesses—she was, as far as they could tell, just stupid, or—as they phrased it in that part of the world—slow. Of course she'd been sick, but that would leave her as she became accustomed to her new home. Some of her debility had undoubtedly been induced by her surroundings: first her family, then the institutions they'd put her in. With kindness and patience there would be some improvement; there always was. She might not become completely well, only recovered enough to believe everything William told her: to adopt his madness in place of her own.

She liked William. She was acquiescent, dreamy, vague. She was like someone asleep. He didn't mind. He liked her quietness. There was nothing to disturb his idea that deep down, under the different face and body, she was Jean.

He told her many times, simply and clearly, how they'd loved each other and been parted. Now that they were together again, their lives were going to be full of joy. He handed her the packet of letters his mother had kept tied with a ribbon. She held the letters to her face and smiled gently. Then she dropped them on the floor. He took her action to mean that as far as she was concerned, the past was over: they would get married and be happy.

The wedding was announced. Coralee was fitted for a wedding dress. The dressmaker called at the house to measure and alter. Coralee delighted in the fitting sessions; she played with the veil, she danced around, holding the partly completed skirt, she tried to sniff the artificial flowers. The dress was made with plenty of tucks that could be let out easily for extra width; Coralee had gained sixteen pounds since leaving Green Mansions and was still putting on weight. Apparently, the inmates had been kept on a meager diet.

The wedding was to be a small affair. He didn't invite Jean's parents—in fact, hardly anyone from his old days in the town went on the list of guests. He could have asked men and women he'd been to school with, but he hadn't kept up with them. He still said hello to people on the street when he ran into them—that was all: he'd made no effort to pick up old friendships again, and when pursued, he declined invitations. He didn't need anyone except Coralee.

He invited his lawyers, the local doctor, the dressmaker and her family, the women he'd hired to work in the house. He didn't bother to notify any of his aunts, uncles, or cousins; he thought he'd write to them afterward. As soon as Coralee got used to married life, they might take some trips, meet people; there would be time for everything. And then he'd get back to his job with the law firm. As an afterthought, he picked up the phone and issued an informal invitation to Harvey.

Harvey said he'd really like to attend, but he just couldn't: he had too much work to do. It was nice of William to ask him, he said. The truth was that after he'd banked his check, Harvey had begun to detest William and his love and the misery of it. He hated fools. He thought of them as people who had the sanction of the law to cause more damage than criminals. He didn't consider them funny or lovable.

William wouldn't have minded if nobody turned up but the preacher and a witness. He'd have had the whole business done in a registry office if he hadn't believed it would be more fun for Coralee, and more like a party, to have a church ceremony. When he saw the way she took to the white dress, with its train and veil and little crown of flowers, he knew he'd been right. She glowed with pleasure.

The dressmaker's two small nieces had been chosen to hold up the train. During the rehearsal Coralee kept turning around to peek at the children and then all three would laugh wildly. The cook's family arrived and sat proudly near the front, as William had told them to.

Other people from around town were scattered among the pews. A bass and soprano sang to piano accompaniment. The pianist was a relic from William's school days; she was blind now and had almost cried with gratitude when William telephoned her. On the day of the wedding she did a good job; the singers, too, suddenly came into their own, delivering without affectation the simple old hymns about belief in the Savior, love of the Lord. *I believe,* they sang. *I believe.* William could feel that beside him, Coralee had realized all at once where she was. He held his arm around her lightly, protectively. The singers' last words rang in the air, stopped, and echoed and left. The minister said afterward that it was one of the most moving betrothals he could remember: sometimes it was like that—the spirit would seem to be fully present. The importance or grandeur of the family made no difference, nor the size of the congregation. Sometimes it was especially touching to have just a few witnesses there, when those few had love in their hearts.

To the people in the first three pews the church didn't seem empty; they sensed only good feeling and friendliness. There were even a few strangers who had wandered in and—seeing that there was a marriage ceremony in progress—had sat down to watch. The minister felt that their presence conferred additional blessings upon the happy pair: it was as if the extra observers stood for the rest of the world, who didn't know the couple being joined together, but wished them well.

Among the uninvited audience, almost on the aisle at about the midway point, was Jean. She'd seen the announcement in the papers.

She had changed: the shape of her body, the way she sat, her hair, the expression on her face where the action of the poison she'd taken had caused scarring. The damage to the skin was mild, but it was there; it made a slight difference to the overall facial look. If her parents had been at the wedding, they would have known her. And Harvey would have recognized her from the many photographs he'd seen of her; he'd been trained to spot resemblances, even if a face had aged or been deliberately disguised.

She wasn't disguised, nor was she disfigured, although she looked old and clumsy. The doctors had told her that she was always going to have trouble with her health, and so maybe it was just as well that she didn't have a husband or children.

When she saw William with his bride, she knew it wasn't her health that was to blame for everything going wrong in her life—it was being without him. It was the fact that he hadn't wanted her.

She watched the whole ritual: the ring being put on, the kiss. She heard the promises: *till death*. And William turned around, his strange, vacant companion on his arm. He shook hands with people in the first rows; he pulled the bride along with him down the aisle, coming nearer. He bowed to a couple of women in front and to the left of Jean, then he looked at her: right into her eyes.

He moved forward, still looking at her face. He came closer, near enough to speak to her. Her lips parted, as if to shape his name: she almost said it out loud.

He smiled, his eyes going to the doorway beyond her. He passed on by. He didn't recognize her.

Steven Millhauser

THE SLEDDING PARTY

Catherine discovered that it was really two parties. The indoor party took place in the warm, lamplit playroom, with its out-of-tune piano that did not quite conceal a folded-up ping-pong table, and the outdoor party took place on the snowy slope of the Anderson back yard. From the top of the slope you could look down across the floodlit driveway to the dark, open garage at the side of the house. Under the floodlight the snow-lumped bushes, glazed and glistening, looked like crusted pastries with rich, soft centers. Now and then the inner door leading to the playroom would open, and there would come a burst of voices, laughter, and rock-and-roll, followed by sudden silence. A few moments later a shadowy, winter-coated figure would step from the garage into the glare of the floodlight, revealing itself to be Linda Shulick or Karen Soltis or Bill Newmeyer or Roger Murray or anyone else who might want to leave the hot crowded room and come into the fresh winter night. The figure would cross the driveway, trudge up the hill, and join the group beside the willow for a smoke in the cold air or a ride down the path in the snow. The good thing about two parties was that you could pass back and forth between them. You never felt trapped.

The sledding path itself was simply a wonder. The path began at the top of the slope, beside the willow, and after a sweeping curve it headed sharply down. Then came a second, lesser curve, and a little more than halfway down, the path forked abruptly. You could steer to the right and continue down to the high snow and half-buried hedge near the bottom of the driveway, or you could steer to the left and pass the wild cherry and end up in the high snow near the mountain laurel in the flat part of the yard. From the bottom of the path you could look up at the yellow windows of the playroom. To everyone who arrived, Len Anderson explained that he and his father had shoveled the path all that day; and after dinner, when the temperature had fallen to twenty-six, Len had carried out pot after pot of water, coating the path carefully with a layer of ice. That was to ensure maximum speed. Mr. Anderson was a mechanical engineer, and Len always said things like "maximum efficiency" and "ensure maximum speed." But Catherine thought it was a lovely path anyway. The snow on both sides was a foot and a half deep.

A new white Studebaker turned into the driveway, and at the same time, from the bottom of the hill, came shouts and laughter: Bob Carwin and Bonnie Baker tumbling into the snow. "Hey, Bobby boy, none of that, now!" "He did that on purpose." The night sky was a rich, dark blue. It seemed to Catherine, taking deep breaths, that she smelled the richness and freshness of the dark-blue winter night. She wondered whether it was possible to know a winter night by its smell, the way you could know a summer night or an autumn night by its smell. The Studebaker stopped at the top of the drive, and under the floodlight Sonia Holmes got out. Perhaps it was possible to smell snow. It would be a white, cool, fresh smell, like the smell of a cool white sheet. Or was snow simply an absence of smell: of the sharp green aroma of grass, the faintly acrid smell of moist earth? Bev Carlotti came over to Catherine. "I can't believe it. Do you see what she's wearing?" Sonia Holmes went into the garage.

Roger said, "Have you seen my sled? I left it against the tree. It's gone."

"Oh, look!" said Catherine. She was stunned. "Was that a rabbit?" A little animal had gone hobbling across the dark upper yard.

"A cat, I think," someone said.

"A rat," someone else said.

"A skirt to go sledding in. Nylons; the whole bit. She kills me. She's probably wearing heels. I suppose she thinks it's the spring dance."

"Well," said Brad, "at least she didn't come in a bathing suit."

"Don't bet on it. She gives me a swift pain I hate to say where. She ought to wear a sign on her chest: Look on my works, ye Mighty, and despair."

"It didn't look like a cat," said Catherine. "Unless cats hop. Cats don't, do they?"

"They might," said Roger, "in the snow. They might have to. Someone stole my sled. This isn't a bad party. At least they let you smoke."

"You sound like my father," said Catherine. "This party is not unwonderful."

"This party," said Roger, "is very unbad."

Sonia Holmes had come to the sledding party wearing nylons. Catherine imagined her long, sleek legs glittering in the moonlight as she sledded down the path, under the dark, rich-blue sky. It seemed festive. Why not?

"Maybe she isn't planning to go sledding," said Brad. "I hope she is, though. It might be worth watching—especially if she falls off."

"I bet she came to the wrong party," said Bev. "Whoops, 'scuse me, folks. I just stopped by to use your convenience. Can someone point the way to the powder room? Cath, what on earth are you doing?"

"I was looking at the moon. My eyes were closed because I was trying to see if I could tell whether the moon was out even if my eyes were closed. Parties make me feel a little insane. Listen, here's what we'll do. We'll call Mr. Holmes. Mr. Holmes, a dreadful accident has occurred. Mr. Holmes, I regret to inform you that your daughter has lost her pants. She's hiding in the cellar, Mr. Holmes. Mr. Holmes, I know we can trust you to be discreet."

"Well, could you?" said Roger.

"What are you talking about?"

"The moon. You said you were trying to tell if the moon—welcome, stranger."

"Ride down with me, Cath?" It was Peter Schiller, holding a sled.

"Sure. But let me steer, all right? Listen, do you know what Bev said? She said Sonia ought to wear a sign around her chest: Look on my works, ye Mighty, and despair."

"Ozymandias," said Peter.

Catherine looked away in sharp irritation.

"She came in a skirt and stockings," he said.

"We know."

"But you don't know what she said. When she came into the room Helen said to her, 'Are you going sledding like *that?*' She gave Helen one of her Sonia looks and said, 'I didn't think you *had* to go.' That was how she said it: 'I didn't think you *had* to go.' " Peter laughed. "Well, come on. Have you done it with two before?"

"Not exactly."

He put down the sled. "Well, it's a little tricky." He bent over the sled, pushed it lightly to the start of the path, and lay down. He looked over his shoulder. "Just think of me as a sled. Try not to get off center. I can't steer much with my hands on the inside, but I can help a little. It's better to get a running start, but we'll ask Brad to push us off this time. O.K.?"

"I'll just think of you as a sled, Peter." As she said it, laughing, Catherine was startled at the cruel and mocking sound of her words, but no one seemed to notice. Peter lay on the sled in his heavy coat and tucked-in scarf. She lay down on top of him, shifted about, and grasped the outside of the steering bar. She felt awfully high up. Her boots kept sliding off his legs. "Put your feet on the sled, Cath, it's safer. O.K., Brad. Give us a push. Easy." Brad bent over them and eased them forward along the flat start of the path. He gave a light push and released them.

Catherine steered clumsily around the curve and felt herself slipping to one side, but she managed to stay on as they swung onto the downward path. The runners rushed over the glazed snow, and she felt

herself still slipping to one side as they took the second curve and came
to the fork. She turned sharply to the left, rocking the sled and feeling
a boot drag against the snowbank. She jerked to the right, and suddenly
they were rushing at the right bank; Catherine braced herself, but
somehow they were back on the path. Half on and half off, they rushed
past the wild cherry and came to an abrupt stop in the high snow.
Catherine fell off. "Damn." She burst into laughter, lying on her back
in the snow. The sky was dark, radiant blue. The moon was so bright
that it seemed lit from within. It reminded her of the eye of a great
cat. The night was a dark-blue cat with a mad moon eye. Snow burned
on her cheeks and a soft powder of snow stirred in the air about her.
She could feel a coil of hair on her snow-wet cheek. She stretched out
her arms and began moving them back and forth in the snow, as if she
were giving semaphore signals. Peter stared down at her. "You'd better
get up, Cath. What are you doing?" "Snow-angels. Didn't you ever do
that as a kid?" He stared down at her and she burst out laughing. "Oh,
Peter, you look so bewildered!" She stood up, dusting off snow.

They trudged uphill, Peter's buckled boots jangling.

The second time it went much better: Catherine took the first curve
smoothly, swung effortlessly onto the left fork, steered past the wild
cherry, and never once felt herself slipping. She drove into their tracks
beside the blurred snow-angel, and brought them to a stop five feet
beyond their first mark.

She was exhilarated as they walked uphill. "Isn't there something
festive about snow? Festive and solemn. I can't explain it. Oh, I can.
It's festive because it turns everything into odd shapes, and solemn
because it's white, like nurses, and hushed, and very smooth and formal,
like a linen tablecloth."

Peter laughed. "That's wild. Have you got your scores back yet?"

"Not yet. Brad got 787 in Math."

"Well, he can always join the Army."

"He had to break the news gently to his mother. I hear Sonia got
an 800 in posture."

Peter burst into loud, nervous laughter.

The third time, it was Peter's turn. Catherine lay on the sled and grasped the inside of the steering bar. "Watch out for that tree, Peter. Remember old Ethan Frome." He pushed the sled, running behind as he bent over it, then threw himself lightly and easily on top of her as he took the outside of the steering bar. She could feel his chin pressing into her thick fur collar. They went much faster, took the curves well, rushed into the left fork, and flew past the wild cherry. At the bottom they came to a halt a few feet past their second mark—a record every time. She felt Peter moving her hair and kerchief away from her ear, and she heard him say "Love you" or "I love you." She stayed very still. Nothing happened. All at once the weight left her body; she heard the jangle of boot buckles and a sharp crunch of snow.

When she was sure he was going away she looked over her shoulder and saw him walking across the driveway toward the garage.

Catherine dragged the sled up the hill and stood beside the willow. He had moved away her hair and said those words. She felt violated, betrayed.

Brad came over. "What happened to Peter?"

"Nothing. He got cold, I guess."

"Would you care for company on the downward path to ruin?"

"Not now, Brad. I've had it, for a while."

"Where's Peter?" asked Bev.

"God, Peter Peter Peter. He just went inside. What's all the commotion about?"

"Nothing. You're standing there with his sled."

"That is not a sled," said Brad. "It is Peter, bewitched. Let us honor the memory of our late friend, Miss Carlotti, by sharing a ride."

Catherine handed him the sled and walked through the soft, hanging twigs of the willow into the snowy flatness of the upper yard. Her red galoshes, black-red in the moonlight, sank almost to their furred tops. The black twig-ends of some buried bush stuck up out of the snow; a small withered leaf still clung to one of the twigs, and shook slightly. The sight of the trembling leaf disturbed Catherine, and she looked away. She came to a tall, broad pine that leaned to one side, as if it had begun to fall but had changed its mind. The long lower branches, heavy with clumps of snow, grew close to the ground. A few of the branches had been broken off, leaving an open space.

Catherine bent over and entered the prickly shelter of the tree. The
outer parts of the branches were heavy with snow, but toward the trunk
the branches showed their bark. She dusted off the bark of a thick
branch and sat down, leaning back against the trunk and laying one
leg along the branch. Through black and snowy pine-needles she could
see the crowd by the willow, the bottom of the sledding path, and the
open, dark garage.

It was not possible that Peter Schiller had said those words. It
was so impossible that she wondered whether he had said something
else, something that sounded like it. She tried to think of something
that sounded like it, and began going through the alphabet: above,
dove, glove—remembering, at "glove," that in the ninth grade she
had written an awful sonnet just that way, and wondering what had
ever happened to that sonnet. Was it in the attic? Maybe he had said
"I'm above you" or "A glove for you." But she knew perfectly well
what he had said. And he had walked away. He had said it and walked
away. He had no right. And he knew it: he was ashamed. She and
Peter Schiller were friends, they had been good friends for more than
three years, but if they were good friends it was precisely because there
was nothing more to it than that. She had never thought of him in that
way. He was sweet, and irritating, and she could almost be herself with
him; she liked to tease him about his horrible French pronunciation,
and he had once written a limerick beginning "There was a young lady
called Cath, Who was better at English than Math." They were comrades. They hit it off. Catherine knew she had a playfulness about her,
even a flirtatiousness, and she needed friends who were playful as well
as intelligent. In the auditorium, where members of the National Honor
Society were allowed to sit after lunch, she enjoyed a sense of light-
heartedness, of pleasurable release from the routines and responsibilities
of school, and not everyone rose to the occasion as Peter Schiller sometimes did. The fact was, they got on well together; and that was all.
He was not her type. No one was her type. She had ridden down
with him on the sled because he had asked her, but she would have
ridden down with Brad or Roger or even Bill Newmeyer. They were
all friends.

He had moved away her hair and whispered it. She had felt his finger on her ear. Suddenly she realized that he must have removed his glove. He had trapped her on the sled and said it.

Catherine heard a jangle of boot buckles; her stomach tightened, as if she were about to be punched. She wanted to run away, over the snow, into the sky, beyond the moon, but it was only Brad. He looked in at her, bending over and resting his gloved hands, leather and wool, on his knees. Bits of snow clung to his thick orange scarf, and a thread of snow hung from one eyebrow.

"Is anything wrong?"

"No, I'm just sitting here." She gave a shrug and hugged herself. "I like it here. Did you make it down?"

"I think we went through the tree and came out the other side, but other than that. You're sure nothing's wrong?"

"I like watching from here. You have snow on your eyebrow. No, now it's worse. You have snow on your glove."

When he left, Catherine felt forlorn. Forlorn! The very word was like a bell. She was sitting alone in a cold tree, and everyone else was laughing, and sledding, and running up and down hills. He had said it, and there was no way he could unsay it. Catherine had vaguely expected to hear those words someday, just as she vaguely expected to hear "Will you marry me?"—she felt it was inevitable, there was no way around it—but they would be uttered by someone she could not even imagine. They had nothing whatever to do with anyone she knew, or with this town, or with this life. When she heard them, she would be somewhere else. She would not even be herself.

He had looked down strangely at her, lying in the snow. Now she would never know what he was thinking. She could never trust him. She wondered whether he had felt that way all of a sudden, or whether he had been feeling that way a long time. Once, in sophomore year, he had drawn a heart in the black wax of her dissecting pan. It had been a frog's heart, with labels like PULMONARY VEINS and RIGHT AURICLE. He had drawn a feathered arrow going through it.

"Hey, are you all right?"

Catherine started; she had not heard Bev come up.

"Yes, I'm fine, I'm fine. What's wrong with everybody tonight?"

"You're sitting in a tree, Cath. Nobody else is sitting in a tree."

"Well, I believe in Nature. I believe Americans ought to get back to Nature, like the Indians. God, can't a poor working girl enjoy Nature without everybody having a conniption fit? Slaving in the factory nine to five, six days a week, ten children, my husband drunk every night—"

"Hell, honey, you think you got problems. My husband don't drink, but I got ten drunk children. Listen, a bunch of us are going inside now, O.K.? I've had enough of Mother Nature for one night. Time to catch a little of the Sonia Holmes show. They've got Potato Frills, Cath. Suit yourself. I tried."

Catherine watched them tramp down to the driveway and into the garage. The inner door opened, and she heard shouts and laughter and music: piano chords, not records. Only Roger and Bill Newmeyer stayed outside, sledding hard, over and over again, with a concentration and seriousness that seemed to her beautiful. Someone smoking a cigarette came up from the house—it was George Silko—and joined them for a time, but the spirit of pure, silent concentration had been broken, and soon all three went down to the house. Catherine was alone, in her tree.

She could never go down there, because Peter Schiller was there. He had pinned her to the sled and put those words inside her, and then he had gone back to the house and left her there with the words inside. It was as if—she tried to think how it was—he had suddenly touched her breast. She felt he had delicately wounded her in some way.

A light went on over the garage: the party had spread to the kitchen. Through a sliver of window between translucent curtains she saw someone pass clearly between blur and blur. Down in the play-room someone must have opened a window, for Catherine could hear the out-of-tune piano coming from the front of the house. A voice cried "I can't find it." There was a burst of laughter. The window shut.

For a moment she had been drawn into the warm room and the laughter, and now she was banished to her cold tree. She remembered standing at the top of the slope, feeling the moonlight pour into her face. It seemed a long time ago. Catherine felt that something strange was happening, that at any moment the house below might start slowly sliding away over the snow, like a great, silent ship with yellow windows.

She heard the piano again: someone was coming to get her. From the garage Len Anderson, wearing a sweater but no coat, stepped onto the driveway. He had his hands in his pockets, and he hunched his shoulders quickly against the cold. He looked up at the willow, and then at the pine, and walked rapidly across the driveway, stopping at the side of the hill. "Catherine?" he called. She wondered if he could see her through the dark branches. "Here," she answered, feeling absurd. Len raised an arm and waved. "O.K.!" he said, and turned around and went back into the house.

She supposed they were all talking about her. Where was Catherine? Sitting in a stupid tree. Everything was strange, all the houses were about to float away, the moon was looking sorrowfully for Catherine, but no one was there.

She hugged herself in the cold, shivered dramatically, as if someone were watching, and tried to understand what had happened. She had been in one of her moods, wide open to the blue mystery of night and the festive, solemn snow. There were times when the world seemed to Catherine a whole series of little explosions, going off one after the other, and all she could do was stand transfixed, feeling it happening all around her. And so they had ridden down on the sled, and she had lain on her back in the snow, looking up at Peter Schiller's bewildered face. And perhaps, without intending to, she had encouraged him to say those words. She had caught him in her wonder. She had bewitched him. She had offered herself to the night and the snow, and poor old Peter had misunderstood. It wasn't his fault. And the longer she stayed in her tree, the more awkward everything was becoming. It seemed to her that she must go down to the house quickly, quickly, and set things right. She would behave as if nothing had happened. And then, in a moment when they were alone, she would explain that she had been touched by what he had said—really touched, Peter—but that she preferred to think of him as a dear friend. She hoped he would think of her that way too. She was not in love with anyone at all.

Catherine was so relieved that she clapped her gloved hands, sending

up a faint snowspray. She felt that if she could see him quickly, and
explain, then the words would go away, as if they had never been
spoken. Everything would be all right between them. Nothing would
have happened at all.

Catherine tried to hurry through the high snow. She had to take
big, awkward steps, and snow got into her boots. She thought of the
rabbit or cat she had seen at the back of the house. She wondered if
it had found a warm, dry place, out of the snow. On the driveway
she looked down at the little mounds of snow on her boot-toes and
stamped each foot hard. As she entered the garage and passed along
the side of a darkly gleaming car, a nervousness came over her, but
she hurried on.

The inner door opened onto a tiny hall. Wooden steps covered with
black rubber led up to the kitchen. Directly on her left was the dark-
red door of the playroom. On her right was a dusky workroom where,
on a long workbench under a dim yellow bulb, dripping coats lay
carelessly heaped.

"The mystery woman returns," said Brad from the couch. He gave
a little wave. The room was hot and dimly lit and full of smoke. She
did not see Peter. She felt her cheeks tightening and tingling in the
warmth, as if her face were being pulled carefully into place over her
skull. Ned Toomey, seated at the piano with a cigarette in the corner
of his mouth and his eyes narrowed in the upstreaming smoke, was
playing "Sloop John B." Beside him, looking intensely at the music and
holding in one outstretched hand an empty glass, stood Richie Jelenik,
singing in a deep, mournful voice. On the other side Ken Jackson stood
with one foot on the piano bench, playing the guitar and leaning close
to the music as he looked back and forth quickly from the notes to his
left hand. The two couches were full, people walked about, on the floor
in a lamplit corner Roger and Bill Newmeyer were building a high
tower with small colored blocks. "They said you were in a tree," said
Nancy Russell, and Catherine noticed that Nancy Russell's eyebrows
were not the same length. A bowl of Potato Frills appeared. A hand
held out a paper cup of ginger ale. Catherine, glancing at a window,
saw with surprise her surprised face. Through herself she saw brilliant
yellowish snow and a yellow-lit lantern on a black pole. Ned Toomey

and Ken Jackson came to the end of "Sloop John B," and Richie Jelenik put his glass down on the piano. They began to play "Goodnight Irene." Catherine moved across the room toward Brad. "I'm back," she said, and sat down next to him as he shoved over. "Isn't it awfully smoky in here?"

"It goes with the décor. We can have a tree brought in for you, if you'd like that. We could set it up by the piano."

"I had a wonderful time in my tree, thanks. All it needed was a heater. Where's Bev?"

"Upstairs, enjoying the absence of smoke, music, and teenage fun."

"I guess Peter fled up there too."

"I don't know. He was here when we came in, moping in that corner. I thought he went out again. What did you say to him, cruel woman? Oh, they're good at this one."

Ned Toomey had broken off "Goodnight Irene" and had passed without pause into a series of climbing, suspenseful phrases with his right hand. There were shouts of applause. The phrases climaxed in harsh rock-and-roll chords, and Richie Jelenik sang deeply, soulfully, soaringly:

"*Ah*
Found
Mah
Thri-hill"

"Louder!" cried Brad. "Sing it, Richie babe!"

"*Own bluebayry hih-ill*"

"Go, Ned!"

"*Own bluebayry hih-ill*"

"These guys are too much." Richie Jelenik's eyes were closed, his head flung back, his face twisted in a parody of passion; and the tense fingers of his outstretched hands were hooked like claws. His cheek glistened,

and Catherine was shocked: she thought he was crying. But she saw
that he was sweating in the close, warm air. All at once she saw a bright
green hill, covered with tall trees, ripe blueberry bushes, and winding
paths. Sunlight streamed in through the leaves and fell in shafts onto
the lovely paths; and all was still and peaceful in the blue summer air.
It was as if the world were waiting for something, waiting and waiting
with held breath for something that was bound to happen, but not yet,
not yet. Suddenly Catherine felt like bursting into tears. She looked
about. Her temples throbbed in the smoke-filled air; she felt a little
sick. "I think I'll go up and say hello to Bev," she said.

"Tell her to come on down and join the party. These guys are
terrific."

Catherine escaped from the room and climbed the wooden stairs
toward the kitchen. On her left at the top of the stairs was the dark,
moonlit living room, glowing like an enchanted cave filled with chests
of precious jewels. You were not allowed to go into the Anderson living
room. In the bright-yellow kitchen to her right, Bev was standing at
the stove, gently shaking a black frying pan containing dark-yellow
corn kernels. She thrust a large potcover over it and shook harder. Sue
Wilson, Linda Shulick, and Joey Musante were sitting at the kitchen
table. On the table stood a large bottle of 7-Up, a bowl containing
crumbs of popcorn, and a smaller bowl filled with thin straight pretzels.
Catherine went over to Bev and, leaning close to her ear, said, "Boo."
Bev gave a little start. "God, you scared me. I thought you were hi-
bernating for the winter. Do you know, Len thought you were angry
at him? Come on, you guys, pop." "Oh no, no. That's crazy. Len?"
Through a door in the kitchen Catherine saw the small dim den,
crowded with people. Sonia Holmes sat on a couch surrounded by her
courtiers. Her glittering legs were tucked under her skirt. You could
not smoke in the den or kitchen, you could not play music in the den,
you could not drink beer, and you could not set foot in the living room.
You could use the top of the stove but not the inside. "It's so hot down
there," Catherine continued. "Have you seen Peter around?"

"Peter? You and Peter are some pair."

Catherine drew back her face sharply, as if she had been struck on
the cheek. "Oh?"

"You go sit in a tree, and Peter goes home."

"Peter went home?"

Sue Wilson said, "He didn't even tell anybody. Janet saw him. She thought he went to get something in his car, but he got in and drove away. I call that rude."

Bev said, "Peter isn't rude."

"He left his sled," said Catherine. A restlessness came over her, and she thought how irritating and boring all these people were, and this kitchen, and this universe, and above all, above all, those little straight pretzels. Why weren't they the three-ring kind?

"It's about time!" said Bev. She tipped up the cover and Catherine saw a kernel burst into flower. Bev banged the cover down and shook the pan; there was a crack-crack-cracking. Catherine went over to the den and looked in quickly. Then she turned, walked across the kitchen, and went downstairs.

Through the half-open door of the playroom Catherine saw drifting smoke and the corner of a couch. She went into the workroom and put on her coat, fumbling with the plump buttons, shaped like half-globes. Pulling on her boots, and tying her kerchief under her chin, she strode through the garage.

When she stepped outside she saw that some of the party had returned to the slope. She had thought only of escaping from the house, and now she was standing in the floodlight, exposed. She felt like putting her hands over her face. The only private place was the leaning pine. She climbed the slope at the back of the house, away from the sledding path, and headed across the deep snow toward her tree. Under the moon and the dark-blue sky the snow was luminous and tinged with blue.

Catherine stopped; in the open space of the pine she saw Bob Carwin, standing with one arm against the trunk as he leaned over Bonnie Baker, who sat on a low branch. Catherine turned back angrily into the upper yard. There was no place where she could be alone. There were people at the willow, people at the bottom of the sledding path, people in the pine. There were people in the playroom, people in the kitchen, people in the den. The party was spreading; soon it would flow across the yard, over the hedge, and into the next yard. It would flow across the town. It would spread into the dark-blue sky, all the way to the snowy moon.

Catherine stood in the empty upper yard. She felt restless, yet there was no place to go. He had walked to his car and driven home. He had not told anyone he was going home. Catherine thought it was a strange, upsetting thing to have done, and all at once she felt an immense pity for Peter Schiller, and for herself, as if someone had done something to them and gone away. But it was Peter Schiller who had gone away. Catherine shook her head, as if to shake out the words. She looked about. Everything seemed suspenseful and mysterious—the blue snow, the deep boot-hollows in the snow, the floodlit black of the driveway, startling as spilled ink rushing across a table. It seemed to her that everything she looked at was about to change shape suddenly. But it all remained peaceful, suspended, still. And the sledders rushing down the slope were part of it too, as if their motion were only another form of stillness. A hill of summer blueberries, sledders in the snow. Catherine felt lifted up into stillness, as if things were about to shift slightly, or crack open like kernels, thrusting up inner blossoms. She felt a faint cracking inside her. In another moment she would understand everything. And as she waited, she bowed her head against the cold, as if in prayer.

A shout from the hill startled her. Catherine hugged herself, and shivered in the cold. It had slipped away, whatever it was. She felt tired, as if she had been running for a long time. It seemed to her that she had been set spinning, like a top that travels across a table, touches an object, and, still spinning, rushes off in another direction. The words had set her spinning to the tree, and from there to the playroom, and from there to the kitchen, and from there to the snowy wasteland of the upper yard. And once you were set spinning, who knew where you would stop? She was spinning, spinning, and now she was about to go spinning off again, because she could not bear to be alone. She no longer knew what was going to happen to her. She no longer knew anything at all.

Gravely, her head bowed slightly, Catherine walked down the hill. But in the glow of the floodlight her spirits revived, and when she stepped into the smoky warmth of the playroom she felt so soothed, so enfolded, that she enjoyed the feel of her own smile as it pushed against her tightening cheeks. Bev and Brad waved from a couch; Catherine waved back. At the piano they were singing "Auld Lang Syne." These were her friends, her dear friends who were waving to her and laughing and playing the piano and singing. There was a clatter of descending footsteps, and Catherine turned to the half-open door. Len Anderson entered, frowning as he lit a cigarette in cupped hands. "You're leaving?" he said, looking up harshly. "Arriving," she answered, and untied her kerchief. "And Len, I can't tell you what a wonderful party it is." Pleasure surged in her; and everyone was surprised when she gave him a big hug.

Andre Dubus

GRADUATION

Sometimes, out in California, she wanted to tell her husband. That was after they had been married for more than two years (by then she was twenty-one) and she had settled into the familiarity so close to friendship but not exactly that either: she knew his sounds while he slept, brought some recognition to the very weight of his body next to her in bed, knew without looking the expressions on his face when he spoke. As their habits merged into common ritual, she began to feel she had never had another friend. Geography had something to do with this too. Waiting for him at the pier after the destroyer had been to sea for five days, or emerging from a San Diego movie theater, holding his hand, it seemed to her that the first eighteen years of her life, in Port Arthur, Texas, had no meaning at all. So, at times like that, she wanted to tell him.

She would look at the photograph, which she had kept hidden for four years now, and think, as though she were speaking to him: *I was seventeen years old, a senior in high school, and I got up that day just like any other day and ate Puffed Wheat or something with my parents and went to school and there it was, on the bulletin board*— But she didn't tell him, for she knew that something was wrong: the photograph and her years in Port Arthur were true, and now her marriage in San Diego was true. But it seemed that for both of them to remain true they had to exist separately, one as history, one as now, and that if she disclosed the history, then those two truths added together would somehow produce a lie which in turn would call for more analysis than she cared to give. Or than she cared for her husband to give. So she would simply look at the picture of herself at sixteen, then put it away, in an old compact at the bottom of her jewelry box.

The picture had been cut out of the high school yearbook. Her blonde hair had been short then, an Italian boy; her face was tilted down to one side, she was smiling at the camera, and beneath her face, across her sweater, was written: *Good piece.*

It had been thumbtacked to the bulletin board approximately two years after she had lost her virginity, parked someplace with a boy she loved. When they broke up she was still fifteen, a long way from marriage, and she wanted her virginity back. But this was impossible, for he had told all his friends. So she gave herself to the next boy whose pledge was a class ring or football sweater, and the one after that (before graduation night there were three of them, all with loose tongues), and everyone knew about Bobbie Huxford and she knew they did.

She never found out who put the picture on the bulletin board. When she got to school that day, a group of students were standing in the hall; they parted to let her through. Then she met the eyes of a girl, and saw neither mischief nor curiosity but fascination. A boy glanced at the bulletin board and quickly to the floor, and Bobbie saw the picture. She walked through them, pulled out the thumbtacks, forcing herself to go slowly, taking out each one and pressing it back into the board. She dropped the picture into her purse and went down the hall to her locker.

So at graduation she was not leaving the camaraderie, the perfunctory education, the ball games and dances and drives on a Sunday afternoon; she was leaving a place where she had always felt watched, except when Sherri King had been seduced by an uncle and somehow

that word had got out. But the Kings had moved within a month, and
Bobbie's classmates went back to watching her again. Still there was
nostalgia: sitting on the stage, looking at the audience in the dark, she
was remembering songs. Each of her loves had had a song, one she
had danced to, pressed sweating and tight-gripped and swaying in dance
halls where they served beer to anyone and the juke box never stopped:
Nat "King" Cole singing "Somewhere Along the Way," "Trying" by
the Hilltoppers, "Your Cheatin' Heart" by Joni James, all of them
plaintive songs: you drank two or three beers and clenched and dipped
and weaved on the dance floor, and you squeezed him, your breasts
against his firm narrow chest feeling like your brassiere and wrinkled
blouse and his damp shirt weren't even there; you kept one hand on
the back of his neck, sweat dripped between your fused cheeks, and
you sang in nearly a whisper with Joni or Nat and you gave him a
hard squeeze and said in his ear: *I love you, I'll love you forever.*

She had not loved any of them forever. With each one something
had gone sour, but she was able to look past that, farther back to the
good times. So there was that: sitting on the stage she remembered the
songs, the love on waxed dance floors. But nostalgia wasn't the best
part. She was happy, as she had been dancing to those songs that
articulated her feelings and sent them flowing back into her blood, her
heart. This time she didn't want to hold anyone, not even love anyone.
She wanted to fly: soar away from everything, go higher than rain. She
wanted to leave home, where bright and flowered drapes hung and
sunlight moved through the day from one end of the maroon sofa to
the other and formed motes in the air but found dustless the coffee
table and the Bible that sat on it.

She was their last child, an older brother with eight years in the
Army and going for twenty, and an older sister married to a pharmacist
in Beaumont, never having gone farther than Galveston in her whole
life and bearing kids now like that was the only thing to do.

In the quiet summer afternoons when her mother was taking a nap
and her father was at work, she felt both them and the immaculate
house stifling her. One night returning from a date she had walked
quietly into the kitchen. From there she could hear them snoring.
Standing in the dark kitchen she smoked a cigarette, flicking the ashes

in her hand (there was only one ash tray in the house and it was used by guests). Then looking at their bedroom door she suddenly wanted to holler: *I drank too much beer tonight and got sick in the john and Bud gave me 7-Up and crème de menthe to settle my stomach and clean my breath so I could still screw and that's what we did:* WE SCREWED. *That's what we always do.*

Now, looking out into the dark, Bobbie wondered if her parents were watching her. Then she knew they were, and they were proud. She was their last child, she was grown now, they had done their duty (college remained but they did not consider it essential) and now in the clean brightly colored house they could wait with calm satisfaction for their souls to be wafted to heaven. Then she was sad. Because from the anxiety and pain of her birth until their own deaths, they had loved her and would love her without ever knowing who she was.

After the ceremony there was an all-night party at Rhonda Miller's camp. Bobbie's date was a tall shy boy named Calvin Tatman, who was popular with the boys but rarely dated; three days before graduation he had called Bobbie and asked her to be his date for Rhonda's party. The Millers' camp was on a lake front, surrounded by woods; behind the small house there was a large outdoor kitchen, screened on all sides. In the kitchen was a keg of beer, paper cups, and Rhonda's record player; that was how the party began. Several parents were there, drinking bourbon from the grown-ups' bar at one side of the kitchen; they got tight, beamed at the young people jitterbugging, and teased them about their sudden liking for cigarettes and beer. After a while Mr. Miller went outside to the barbecue pit and put on some hamburgers.

At first Bobbie felt kindly toward Calvin and thought since it was a big night, she would let him neck with her. But after Calvin had a few tall cups of beer she changed her mind. He stopped jitterbugging with her, dancing only the slow dances, holding her very close; then, a dance ended, he would join the boys at the keg. He didn't exactly leave her on the dance floor; she could follow him to the keg if she wanted to, and she did that a couple of times, then stopped. Once she watched him talking to the boys and she knew exactly what was going on: he had brought her because he couldn't get another date (she had already known that, absorbed it, spent a long time preparing her face and hair anyway), but now he was saving face by telling people he had brought her because he wanted to get laid.

Then other things happened. She was busy dancing, so she didn't notice for a while that she hadn't really had a conversation with anyone. She realized this when she left Calvin at the beer keg and joined the line outside at the barbecue pit, where Mr. Miller was serving hamburgers. She was last in line. She told Mr. Miller it was a wonderful party, then she went to the table beside the barbecue pit and made her hamburger. When she turned to go back to the kitchen, no one was waiting: two couples were just going in the door, and Bobbie was alone with Mr. Miller. She hesitated, telling herself that it meant nothing, that no one waited for people at barbecue pits. Still, if she went in alone, who would she sit with? She sat on the grass by the barbecue pit and talked to Mr. Miller. He ate a hamburger with her and gave her bourbon and water from the one-man bar he had set up to get him through the cooking. He was a stout, pleasant man, and he told her she was the best-looking girl at the party.

As soon as she entered the kitchen she knew people had been waiting for her. The music and talk were loud, but she also felt the silence of waiting; looking around, she caught a few girls watching her. Then, at her side, Rhonda said: "Where you been, Bobbie?"

She glanced down at Rhonda, who sat with her boyfriend, a class ring dangling from a chain around her neck, one possessive hand on Charlie Wright's knee. She doubted that Rhonda was a virgin but she had heard very little gossip because she had no girlfriends. Now she went to the keg, pushed through the boys, and filled a cup.

Some time later, when the second keg had been tapped and both she and Calvin were drunk, he took her outside. She knew by now that everyone at the party was waiting to see if Calvin would make out. She went with him as far as the woods, kissed him standing up, worked her tongue in his mouth until he trembled and gasped; when he touched her breast she spun away and went back to the kitchen, jerking out of his grasp each time he clutched her arm. He was cursing her but she wasn't afraid. If he got rough, they were close enough to the kitchen so she could shout for Mr. Miller. Then Calvin was quiet anyway, realizing that if anyone heard they would know what had happened. When they stepped into the kitchen people were grinning at them. Bobbie went to the beer keg and Calvin danced with the first girl he saw.

When Charlie Wright got drunk he came over and danced with her. They swayed to "Blue Velvet," moved toward the door, and stumbled outside. They lay on the ground just inside the woods; because of the beer he took a long time and Bobbie thought of Rhonda waiting, faking a smile, dancing, waiting . . . Charlie told her she did it better than Rhonda. When they returned to the kitchen, Rhonda's face was pale; she did not dance with Charlie for the rest of the night.

At breakfast, near dawn, she sat on the bar and ate bacon and eggs with Mr. Miller, hoping Rhonda would worry about that too. Calvin tried to leave without her, but she had taken his car key, so he had to drive her home. It was just after sunrise, he was drunk, and he almost missed two curves.

"Hell, Calvin," she said, "just 'cause you can't make out doesn't mean you got to kill us."

He swung at her, the back of his open hand striking her cheekbone, and all the way home she cried. Next day there was not even a bruise.

The lawnmower woke her that afternoon. She listened to it, knowing she had been hearing it for some time, had been fighting it in her sleep. Then she got up, took two aspirins which nearly gagged her, and made coffee and drank it in the kitchen, wanting a cigarette but still unable to tell her parents that she smoked. So she went outside and helped her father rake the grass. The day was hot; bent over the rake she sweated and fought with her stomach and shut her eyes to the pain pulsing in her head and she wished she had at least douched with a Coke, something she had heard about but had never done. Then she wished she had a Coke right now, with ice, and some more aspirin and a cool place in the house to sit very still. She did not want to marry Charlie Wright. Then she had to smile at herself, looking down at the grass piling under her rake. Charlie would not marry her. By this time everyone in school knew she had done it with him last night, and they probably thought she had done it with Calvin too. If she were pregnant, it would be a joke.

That night she told her parents she wanted to finish college as soon
as possible so she could earn her own money. They agreed to send her
to summer school at L.S.U., and two weeks later they drove her to
Baton Rouge. During those two weeks she had seen no one; Charlie
had called twice for dates, but she had politely turned him down, with
excuses; she had menstruated, felt the missed life flowing as a new life
for herself. Then she went away. Sitting in the back of the car, driving
out of Port Arthur, she felt incomplete: she had not told anyone she
was going to summer school, had not told anyone goodbye.

She went home after the summer term, then again at Thanksgiving,
each time feeling more disengaged from her house and the town. When
she went home for Christmas vacation, her father met her at the bus
station. It was early evening. She saw him as the bus turned in: wiry,
a little slumped, wearing the hat that wasn't a Stetson but looked like
one. He spoke of the Christmas lights being ready and she tried to
sound pleased. She even tried to feel pleased. She thought of him going
to all that trouble every Christmas and maybe part of it was for her;
maybe it had all started for her delight, long ago when she was a child.
But when they reached the house she was again appalled by the lights
strung on its front and the lighted manger her father had built years
before and every Christmas placed on the lawn: a Nativity absurdly
without animals or shepherds or wise men or even parents for the Child
Jesus (a doll: Bobbie's) who lay utterly alone, wrapped in blankets on
the straw floor of the manger. Holding her father's arm she went into
the kitchen and hugged her mother, whose plumpness seemed em-
blematic of a woman who was kind and good and clean. Bobbie mar-
velled at the decorated house, then sat down to supper and talk of food
and family news. After supper she told them, with even more nervousness than she had anticipated, that she had started smoking and
she hoped they didn't mind. They both frowned, then her mother sighed
and said:

"Well, I guess you're a big girl now."

She was. For at L.S.U. she had learned this: you could become a
virgin again. She finally understood that it was a man's word. They
didn't mean you had done it once; they meant you did it, the lost hymen
testimony not of the past but the present, and you carried with you a

flavor of accessibility. She thought how much she would have been spared if she had known it at fifteen when she had felt changed forever, having focused on the word *loss* as though an arm or a leg had been amputated, so she had given herself again, trying to be happy with her new self, rather than backing up and starting over, which would have been so easy because Willie Sorrells—her first lover—was not what you would call irresistible. Especially in retrospect.

But at L.S.U. she was a virgin; she had dated often in summer and fall, and no one had touched her. Not even Frank Mixon, whom she planned to marry, though he hadn't asked her yet. He was an economics major at Tulane, and a football player. He was also a senior. In June he was going into the Navy as an ensign and this was one of her reasons for wanting to marry him. And she had him fooled.

One night, though, she had scared herself. It was after the Tulane-L.S.U. game, the traditional game which Tulane traditionally lost. It was played in Baton Rouge. After the game Bobbie and Frank double-dated with the quarterback, Roy Lockhart, and his fiancée, Annie Broussard. Sometime during the evening of bar-hopping, when they were all high, Roy identified a girl on the dance floor by calling her Jack Shelton's roommate of last year.

"What?" Bobbie said. "What did you say?"

"Never mind," Roy said.

"No: listen. Wait a minute."

Then she started. All those things she had thought about and learned in silence came out, controlled, lucid, as though she had been saying them for years. At one point she realized Frank was watching her, quiet and rather awed, but a little suspiciously too. She kept talking, though.

"You fumbled against Vanderbilt," she said to Roy. "Should we call you fumbler for the rest of your life?"

Annie, the drunkest of the four, kept saying: That's *right,* that's *right.* Finally Bobbie said:

"Anyway, that's what *I* think."

Frank put his arm around her.

"That takes care of gossip for tonight," he said. "Anybody want to talk about the game?"

"We tied 'em till the half," Roy said. "Then we should have gone home."

"It wasn't your fault, fumbler," Annie said, and she was still laughing when the others had stopped and ordered more drinks.

When Frank took Bobbie to the dormitory, they sat in the car, kissing. Then he said:

"You were sort of worked up tonight."

"It happened to a friend of mine in high school. They ruined her. It's hard to believe, that you can ruin somebody with just talking, but they did it."

He nodded, and moved to kiss her, but she pulled away.

"But that's not the only reason," she said.

She shifted on the car seat and looked at his face, a good ruddy face, hair neither long nor short and combed dry, the college cut that would do for business as well; he was a tall strong young man, and because of his size and strength she felt that his gentleness was a protective quality reserved for her alone; but this wasn't true either, for she had never known him to be unkind to anyone and, even tonight, as he drank too much in post-game defeat, he only got quieter and sweeter.

"I don't have one either," she said.

At first he did not understand. Then his face drew back and he looked out the windshield.

"It's not what you think. It's awful, and I'll never forget it, but I've never told anyone, no one knows, they all think—"

Then she was crying into his coat, not at all surprised that her tears were real, and he was holding her.

"I was twelve years old," she said.

She sat up, dried her cheeks, and looked away from him.

"It was an uncle, one of those uncles you never see. He was leaving someplace and going someplace else and he stopped off to see us for a couple of days. On the second night he came to my room and when I woke up he was doing it—"

"Hush," he said. "Hush, baby."

She did not look at him.

"I was so scared, so awfully *scared*. So I didn't tell. Next morning

I stayed in bed till he was gone. And I felt so rotten. Sometimes I still do, but not the way I did then. He's never come back to see us, but once in a while they mention him and I feel sick all over again, and I think about telling them but it's too late now, even if they did something to him it's too late, I can never get it back—"

For a long time that night Frank Mixon held his soiled girl in his arms, and, to Bobbie, those arms seemed quite strong, quite capable. She knew that she would marry him.

Less than a month later she was home for Christmas, untouched, changed. She spent New Year's at Frank's house in New Orleans. In the cold dusk after the Sugar Bowl game they walked back to his house to get the car and go to a party. Holding his arm, she watched a trolley go by, looked through car windows at attractive people leaving the stadium, breathed the smell of exhaust which was somehow pleasing, and the damp winter air, and another smell as of something old, as though from the old lives of the houses they passed. She knew that if she lived in New Orleans only a few months, Port Arthur would slide away into the Gulf. Climbing a gentle slope to his house, she was very tired, out of breath. The house was dark. Frank turned on a light and asked if she wanted a drink.

"God, no," she said. "I'd like to lie down for a few minutes."

"Why don't you? I'll make some coffee."

She climbed the stairs, turned on the hall light, and went to the guest room. She took off her shoes, lay clothed on the bed, and was asleep. His voice woke her: he stood at the bed, blocking the light from the hall. She propped on an elbow to drink the coffee, and asked him how long she had been asleep.

"About an hour."

"What did you do?"

"Watched some of the Rose Bowl."

"That was sweet. I'll hurry and get freshened up so we won't be too late."

But when she set the empty cup on the bedside table he kissed her; then he was lying on top of her.

"Your folks—"

"They're at a party."

She was yielding very slowly, holding him off tenderly then murmuring when his hand slipped into her blouse, stayed there, then withdrew to work on the buttons. She delayed, gave in, then stalled so that it took a long while for him to take off the blouse and brassiere. Finally they were naked, under the covers, and her hands on his body were shy. Then she spoke his name. With his first penetration she stiffened and he said, "It's all right, sweet darling Bobbie, it's all right now"— and she eased forward, wanting to enfold him with her legs, but she kept them outstretched, knees bent, and gave only tentative motion to her hips. When he was finished she held him there, his lips at her ear; she moved slowly as he whispered; then, whimpering, shuddering, and concealing, she came.

"Will you?" he said. "Will you marry me this June?"

"Oh *yes,*" she said, and squeezed his ribs. "Yes I will. This is my first time and that other never happened, not ever, it's all over now— Oh I'm so *happy,* Frank, I'm so *happy*—"

Charles Bukowski

THE MOST BEAUTIFUL WOMAN IN TOWN

Cass was the youngest and most beautiful of five sisters. Cass was the most beautiful girl in town, one-half Indian, with a supple and strange body, a snake-like and fiery body with eyes to go with it. Cass was fluid moving fire. She was like a spirit stuck into a form that would not hold her. Her hair was black and long and silken and moved and whirled about as did her body. Her spirit was either very high or very low. There was no in between for Cass. Some said she was crazy. The dull ones said that. The dull ones would never understand Cass. To the men she simply seemed a sex machine and they didn't care whether she was crazy or not. And Cass danced and flirted, kissed the men, but except for an instance or two, when it came time to make it with Cass, Cass had somehow slipped away, eluded the men.

Her sisters accused her of misusing her beauty, of not using her mind enough, but Cass had mind and spirit; she painted, she danced, she sang, she made things of clay, and when people were hurt either in the spirit or in the flesh, Cass felt a deep grieving for them. Her mind was simply different; her mind was simply not practical. Her sisters were jealous of her because she attracted their men, and they were angry because they felt she didn't make the best use of them. She had a habit of being kind to the uglier ones; the so-called handsome men revolted her—"No guts," she said, "no zap. They are riding on their perfect little earlobes and their well-shaped nostrils . . . All surface and no insides . . ." She had a temper that came close to insanity; she had a temper that some called insanity.

Her father had died of alcohol and her mother had run off leaving the girls alone. The girls went to a relative who placed them in a convent. The convent had been an unhappy place, more for Cass than the sisters. The girls were jealous of Cass and Cass fought most of them. She had razor marks all along her left arm from defending herself in two fights. There was also a permanent scar along the left cheek but the scar rather than lessening her beauty only seemed to highlight it.

I met her at the West End Bar several nights after her release from the convent. Being youngest, she was the last of the sisters to be released. She simply came in and sat next to me. I was probably the ugliest man in town and this might have had something to do with it.

"Drink?" I asked.

"Sure, why not?"

I don't suppose there was anything unusual in our conversation that night, it was simply in the feeling Cass gave. She had chosen me and it was as simple as that. No pressure. She liked her drinks and had a great number of them. She didn't seem quite of age but they served her anyhow. Perhaps she had a forged ID, I don't know. Anyhow, each time she came back from the restroom and sat down next to me, I did feel some pride. She was not only the most beautiful woman in town but also one of the most beautiful women I had ever seen. I placed my arm about her waist and kissed her once.

"Do you think I'm pretty?" she asked.

"Yes, of course, but there's something else . . . there's more than your looks . . ."

"People are always accusing me of being pretty. Do you really think I'm pretty?"

"Pretty isn't the word, it hardly does you fair."

Cass reached into her handbag. I thought she was reaching for her handkerchief. She came out with a long hatpin. Before I could stop her she had run this long hatpin through her nose, sideways, just above the nostrils. I felt disgust and horror.

She looked at me and laughed. "Now do you think me pretty? What do you think now, man?"

I pulled the hatpin out and held my handkerchief over the bleeding. Several people, including the bartender, had seen the act. The bartender came down.

"Look," he said to Cass, "you act up again and you're out. We don't need your dramatics here."

"Oh, fuck you, man!" she said.

"Better keep her straight," the bartender said to me.

"She'll be all right," I said.

"It's *my* nose," said Cass. "I can do what I want with my nose."

"No," I said, "it hurts me."

"You mean it hurts you when I stick a pin in my nose?"

"Yes, it does. I mean it."

"All right, I won't do it again. Cheer up."

She kissed me, rather grinning through the kiss and holding the handkerchief to her nose. We left for my place at closing time. I had some beer and we sat there talking. It was then that I got the perception of her as a person full of kindness and caring. She gave herself away without knowing it. At the same time she would leap back into areas of wildness and incoherence. Schitzi. A beautiful and spiritual *schitzi*. Perhaps some man, something, would ruin her forever. I hoped that it wouldn't be me.

We went to bed and after I turned out the lights Cass asked me, "When do you want it? Now or in the morning?"

"In the morning," I said and turned my back.

In the morning I got up and made a couple of coffees, brought her one in bed.

She laughed. "You're the first man I've met who has turned it down at night."

"It's O.K.," I said, "we needn't do it at all."

"No, wait, I want to now. Let me freshen up a bit."

Cass went to the bathroom. She came out shortly, looking quite wonderful, her long black hair glistening, her eyes and lips glistening, *her* glistening . . . She displayed her body calmly, as a good thing. She got under the sheet.

"Come on, lover man."

I got on in.

She kissed with abandon but without haste. I let my hands run over her body, through her hair. I mounted. It was hot, and tight. I began to stroke slowly, wanting to make it last. Her eyes looked directly into mine.

"What's your name?" I asked.

"What the hell difference does it make?" she asked.

I laughed and went on ahead. Afterwards she dressed and I drove her back to the bar but she was difficult to forget. I wasn't working and I slept until 2 P.M., then got up and read the paper. I was in the bathtub when she came in with a large leaf—an elephant ear.

"I knew you'd be in the bathtub," she said, "so I brought you something to cover that thing with, nature boy."

She threw the elephant leaf down on me in the bathtub.

"How did you know I'd be in the tub?"

"I knew."

Almost every day Cass arrived when I was in the tub. The times were different but she seldom missed, and there was the elephant leaf. And then we'd make love.

One or two nights she phoned and I had to bail her out of jail for drunkenness and fighting.

"These sons of bitches," she said, "just because they buy you a few drinks they think they can get into your pants."

"Once you accept a drink you create your own trouble."

"I thought they were interested in *me,* not just my body."

"I'm interested in you *and* your body. I doubt, though, that most men can see beyond your body."

I left town for six months, bummed around, came back. I had never forgotten Cass, but we'd had some type of argument and I felt like moving on anyhow, and when I got back I figured she'd be gone, but

I had been sitting in the West End Bar about thirty minutes when she walked in and sat down next to me.

"Well, bastard, I see you've come back."

I ordered her a drink. Then I looked at her. She had on a high-necked dress. I had never seen her in one of those. And under each eye, driven in, were two pins with glass heads. All you could see were the glass heads of the pins, but the pins were driven down into her face.

"God damn you, still trying to destroy your beauty, eh?"

"No, it's the *fad,* you fool."

"You're crazy."

"I've missed you," she said.

"Is there anybody else?"

"No, there isn't anybody else. Just you. But I'm hustling. It costs ten bucks. But you get it free."

"Pull those pins out."

"No, it's the fad."

"It's making me very unhappy."

"Are you sure?"

"Hell yes, I'm sure."

Cass slowly pulled the pins out and placed them in her purse.

"Why do you haggle your beauty?" I asked. "Why don't you just live with it?"

"Because people think it's all I have. Beauty is nothing, beauty won't stay. You don't know how lucky you are to be ugly, because if people like you then you know it's for something else."

"O.K.," I said, "I'm lucky."

"I don't mean you're ugly. People just think you're ugly. You have a fascinating face."

"Thanks."

We had another drink.

"What are you doing?" she asked.

"Nothing. I can't get on to anything. No interest."

"Me neither. If you were a woman you could hustle."

"I don't think I'd want to make that close a contact with so many strangers. It's wearing."

"You're right, it's wearing, everything is wearing."

We left together. People still stared at Cass on the streets. She was still a beautiful woman, perhaps more beautiful than ever.

We made it to my place and I opened a bottle of wine and we talked. With Cass and me, the talk always came easy. She talked a while and I would listen and then I would talk. Our conversation simply went along without strain. We seemed to discover secrets together. When we discovered a good one Cass would laugh that laugh—only the way she could. It was like joy out of fire. Through the talking we kissed and moved closer together. We became quite heated and decided to go to bed. It was then Cass took off her high-necked dress and I saw it—the ugly jagged scar across her throat. It was large and thick.

"God damn you, woman," I said from the bed, "god damn you, what have you done?"

"I tried it with a broken bottle one night. Don't you like me anymore? Am I still beautiful?"

I pulled her down on the bed and kissed her. She pushed away and laughed. "Some men pay me that ten and then I undress and they don't want to do it. I keep the ten. It's very funny."

"Yes," I said, "I can't stop laughing . . . Cass, bitch, I love you . . . stop destroying yourself; you're the most alive woman I've ever met."

We kissed again. Cass was crying without sound. I could feel the tears. That long black hair lay behind me like a flag of death. We conjoined and made slow and somber and wonderful love.

In the morning Cass was up making breakfast. She seemed quite calm and happy. She was singing. I stayed in bed and enjoyed her happiness. Finally she came over and shook me. "Up, bastard! Throw some cold water on your face and pecker and come enjoy the feast!"

I drove her to the beach that day. It was a weekday and not yet summer so things were splendidly deserted. Beach bums in rags slept on the lawns above the sand. Others sat on stone benches sharing a lone bottle. The gulls whirled about, mindless yet distracted. Old ladies in their seventies and eighties sat on the benches and discussed selling real estate left behind by husbands long ago killed by the pace and stupidity of survival. For it all, there was peace in the air and we walked about and stretched on the lawns and didn't say much. It simply felt good being together. I bought a couple of sandwiches, some chips and drinks, and we sat on the sand eating. Then I held Cass and we slept together about an hour. It was somehow better than lovemaking. There was a flowing together without tension. When we awakened we drove back to my place and I cooked a dinner. After dinner I suggested to Cass that we shack together. She waited a long time, looking at me, then she slowly said, "No." I drove her back to the bar, bought her a drink and walked out. I found a job as a packer in a factory the next day and the rest of the week went to working. I was too tired to get about much but that Friday night I did get to the West End Bar. I sat and waited for Cass. Hours went by. After I was fairly drunk the bartender said to me, "I'm sorry about your girl friend."

"What is it?" I asked.

"I'm sorry. Didn't you know?"

"No."

"Suicide. She was buried yesterday."

"Buried?" I asked. It seemed as if she would walk through the doorway at any moment. How could she be gone?

"Her sisters buried her."

"A suicide? Mind telling me how?"

"She cut her throat."

"I see. Give me another drink."

I drank until closing time, Cass, the most beautiful of five sisters, the most beautiful in town. I managed to drive to my place and I kept thinking, I should have *insisted* she stay with me instead of accepting that "no." Everything about her had indicated that she had cared. I had simply been too offhand about it, lazy, too unconcerned. I deserved my death and hers. I was a dog. No, why blame the dogs? I got up and found a bottle of wine and drank from it heavily. Cass the most beautiful girl in town was dead at twenty.

Outside somebody honked their automobile horn. They were very loud and persistent. I set the bottle down and screamed out: "GOD DAMN YOU, YOU SON OF A BITCH, SHUT UP!"

The night kept coming on in and there was nothing I could do.

Harold Brodkey

INNOCENCE

1. ORRA AT HARVARD

Orra Perkins was a senior. Her looks were like a force that struck you. Truly, people on first meeting her often involuntarily lifted their arms as if about to fend off the brightness of the apparition. She was a somewhat scrawny, tulip-like girl of middling height. To see her in sunlight was to see Marxism die. I'm not the only one who said that. It was because seeing someone in actuality who has such a high immediate worth meant you had to decide whether such personal distinction had a right to exist or if she belonged to the state and ought to be shadowed in, reduced in scale, made lesser, laughed at.

Also, it was the case that you had to be rich and famous to get your hands on her; she could not fail to be a trophy and the question was whether the trophy had to be awarded on economic and political grounds or whether chance could enter in.

I was a senior too, and ironic. I had no money. I was without lineage. It seemed to me Orra was proof that life was a terrifying phenomenon of surface immediacy. She made any idea I had of psychological normalcy or of justice absurd since normalcy was not as admirable or as desirable as Orra; or rather she was normalcy and everything else was a falling off, a falling below; and justice was inconceivable if she, or someone equivalent to her if there was an equivalent once you had seen her, would not sleep with you. I used to create general hilarity in my room by shouting her name at my friends and then breaking up into laughter, gasping out, "God, we're so small time." It was grim that she existed and I had not had her. One could still prefer a more ordinary girl but not for simple reasons.

A great many people avoided her, ran away from her. She was, in part, more knowing than the rest of us because the experiences offered her had been so extreme, and she had been so extreme in response—scenes in Harvard Square with an English marquess, slapping a son of a billionaire so hard he fell over backwards at a party in Lowell House, her saying then and subsequently, "I never sleep with anyone who has a fat ass." Extreme in the humiliations endured and meted out, in the crassness of the publicity, of her life defined as those adventures, extreme in the dangers survived or not entirely survived, the cheapness undergone so that she was on a kind of frightening eminence, an eminence of her experiences and of her being different from everyone else. She'd dealt in intrigues, major and minor, in the dramas of political families, in passions, deceptions, folly on a large, expensive scale, promises, violence, the genuine pain of defeat when defeat is to some extent the result of your qualities and not of your defects, and she knew the rottenness of victories that hadn't been final. She was crass and impaired by beauty. She was like a giant bird, she was as odd as an ostrich walking around the Yard, in her absurd gorgeousness, she was so different from us in kind, so capable of a different sort of progress through the yielding medium of the air, through the strange rooms of our minutes on this earth, through the gloomy circumstances of our lives in those years.

People said it was worth it to do this or that just in order to see her—seeing her offered some kind of encouragement, was some kind of testimony that life was interesting. But not many people cared as much about knowing her. Most people preferred to keep their distance.

I don't know what her having made herself into what she was had done for her. She could have been ordinary if she'd wished.

She had unnoticeable hair, a far from arresting forehead, and extraordinary eyes, deep-set, longing, hopeful, angrily bored behind smooth, heavy lids that fluttered when she was interested and when she was not interested at all. She had a great desire not to trouble or be troubled by supernumeraries and strangers. She has a proud, too large nose that gives her a noble, stubborn dog's look. Her mouth has a disconcertingly lovely set to it—it is more immediately expressive than her eyes and it shows her implacability: it is the implacability of her knowledge of life in her. People always stared at her. Some giggled nervously. *Do you like me, Orra? Do you like me at all?* They stared at the great hands of the Aztec priest opening them to feelings and to awe, exposing their hearts, the dread cautiousness of their lives. They stared at the incredible symmetries of her sometimes anguishedly passionate face, the erratic pain for her in being beautiful that showed on it, the occasional plunging gaiety she felt because she was beautiful. I like beautiful people. The symmetries of her face were often thwarted by her attempts at expressiveness—beauty was a stone she struggled free of. A ludicrous beauty. A cruel clown of a girl. Sometimes her face was absolutely impassive as if masked in dullness and she was trying to move among us incognito. I was aware that each of her downfalls made her more possible for me. I never doubted that she was privately a pedestrian shitting-peeing person. Whenever I had a chance to observe her for any length of time, in a classroom for instance, I would think, *I understand her.* Whenever I approached her, she responded up to a point and then even as I stood talking to her I would fade as a personage, as a sexual presence, as someone present and important to her into greater and greater invisibility. That was when she was a freshman, a sophomore, and a junior. When we were seniors, by then I'd learned how to avoid being invisible even to Orra. Orra was, I realized, hardly more than a terrific college girl, much vaunted, no more than that yet. But my god, my god, in one's eyes, in one's thoughts, she strode like a *Nike,* she entered like a blast of light, the thought of her was as vast as a desert. Sometimes in an early winter twilight in the Yard, I would see her in her coat, unbuttoned even in cold weather as if she burned slightly always, see her move clumsily along a walk looking like a scrawny field hockey player, a great athlete of a girl half-stumbling, uncoordinated off the playing field, yet with reserves of strength, do you know? and her face, as she walked along, might twitch like a dog's when the dog is asleep, twitching with whatever dialogue or adventure or daydream she was having in her head. Or she might in the early darkness stride along, cold-faced, haughty, angry, all the worst refusals one would ever receive bound up in one ridiculously beautiful girl. One always said, *I wonder what will become of her.* Her ignoring me marked me as a sexual nonentity. She was proof of a level of sexual adventure I had not yet with my best efforts reached: that level existed because Orra existed.

What is it worth to be in love in this way?

2. ORRA WITH ME

I distrust summaries, any kind of gliding through time, any too great a claim that one is in control of what one recounts; I think someone who claims to understand but who is obviously calm, someone who claims to write with emotion recollected in tranquillity, is a fool and a liar. To understand is to tremble. To recollect is to reenter and be riven. An acrobat after spinning through the air in a mockery of flight stands erect on his perch and mockingly takes his bow as if what he is being applauded for was easy for him and cost him nothing, although meanwhile he is covered with sweat and his smile is edged with a relief chilling to think about; he is indulging in a show business style; he is pretending to be superhuman. I am bored with that and with where it has brought us. I admire the authority of being on one's knees in front of the event.

In the last spring of our being undergraduates, I finally got her. We had agreed to meet for dinner in my room, to get a little drunk cheaply before going out to dinner. I left the door unlatched; and I lay naked on my bed under a sheet. When she knocked on the door, I said, "Come in," and she did. She began to chatter right away, to complain that I was still in bed; she seemed to think I'd been taking a nap and had forgotten to wake up in time to get ready for her arrival.

I said, "I'm naked, Orra, under this sheet. I've been waiting for you. I haven't been asleep."

Her face went empty. She said, "Damn you—why couldn't you wait?" But even while she was saying that, she was taking off her blouse.

I was amazed that she was so docile; and then I saw that it was maybe partly that she didn't want to risk saying no to me—she didn't want me to be hurt and difficult, she didn't want me to explode; she had a kind of hope of making me happy so that I'd then appreciate her and be happy with her and let her know me: I'm putting it badly. But her not being able to say no protected me from having so great a fear of sexual failure that I would not have been able to be worried about her pleasure, or to be concerned about her in bed. She was very amateurish and uninformed in bed, which touched me. It was really sort of poor sex; she didn't come or even feel much that I could see. Afterwards, lying beside her, I thought of her eight or ten or fifteen lovers being afraid of her, afraid to tell her anything about sex in case they might be wrong. I had an image of them protecting their own egos, holding their arms around their egos and not letting her near them. It seemed a kindness embedded in the event that she was, in quite an obvious way, with a little critical interpretation, a virgin. And impaired, or crippled by having been beautiful, just as I'd thought. I said to myself that it was a matter of course that I might be deluding myself. But what I did for the rest of that night—we stayed up all night; we talked, we quarreled for a while, we confessed various things, we argued about sex, we fucked again (the second one was a little better)—I treated her with the justice with which I'd treat a boy my age, a young man, and with a rather exact or measured patience and tolerance, as if she was a paraplegic and had spent her life in a wheelchair and was tired of sentiment. I showed her no sentiment at all. I figured she'd been asphyxiated by the sentiments and sentimentality of people impressed by her looks. She was beautiful and frightened and empty and shy and alone and wounded and invulnerable (like a cripple: what more can you do to a cripple?). She was Caesar and ruler of the known world and not Caesar and no one as well.

It was a fairly complicated, partly witty thing to do. It meant I could not respond to her beauty but had to ignore it. She was a curious sort of girl; she had a great deal of isolation in her, isolation as a woman. It meant that when she said something on the order of "You're very defensive," I had to be a debater, her equal, take her seriously, and say, "How do you mean that?" and then talk about it, and alternately deliver a blow ("You can't judge defensiveness, you have the silly irresponsibility of women, the silly disconnectedness: I *have* to be defensive.") and defer to her: "You have a point: you think very clearly. All right, I'll adopt that as a premise." Of course, much of what we said was incoherent and nonsensical on examination but we worked out in conversation what we meant or thought we meant. I didn't react to her in any emotional way. She wasn't really a girl, not really quite human: how could she be? She was a position, a specific glory, a trophy, our local upper-middle-class pseudo Cleopatra. Or not pseudo. I couldn't revel in my luck or be unself-consciously vain. I could not strut horizontally or loll as if on clouds, a demi-god with a goddess, although it was clear we were deeply fortunate, in spite of everything, the poor sex, the difference in attitude which were all we seemed to share, the tensions and the blundering. If I enjoyed her more than she enjoyed me, if I lost consciousness of her even for a moment, she would be closed into her isolation again. I couldn't love her and have her too. I could love her and have her if I didn't show love or the symptoms of having had her. It was like lying in a very lordly way, opening her to the possibility of feeling by making her comfortable inside the calm lies of my behavior, my inscribing the minutes with false messages. It was like meeting a requirement in Greek myth, like not looking back at Eurydice. The night crept on, swept on, late minutes, powdered with darkness, in the middle of a sleeping city, spring crawling like a plague of green snakes, bits of warmth in the air, at four A.M. smells of leaves when the stink of automobiles died down. Dawn came, so pink, so pastel, so silly: we were talking about the possibility of innate grammatical structures; I said it was an unlikely notion, that Jews really were God-haunted (the idea had been broached by a Jew), and the great difficulty was to invent a just God, that if God appeared at a moment of time or relied on prophets, there had to be degrees in the possibility of knowing him so that he was by definition unjust; the only just God

would be one who consisted of what had always been known by everyone; and that you could always identify a basically Messianic, a hugely
religious, fraudulent thinker by how much he tried to anchor his doc-
trine to having always been true, to be innate even in savage man;
whereas an honest thinker, a nonliar, was caught in the grip of the
truth of process and change and the profound absence of justice except
as an invention, an attempt by the will to live with someone, or with
many others without consuming them. At that moment Orra said, "I
think we're falling in love."

I figured I had kept her from being too depressed after fucking—
it's hard for a girl with any force in her and any brains to accept the
whole thing of fucking, of being fucked without trying to turn it on
its end, so that she does some fucking, or some fucking up; I mean the
mere power of arousing the man so he wants to fuck isn't enough: she
wants him to be willing to die in order to fuck. There's a kind of strain
or intensity women are bred for, as beasts, for childbearing when childbearing might kill them, and childrearing when the child might die at
any moment: it's in women to live under that danger, with that risk,
that close to tragedy, with that constant taut or casual courage. They
need death and nobility near. To be fucked when there's no drama
inherent in it, when you're not going to rise to a level of nobility and
courage forever denied the male, is to be cut off from what is inherently
female, bestially speaking. I wanted to be halfway decent company for
her. I don't know that it was natural to me. I am psychologically,
profoundly, a transient. A form of trash. I am incapable of any contin-
uing loyalty and silence; I am an informer. But I did all right with her.
It was dawn, as I said. We stood naked by the window silently watching
the light change. Finally she said, "Are you hungry? Do you want
breakfast?"

"Sure. Let's get dressed and go—"

She cut me off; she said with a funny kind of firmness, "No! Let
me go and get us something to eat."

"Orra, don't wait on me. Why are you doing this? Don't be like
this."

But she was in a terrible hurry to be in love. After those few hours,
after that short a time.

She said, "I'm not as smart as you, Wiley. Let me wait on you. Then things will be even."

"Things are even, Orra."

"No. I'm boring and stale. You just think I'm not because you're in love with me. Let me go."

I blinked. After a while, I said, "All right."

She dressed and went out and came back. While we ate, she was silent; I said things but she had no comment to make; she ate very little; she folded her hands and smiled mildly like some nineteenth-century portrait of a handsome young mother. Every time I looked at her, when she saw I was looking at her, she changed the expression on her face to one of absolute and undeviating welcome to me and to anything I might say.

So, it had begun.

3. ORRA

She hadn't come. She said she had never come with anyone at any time. She said it didn't matter.

After our first time, she complained. "You went twitch, twitch, twitch—just like a grasshopper." So she had wanted to have more pleasure than she'd had. But after the second fuck and after the dawn, she never complained again—unless I tried to make her come, and then she complained of that. She showed during sex no dislike for any of my sexual mannerisms or for the rhythms and postures I fell into when I fucked. But I was not pleased or satisfied; it bothered me that she didn't come. I was not pleased or satisfied on my own account either. I thought the reason for that was she attracted me more than she could satisfy me, maybe more than fucking could ever satisfy me, that the more you cared, the more undertow there was, so that the sexual thing drowned—I mean the sharpest sensations, and yet the dullest, are when you masturbate—but when you're vilely attached to somebody, there are noises, distractions that drown out the sensations of fucking. For a long time, her wanting to fuck, her getting undressed, and the soft horizontal bobble of her breasts as she lay there, and the soft wavering, the kind of sinewlessness of her legs and lower body with which she more or less showed me she was ready, that was more

moving, was more immensely important to me than any mere ejacu-
lation later, any putt-putt-putt in her darkness, any hurling of future
generations into the clenched universe, the strict mitten inside her: I
clung to her and grunted and anchored myself to the most temporary
imaginable relief of the desire I felt for her; I would be hungry again
and anxious to fuck again in another twenty minutes; it was pitiable,
this sexual disarray. It seemed to me that in the vast spaces of the
excitement of being welcomed by each other, we could only sightlessly
and at best half-organize our bodies. But so what? We would probably
die in these underground caverns; a part of our lives would die; a
certain innocence and hope would never survive this: we were too open,
too clumsy, and we were the wrong people: so what did a fuck matter?
I didn't mind if the sex was always a little rasping, something of a
failure, if it was just preparation for more sex in half an hour, if coming
was just more foreplay. If this was all that was in store for us, fine. But
I thought she was getting gypped in that she felt so much about me,
she was dependent, and she was generous, and she didn't come when
we fucked.

She said she had never come, not once in her life, and that she
didn't need to. And that I mustn't think about whether she came or
not. "I'm a sexual tigress," she explained, "and I like to screw but I'm
too sexual to come: I haven't that kind of daintiness. I'm not selfish
that way."

I could see that she had prowled around in a sense and searched
out men and asked them to be lovers as she had me rather than wait
for them or plot to capture their attention in some subtle way; and in
bed she was sexually eager and a bit more forward and less afraid than
most girls; but only in an upper-middle-class frame of reference was
she *a sexual tigress.*

It seemed to me—my whole self was focused on this—that her not
coming said something about what we had, that her not coming was
an undeniable fact, a measure of the limits of what we had. I did not
think we should think we were great lovers when we weren't.

Orra said we were, that I had no idea how lousy the sex was other
people had. I told her that hadn't been my experience. We were, it
seemed to me, two twenty-one-year-olds, overeducated, irrevocably shy

beneath our glaze of sexual determination and of sexual appetite, and psychologically somewhat slashed up and only capable of being partly useful to each other. We weren't the king and queen of Cockand-cuntdom yet.

Orra said coming was a minor part of sex for a woman and was a demeaning measure of sexuality. She said it was imposed as a measure by people who knew nothing about sex and judged women childishly.

It seemed to me she was turning a factual thing, coming, into a public relations thing. But girls were under fearful public pressures in these matters.

When she spoke about them, these matters, she had a little, superior inpuckered look, a don't-make-me-make-mincemeat-of-you-in-argument look—I thought of it as her Orra-as-Orra look, Orra alone, Orra-without-Wiley, without me, Orra isolated and depressed, a terrific girl, an Orra who hated cowing men.

She referred to novels, to novels by women writers, to specific scenes and remarks about sex and coming for women, but I'd read some of those books, out of curiosity, and none of them were literature, and the heroines in them invariably were innocent in every relation; but very strong and very knowing and with terrifically good judgment; and the men they loved were described in such a way they appeared to be examples of the woman's sexual reach, or of her intellectual value, rather than sexual companions or sexual objects; the women had sex generously with men who apparently bored them physically; I had thought the books and their writers and characters sexually naïve.

Very few women, it seemed to me, had much grasp of physical reality. Still, very strange things were often true, and a man's notion of orgasm was necessarily specialized.

When I did anything in bed to excite her with an eye to making her come, she asked me not to, and that irritated the hell out of me. But no matter what she said, it must be bad for her after six years of fucking around not to get to a climax. It had to be that it was a run on her neural patience. How strong could she be?

I thought about how women coming were at such a pitch of uncontrol they might prefer a dumb, careless lover, someone very unlike me: I had often played at being a strong, silent dunce. Some girls became

fawning and doglike after they came, even toward dunces. Others
jumped up and became immediately tough, proud of themselves as if
the coming was *all* to their credit, and I ought to be flattered. God, it
was a peculiar world. Brainy girls tended to control their comes, doling
out one to a fuck, just like a man; and often they would try to keep
that one under control, they would limit it to a single nozzle-contracted
squirt of excitement. Even that sometimes racked and emptied them
and made them curiously weak and brittle and embarrassed and delicate
and lazy. Or they would act bold and say, "God, I needed that."

I wondered how Orra would look, in what way she would do it,
a girl like that going off, how she'd hold herself, her eyes, how she'd
act toward me when it was over.

To get her to talk about sex at all, I argued that analyzing something
destroyed it, of course, but leaves rotted on the ground and prepared
the way for what would grow next. So she talked.

She said I was wrong in what I told her I saw and that there was
no difference in her between mental and physical excitement, that it
wasn't true her mind was excited quickly, and her body slowly, if at
all. I couldn't be certain I was right, but when I referred to a moment
when there had seemed to be deep physical feeling in her, she sometimes
agreed that had been a good moment in her terms; but sometimes she
said, no, it had only been a little irritating then, like a peculiarly unpleasant tickle. In spite of her liking my mind, she gave me no authority
for what I knew—I mean when it turned out I was right. She kept
the authority for her reactions in her own hands. Her self-abnegation
was her own doing. I liked that: some people just give you themselves,
and it is too much to keep in your hands: your abilities aren't good
enough. I decided to stick with what I observed and to think her
somewhat mistaken and not to talk to her about sex any more.

I watched her in bed; her body was doubting, grudging, tardy,
intolerant—and intolerably hungry—I thought. In her pride and self-
consciousness and ignorance she hated all that in herself. She preferred
to think of herself as quick, to have pleasure as she willed rather than
as she actually had it, to have it on her own volition, to her own
prescription, and almost out of politeness, so it seemed to me, to give
herself to me, to give me pleasure, to ignore herself, to be a nice girl

because she was in love. She insisted on that but that was too sentimental and she also insisted she was, she persuaded herself, she passed herself off as dashing.

In a way, sexually, she was a compulsive liar.

I set myself to remove every iota of misconception I had about Orra in bed, any romanticism, any pleasurable hope. It seemed to me what had happened to her with other boys was that she was distrustful to start with and they had overrated her, and they'd been overwrought and off-balance and uneasy about her judgment of them, and they'd taken their pleasure and run.

And then she had in her determination to have sex become more and more of a sexual fool. (I was all kinds of fool: I didn't mind her being a sexual fool.) The first time I'd gone to bed with her, she'd screamed and thrown herself around, a good two or three feet to one side or another, as she thought a sexual tigress would, I supposed. I'd argued with her afterwards that no one was that excited especially without coming; she said she had come, sort of. She said she was too sexual for most men. She said her reactions weren't fake but represented a real sexuality, a real truth. That proud, stubborn, stupid girl.

But I told her that if she and a man were in sexual congress, and she heaved herself around and threw herself a large number of inches to either the left or the right or even straight up, the man was going to be startled; and if there was no regular pattern or predictability, it was easy to lose an erection; that if she threw herself to the side, there was a good chance she would interrupt the congress entirely unless the man was very quick and scrambled after her, and scrambling after her was not likely to be sexual for him: it would be more like playing tag. The man would have to fuck while in a state of siege; not knowing what she'd do next, he'd fuck and hurry to get it over and to get out.

Orra had said on that first occasion, "That sounds reasonable. No one ever explained that to me before, no one ever made it clear. I'll try it your way for a while."

After that, she had been mostly shy and honest, and honestly lecherous in bed but helpless to excite herself or to do more to me than she did just by being there and welcoming me. As if her hands were webbed and her mind was glued, as if I didn't deserve more, or as if she was

such a novice and so shy she could not begin to do anything *sexual*. I
did not understand: I'd always found that anyone who *wanted* to give
pleasure, could: it didn't take skill, just the desire to please and a kind
of, I-don't-know, a sightless ability to feel one's way to some extent in
the lightless maze of pleasure. But upper-middle-class girls might be
more fearful of tying men to them by bands of excessive pleasure; such
girls were careful and shy.

I set myself for her being rude and difficult although she hadn't
been rude and difficult to me for a long time but those traits were in
her like a shadow giving her the dimensionality that made her valuable
to me, that gave point to her kindness toward me. She had the sloppiest
and most uncertain and silliest and yet bravest and most generous ego
of anyone I'd ever known; and her manners were the most stupid
imaginable alternation between the distinguished, the sensitive, the intelligent, with a rueful, firm, almost snotty delicacy and kindness and
protectiveness toward you, and the really selfish and bruising. The
important thing was to prevent her from responding falsely, as if in a
movie, or in some imitation of the movies she'd seen and the books
she'd read—she had a curious faith in movies and in books; she admired
anything that made her feel and that did not require responsibility from
her because then she produced happiness like silk for herself and others.
She liked really obscure philosophers, like Hegel, where she could
admire the thought but where the thought didn't demand anything
from her. Still, she was a realist, and she would probably learn what I
knew and would surpass me. She had great possibilities. But she was
also merely a good-looking, pseudo-rich girl, a paranoid, a Perkins. On
the other hand she was a fairly marvelous girl a lot of the time, brave,
eye-shattering, who could split my heart open with one slightly shaky
approving-of-me brainy romantic heroine's smile. The romantic splen-
dor of her face. So far in her life she had disappointed everyone. I had
to keep all this in mind, I figured. She was fantastically alive and eerily
dead at the same time. I wanted for my various reasons to raise her
from the dead.

4. ORRA: THE SAME WORLD, A DIFFERENT TIME SCALE

One afternoon, things went well for us. We went for a walk, the air was plangent, there was the amazed and polite pleasure we had sometimes merely at being together. Orra adjusted her pace now and then to mine; and I kept mine adjusted to her most of the time. When we looked at each other, there would be small soft puffs of feeling as of toy explosions or sparrows bathing in the dust. Her willed softness, her inner seriousness or earnestness, her strength, her beauty muted and careful now in her anxiety not to lose me yet, made the pleasure of being with her noble, contrapuntal, and difficult in that one had to live up to it and understand it and protect it, against my clumsiness and Orra's falsity, kind as that falsity was; or the day would become simply an exploitation of a strong girl who would see through that sooner or later and avenge it. But things went well; and inside that careless and careful goodness, we went home; we screwed; I came—to get my excitement out of the way; she didn't know I was doing that; she was stupendously polite; taut; and very admiring. "How pretty you are," she said. Her eyes were blurred with half-tears. I'd screwed without any fripperies, coolly, in order to leave in us a large residue of sexual restlessness but with the burr of immediate physical restlessness in me removed: I still wanted her; I always wanted Orra; and the coming had been dull; but my body was not very assertive, was more like a glove for my mind, for my will, for my love for her, for my wanting to make her feel more.

She was slightly tearful, as I said, and gentle, and she held me in her arms after I came, and I said something like, "Don't relax. I want to come again," and she partly laughed, partly sighed, and was flattered, and said, "Again? That's nice." We had a terrific closeness, almost like a man and a secretary—I was free and powerful, and she was devoted: there was little chance Orra would ever be a secretary: she'd been offered executive jobs already for when she finished college, but to play at being a secretary who had no life of her own was a romantic thing for Orra. I felt some apprehension, as before a game of tennis that I wanted to win, or as before stealing something off a counter in a store: there was a dragging enervation, a fear and silence, and there was a lifting, a

preparation, a willed and then unwilled, self-contained fixity of purpose;
it was a settled thing; it would happen.

After about ten minutes or so, perhaps it was twenty, I moved in
her: I should say that while I'd rested, I'd stayed in her (and she'd held
on to me). As I'd expected—and with satisfaction and pride that everything was working, my endowments were cooperating—I felt my prick
come up; it came up at once with comic promptness but it was sore—
Jesus, was it sore. It, its head, ached like hell, with a dry, burning, red-
dish pain.

The pain made me chary and prevented me from being excited
except in an abstract way; my mind was clear; I was idly smiling as I
began, moving very slowly, just barely moving, sort of pressing on her
inside her, moving around, lollygagging around, feeling out the reaches
in there, arranging the space inside her, as if to put the inner soft-oiled
shadows in her in order; or like stretching out your hand in the dark
and pressing a curve of a blanket into familiarity or to locate yourself
when you're half-asleep, when your eyes are closed. In fact, I did close
my eyes and listened carefully to her breathing, concentrating on her
but trying not to let her see I was doing that because it would make
her self-conscious.

Her reaction was so minimal that I lost faith in fucking for getting
her started, and I thought I'd better go down on her; I pulled out of
her, which wasn't too smart, but I wasn't thinking all that consequen-
tially; she'd told me on other occasions she didn't like "all that foreign
la-di-dah," that it didn't excite her, but I'd always thought it was only
that she was ashamed of not coming and that made being gone down
on hard for her. I started in on it; she protested; and I pooh-poohed
her objections and did it anyway; I was raw with nerves, with stifled
amusement because of the lying and the tension, so much of it. I
remarked to her that I was going down on her for my own pleasure;
I was jolted by touching her with my tongue there when I was so raw-
nerved but I hid that. It seemed to me physical unhappiness and readiness were apparent in her skin—my lips and tongue carried the currents
of a jagged unhappiness and readiness in her into me; echoes of her
stiffness and dissatisfaction sounded in my mouth, my head, my feet,

my entire tired body was a stethoscope. I was entirely a stethoscope; I listened to her with my *bones;* the glimmers of excitement in her traveled to my *spine;* I felt her grinding sexual haltedness, like a car's broken starter motor grinding away in her, in my *stomach,* in my *knees.* Every part of me listened to her; every goddamned twinge of muscular contraction she had that I noticed or that she should have had because I was licking her clitoris and she didn't have, every testimony of excitement or of no-excitement in her, I listened for it so hard it was amazing it didn't drive her out of bed with self-consciousness; but she probably couldn't tell what I was doing, since I was out of her line of sight, was down in the shadows, in the basement of her field of vision, in the basement with her sexual feelings where they lay, strewn about.

When she said, "No . . . No, Wiley . . . Please don't. No . . ." and wiggled, although it wasn't the usual pointless protest that some girls might make—it was real, she wanted me to stop—I didn't listen because I could feel she responded to my tongue more than she had to the fucking a moment before. I could feel beads sliding and whispering and being strung together rustlingly in her; the disorder, the scattered or strewn sexual bits, to a very small extent, were being put in order. She shuddered. With discomfort. She produced, was subjected to, her erratic responses. And she made odd, small cries, protests mostly, uttered little exclamations that mysteriously were protests although they were not protests too, cries that somehow suggested the ground of protest kept changing for her.

I tried to string a number of those cries together, to cause them to occur in a mounting sequence. It was a peculiar attempt: it seemed we moved, I moved with her, on dark water, between two lines of buoys, dark on one side, there was nothingness there, and on the other, lights, red and green, the lights of the body advancing on sexual heat, the signs of it anyway, nipples like scored pebbles, legs lightly thrashing, little *ohs;* nothing important, a body thing; you go on: you proceed.

When we strayed too far, there was nothingness, or only a distant flicker, only the faintest guidance. Sometimes we were surrounded by the lights of her responses, widely spaced, bobbing unevenly, on some darkness, some ignorance we both had, Orra and I, of what were the responses of her body. To the physical things I did and to the atmosphere of the way I did them, to the authority, the argument I made that this was sexual for her, that the way I touched her and concentrated on her, on the partly dream-laden dark water or underwater thing, she responded; she rested on that, rolled heavily on that. Everything I did was speech, was hieroglyphics, pictures on her nerves; it was what masculine authority was for, was what bravery and a firm manner and musculature were supposed to indicate that a man could bring to bed. Or skill at dancing; or musicianliness; or a sad knowingness. Licking her, holding her belly, stroking her belly pretty much with unthought-out movements—sometimes just moving my fingers closer together and spreading them again to show my pleasure, to show how rewarded I felt, not touching her breasts or doing anything so intensely that it would make her suspect me of being out to make her come—I did those things but it seemed like I left her alone and was private with my own pleasures. She felt unobserved with her sensations, she had them without responsibility, she clutched at them as something round and slippery in the water, and she would fall off them, occasionally gasping at the loss of her balance, the loss of her self-possession too.

I'd flick, idly almost, at her little spaghetti-ending with my tongue, then twice more idly, then three or four or five times in sequence, then settle down to rub it or bounce it between lip and tongue in a steadily more earnest way until my head, my consciousness, my lips and tongue were buried in the dark of an ascending and concentrated rhythm, in the way a stoned dancer lets a movement catch him and wrap him around and become all of him, become his voyage and not a collection of repetitions at all.

Then some boring stringy thing, a sinew at the base of my tongue, would begin to ache, and I'd break off that movement, and sleepily lick her, or if the tongue was too uncomfortable, I'd worry her clit, I'd nuzzle it with my pursed lips until the muscles that held my lips pursed grew tired in their turn; and I'd go back and flick at her tiny clitoris with my tongue, and go on as before, until the darkness came; she sensed the darkness, the privacy for her, and she seemed like someone in a hallway, unobserved, moving her arms, letting her mind stroke itself, taking a step in that dark.

But whatever she felt was brief and halting; and when she seemed to halt or to be dead or jagged, I authoritatively, gesturally accepted that as part of what was pleasurable to me and did not let it stand as hint or foretaste of failure; I produced sighs of pleasure, even gasps, not all of them false, warm nuzzlings, and caresses that indicated I was rewarded—I produced rewarded strokings; I made elements of sexual pleasure out of moments that were unsexual and that could be taken as the collapse of sexuality.

And she couldn't contradict me because she thought I was working on my own coming, and she loved me and meant to be cooperative.

What I did took nerve because it gave her a tremendous ultimate power to laugh at me, although what the courtship up until now had been for was to show that she was not an enemy, that she could control the hysteria of fear or jealousy in her or the cold judgments in her of me that would lead her to say or do things that would make me hate or fear her; what was at stake included the risk that I would look foolish in my own eyes—and might then attack her for failing to come—and then she would be unable to resist the inward conviction I was a fool. Any attempted act confers vulnerability on you but an act devoted to her pleasure represented doubled vulnerability since only she could judge it; and I was safe only if I was immune or insensitive to her; but if I was immune or insensitive I could not hope to help her come; by making myself vulnerable to her, I was in a way being a sissy or a creep because Orra wasn't organized or trained or prepared to accept responsibility for how I felt about myself: she was a woman who wanted to be left alone; she was paranoid about the inroads on her life men in their egos tried to make: there was dangerous masochism, dangerous hubris, dangerous hopefulness, and a form of love in my doing what I did: I nuzzled nakedly at the crotch of the sexual tigress; any weakness in her ego or her judgment and she would lash out at *me;* and the line was very frail between what I was doing as love and as intrusion, exploitation, and stupid boastfulness. There was no way for me even to begin to imagine the mental pain—or the physical pain—for her if I should fail, and, then to add to that, if I should withdraw from her emotionally too, because of my failure and hers and our pain. Or merely because the failure might make me so uncomfortable I couldn't go on unless she nursed my ego, and she couldn't nurse my ego, she didn't know how to do it, and probably was inhibited about doing it.

Sometimes my hands, my fingers, not just the tips, but all of their inside surface and the palms, held her thighs, or cupped her little belly, or my fingers moved around the lips, the labia or whatever, or even poked a little into her, or with the nails or tips lightly nudged her clitoris, always within a fictional frame of my absolute sexual pleasure, of my admiration for this sex, of there being no danger in it for us. No tongues or brains handy to speak unkindly, I meant. My God, I felt exposed and noble. This was a great effort to make for her.

Perhaps that only indicates the extent of my selfishness. I didn't mind being feminized except for the feeling that Orra would not ever understand what I was doing but would ascribe it to the power of my or our sexuality. I minded being this self-conscious and so conscious of her; I was separated from my own sexuality, from any real sexuality; a poor sexual experience, even one based on love, would diminish the ease of my virility with her at least for a while; and she wouldn't understand. Maybe she would become much subtler and shrewder sexually and know how to handle me but that wasn't likely. And if I apologized or complained or explained in that problematic future why I was sexually a little slow or reluctant with her, she would then blame my having tried to give her orgasm, she would insist I must not be bored again, so I would in that problematic future, if I wanted her to come, have to lie and say I was having more excitement than I felt, and that too might diminish my pleasure. I would be deprived even of the chance for honesty: I would be further feminized in that regard. I thought all this while I went down on her. I didn't put it in words but thought in great misty blocks of something known or sensed. I felt an inner weariness I kept working in spite of. This ignoring myself gave me an odd, starved feeling, a mixture of agony and helplessness. I didn't want to feel like that. I suddenly wondered why in the Theory of Relativity the speed of light is given as a constant: was that more Jewish absolutism? Surely in a universe as changeable and as odd as this one, the speed of light, considering the variety of experiences, must vary;

there must be a place where one could see a beam of light struggle to move. I felt silly and selfish; it couldn't be avoided that I felt like that—I mean it couldn't be avoided by *me*.

Whatever she did when I licked her, if she moved at all, if a muscle twitched in her thigh, a muscle twitched in mine, my body imitated hers as if to measure what she felt or perhaps for no reason but only because the sympathy was so intense. The same things happened to each of us but in amazingly different contexts as if we stood at opposite ends of the room and reached out to touch each other and to receive identical messages which then diverged as they entered two such widely separated sensibilities and two such divergent and incomplete ecstasies. The movie we watched was of her discovering how her sexual responses worked: we were seated far apart. My tongue pushed at her erasure, her wronged and heretofore hardly existent sexual powers. I stirred her with varieties of kisses far from her face. A strange river moved slowly, bearing us along, reeds hid the banks, willows braided and unbraided themselves, moaned and whispered, raveled and faintly clicked. Orra groaned, sighed, shuddered, shuddered harshly or liquidly; sometimes she jumped when I changed the pressure or posture of my hands on her or when I rested for a second and then resumed. Her body jumped and contracted interestingly but not at any length or in any pattern that I could understand. My mind grew tired. There is a limit to invention, to mine anyway: I saw myself (stupidly) as a Roman trireme, my tongue as the prow, *bronze,* pushing at her; she was the Mediterranean. Tiers of slaves, my god, the helplessness of them, pulled oars, long stalks that metaphorically and rhythmically bloomed with flowing clusters of short-lived lilies at the water's surface. The pompous and out-of-proportion boat, all of me hunched over Orra's small sea—not actually hunched: what I was, was lying flat, the foot of the bed was at my waist or near there, my legs were out, my feet were propped distantly on the floor, all of me was concentrated on the soft, shivery, furry delicacies of Orra's twat, the pompous boat advanced lickingly, leaving a trickling, gurgling wake of half-response, the ebbing of my will and activity into that fluster subsiding into the dark water of this girl's passivity, taut storminess, and self-ignorance.

The whitish bubbling, the splash of her discontinuous physical response: those waves, ah, that wake rose, curled outward, bubbled, and fell. Rose, curled outward, bubbled, and fell. The white fell of a naiad. In the vast spreading darkness and silence of the sea. There was nothing but that wake. The darkness of my senses when the rhythm absorbed me (so that I vanished from my awareness, so that I was blotted up and was a stain, a squid hidden, stroking Orra) made it twilight or night for me; and my listening for her pleasure, for our track on that markless ocean, gave me the sense that where we were was in a lit-up, great, ill-defined oval of night air and sea and opalescent fog, rainbowed where the lights from the portholes of an immense ship were altered prismatically by droplets of mist—as in some 1930's movie, as in some dream. Often I was out of breath; I saw spots, colors, ocean depths. And her protests, her doubts! My God, her doubts! Her *No don't, Wiley*'s and her *I don't want to do this*'s and her *Wiley, don't*'s and *Wiley, I can't come—don't do this—I don't like this*'s. Mostly I ignored her. Sometimes I silenced her by leaning my cheek on her belly and watching my hand stroke her belly and saying to her in a sex-thickened voice, "Orra, I like this—this is for me."

Then I went down on her again with unexpectedly vivid, real pleasure, as if merely thinking about my own pleasure excited and refreshed me, and there was yet more pleasure, when she—reassured or strengthened by my putative selfishness, by the conviction that this was all for me, that nothing was expected of her—cried out. Then a second later she *grunted*. Her whole body rippled. Jesus, I loved it when she reacted to me. It was like causing an entire continent to convulse, Asia, South America. I felt huge and tireless.

In her excitement, she threw herself into the air; but my hands happened to be on her belly; and I fastened her down, I held that part of her comparatively still with her twat fastened to my mouth, and I licked her while she was in mid-heave; and she yelled; I kept my mouth there as if I were drinking from her; I stayed like that until her upper body fell back on the bed and bounced, she made the whole bed bounce; then my head bounced away from her; but I still held her down with my hands; and I fastened myself, my mouth, on her twat again; and she yelled in a deep voice, *"Wiley, what are you doing!"*

Her voice was deep, as if her impulses at that moment were masculine, not out of neurosis but in generosity, in an attempt to improve on the sickliness she accused women of; she wanted to meet me halfway, to share; to share my masculinity: she thought men were beautiful: she cried out, *"I don't want you to do things to me! I want you to have a good fuck!"*

Her voice was deep and despairing, maybe with the despair that goes with surges of sexuality, but then maybe she thought I would make her pay for this. I said, "Orra, I like this stuff, this stuff is what gets me excited." She resisted, just barely, for some infinitesimal fragment of a second, and then her body began to vibrate; it twittered as if in it were the strings of a musical instrument set jangling; she said foolishly—but sweetly—"Wiley, I'm embarrassed, Wiley, this embarrasses *me* . . . Please stop . . . No . . . No . . . No . . . Oh . . . Oh . . . Oh . . . I'm very sexual, I'm too sexual to have orgasms, Wiley, stop, please . . . Oh . . . Oh . . . Oh . . ." And then a deeper shudder ran through her; she gasped; then there was a silence; then she gasped again; she cried out in an extraordinary voice, *"I FEEL SOMETHING!"* The hair stood up on the back of my neck; I couldn't stop; I hurried on; I heard a dim moaning come from her. What had she felt before? I licked hurriedly. How unpleasant for her, how unreal and twitchy had the feelings been that I'd given her? In what way was this different? I wondered if there was in her a sudden swarming along her nerves, a warm conviction of the reality of sexual pleasure. She heaved like a whale—no: not so much as that. But it was as if half an ocean rolled off her young flanks; some element of darkness vanished from the room; some slight color of physical happiness tinctured her body and its thin coating of sweat; I felt it all through me; she rolled on the surface of a pale blue, a pink and blue sea; she was dark and gleaming, and immense and wet. And warm.

She cried, *"Wiley, I feel a lot!"*

God, she was happy.

I said, "Why not?" I wanted to lower the drama quotient; I thought the excess of drama was a mistake, would overburden her. But also I wanted her to defer to me, I wanted authority over her body now, I wanted to make her come.

But she didn't get any more excited than that: she was rigid, almost boardlike, after a few seconds. I licked at her thing as best I could but the sea was dry; the board collapsed. I faked it that I was very excited; actually I was so caught up in being sure of myself, I didn't know what I really felt. I thought, as if I was much younger than I was, Boy, if this doesn't work, is my name mud. Then to build up the risk, out of sheer hellish braggadocio, instead of just acting out that I was confident—and in sex, everything unsaid that is portrayed in gestures instead is twice as powerful—when she said, because the feeling was less for her now, the feeling she liked having gone away, "Wiley, I can't—this is silly—" I said, "Shut up, Orra, I know what I'm doing. . . ." But I didn't know.

And I didn't like that tone for sexual interplay either, except as a joke, or as role-playing, because pure authority involves pure submission, and people don't survive pure submission except by being slavishly, possessively, vindictively in love; when they are in love like that, they can *give* you nothing but rebellion and submission, bitchiness and submission; it's a general rottenness: you get no part of them out of bed that has any value; and in bed, you get a grudging submission, because what the slave requires is your total attention, or she starts paying you back; I suppose the model is childhood, that slavery. Anyway I don't like it. But I played at it, then, with Orra, as a gamble.

Everything was a gamble. I didn't know what I was doing; I figured it out as I went along; and how much time did I have for figuring things out just then? I felt strained as at poker or roulette, sweaty and a little stupid, placing bets—with my tongue—and waiting to see what the wheel did, risking my money when no one forced me to, hoping things would go my way, and I wouldn't turn out to have been stupid when this was over.

Also, there were sudden fugitive convulsions of lust now, in sympathy with her larger but scattered responses, a sort of immediate and automatic sexuality—I was at the disposal, inwardly, of the sexuality in her and could not help myself, could not hold it back and avoid the disappointments, and physical impatience, the impatience in my skin and prick, of the huge desire that unmistakably accompanies love, of a primitive longing for what seemed her happiness, for closeness to her as to something I had studied and was studying and had found more and more of value in—what was of value was the way she valued me, a deep, and no doubt limited (but in the sexual moment it seemed illimitable), permissiveness toward me, a risk she took, an allowance she made as if she'd let me damage her and use her badly.

Partly what kept me going was stubbornness because I'd made up my mind before we started that I wouldn't give up; and partly what it was was the feeling she aroused in me, a feeling that was, to be honest, made up of tenderness and concern and a kind of mere affection, a brotherliness, as if she was my brother, not different from me at all.

Actually this was brought on by an increasing failure, as the sex went on, of one kind of sophistication—of worldly sophistication—and by the increase in me of another kind, of a childish sophistication, a growth of innocence: Orra said, or exclaimed, in a half-harried, half-amazed voice, in a hugely admiring, gratuitous way, as she clutched at me in approval, "Wiley, I never had feelings like these before!"

And to be the first to have caused them, you know? It's like being a collector, finding something of great value, where it had been unsuspected and disguised, or like earning any honor; this partial success, this encouragement, gave rise to this pride, this inward innocence.

Of course that lessened the risk for this occasion; I could fail now and still say, *It was worth it,* and she would agree; but it lengthened the slightly longer-term risk; because I might feel trebly a fool someday. Also it meant we might spend months making love in this fashion—I'd get impotent, maybe not in terms of erection, but I wouldn't look forward to sex—still, that was beautiful to me in a way too, and exciting. I really didn't know what I was thinking: whatever I thought was part of the sex.

I went on, I wanted to hit the jackpot now. Then Orra shouted, "It's *there!* It's *THERE!*" I halted, thinking she meant it was in some specific locale, in some specific motion I'd just made with my tired tongue and jaw; I lifted my head—but couldn't speak: in a way, the sexuality pressed on me too hard for me to speak; anyway I didn't have to; she had lifted her head with a kind of overt twinship and she was looking at me down the length of her body; her face was askew and boyish—every feature was wrinkled; she looked angry and yet naïve and swindleable; she said angrily, naïvely, "*Wiley, it's there!*"

But even before she spoke that time, I knew she'd meant it was in her; the fox had been startled from its covert again; she had seen it, had felt it run in her again. She had been persuaded that it was in her for good.

I started manipulating her delicately with my hand; and in my own excitement, and thinking she was ready, I sort of scrambled up and, covering her with myself, and playing with her with one hand, guided my other self, my lower consciousness, into her. My God, she was warm and restless inside; it was heated in there and smooth, insanely smooth, and oiled, and full of movements. But I knew at once I'd made a mistake: I should have gone on licking her; there were no regular contractions; she was anxious for the prick, she rose around it, closed around it, but in a rigid, dumb, far-away way; and her twitchings played on it, ran through it, through the walls of it and into me; and they were uncontrolled and not exciting, but empty; she didn't know what to do, how to be fucked and come. I couldn't pull out of her, I didn't want to, I couldn't pull out; but if there were no contractions for me to respond to, how in hell would I find the rhythm for her? I started slowly with what seemed infinite suggestiveness to me, with great dirtiness, a really grownup sort of fucking—just in case she was far along—and she let out a huge, shuddering hour-long sigh and cried out my name and then in a sobbing, exhausted voice, said, "I lost it . . . Oh Wiley, I lost it . . . Let's stop . . ." My face was above hers; her face was wet with tears; why was she crying like that? She had changed her mind; now she wanted to come; she turned her head back and forth; she said, "I'm no good . . . I'm no good . . . Don't worry about me . . . You come . . ."

No matter what I mumbled, "Hush," and "Don't be silly," and in a whisper, "Orra, I love you," she kept on saying those things until I slapped her lightly and said, *"Shut up, Orra."*

Then she was silent again.

The thing was, apparently, that she was arrhythmic: at least that's what I thought; and that meant there weren't going to be regular contractions, any rhythm for me to follow; and any rhythm I set up as I fucked, she broke with her movements: so that it was that when she moved, she made her excitement go away: it would be best if she moved very smally: but I was afraid to tell her that, or even to try to hold her hips firmly, and guide them, to instruct her in that way for fear she'd get self-conscious and lose what momentum she'd won. And also I was ashamed that I'd stopped going down on her. I experimented—doggedly, sweatily, to make up for what I'd done—with fucking in different ways, and I fantasized about us being in Mexico, some place warm and lushly colored where we made love easily and filthily and graphically. The fantasy kept me going. That is, it kept me hard. I kept acting out an atmosphere of sexual pleasure—I mean of my sexual pleasure—for her to rest on, so she could count on that. I discovered that a not very slow sort of one-one-one stroke, or fuck-fuck-fuck-Orra-now-now-now really got to her; her feelings would grow heated; and she could shift up from that with me into a one-two, one-two, one-two, her excitement rising; but if she or I then tried to shift up farther to one-two-three, one-two-three, one-two-three, she'd lose it all. That was too complicated for her: my own true love, my white American. But her feelings when they were present were very strong, they came in gusts, huge squalls of heat as if from a furnace with a carelessly banging door, and they excited and allured both of us. That excitement and the dit-dit-ditting got to her; she began to be generally, continuingly sexual. It's almost standard to compare sexual excitement to holiness; well, after a while, holiness seized her; she spoke with tongues, she testified. She was shaking all over; she was saved temporarily and sporadically; that is, she kept lapsing out of that excitement too. But it would recur. Her hands would flutter; her face would be pale and then red, then very, very red; her eyes would stare at nothing; she'd call my name. I'd plug on one-one-one, then one-two, one-two, then I'd go back to one-one-one: I could see as before—in the deep pleasure I felt even in the midst of the labor—why a man might kill her in order to stimulate in her (although he might not know this was why he did it) these signs of pleasure. The familiar Orra had vanished; she said, "GodohGodohGod"; it was sin and redemption and holiness and visions time. Her throbs were very direct, easily comprehensible, but without any pattern; they weren't in any regular sequence; still, they were exciting to me, maybe all the more exciting because of the piteousness of her not being able to regulate them, of their being like blows delivered inside her by an enemy whom she couldn't even half-domesticate or make friendly to herself or speak to. She was the most out-of-control girl I ever screwed. She would at times start to thrust like a woman who had her sexuality readied and well-understood at last and I'd start to distend with anticipation and a pride and relief as large as a house; but after two thrusts—or four, or six—she'd have gotten too excited, she'd be shaking, she'd thrust crookedly and out of tempo, the movement would collapse; or she'd suddenly jerk in mid-movement without warning and crash around with so great and so meaningless a violence that she'd lose her thing; and she'd start to cry. She'd whisper wetly, "I lost it"; so I'd say, "No you didn't," and I'd go on or start over, one-one-one; and of course, the excitement would come back; sometimes it came back at once; but she was increasingly afraid of herself, afraid to move her lower body; she would try to hold still and just *receive* the excitement; she would let it pool up in her; but then too she'd begin to shake more and more; she'd leak over into spasmodic and oddly sad, too large movements; and she'd whimper, knowing, I suppose, that those movements were breaking the tempo in herself; again and again, tears streamed down her cheeks; she said in a not quite hoarse, in a sweet, almost hoarse whisper, "I don't want to come, Wiley, you go ahead and come."

My mind had pretty much shut off; it had become exhausted; and I didn't see how we were going to make this work; she said, "Wiley, it's all right—please, it's all right—I don't want to come."

I wondered if I should say something and try to trigger some fantasy in her; but I didn't want to risk saying something she'd find unpleasant or think was a reproach or a hint for her to be sexier. I thought if I just kept on dit-dit-ditting, sooner or later, she'd find it in herself, the trick of riding on her feelings, and getting them to rear up, crest, and topple. I held her tightly, in sympathy and pity, and maybe fear, and admiration: she was so unhysterical; she hadn't yelled at me or broken anything; she hadn't ordered me around: she was simply alone and shaking in the middle of a neural storm in her that she seemed to have no gift for handling. I said, "Orra, it's OK: I really prefer long fucks," and I went on, dit-dit-dit-dit, then I'd shift up to dit-dot, dit-dot, dit-dot, dit-dot . . . My back hurt, my legs were going; if sweat was sperm, we would have looked like liquefied snow fields.

Orra made noises, more and more quickly, and louder and louder; then the noises she made slackened off. Then, step by step, with shorter and shorter strokes, then out of control and clumsy, simply reestablishing myself inside the new approach, I settled down, fucked slowly. The prick was embedded far in her; I barely stirred; the drama of sexual movement died away, the curtains were stilled; there was only sensation on the stage.

I bumped against the stone blocks and hidden hooks that nipped and bruised me into the soft rottenness, the strange, glowing, breakable hardness of coming, of the sensations at the approaches to coming.

I panted and half-rolled and pushed and edged it in, and slid it back, sweatily—I was semi-expert, aimed, intent: sex can be like a wilderness that imprisons you: the daimons of the locality claim you: I was achingly nagged by sensations; my prick had been somewhat softened before and now it swelled with a sore-headed, but fine distension: Orra shuddered and held me cooperatively; I began to forget her.

I thought she was making herself come on the slow fucking, on the prick which, when it was seated in her like this, when I hardly moved it, seemed to belong to her as much as to me; the prick seemed to *enter* me too; we both seemed to be sliding on it, the sensation was like that; but there was the moment when I became suddenly aware of her again, of the flesh and blood and bone in my arms, beneath me. I had a feeling of grating on her, and of her grating on me. I didn't recognize the unpleasantness at first. I don't know how long it went on before I felt it as a withdrawal in her, a withdrawal that she had made, a patient and restrained horror in her, and impatience in me: our arrival at sexual shambles.

My heart filled suddenly—filled; and then all feeling ran out of it—it emptied itself.

I continued to move in her slowly, numbly, in a shabby hubbub of faceless shudderings and shufflings of the mid-section and half-thrusts, half-twitches; we went on holding each other, in silence, without slackening the intensity with which we held each other; our movements, that flopping in place, that grinding against each other, went on; neither of us protested in any way. Bad sex can be sometimes stronger and more moving than good sex. She made sobbing noises—and held on to me. After a while sex seemed very ordinary and familiar and unromantic. I started going dit-dit-dit again.

Her hips jerked up half a dozen times before it occurred to me again that she liked to thrust like a boy, that she wanted to thrust, and then it occurred to me she wanted me to thrust.

I maneuvered my ass slightly and tentatively delivered a shove, or rather, delivered an authoritative shove, but not one of great length, one that was exploratory; Orra sighed, with relief it seemed to me; and jerked, encouragingly, too late, as I was pulling back. When I delivered a second thrust, a somewhat more obvious one, more amused, almost boyish, I was like a boy whipping a fairly fast ball in a game, at a first baseman—she jerked almost wolfishly, gobbling up the extravagant power of the gesture, of the thrust; with an odd shudder of pleasure, of irresponsibility, of boyishness, I suddenly realized how physically strong Orra was, how well-knit, how well put together her body was, how great the power in it, the power of endurance in it; and a phrase—absurd and demeaning but exciting just then—came into my head: *to throw a fuck;* and I settled myself atop her, braced my toes and knees and elbows and hands on the bed and half-scramblingly worked *it—it* was clearly mine; but I was Orra's—worked *it* into a passionate shove, a curving stroke about a third as long as a full stroke; but amateur and gentle, that is, tentative still; and Orra screamed then; how she screamed; she made known her readiness: then the next time, she grunted: "Uhnnn-nahhhhhh . . ." a sound thick at the beginning but that trailed into refinement, into sweetness, a lingering sweetness.

It seemed to me I really wanted to fuck like this, that *I* had been waiting for this all my life. But it wasn't really my taste, that kind of fuck: I liked to throw a fuck with less force and more gradations and implications of force rather than with the actual thing; and with more immediate contact between the two sets of pleasures and with more admissions of defeat and triumph; my pleasure was a thing of me reflecting her; her spirit entering me; or perhaps it was merely a mistake, my thinking that; but it seemed shameful and automatic, naïve and animal: to throw the prick into her like that.

She took the thrust: she convulsed a little; she fluttered all over; her skin fluttered; things twitched in her, in the disorder surrounding the phallic blow in her. After two thrusts, she collapsed, went flaccid, then toughened and readied herself again, rose a bit from the bed, aimed the flattened, mysteriously funnel-like container of her lower end at me, too high, so that I had to pull her down with my hands on her butt or on her hips; and her face, when I glanced at her beneath my lids, was fantastically pleasing, set, concentrated, busy, harassed; her body was strong, was stone, smooth stone and wet-satin paper bags and snaky webs, thin and alive, made of woven snakes that lived, thrown over the stone; she held the great, writhing-skinned stone construction toward me, the bony marvel, the half-dish of bone with its secretive, gluey-smooth entrance, *the place where I was*—it was undefined, except for that: *the place where I was:* she took and met each thrust—and shuddered and collapsed and rose again: she seemed to rise to the act of taking it; I thought she was partly mistaken, childish, to think that the center of sex was to meet and take the prick thrown into her as hard as it could be thrown, now that she was excited; but there was a weird wildness, a wild freedom, like children cavorting, uncontrolled, set free, but not hysterical merely without restraint; the odd, thickened, knobbed pole springing back and forth as if mounted on a web of wide rubber bands; it was a naïve and a complete release. I whomped it in and she went, "UHNNN!" and a half-iota of a second later, I was seated all the way in her, I jerked a minim of an inch deeper in her, and went "UHNNN!" too. Her whole body shook. She would go, "UHN!" And I would go, "UHN!"

Then when it seemed from her strengthening noises and her more rapid and jerkier movements that she was near the edge of coming, I'd start to place whomps, in neater and firmer arrangements, more obviously in a rhythm, more businesslike, more teasing with pauses at each end of a thrust; and that would excite her up to a point; but then her excitement would level off, and not go over the brink. So I would speed up: I'd thrust harder, then harder yet, then harder and faster; she made her noises and half-thrust back. She bit her lower lip; she set her teeth in her lower lip; blood appeared. I fucked still faster, but on a shorter stroke, almost thrumming on her, and angling my abdomen hopefully to drum on her clitoris; sometimes her body would go limp; but her cries would speed up, bird after bird flew out of her mouth while she lay limp as if I were a boxer and had destroyed her ability to move; then when the cries did not go past a certain point, when she didn't come, I'd slow and start again. I wished I'd been a great athlete, a master of movement, a woman, a lesbian, a man with a gigantic prick that would explode her into coming. I moved my hands to the corners of the mattress; and spread my legs; I braced myself with my hands and feet; and braced like that, free-handed in a way, drove into her; and the new posture, the feeling she must have had of being covered, and perhaps the difference in the thrust got to her; but Orra's body began to set up a babble, a babble of response then—I think the posture played on her mind.

But she did not come.

I moved my hands and held the dish of her hips so that she couldn't wiggle or deflect the thrust or pull away: she began to "Uhn" again but interspersed with small screams: we were like kids playing catch (her poor brutalized clitoris), playing hard hand: this was what she thought sex was; it was sexual, as throwing a ball hard is sexual; in a way, too, we were like acrobats hurling ourselves at each other, to meet in mid-air, and fall entangled to the net. It was like that.

Her mouth came open, her eyes had rolled to one side and stayed there—it felt like twilight to me—I knew where she was sexually, or thought I did. She pushed, she egged us on. She wasn't breakable this way. Orra. I wondered if she knew, it made me like her how naïve this was, this American fuck, this kids-playing-at-twilight-on-the-neighborhood-street fuck. After I seated it and wriggled a bit in her and moozed on her clitoris with my abdomen, I would draw it out not in a straight line but at some curve so that it would press against the walls of her cunt and she could keep track of where it was; and I would pause fractionally just before starting to thrust, so she could brace herself and expect it; I whomped it in and understood her with an absurd and probably unfounded sense of my sexual virtuosity; and she became silent suddenly, then she began to breathe loudly, then something in her toppled; or broke, then all at once she shuddered in a different way. It really was as if she lay on a bed of wings, as if she had a half-dozen wings folded under her, six huge wings, large, veined, throbbing, alive wings, real ones, with fleshy edges from which glittering feathers sprang backwards; and they all stirred under her.

She half-rose; and I'd hold her so she didn't fling herself around and lose her footing, or her airborneness, on the uneasy glass mountain she'd begun to ascend, the frail transparency beneath her, that was forming and growing beneath her, that seemed to me to foam with light and darkness, as if we were rising above a landscape of hedges and moonlight and shadows: a mountain, a sea that formed and grew; it grew and grew; and she said "OH!" and "OHHHH!" almost with vertigo, as if she was airborne but unsteady on the vans of her wings, and as if I was there without wings but by some magic dispensation and by some grace of familiarity; I thunked on and on, and she looked down and was frightened; the tension in her body grew vast; and suddenly a great, a really massive violence ran through her but now it was as if, in fear at her height or out of some automatism, the first of her three pairs of wings began to beat, great fans winnowingly, great wings of flesh out of which feathers grew, catching at the air, stabilizing and yet lifting her: she whistled and rustled so; she was at once so still and so violent; the great wings engendered, their movement engendered in her, patterns of flexed and crossed muscles: her arms and legs and breasts echoed or carried out the strain, or strained to move the weight of those winnowing, moving wings. Her breaths were wild but not loud and slanted every which way, irregular and new to this particular dream, and very much as if she looked down on great spaces of air; she grabbed at me, at my shoulders, but she had forgotten how to work her hands, her hands just made the gestures of grabbing, the gestures of a well-meaning, dark but beginning to be luminous, mad, amnesiac angel. She called out, "Wiley, Wiley!" but she called it out in a *whisper,* the whisper of someone floating across a night sky, of someone crazily ascending, someone who was going crazy, who was taking on the mad purity and temper of angels, someone who was tormented unendurably by this, who was unendurably frightened, whose pleasure was enormous, half-human, mad. Then she screamed in rebuke, "Wiley!" She screamed my name: "*Wiley!*"—she did it hoarsely and insanely, asking for help, but blaming me, and merely as exclamation; it was a gutter sound in part, and ugly; the ugliness, when it destroyed nothing, or maybe it had an impetus of its own, but it whisked away another covering, a membrane of ordinariness—I don't know—and her second pair of wings began to beat; her whole body was aflutter on the bed. I was as wet as—as some fish, thonking away, sweatily. Grinding away. I said, "It's OK, Orra. It's OK." And poked on. In mid-air. She shouted, "*What is this!*" She shouted it in the way a tremendously large person who can defend herself might shout at someone who was unwisely beating her up. She shouted—angrily, as an announcement of anger, it seemed—"*Oh my God!*" Like: *Who broke this cup?* I plugged on. She raised her torso, her head, she looked me clearly in the eye, her eyes were enormous, were bulging, and she said, "*Wiley, it's happening!*" Then she lay down again and screamed for a couple of seconds. I said a little dully, grinding on, "It's OK, Orra. It's OK." I didn't want to say *Let go* or to say anything lucid because I didn't know a damn thing about female orgasm after all, and I didn't want to give her any advice and wreck things; and also I didn't want to commit myself in case this turned out to be a false alarm; and we had to go on. I pushed in, lingered, pulled back, went in, only half on beat, one-thonk-one-thonk, then one-one-one, saying, "This is sexy, this is good for me, Orra, this is very good for me," and then, "Good Orra," and she trembled in a new way at that, "*Good* Orra," I said, "*Good . . . Orra*," and then all at once, it happened. Something pulled her over; and something gave in; and all three pairs of wings began to beat: she was the center and the source and the victim of a storm of wing beats; we were at the top of the world; the huge bird of God's body in us hovered; the great miracle pounded on her back, pounded around us; she was straining and agonized and distraught, estranged within this corporeal-incorporeal thing, this angelic other avatar, this other substance of herself: the wings were outspread; they thundered and gaspily galloped with her; they half broke her; and she screamed, "*Wiley!*" and "*My-godmygod*" and "*IT'S NOT STOPPING, WILEY, IT'S NOT STOP-PING!*" She was pale *and* red; her hair was everywhere; her body was wet, and thrashing. It was as if something unbelievably strange and fierce—like the holy temper—lifted her to where she could not breathe or walk: she choked in the ether, a scrambling seraph, tumbling, and aflame and alien, powerful beyond belief, hideous and frightening and beautiful beyond the reach of the human. A screaming child, an angel howling in the Godly sphere: she churned without delicacy, as wild as an angel bearing threats; her body lifted from the sheets, fell back, lifted again; her hands beat on the bed; she made very loud hoarse tearing noises—I was frightened for her: this was her first time after six years of playing around with her body. It hurt her; her face looked like something made of stone, a monstrous carving; only her body was alive; her arms and legs were outspread and tensed and they beat or they were weak and fluttering. She was an angel as brilliant as a beautiful insect infinitely enlarged and irrevocably foreign: she was unlike me: she was a girl making rattling, astonished, uncontrolled, unhappy noises, a girl looking shocked and intent and harassed by the variety and viciousness of the sensations, including relief, that attacked her. I sat up on my knees and moved a little in her and stroked her breasts, with smooth sideways, winglike strokes. And she screamed, *Wiley, I'm coming!*" and with a certain idiocy entered on her second orgasm or perhaps her third since she'd started to come a few minutes before; and we should have gone on for hours but she said, "It hurts, Wiley, I hurt, make it stop . . ." So I didn't move; I just held her thighs with my hands; and her things began to trail off, to trickle down, into little shiverings; the stoniness left her face; she calmed into moderated shudders, and then she said, she started to speak with wonder but then it became an exclamation and ended on a kind of hollow note, the prelude to a small scream: she said, "I *came* . . ." Or "I ca-a-a-ammmmmmmme . . ." What happened was that she had another orgasm at the thought that she'd had her first.

That one was more like three little ones, diminishing in strength. When she was quieter, she was gasping, she said, "Oh you *love* me . . ."

That too excited her. When that died down, she said—angrily—"I always knew they were doing it wrong, I always knew there was nothing wrong with me . . ." And that triggered a little set of ripples. Some time earlier, without knowing it, I'd begun to cry. My tears fell

on her thighs, her belly, her breasts, as I moved up, along her body,
above her, to lie atop her. I wanted to hold her, my face next to hers;
I wanted to hold her. I slid my arms in and under her, and she said,
"Oh, Wiley," and she tried to lift her arms, but she started to shake
again; then trembling anyway, she lifted her arms and hugged me with
a shuddering sternness that was unmistakable; then she began to
cry too.

Mary Gaitskill

A Romantic Weekend

She was meeting a man she had recently and abruptly fallen in love with. She was in a state of ghastly anxiety. He was married, for one thing, to a Korean woman whom he described as the embodiment of all that was feminine and elegant. Not only that, but a psychic had told her that a relationship with him could cripple her emotionally for the rest of her life. On top of this, she was tormented by the feeling that she looked inadequate. Perhaps her body tilted too far forward as she walked, perhaps her jacket made her torso look bulky in contrast to her calves and ankles, which were probably skinny. She felt like an object unraveling in every direction. In anticipation of their meeting, she had not been able to sleep the night before; she had therefore eaten some amphetamines and these had heightened her feeling of disintegration.

When she arrived at the corner he wasn't there. She stood against a building, trying to arrange her body in the least repulsive configuration possible. Her discomfort mounted. She crossed the street and stood on the other corner. It seemed as though everyone who walked by was eating. A large, distracted businessman went by holding a half-eaten hot dog. Two girls passed, sharing cashews from a white bag. The eating added to her sense that the world was disorderly and unbeautiful. She became acutely aware of the garbage on the street. The wind stirred it; a candy wrapper waved forlornly from its trapped position in the mesh of a jammed public wastebasket. This was all wrong, all horrible. Her meeting with him should be perfect and scrap-free. She couldn't bear the thought of flapping trash. Why wasn't he there to meet her? Minutes passed. Her shoulders drew together.

She stepped into a flower store. The store was clean and white, except for a few smudges on the linoleum floor. Homosexuals with low voices stood behind the counter. Arranged stalks bearing absurd blossoms protruded from sedate round vases and bristled in the aisles. She had a paroxysm of fantasy. He held her, helpless and swooning, in his arms. They were supported by a soft ball of puffy blue stuff. Thornless roses surrounded their heads. His gaze penetrated her so thoroughly, it was as though he had thrust his hand into her chest and begun feeling her ribs one by one. This was all right with her. "I have never met anyone I felt this way about," he said. "I love you." He made her do things she'd never done before, and then they went for a walk and looked at the new tulips that were bound to have grown up somewhere. None of this felt stupid or corny, but she knew that it was. Miserably, she tried to gain a sense of proportion. She stared at the flowers. They were an agony of bright, organized beauty. She couldn't help it. She wanted to give him flowers. She wanted to be with him in a room full of flowers. She visualized herself standing in front of him, bearing a handful of blameless flowers trapped in the ugly pastel paper the florist would staple around them. The vision was brutally embarrassing, too much so to stay in her mind for more than seconds.

She stepped out of the flower store. He was not there. Her anxiety approached despair. They were supposed to spend the weekend together.

He stood in a cheap pizza stand across the street, eating a greasy slice and watching her as she stood on the corner. Her anxiety was visible to him. It was at once disconcerting and weirdly attractive. Her appearance otherwise was not pleasing. He couldn't quite put his finger on why this was. Perhaps it was the suggestion of meekness in her dress, of a desire to be inconspicuous, or worse, of plain thoughtlessness about how clothes looked on her.

He had met her at a party during the previous week. She immediately reminded him of a girl he had known years before, Sharon, a painfully serious girl with a pale, gentle face whom he had tormented off and on for two years before leaving for his wife. Although it had gratified him enormously to leave her, he had missed hurting her for years, and had been half-consciously looking for another woman with a similarly fatal combination of pride, weakness and a foolish lust for something resembling passion. On meeting Beth, he was astonished at how much she looked, talked and moved like his former victim. She was delicately morbid in all her gestures, sensitive, arrogant, vulnerable to flattery. She veered between extravagant outbursts of opinion and sudden, uncertain halts, during which she seemed to look to him for approval. She was in love with the idea of intelligence, and she overestimated her own. Her sense of the world, though she presented it aggressively, could be, he sensed, snatched out from under her with little or no trouble. She said, "I hope you are a savage."

He went home with her that night. He lay with her on her sagging, lumpy single mattress, tipping his head to blow smoke into the room. She butted her forehead against his chest. The mattress squeaked with every movement. He told her about Sharon. "I had a relationship like that when I was in college," she said. "Somebody opened me up in a way that I had no control over. He hurt me. He changed me completely. Now I can't have sex normally."

The room was pathetically decorated with postcards, pictures of huge-eyed Japanese cartoon characters, and tiny, maddening toys that she had obviously gone out of her way to find, displayed in a tightly arranged tumble on her dresser. A frail model airplane dangled from the light above her dresser. Next to it was a pasted-up cartoon of a pink-haired girl cringing open-mouthed before a spike-haired boy-villain in shorts and glasses. Her short skirt was blown up by the force of his threatening expression, and her panties showed. What kind of person would put crap like this up on her wall?

"I'm afraid of you," she murmured.

"Why?"

"Because I just am."

"Don't worry. I won't give you any more pain than you can handle."

She curled against him and squeezed her feet together like a stretching cat. Her socks were thick and ugly, and her feet were large for her size. Details like this could repel him, but he felt tenderly toward the long, grubby, squeezed-together feet. He said, "I want a slave."

She said, "I don't know. We'll see."

He asked her to spend the weekend with him three days later.

It had seemed like a good idea at the time, but now he felt an irritating combination of guilt and anxiety. He thought of his wife, making breakfast with her delicate, methodical movements, or in the bathroom, painstakingly applying kohl under her huge eyes, flicking away the excess with pretty, birdlike finger gestures, her thin elbows raised, her eyes blank with concentration. He thought of Beth, naked and bound, blindfolded and spread-eagled on the floor of her cluttered apartment. Her cartoon characters grinned as he beat her with a whip. Welts rose on her breasts, thighs, stomach and arms. She screamed and twisted, wrenching her neck from side to side. She was going to be scarred for life. He had another picture of her sitting across from him at a restaurant, very erect, one arm on the table, her face serious and intent. Her large glasses drew her face down, made it look somber and elegant. She was smoking a cigarette with slow, mournful intakes of breath. These images lay on top of one another, forming a hideously confusing grid. How was he going to sort them out? He managed to separate the picture of his wife and the original picture of blindfolded Beth and hold them apart. He imagined himself traveling happily between the two. Perhaps, as time went on, he could bring Beth home and have his wife beat her too. She would do the dishes and serve them dinner. The grid closed up again and his stomach went into a moil. The thing was complicated and potentially exhausting. He looked at the anxious girl on the corner. She had said that she wanted to be hurt, but he suspected that she didn't understand what that meant.

He should probably just stay in the pizza place and watch her until she went away. It might be entertaining to see how long she waited. He felt a certain pity for her. He also felt, from his glassed-in vantage point, as though he were torturing an insect. He gloated as he ate his pizza.

At the height of her anxiety she saw him through the glass wall of the pizza stand. She immediately noticed his gloating countenance. She recognized the coldly scornful element in his watching and waiting as opposed to greeting her. She suffered, but only for an instant; she was then smitten by love. She smiled and crossed the street with a senseless confidence in the power of her smile.

"I was about to come over," he said. "I had to eat first. I was starving." He folded the last of his pizza in half and stuck it in his mouth.

She noticed a piece of bright orange pizza stuck between his teeth, and it endeared him to her.

They left the pizza stand. He walked with wide steps, and his heavy black overcoat swung rakishly, she thought, above his boots. He was a slight, slender boy with a pale, narrow face and blond hair that wisped across one brow. In the big coat he looked like the young pet of a budding secret police force. She thought he was beautiful.

He hailed a cab and directed the driver to the airport. He looked at her sitting beside him. "This is going to be a disaster," he said. "I'll probably wind up leaving you there and coming back alone."

"I hope not," she said. "I don't have any money. If you left me there, I wouldn't be able to get back by myself."

"That's too bad. Because I might." He watched her face for a reaction. It showed discomfort and excitement and something that he could only qualify as foolishness, as if she had just dropped a tray full of glasses in public. "Don't worry, I wouldn't do that," he said. "But I like the idea that I could."

"So do I." She was terribly distressed. She wanted to throw her arms around him.

He thought: There is something wrong. Her passivity was pleasing, as was her silence and her willingness to place herself in his hands. But he sensed another element present in her that he could not define and did not like. Her tightly folded hands were nervous and repulsive. Her public posture was brittle, not pliant. There was a rigidity that if cracked would yield nothing. He was disconcerted to realize that he didn't know if he could crack it anyway. He began to feel uncomfortable. Perhaps the weekend would be a disaster.

They arrived at the airport an hour early. They went to a bar and drank. The bar was an open-ended cube with a red neon sign that said "Cocktails." There was no sense of shelter in it. The furniture was spindly and exposed, and there were no doors to protect you from the sight of dazed, unattractive passengers wandering through the airport with their luggage. She ordered a Bloody Mary.

"I can't believe you ordered that," he said.

"Why not?"

"Because I want a bloody Beth." He gave her a look that made her think of a neurotic dog with its tongue hanging out, waiting to bite someone.

"Oh," she said.

He offered her a cigarette.

"I don't smoke," she said. "I told you twice."

"Well, you should start."

They sat quietly and drank for several minutes.

"Do you like to look at people?" she asked.

She was clearly struggling to talk to him. He saw that her face had become very tense. He could've increased her discomfort, but for the moment he had lost the energy to do so. "Yes," he said. "I do."

They spent some moments regarding the people around them. They were short on material. There were only a few customers in the bar; most of them were men in suits who sat there seemingly enmeshed in a web of habit and accumulated rancor that they called their personalities, so utterly unaware of their entanglement that they clearly considered themselves men of the world, even though they had long ago stopped noticing it. Then a couple walked through the door, carrying luggage. The woman's bright skirt flashed with each step. The man walked ahead of her. He walked too fast for her to keep up. She looked harried. Her eyes were wide and dark and clotted with makeup; there was a mole on her chin. He paused, as though considering whether he could stop for a drink. He decided not to and strode again. Her earrings jiggled as she followed. They left a faint trail of sex and disappointment behind them.

Beth watched the woman's hips move under her skirt. "There was something unpleasant about them," she said.

"Yes, there was."

It cheered her to find this point of contact. "I'm sorry I'm not more talkative," she said.

"That's all right." His narrow eyes became feral once again. "Women should be quiet." It suddenly struck her that it would seem completely natural if he lunged forward and bit her face.

"I agree," she said sharply. "There aren't many men around worth talking to."

He was nonplussed by her peevish tone. Perhaps, he thought, he'd imagined it.

He hadn't.

They had more drinks on the plane. They were served a hunk of white-frosted raisin pastry in a red paper bag. He wasn't hungry, but the vulgar cake appealed to him so he stuck it in his baggage.

They had a brief discussion about shoes, from the point of view of expense and aesthetics. They talked about intelligence and art. There were large gaps of silence that were disheartening to both of them. She began talking about old people, and how nice they could be. He had a picture of her kneeling on the floor in black stockings and handcuffs. This picture became blurred, static-ridden, and then obscured by their conversation. He felt a ghastly sense of longing. He called back the picture, which no longer gave him any pleasure. He superimposed it upon a picture of himself standing in a nightclub the week before, holding a drink and talking to a rather combative girl who wanted his number.

"Some old people are beautiful in an unearthly way," she continued. "I saw this old lady in the drugstore the other day who must've been in her nineties. She was so fragile and pretty, she was like a little elf."

He looked at her and said, "Are you going to start being fun to be around or are you going to be a big drag?"

She didn't answer right away. She didn't see how this followed her comment about the old lady. "I don't know."

"I don't think you're very sexual," he said. "You're not the way I thought you were when I first met you."

She was so hurt by this that she had difficulty answering. Finally, she said, "I can be very sexual or very unsexual depending on who I'm with and in what situation. It has to be the right kind of thing. I'm sort of a cerebral person. I think I respond to things in a cerebral way, mostly."

"That's what I mean."

She was struck dumb with frustration. She had obviously disappointed him in some fundamental way, which she felt was completely due to misunderstanding. If only she could think of the correct thing to say, she was sure she could clear it up. The blue puffball thing unfurled itself before her with sickening power. It was the same image of him holding her and gazing into her eyes with bone-dislodging intent, thinly veiling the many shattering events that she anticipated between them. The prospect made her disoriented with pleasure. The only problem was, this image seemed to have no connection with what was happening now. She tried to think back to the time they had spent in her apartment, when he had held her and said, "You're cute." What had happened between then and now to so disappoint him?

She hadn't yet noticed how much he had disappointed her.

He couldn't tell if he was disappointing her or not. She completely mystified him, epecially after her abrupt speech on cerebralism. It was now impossible to even have a clear picture of what he wanted to do to this unglamorous creature, who looked as though she bit her nails and read books at night. Dim, half-formed pictures of his wife, Sharon, Beth and a sixteen-year-old Chinese hooker he'd seen a month before crawled aimlessly over each other. He sat and brooded in a bad-natured and slightly drunken way.

She sat next to him, diminished and fretful, with idiot radio songs about sex in her head.

They were staying in his grandmother's deserted apartment in Washington, D.C. The complex was a series of building blocks seemingly arranged at random, stuck together and painted the least attractive colors available. It was surrounded by bright green grass and a circular driveway, and placed on a quiet highway that led into the city. There was a drive-in bank and an insurance office next to it. It was enveloped in the steady continuous noise of cars driving by at roughly the same speed.

"This is a horrible building," she said, as they traveled up in the elevator.

The door slid open and they walked down a hall carpeted with dense brown nylon. The grandmother's apartment opened before them. Beth found the refrigerator and opened it. There was a crumpled package of French bread, a jar of hot peppers, several lumps covered with aluminum foil, two bottles of wine and a six-pack. "Is your grandmother an alcoholic?" she asked.

"I don't know." He dropped his heavy leather bag and her white canvas one in the living room, took off his coat and threw it on the bags. She watched him standing there, pale and gaunt in a black leather shirt tied at his waist with a leather belt. That image of him would stay with her for years for no good reason and with no emotional significance. He dropped into a chair, his thin arms flopping lightly on its arms. He nodded at the tray of whiskey, Scotch and liqueurs on the coffee table before him. "Why don't you make yourself a drink?"

She dropped to her knees beside the table and nervously played with the bottles. He was watching her quietly, his expression hooded. She plucked a bottle of thick chocolate liqueur from the cluster, poured herself a glass and sat in the chair across from his with both hands around it. She could no longer ignore the character of the apartment. It was brutally ridiculous, almost sadistic in its absurdity. The couch and chairs were covered with a floral print. A thin maize carpet zipped across the floor. There were throw rugs. There were artificial flowers. There was an abundance of small tables and shelves housing a legion of figures; grinning glass maidens in sumptuous gowns bore baskets of glass roses, ceramic birds warbled from the ceramic stumps they clung to, glass horses galloped across teakwood pastures. A ceramic weather poodle and his diamond-eyed kitty-cat companions silently watched the silent scene in the room.

"Are you all right?" he asked.

"I hate this apartment. It's really awful."

"What were you expecting? Jesus Christ. It's a lot like yours, you know."

"Yes. That's true, I have to admit." She drank her liqueur.

"Do you think you could improve your attitude about this whole thing? You might try being a little more positive."

Coming from him, this question was preposterous. He must be so pathologically insecure that his perception of his own behavior was thoroughly distorted. He saw rejection everywhere, she decided; she must reassure him. "But I do feel positive about being here," she said. She paused, searching for the best way to express the extremity of her positive feelings. She invisibly implored him to see and mount their blue puffball bed. "It would be impossible for you to disappoint me. The whole idea of you makes me happy. Anything you do will be all right."

Her generosity unnerved him. He wondered if she realized what she was saying. "Does anybody know you're here?" he asked. "Did you tell anyone where you were going?"

"No." She had in fact told several people.

"That wasn't very smart."

"Why not?"

"You don't know me at all. Anything could happen to you."

She put her glass on the coffee table, crossed the floor and dropped to her knees between his legs. She threw her arms around his thighs. She nuzzled his groin with her nose. He tightened. She unzipped his pants. "Stop," he said. "Wait." She took his shoulders—she had a surprisingly strong grip—and pulled him to the carpet. His hovering brood of images and plans was suddenly upended, as though it had been sitting on a table that a rampaging crazy person had flipped over. He felt assaulted and invaded. This was not what he had in mind, but to refuse would make him seem somehow less virile than she. Queasily, he stripped off her clothes and put their bodies in a viable position. He fastened his teeth on her breast and bit her. She made a surprised noise and her body stiffened. He bit her again, harder. She screamed. He wanted to draw blood. Her screams were short and stifled. He could tell that she was trying to like being bitten, but that she did not. He gnawed her breast. She screamed sharply. They screwed. They broke apart and regarded each other warily. She put her hand on his tentatively. He realized what had been disturbing him about her. With other women whom he had been with in similar situations, he had experienced a relaxing sense of emptiness within them that had made it easy for him to get inside them and, once there, smear himself all over their innermost territory until it was no longer theirs but his. His wife did not have this empty quality, yet the gracious way in which she emptied herself for him made her submission, as far as it went, all the more poignant. This exasperating girl, on the other hand, contained a tangible somethingness that she not only refused to expunge, but that seemed to willfully expand itself so that he banged into it with every attempt to invade her. He didn't mind the somethingness; he rather liked it, in fact, and had looked forward to seeing it demolished. But she refused to let him do it. Why had she told him she was a masochist? He looked at her body. Her limbs were muscular and alert. He considered taking her by the neck and bashing her head against the floor.

He stood abruptly. "I want to get something to eat. I'm starving."

She put her hand on his ankle. Her desire to abase herself had been completely frustrated. She had pulled him to the rug certain that if only they could fuck, he would enter her with overwhelming force and take complete control of her. Instead she had barely felt him, and what she had felt was remote and cold. Somewhere on her exterior he'd been doing some biting thing that meant nothing to her and was quite unpleasant. Despairing, she held his ankle tighter and put her forehead on the carpet. At least she could stay at his feet, worshiping. He twisted free and walked away. "Come on," he said.

The car was in the parking lot. It was because of the car that this weekend had come about. It was his wife's car, an expensive thing that her ex-husband had given her. It had been in Washington for over a year; he was here to retrieve it and drive it back to New York.

Beth was appalled by the car. It was a loud yellow monster with a narrow, vicious shape and absurd doors that snappd up from the roof and out like wings. In another setting it might have seemed glamorous, but here, behind this equally monstrous building, in her unsatisfactory clothing, the idea of sitting in it with him struck her as comparable to putting on a clown nose and wearing it to dinner.

They drove down a suburban highway lined with small businesses, malls and restaurants. It was twilight; several neon signs blinked consolingly.

"Do you think you could make some effort to change your mood?" he said.

"I'm not in a bad mood," she said wearily. "I just feel blank."

Not blank enough, he thought.

He pulled into a Roy Rogers fast food cafeteria. She thought: He is not even going to take me to a nice place. She was insulted. It seemed as though he was insulting her on purpose. The idea was incredible to her.

She walked through the line with him, but did not take any of the shiny dishes of food displayed on the fluorescent-lit aluminum shelves. He felt a pang of worry. He was no longer angry, and her drawn white face disturbed him.

"Why aren't you eating?"

"I'm not hungry."

They sat down. He picked at his food, eyeing her with veiled alarm. It occurred to her that it might embarrass him to eat in front of her while she ate nothing. She asked if she could have some of his salad. He eagerly passed her the entire bowl of pale leaves strewn with orange dressing. "Have it all."

He huddled his shoulders orphanlike as he ate; his blond hair stood tangled like pensive weeds. "I don't know why you're not eating," he said fretfully. "You're going to be hungry later on."

Her predisposition to adore him was provoked. She smiled.

"Why are you staring at me like that?" he asked.

"I'm just enjoying the way you look. You're very airy."

Again, his eyes showed alarm.

"Sometimes when I look at you, I feel like I'm seeing a tank of small, quick fish, the bright darting kind that go every which way."

He paused, stunned and dangle-forked over his pinched, curled-up steak. "I'm beginning to think you're out of your fucking mind."

Her happy expression collapsed.

"Why can't you talk to me in a half-normal fucking way?" he continued. "Like the way we talked on the plane. I liked that. That was a conversation." In fact, he hadn't liked the conversation on the plane either, but compared to this one, it seemed quite all right.

When they got back to the apartment, they sat on the floor and drank more alcohol. "I want you to drink a lot," he said. "I want to make you do things you don't want to do."

"But I won't do anything I don't want to do. You have to make me want it."

He lay on his back in silent frustration.

"What are your parents like?" she asked.

"What?"

"Your parents. What are they like?"

"I don't know. I don't have that much to do with them. My mother is nice. My father's a prick. That's what they're like." He put one hand over his face; a square-shaped album-style view of his family presented itself. They were all at the breakfast table, talking and reaching for things. His mother moved in the background, a slim, worried shadow in her pink robe. His sister sat next to him, tall, blond and arrogant, talking and flicking at toast crumbs in the corners of her mouth. His father sat at the head of the table, his big arms spread over everything, leaning over his plate as if he had to defend it, gnawing his breakfast. He felt unhappy and then angry. He thought of a little Italian girl he had met in a go-go bar a while back, and comforted himself with the memory of her slim haunches and pretty high-heeled feet on either side of his head as she squatted over him.

"It seems that way with my parents when you first look at them. But in fact my mother is much more aggressive and, I would say, more cruel than my father, even though she's more passive and soft on the surface."

She began a lengthy and, in his view, incredible and unnecessary history of her family life, including descriptions of her brother and sister. Her entire family seemed to have a collectively disturbed personality characterized by long brooding silences, unpleasing compulsive sloppiness (unflushed toilets, used Kleenex abandoned everywhere, dirty underwear on the floor) and outbursts of irrational, violent anger. It was horrible. He wanted to go home.

He poked himself up on his elbows. "Are you a liar?" he asked. "Do you lie often?"

She stopped in midsentence and looked at him. She seemed to consider the question earnestly. "No," she said. "Not really. I mean, I can lie, but I usually don't about important things. Why do you ask?"

"Why did you tell me you were a masochist?"

"What makes you think I'm not?"

"You don't act like one."

"Well, I don't know how you can say that. You hardly know me. We've hardly done anything yet."

"What do you want to do?"

"I can't just come out and tell you. It would ruin it."

He picked up his cigarette lighter and flicked it, picked up her shirt and stuck the lighter underneath. She didn't move fast enough. She screamed and leapt to her feet.

"Don't do that! That's awful!"

He rolled over on his stomach. "See. I told you. You're not a masochist."

"Shit! That wasn't erotic in the least. I don't come when I stub my toe either."

In the ensuing silence it occurred to her that she was angry, and had been for some time.

"I'm tired," she said. "I want to go to bed." She walked out of the room.

He sat up. "Well, we're making decisions, aren't we?"

She reentered the room. "Where are we supposed to sleep, anyway?"

He showed her the guest room and the fold-out couch. She immediately began dismantling the couch with stiff, angry movements. Her body seemed full of unnatural energy and purpose. She had, he decided, ruined the weekend, not only for him but for herself. Her willful, masculine, stupid somethingness had obstructed their mutual pleasure and satisfaction. The only course of action left was hostility. He opened his grandmother's writing desk and took out a piece of paper and a Magic Marker. He wrote the word "stupid" in thick black letters. He held it first near her chest, like a placard, and then above her crotch. She ignored him.

"Where are the sheets?" she asked.

"How'd you get so tough all of a sudden?" He threw the paper on the desk and took a sheet from a dresser drawer.

"We'll need a blanket too, if we open the window. And I want to open the window."

He regarded her sarcastically. "You're just keeping yourself from getting what you want by acting like this."

"You obviously don't know what I want."

They got undressed. He contemptuously took in the muscular, energetic look of her body. She looked more like a boy than a girl, in spite of her pronounced hips and round breasts. Her short, spiky red hair was more than enough to render her masculine. Even the dark bruise he had inflicted on her breast and the slight burn from his lighter failed to lend her a more feminine quality.

She opened the window. They got under the blanket on the foldout couch and lay there, not touching, as though they really were about to sleep. Of course, neither one of them could.

"Why is this happening?" she asked.

"You tell me."

"I don't know. I really don't know." Her voice was small and pathetic.

"Part of it is that you don't talk when you should, and then you talk too much when you shouldn't be saying anything at all."

In confusion, she reviewed the various moments they had spent together, trying to classify them in terms of whether or not it had been appropriate to speak, and to rate her performance accordingly. Her confusion increased. Tears floated on her eyes. She curled her body against his.

"You're hurting my feelings," she said, "but I don't think you're doing it on purpose."

He was briefly touched. "Accidental pain," he said musingly. He took her head in both hands and pushed it between his legs. She opened her mouth compliantly. He had hurt her after all, he reflected. She was confused and exhausted, and at this instant, anyway, she was doing what he wanted her to do. Still, it wasn't enough. He released her and she moved upward to lie on top of him, resting her head on his shoulder. She spoke dreamily. "I would do anything with you."

"You would not. You would be disgusted."

"Disgusted by what?"

"You would be disgusted if I even told you."

She rolled away from him. "It's probably nothing."

"Have you ever been pissed on?"

He gloated as he felt her body tighten.

"No."

"Well, that's what I want to do to you."

"On your grandmother's rug?"

"I want you to drink it. If any got on the rug, you'd clean it up."

"Oh."

"I knew you'd be shocked."

"I'm not. I just never wanted to do it."

"So? That isn't any good to me."

In fact, she was shocked. Then she was humiliated, and not in the way she had planned. Her seductive puffball cloud deflated with a flaccid hiss, leaving two drunken, bad-tempered, incompetent, malodorous people blinking and uncomfortable on its remains. She stared at the ugly roses with their heads collapsed in a dead wilt and slowly saw what a jerk she'd been. Then she got mad.

"Do you like people to piss on you?" she asked.

"Yeah. Last month I met this great girl at Billy's Topless. She pissed in my face for only twenty bucks."

His voice was high-pitched and stupidly aggressive, like some weird kid who would walk up to you on the street and offer to take care of your sexual needs. How, she thought miserably, could she have mistaken this hostile moron for the dark, brooding hero who would crush her like an insect and then talk about life and art?

"There's a lot of other things I'd like to do too," he said with odd self-righteousness. "But I don't think you could handle it."

"It's not a question of handling it." She said these last two words very sarcastically. "So far everything you've said to me has been incredibly banal. You haven't presented anything in a way that's even remotely attractive." She sounded like a prim, prematurely adult child complaining to her teacher about someone putting a worm down her back.

He felt like an idiot. How had he gotten stuck with this prissy, reedy-voiced thing with a huge forehead who poked and picked over everything that came out of his mouth? He longed for a dim-eyed little slut with a big, bright mouth and black vinyl underwear. What had he had in mind when he brought this girl here, anyway? Her serious, desperate face, panicked and tear-stained. Her ridiculous air of sacrifice and abandonment as he spread-eagled and bound her. White skin that marked easily. Frightened eyes. An exposed personality that could be yanked from her and held out of reach like . . . oh, he could see it only in scraps; his imagination fumbled and lost its grip. He looked at her hatefully self-possessed, compact little form. He pushed her roughly. "Oh, I'd do anything with you," he mimicked. "You would not."

She rolled away on her side, her body curled tightly. He felt her trembling. She sniffed.

"Don't tell me I've broken your heart."

She continued crying.

"This isn't bothering me at all," he said. "In fact, I'm rather enjoying it."

The trembling stopped. She sniffed once, turned on her back and looked at him with puzzled eyes. She blinked. He suddenly felt tired. I shouldn't be doing this, he thought. She is actually a nice person. For a moment he had an impulse to embrace her. He had a stronger impulse to beat her. He looked around the room until he saw a light wood stick that his grandmother had for some reason left standing in the corner. He pointed at it.

"Get me that stick. I want to beat you with it."

"I don't want to."

"Get it. I want to humiliate you even more."

She shook her head, her eyes wide with alarm. She held the blanket up to her chin.

"Come on," he coaxed. "Let me beat you. I'd be much nicer after I beat you."

"I don't think you're capable of being as nice as you'd have to be to interest me at this point."

"All right. I'll get it myself." He got the stick and snatched the blanket from her body.

She sat, her legs curled in a kneeling position. "Don't," she said. "I'm scared."

"You should be scared," he said. "I'm going to torture you." He brandished the stick, which actually felt as though it would break on the second or third blow. They froze in their positions, staring at each other.

She was the first to drop her eyes. She regarded the torn-off blanket meditatively. "You have really disappointed me," she said. "This whole thing has been a complete waste of time."

He sat on the bed, stick in lap. "You don't care about my feelings."

"I think I want to sleep in the next room."

They couldn't sleep separately any better than they could sleep together. She lay curled up on the couch pondering what seemed to be the ugly nature of her life. He lay wound in a blanket, blinking in the dark, as a dislocated, manic and unpleasing revue of his sexual experiences stumbled through his memory in a queasy scramble.

In the morning they agreed that they would return to Manhattan immediately. Despite their mutual ill humor, they fornicated again, mostly because they could more easily ignore each other while doing so.

They packed quickly and silently.

"It's going to be a long drive back," he said. "Try not to make me feel like too much of a prick, okay?"

"I don't care what you feel like."

He would have liked to dump her at the side of the road somewhere, but he wasn't indifferent enough to societal rules to do that. Besides, he felt vaguely sorry that he had made her cry, and while this made him view her grudgingly, he felt obliged not to worsen the situation. Ideally she would disappear, taking her stupid canvas bag with her. In reality, she sat beside him in the car with more solidarity and presence than she had displayed since they met on the corner in Manhattan. She

seemed fully prepared to sit in silence for the entire six-hour drive. He
turned on the radio.

"Would you mind turning that down a little?"

"Anything for you."

She rolled her eyes.

Without much hope, he employed a tactic he used to pacify his wife
when they argued. He would give her a choice and let her make it.
"Would you like something to eat?" he asked. "You must be starving."

She was. They spent almost an hour driving up and down the
available streets trying to find a restaurant she wanted to be in. She
finally chose a small, clean egg-and-toast place. Her humor visibly
improved as they sat before their breakfast. "I like eggs," she said.
"They are so comforting."

He began to talk to her out of sheer curiosity. They talked about
music, college, people they knew in common and drugs they used to
take as teenagers. She said that when she had taken LSD, she had often
lost her sense of identity so completely that she didn't recognize herself
in the mirror. This pathetic statement brought back her attractiveness
in a terrific rush. She noted the quick dark gleam in his eyes.

"You should've let me beat you," he said. "I wouldn't have hurt
you too much."

"That's not the point. The moment was wrong. It wouldn't have
meant anything."

"It would've meant something to me." He paused. "But you probably would've spoiled it. You would've started screaming right away
and made me stop."

The construction workers at the next table stared at them quizzically. She smiled pleasantly at them and returned her gaze to him.
"You don't know that."

He was so relieved at the ease between them that he put his arm
around her as they left the restaurant. She stretched up and kissed his
neck.

"We just had the wrong idea about each other," she said. "It's
nobody's fault that we're incompatible."

"Well, soon we'll be in Manhattan, and it'll be all over. You'll never
have to see me again." He hoped she would dispute this, but she didn't.

They continued to talk in the car, about the nature of time, their parents and the injustice of racism.

She was too exhausted to extract much from the pedestrian conversation, but the sound of his voice, the position of his body and his sudden receptivity were intoxicating. Time took on a grainy, dreamy aspect that made impossible conversations and unlikely gestures feasible, like a space capsule that enables its inhabitants to happily walk up the wall. The peculiar little car beamed a warm, humming cocoon, like a miniature house she had, as a little girl, assembled out of odds and ends for invented characters. She felt as if she were a very young child, when every notion that appeared in her head was new and naked of association and thus needed to be expressed carefully so it didn't become malformed. She wanted to set every one of them before him in a row, as she had once presented crayon drawings to her father in a neat many-colored sequence. Then he would shift his posture slightly or make a gesture that suddenly made him seem so helpless and frail that she longed to protect him and cosset him away, like a delicate pet in a matchbox filled with cotton. She rested her head on his shoulder and lovingly regarded the legs that bent at the knee and tapered to the booted feet resting on the brakes or the accelerator. This was as good as her original fantasy, possibly even better.

"Can I abuse you some more now?" he asked sweetly. "In the car?"

"What do you want to do?"

"Gag you? That's all, I'd just like to gag you."

"But I want to talk to you."

He sighed. "You're really not a masochist, you know."

She shrugged. "Maybe not. It always seemed like I was."

"You might have fantasies, but I don't think you have any concept of a real slave mentality. You have too much ego to be part of another person."

"I don't know, I've never had the chance to try it. I've never met anyone I wanted to do that with."

"If you were a slave, you wouldn't make the choice."

"All right, I'm not a slave. With me it's more a matter of love."

She was just barely aware that she was pitching her voice higher and

softer than it was naturally, so that she sounded like a cartoon girl.
"It's like the highest form of love."

He thought this was really cute. Sure it was nauseating, but it was
feminine in a radio-song kind of way.

"You don't seem interested in love. It's not about that for you."

"That's not true. That's not true at all. Why do you think I was
so rough back there? Deep down, I'm afraid I'll fall in love with you,
that I'll need to be with you and fuck you . . . forever." He was enjoying
himself now. He was beginning to see her as a locked garden that he
could sneak into and sit in for days, tearing the heads off the flowers.

On one hand, she was beside herself with bliss. On the other, she
was scrutinizing him carefully from behind an opaque facade as he
entered her pasteboard scene of flora and fauna. Could he function as
a character in this landscape? She imagined sitting across from him in
a Japanese restaurant, talking about anything. He would look intently
into her eyes. . . .

He saw her apartment and then his. He saw them existing a nice
distance apart, each of them blocked off by cleanly cut boundaries. Her
apartment bloomed with scenes that spiraled toward him in colorful
circular motions and then froze suddenly and clearly in place. She was
crawling blindfolded across the floor. She was bound and naked in an
S&M bar. She was sitting next to him in a taxi, her skirt pulled up, his
fingers in her vagina.

. . . and then they would go back to her apartment. He would beat
her and fuck her mouth.

Then he would go home to his wife, and she would make dinner
for him. It was so well balanced, the mere contemplation of it gave
him pleasure.

The next day he would send her flowers.

He let go of the wheel with one hand and patted her head. She
gripped his shirt frantically.

He thought: This could work out fine.

Joyce Carol Oates
Morning

The evening of the day her lover first took her to see his farm nine miles out in the country, an insect resembling a tiny spider, but less quick-witted than a spider, appeared seemingly out of nowhere on Lydia Freeman's back, between her shoulder blades, crawling in the direction of her bare neck. "What's this?" her husband said, picking the insect carefully off. "What is it?" Lydia asked, twisting and cringing like a guilty child. "It looks like a spider," Meredith said. He held the creature aloft between his clean bitten-down fingernails. It was a tick: Lydia's lover had discovered one on his bare leg, a tiny black spot like a mole on his fair fuzzy leg as, awkwardly, with deliberate clownishness, he'd stumbled about hauling up his trousers. They were in an upstairs room of the old derelict house. He'd picked the insect off his leg and held it as Meredith was doing to show Lydia; most ticks were harmless, he said, but some were infected and carried serious diseases. "A spider," Lydia said, taking the insect from her husband and running off to flush it down the toilet.

127

Her lover had told her the tick is such a hardy creature, flushing it down a toilet is about all you can do to get rid of it. That, or setting it on fire.

It was an adventure of the early sixties, that time of innocence. She was twenty-six, married, a graduate student in philosophy at a midwestern land-grant university of some distinction, and a Platonist. She had come to Platonism late but with ferocity, a passion for truth licking about her like erotic flames. *I want to learn! I want to know! I want, want!*

Those days, in her philosophy seminars, she was brilliant. A handsome young woman with a solid, supple body, back straight, neck a fine pale stalk, eyes very dark, bright, suspicious, her brown hair already streaked with gray like spikes, a horsy sort of hair, crackling as if with static electricity about her head. Contentious, easily excitable and easily wounded, but on the whole brilliant. One or two of her professors were in love with her—with the idea of her, that is.

In each generation of graduate students in philosophy there were roles, as if by Platonic decree, to be filled. The brilliant young man. The brilliant young woman. The troubled young man. The neurotic young woman. The young man in-over-his-head, the young woman desperate-to-please. Lydia Freeman, née Sebera, was the brilliant but temperamental young woman.

It had not occurred to her—it would not occur to her for years—that, for all her brains and passion, professional philosophy was no field for a woman. None of the texts were by women. None of the important commentaries were by women. None of her professors were women. Lydia could be only a ministering angel, a sainted drudge, a Nightingale of the trenches, bringing life and healing to others while remaining incomplete and tainted herself. When, speaking of other things, her lover happened to inquire, "Isn't it difficult for a woman, in philosophy?" Lydia did not seem to hear. She said carelessly, "I'm not a woman when I'm doing philosophy!"

This led naturally to a spate of kisses, embracing and cuddling and cozying of the kind that frequently inspires lovers to observe, *What a good, happy world it is!* For all lovers' talk leads to a single rush of a conclusion, like great rivers emptying themselves in the ocean.

And Lydia's lover Scott, a long-married man and a father several
times over, was by both nature and practice so comfortable in his
physicality, so instinctive in ways of demonstrating love, it scarcely
mattered what "subject" the two of them discussed—it led to a single
conclusion.

Those were years when for hours each day, day following day, Lydia
Freeman dwelt inside a skull.

Her work was reading, thinking, writing: a buzzing hive of ideas,
propositions, syllogisms, symbols, words. In the bowels of the university
library where it was neither day nor night she lost herself in the text
before her, fluorescent-lit, framed by her grasping hands. A head upon
a stalk, a brain inside a skull—what need of a body?

Form precedes content. Essence precedes existence. The phenomenal
world is a sort of skeleton upon which things, actual *things* in their
thingness, are draped. If you know the skeleton, the outer appearances
become transparent, invisible. You can look right through them.

It was a way for Lydia to be religious again without being religious.
She'd left her working-class Methodism behind when she left her family
behind, aged eighteen. A lifetime ago.

Denying her womanliness for so many hours of the day, she almost
dreaded the violence of its return. *Passion is faceless and mere blindness
of will*—thus Schopenhauer. But she was newly in love and did not
heed. When the university library closed she walked swiftly, half ran,
a mile across the darkened campus to the warren of prefabricated
housing for married students known as the Barracks, in which she and
her thirty-year-old husband, Meredith Freeman, a graduate student in
economics, lived in a duplex apartment. (Rarely, that first year, did
Lydia meet her lover in the evenings—a family man finds it difficult
to get away after dinner.) How her heart pounded with joy, with dread
and guilt! How happy she was! She saw her lover, when she saw him,
late afternoons; spoke with him, when she spoke with him, at unpre-
dictable hours of the day. Then there was the long chaste stretch of
evening. And night. And awaiting her, in duplex 9-B, her husband,
Meredith, who would be working at the kitchen table on his dissertation,
books and papers spread before him, manual typewriter, hand calculator,

pencils, coffeepot and cup, ashtray, cigarettes: Meredith with his monk-ish Dürer face, bare bony toes twined around the legs of his chair, ambitious and hard-working and "brilliant" too. Meredith's moods rose and fell with abrupt seismic shifts in his assessment of himself, and Lydia could not predict if he might greet her with a distracted peck of a kiss (if she bent her cheek to him) or with his cool smile and voice faint, querulously lifted: "Lydia? So soon? Is it that late?"

Still, when Lydia approached their duplex apartment, hurrying across the barren toy-littered yards, hearing the raised voices of their neighbors, radios, crying babies, and smelling the familiar odors of grease and diapers, she knew herself happy. The world was a good place! Her nostrils widened with desire, her mouth watered. *I want, I want, I want.*

In her paperback copy of Spinoza's *Ethics,* Lydia underlined *He who repents is twice unhappy and doubly weak.*

At the time she fell in love with another woman's husband, she and her own husband had been married five years.

Five years: she could not decide if that was a brief space of time or a small eternity.

Meredith Freeman was a tall, angular, self-conscious young man with a boy's face, thinning pale hair, shrewd ghostly eyes. His forehead creased frequently with currents of dissatisfaction; he saw much in the world that fell short of his standards. He had insisted upon marriage immediately after Lydia graduated from the small church-related liberal arts college in Michigan where they'd met—Meredith had been an instructor in economics and political science. He loved her, he'd said, but he was no romantic: he valued women for depth of character and intelligence; he wanted someone as career-minded as himself. By his mid-twenties he had plotted the trajectory of his life: the Ph.D. written under a famous economist; the subsequent move to the East, to one of the Ivy League universities or their equivalent; eventually, perhaps, to Washington.

In due time, Meredith said, they'd start a family.

It had been he who'd guided their joint move from Michigan—the acquisition of their graduate fellowships—to this university. On her

own, where might Lydia have gone? She'd discovered she loved
philosophy—she loved the life of the mind, the life of books—but she
was too vague about specifics to have chosen well. One day three years
ago Meredith had said, "Here, Lydia, look through this." He'd brought
home a graduate school catalog and application forms. That night, they'd
made them out together like children doing homework.

Lydia, brainy and absentminded, took to housewifery with unexpected fervor. She did most of the meal preparation and most of the
kitchen cleanup; she vacuumed, dusted, scrubbed. At such times, her
hands usefully occupied, her mind was free to apply itself to philosophic
abstractions. Her short-term memory was so acute she could envision
columns of print; could deftly proofread and revise her own knotty
papers; while washing dishes or sponging clean the sticky linoleum floor
she rehearsed razor-sharp arguments for her seminars, coruscating quer-
ies to be brought to bear upon vulnerable propositions of Aristotle,
Kant, Schopenhauer, Berkeley. Meredith, whose nerves were sensitive,
sometimes pointedly asked her to stop her housework, to sit down or
go to the library: just be *still*.

"Your energy wears me out," he complained.

He complained, laughingly, "Do you do it on purpose, Lydia?"

Lydia had married at the age of twenty-one: too young.

And knowing virtually nothing about marriage, "marital relations";
acute embarrassment shrouded such matters in her family. (As in her
husband's family: Meredith's father was pastor of a Lutheran church
in a small city in Minnesota.) Not only had Lydia Sebera no one from
whom she might ask advice, she would not have known to ask advice, trusting to mere good intentions, mutual respect and affection
and "love." For, as Meredith promised, things would work out in due
time.

For the first year or two they worried Lydia might get pregnant,
despite Meredith's fussy precautions, but with the passage of time, and
fairly quickly, that ceased to be an issue. Early in the marriage they'd
often lain wordless together, in bed, like hungry children, eager to suck
life and solace from the other's body. If Meredith were sexually attentive
and if Lydia warmly responded, the next day, and the days following,
he would seem to avoid her: staying up late to work as she slept, slipping

out of bed early in the morning as she slept. Meredith had his own life, his interior passions, and Lydia must not interfere! She felt rebuffed, of course, but also relieved. For his behavior exempted her from the obligation of being a wife, a woman, a physical being. She told herself that wasn't her, really. Her body, perhaps, but not *her*.

Then she fell in love with Scott Chaudry, and it seemed to her an impersonal event: fated, inevitable.

As one might think, transported to the moon, *So—this is how it is!*

When they were first alone together in Chaudry's office at the university (the door locked, the overhead lights off, pellets of snow blowing frantically against the windows), Chaudry gripped her shoulders and asked hesitantly, "Are you certain you want to . . . ?" His voice, kindly at even this passionate moment, lifted quizzically. "Lydia. Dear. Are you absolutely certain?" He meant was she certain she wanted to risk her marriage for him: for this.

Her face shone with tears. She could only plead, "Oh, I can't help it; I love *you*."

That was the first of many times the two were to meet in Scott's office at the dead time of day, late afternoon easing to dusk when no one was around. Together, breathless and nimble as gymnasts, they lay on the braided thrift-basement rug to make love; Lydia imagined nothing surrounding them beyond the room's four concrete-block walls but the midwestern plains, a *nothingness* palpable as any substance. Where lovemaking with Meredith was stark and unadorned and usually wordless, lovemaking with Scott Chaudry had always its element of playful discourse, of talk. Was not making love with someone you loved another form of talk, an extension of talk? Scott was a man who liked to laugh and in his company you laughed a good deal, so Lydia learned. And how quickly they were cozily compatible, tender, daring, passionate, rapt with love. Wasn't it love? Lydia had never felt anything like it; she shut her eyes, bit her lips to keep from crying out.

She saw herself illuminated, veins and arteries, skeleton, like a Christmas tree.

.   .   .

Scott Chaudry made no secret of the fact that he was forty-three years
old. And married, as he said, one year short of half his life. Could Lydia
guess what that might mean?

No, Lydia confessed, she could not. Her marriage with Meredith
Freeman felt, now, like yesterday. That brief and that shallow.

"You're like two trees growing side by side," Scott said, resting his
elbows on his desk, lightly flexing his fists. "Not touching. But underground your roots are inextricably tangled together."

Lydia stared. What was he telling her? Warning her?

"I realize it sounds corny," Scott said, laughing. "But, dear, it happens to be true: *tangledness* as the primary fact of life."

Lydia said, hurt, "It doesn't sound corny."

Scott Chaudry and his wife had four children, the eldest sixteen,
the youngest seven. Showing Lydia snapshots in his wallet he smiled
with pleasure, with love, the clearest sort of familial pride. Lydia stared,
and swallowed, and pronounced the children beautiful, which was true.
Her lover did not show her, nor did she ask to see, snapshots of the
wife.

American philosophy was not formally taken up in the graduate seminars offered by Lydia's department, so she audited a course taught by
a popular history lecturer named Chaudry of whom she had not previously heard: the course was Intellectual Currents in American History:
Emerson, William James, Charles Peirce, John Dewey, Santayana,
among others. When Lydia first sought Chaudry out, knocking hesitantly at the door of his office, she thought, Do I want to do this? But
what am I doing?

Eventually, she would translate it all into fate: that which could not
not be, like Spinoza's closed universe.

It seemed that marriage had made her reckless. She had a vague
unarticulated sense that, since she was no longer a virgin, and since she
had been a virgin up to the moment of her painful and punctilious
deflowering by her bridegroom, it did not matter greatly what she did
with that part of her body designated as "sexual."

Scott Chaudry was a historian of no scholarly ambitions but a superb teacher. He was affable, witty, good-hearted, keenly attuned to his students' moods. (Two hundred students were enrolled in his course; the lecture hall was filled.) Lydia had guessed his age as older than forty-three: he was of moderate height and build, beginning to thicken at the waist, with dense wiry hair that had gone completely gray, a broad freckled face, sweet, open, frank as a sunflower, etched with tiny dents and creases. How authoritatively, Lydia thought, he inhabited his body.

And if he had a reputation for attracting the interest of young women students, Lydia did not know of it and did not wish to know.

Later, he told Lydia that he'd had no idea she was married, at first. And that that might have made a considerable difference. At first.

It wasn't until the spring—May, prematurely warm, fragrant, and damply lush—that Scott Chaudry took Lydia Freeman to see his farm out in the country. He'd been talking of it quite a bit; he'd bought the property at a bankruptcy auction years ago. Lydia noted that whenever he spoke of the farm—"my place out in the country"—his tone became subtly defensive.

"Is it a working farm?" Lydia asked.

"Hardly," Scott said. "It's a"—he paused, seeking the precise term—"a place. A state of being."

So in Scott's station wagon they drove out into the township of Merced, taking a circumlocutory route to get out of the university town unseen. Lydia said laughingly, "Would you like me to hunch down? Hide in the back seat, maybe?" Scott winced and did not reply.

The farm was nine miles out in the country; the drive was achingly beautiful; Lydia wanted it never to end. This was the first time she'd ever been in Scott Chaudry's car. Evidence of children, family life, domesticity—what envy she felt! Scott was speaking animatedly of the farm, which consisted of twelve acres of land and a broken-down old house, a barn, several outbuildings, rusted farm equipment, an aged orchard: he'd grown up in Chicago, spent his entire life in urban areas, wanted with all his heart to live in the country, in the real country— "Though I know it's absurdly romantic." He had planned to renovate the house so they could come out on weekends at least, eventually live there, but somehow there was never money for it, or it wasn't the right time, or the children were the wrong ages or not so interested as they'd once been, or Vivian wasn't well, or—one thing or another. For a while, Scott said, his wife urged him to sell it but lately she seemed to have forgotten about it, as if, being his, his folly so exclusively, it had passed out of her consciousness altogether. He paused. He said, "I wonder what you'll think of it, Lydia."

Lydia thought, I will fall in love with it.

Lydia came from a rural town in western Michigan. Her earliest memories were of her grandparents' farm, of the crude hearty smells of the barnyard, the tall rows of corn, bees buzzing treacherously around fallen, rotting pears, her German-speaking grandfather laughing and cursing as he sheared a bleating sheep's filthy wool.

To her relief, Scott's farm was beautiful, though shabbier, more remote and overgrown than she had imagined.

It was at the end of a badly rutted lane that descended to a sort of shallow, like an old glacier lake. The house and outbuildings were close together; fences were fallen or hidden in weeds; it looked as if pastureland had run up to the house itself, virtually to the windows. The barn was partly collapsed, the corncrib had gone skeletal. In the near distance, in bright sunshine, tall grasses, yellow wildflowers, and thistles grew lushly, undulating in the wind like coarse hair. And there was the house.

Lydia stared. It was like many farmhouses out of her childhood, empty, going to ruin. She felt both a shiver of dread and a sense of coming home.

Scott sighed with pleasure. "Well: my dream house!"

The house was made of wood, foursquare, modest, with a look of having contracted in upon itself. The date 1871 had been etched in its stone foundation. There was a sloping veranda; there were antiquated lightning rods atop the highest peak of the roof; patches of lurid mossy green grew on the shingle boards. The windows had been neatly boarded up, and a NO TRESPASSING notice (peppered with gunshot) had been posted prominently on the front door. Lydia exclaimed, "But it's beautiful!"

She was thinking that, like most abandoned houses, it had a look of being occupied. Though knowing better, she began to feel nervous about going in.

The only sound was from crows, noisily cawing as they circled overhead.

Scott had a key for the side door and they stepped inside. He was saying, "I always have this eerie feeling, every time I come here, that I'm intruding . . . that someone is here."

Lydia said nervously, gripping his arm, "Oh, but not really. The house is *yours.*"

"Yes. But it wasn't always."

Inside there was broken glass underfoot, and the wallpaper hung in shreds. Gauzy slatted sunlight fell through the windows.

Holding hands like adventuresome children, they walked through the house. Rain-soaked sofa, broken-backed chairs, exposed wiring, sagging floorboards, a steep staircase to the second floor, and, there, filthy mattresses, cobwebs brushing against their faces, mouse droppings, the husks of dead insects underfoot, a rich sweetish odor of dirt and rot. Lydia was thinking with a peculiar sort of satisfaction, No other woman has been here, like this. Though she knew that Scott's wife had certainly been here, and had passed judgment, and had withdrawn. Still, she thought, no other woman has been here. Like this.

Scott talked excitedly, rather boyishly. He still had hopes for the farm! He wasn't totally disillusioned, or discouraged!

Lydia knew by his keyed-up mood that they would make love. She cast her eyes about, seeking the least uncomfortable and demeaning of spots. That filthy mattress?

But if she didn't remove most of her clothing, why not?

Afterward, there was the incident of the tick, already embedded in Scott's leg just below the knee. He'd picked it off with his fingernails, a look of distaste contorting his face. "Filthy little bugger," he said.

He told Lydia that the elderly owners of the farm had sold off most of its acreage over the years. The original homestead had consisted of more than one hundred acres, but by degrees it had been whittled away to the few he'd bought, these the least farmable, he supposed: hilly fields studded with rock, woods, shallows, swampy soil. Evidently there

were no children to inherit; the family was dying out. The old man,
suffering from senile dementia, had hoped to subvert fate, so he shot
himself with his twelve-gauge shotgun in a way meant to be considerate
to his wife and others; he'd lain in a shallow creek bed, head down-
stream, and manipulated the trigger with his toe.

His wife had died within a week or two. She'd never recovered
from the shock of finding him.

Lydia said, shivering, "They loved each other."

Scott said lightly, "A good argument, then, for not falling in love."

They straightened their clothes and walked out into the sunshine,
blinking in surprise. Was it still daylight? Still so bright? Their lovemaking took them so far.

Lydia ran in the grass, following the vague trampled path of a deer
trail. Fat horseflies buzzed about her head, airborne, glittering. The
grass was damp beneath, dry and acrid-smelling above, so tall, so coarse,
so twined, flattened, she felt she could swim in it! She could walk on
top of it! Scott called to her, laughing.

They investigated the hay barn. The old, old smells made her nostrils pinch: ammoniac, hay-warm, manure and dirt and rotting wood.
Lydia said softly, laying her head on Scott's shoulder, "I love it here.
This—" She did not know what she said or meant to say; words tumbled
from her like her heart's blood pumping out of her body to soak in
the filthy floor. "This place you've brought me to."

Scott said quietly, "I love it too."

There are cultures that make a fetish of history, honoring the departed
as if the very point of life were posthumous renown, like the ancient
Romans; there are cultures with no history at all, no memory, desperate
to live in a continual present, out of a horror of duration—the so-called
savage cultures. Lydia Freeman read of such things and felt the sharp
deflating pang of recognition.

Yes, she thought, if you're a savage you can't bear to contemplate
predecessors. About who got there first, and what's to come.

Passion is faceless and mere blindness of will so there were nights when
Lydia made love with the man who was her husband and took a harsh

sort of pleasure from the act, greedy, desperate, afterward ashamed. She did not even think of Scott; the effort was purely genital, a matter of precision timing like, say, diving from a high board, executing a flawless plunge. With Scott, lovemaking was often too emotional. She clutched at his body as if clutching to keep from sinking, drowning.

She thought, It's a mistake.

She thought, I will die if he stops loving me.

She was waiting for him to say that they must tell the others: her husband, his wife. She rehearsed the words with which she would greet his words.

But rarely did he speak of his wife. And never of her husband.

So, sometimes, she made love with Meredith, never initiating the brief wordless act but not resisting it either. And afterward they lay apart, sweaty, panting, subdued, like swimmers collapsed on the same beach. Comrades of a sort: sister, brother.

Meredith Freeman, alert to atmospheric changes, sensed in Lydia what he could not have named or would not in his Lutheran pride have wished to name. As if making an observation about a third party held in no great esteem by either of them, he remarked to Lydia, "*You're in odd moods these days. You don't seem to know if you're ecstatic or depressed.*"

To which Lydia had only a vague stammering reply, conciliatory words that trailed off into silence as if losing momentum, or purpose. She said she was sorry. She said it was her work: reading Croce, Peirce, Kant's *Metaphysics of Morals* in nightmare juxtaposition. She said it was the pressure. She avoided the apartment for as many hours as she dared; and several times, returning late, dreading that calm sardonic smile of her husband's, that "Hello, Lydia!" of nominal courtesy, she was surprised to see that the apartment was empty: a kitchen light burning, a radio bristling with voices, mere cautionary ploys Meredith's father had trained him to observe whenever he left home, to discourage burglars.

Some meals they ate together. Some they ate apart: the Freemans meeting for supper in the student union cafeteria, sitting together but not by design.

When Lydia's head was about to burst with too much abstraction, she fled the library and walked into the night: walked swiftly, broke

into a run, purposeless and headlong as she'd been as a child, enraptured
by the phenomenon of motion, the legs' unthinking strength, the canny
muscles. *I do what I want to do, therefore what I do is what I want. Isn't
it?* Without intending it she found herself standing in the shadows of
a residential street staring at the house in which the man who was her
lover lived with wife, sons, young daughter. The house was a trim
decent colonial in no way distinguished from its neighbors. Windows
were warm rectangles of light, the blinds discreetly drawn. Were she
primitive enough for such nonsense she would have willed him to leave
that interior coziness to come to *her*.

That afternoon after love they'd set their watches in tandem.

It was summer and there was a rumor that Professor Chaudry's wife
was "unwell," but Lydia knew nothing of it; her intimacy with the
man excluded certain points of information.

They began to argue, as if arguing were the next logical step. Scott's
philosophy of history was, he said, quite simple: things happen, or they
don't happen. He knew, yes, that men made their reputations ham-
mering away at "precipitating factors" and amassing great quantities
of data to support their hypotheses, certainly he knew; he'd gone through
such stages himself, and eventually he'd come to the conclusion that
each event had a thousand thousand causes or, conversely, none at all:
"Call it God, call it fate." Lydia was incensed; Lydia was baffled. She
accused him of taking ideas too lightly just because he had a settled
position in life, a full professorship with tenure. In turn he accused her
of taking ideas too seriously. "You remind me," he said, smiling at her
with the fondness of watching a child clambering about in its bath, "of
myself at your age." Lydia, smarting, insulted, but smiling too, said,
"So that diminishes us both!"

It was the peak of their physical passion for each other, however,
and very little else seemed really to matter. Chaudry was so thoroughly
husband and father and lover there was nothing he might not do, no
ardor of which, puppylike, stallionlike, he was not capable: loving her
with hands, mouth, tongue, penis, burrowing into her, pumping his life
into her, prodigious and wasteful. He was a big-boned man gone soft
around the waist but heavy with muscle elsewhere, the torso and thighs

particularly. Again and again Lydia heard herself cry *I love you, I love, love you,* the words senseless, mere anguished sound. Again and again she was shaken by the power of the sensations Chaudry caused her to feel, as if such sensations were in fact impersonal, marauding, violating her deepest self, the *I, I, I.*

On the eve of Scott's departure for an August vacation with his children in Colorado (the wife, the mysterious wife, preferred to remain home alone) they were in a motel room five miles from town and it had become late suddenly; they'd slept and woke and it was nearly seven o'clock and Lydia in a panic telephoned Meredith (the Freemans were going out that evening, or had planned to—a rare evening with another couple) to say he should go on without her, she'd meet him and their friends at the restaurant, and Meredith sounded frightened, as if finally things had gone too far, beyond mending. What was wrong? he asked, had he done something wrong? he begged, and Lydia said no, no, she would explain later it had nothing to do with him he should simply go to the restaurant without her and she'd meet him there, and Scott had come up behind her and begun playfully to run his hands over her as, naked, her hair in her face, her voice pleading, she spoke with Meredith, who no longer sounded like Meredith but like a young aggrieved husband who did not understand what was happening to his marriage and was begging to know. Scott buried his face in Lydia's neck, prodded himself against her buttocks, poked and pushed and, growing hard again, eased himself into her, where she was wet, dilated, open; yet Lydia could not put the telephone receiver down, she could not break the connection with Meredith, trying to talk, to give comfort of a kind, to murmur words of assent or promise, as Meredith asked, What was it? Where was she? Who was she with? When was she coming home? What had he done wrong? Had he offended her that morning, had he hurt her, had he said the wrong thing? Would she forgive him?

The receiver slipped from Lydia's hand and fell to the carpet and she did not retrieve it.

They sat on the rear steps drinking beer from cans, the long slow night hours shifting to dawn.

"But *why . . . ?*"

"I don't know why."

"You don't love him?"

"It isn't that."

"You *do* love him?"

"No. It isn't that."

"But you either love him or you don't." Meredith paused. All this was new to him; he was a man picking his way with infinite care across a terrain of incalculable danger. Drinking too, in such excess, was new to him. "You either love me or you don't."

"It isn't that."

Lydia jammed her knuckles against her mouth. She was thinking, Aristotle's logic! How old, how dull and discredited, how dead!

Meredith spoke slowly to avoid slurring his words. "You either want the marriage to continue or you don't. I see no other possibility."

"I do. I do want it to continue."

"And what about him? You either love him . . . or you don't."

"There are degrees of loving. You must know."

"Not when marriage is involved."

"Especially when marriage is involved."

"How long has this been going on? At first you said—"

"It doesn't matter. For God's sake."

"Yes, it matters. It matters to me."

"To your pride!"

"Yes. To my pride."

Lydia wept. As if weeping were a way of being forgiven. Or an exorcism. Or a plea for repudiation. *Now he will raise his hand and strike me.*

After a moment's hesitation Meredith laid his arm across her shoulders, to comfort her. They were both breathing quickly; they were both very warm. She heard herself say, choking, "I love you. Oh, God, I'm sick with the thought of having hurt you."

Was it true? Meredith decided to believe. "Are you, Lydia? Are you really?" The childlike lift of his voice.

How tender he was, suddenly, her young husband! As if broken open. Holding Lydia in both his arms and gallant enough not to notice how, as if involuntarily, she stiffened against him.

So it went. The hours that night, and the following day, and the following. Each of their exchanges was about their new terrible subject, a light burning fiercely in their faces, even when they were speaking of other things: What would Meredith like for dinner? Should Lydia do the laundry this morning or Saturday? As if the element in which husband and wife dwelled, the very air of the cramped apartment that constituted "home," had been subtly and irrevocably altered, thickened. They had to push themselves through it; it offered some natural resistance, like water.

Never did Meredith ask the name of Lydia's lover.

His shrewd logic being: since Lydia assured him she was finished with the man, should he not be finished with the man too? Meredith knew only that X was married, had children, was a good kind likable man, an easygoing sort of man, not a seducer. Not one of Lydia's professors. No one Meredith knew or was required to know.

Instead of typing out a draft for her dissertation Lydia composed an eight-page letter, a masterpiece of a letter, for Scott Chaudry. Affirming her love for him—for otherwise wouldn't she be a hypocrite? a liar? a fool?—while simultaneously informing him that she could not see him again when he returned in September.

She hadn't left the apartment for days. She was pale, subdued, repentant. She felt herself cleansed—no, more than cleansed, *scoured*. As if with a pad of crinkly steel wool.

Lydia rather liked the sensation, for once. Meredith liked it in her, too.

It was September, and Scott Chaudry had returned, and if he'd received and read Lydia's letter he gave no sign; he did not call. So, chagrined, she understood that he too had wanted it to end, though at their last meeting he'd seemed to love her so, and had spoken of hating to leave her.

And then finally he called—there'd been a domestic crisis, he said, but did not further explain, though he sounded sincere enough, and shaken—and Lydia was overcome with rage, saying, "You don't love me so why keep up the pretense? You never did, did you! I know what you are! I know! I hate you! I wish we were both dead!" So naturally they had to meet, a final time.

It was a lovely autumn day, one of those heartbreak days when you realize you must die though you want to live forever: so Lydia saw, and wept. She was unpracticed in adult weeping and surely looked ugly, but still her lover saw her as beautiful and she in turn saw it in his face, his love for her: his desire.

"My God. I've missed you."

"I've missed *you*."

He was hurriedly undressing, his penis erect from a tangle of silvery glinting hair. He had the look of a creature impaled upon its own flesh.

Afterward they lay together on the rug, the familiar braided rug, like swimmers collapsed on the sand. Oh, they were comrades, conspirators: Scott kissing her damp eyelids, stroking her body, comforting her. "But I do love you, Lydia. My darling. My dear one. How could you ever doubt me?"

Meredith Freeman was trying to do the right thing so years later he might tell himself, reflecting, *I did the right thing.* He was a minister's son after all, and though he no longer believed in the revealed truths of Christianity there lingered in him the urge, perhaps the need, to forgive: to be charitable and not-sinning and martyrish, thereby superior. Yes, and to punish too. In the end when forgiveness ran its course there would have to be some punishing too.

The dishes left all day in the sink, for instance. The toilet left unflushed.

Lydia knew the import of these clues. She had lied persuasively to Meredith and she could not think that he did not believe her, yet she knew the import of these clues, though breezing over them as mere accidents, aberrations. She was reading in anthropology: Mead, Bateson, Lévi-Strauss. These names her philosophy professors scarcely knew, or knew only to deride. But here was Lévi-Strauss: newly translated, smart laminated paperback editions, the critical imprimatur of the eastern establishment press. Lydia was growing out of Platonism, not understanding that in fact she was moving into a new species of Platonism, but this had at least the weight of scientific evidence, or seemingly. So much data amassed "in the field" to be hung upon structure's skeleton!

Thus she learned of manners, the significance of manners. What are manners but devices to control and calibrate impurity, strategies of protecting oneself from others and protecting others from oneself? The breakdown in a culture is signaled by, and in turn signals, a breakdown in ordinary manners. For instance the dirty dishes in the sink, not even soaking in water. The scattered pages of the newspaper, the soiled socks and towels, heaping ashtrays, the shockingly unflushed toilet. Lydia tried to transform it into something light, anecdotal, telling Scott, "My husband is turning savage!" Though for a long time she said nothing to Meredith. Not a word!

Then one day, unable to bear it any longer, she confronted him with, "Please don't."

Immediately Meredith said, "Don't what?" His voice uninflected, innocent.

"The toilet, for one thing."

"What? What about the toilet?"

"It isn't like you, Meredith, so why do it?"

"Why do what?"

"Oh, for God's sake, you *know!*"

And suddenly they were shouting. Walls in the Barracks were famously thin but what did the Freemans care, empowered by rage, mutual loathing? In the end Meredith was laughing as if drunk, thoroughly enjoying himself as Lydia had never before witnessed. His face was slit as with a jack-o'-lantern's grin. He said, "What's the difference? Why so sensitive? Do you think my shit is any different from his, sweetheart? From *yours?*"

So it went.

Lydia knew herself watched. Nowhere in this place could she move among people who knew her—along certain sidewalks, into certain buildings, through the maze of carrels on B-level of the library— without being observed, assessed, commented upon, judged. *There she is. That's the one. See her? Lydia Freeman.* Her professors who had such hopes for her, or who'd once had such hopes for her: they now looked upon her with fastidious disdain or ribald interest.

Scott assured her she was imagining things. Scott, nervous himself, insisted she was imagining things, "Exaggerating it all."

She walked a good deal, those weeks. Along the margins of muddy playing fields, in scrubby land along the river, miles from the campus in neighborhoods unknown to her: warehouses, slum tenements, railroad yards. Sometimes she stood for long minutes as if she'd lost all volition or awareness, a stroke victim yet still on her feet. What had she done, and why? She could not remember.

What had she done, what had been the actual sequence of events, actions, beginning with that knock on Scott Chaudry's office door? She could not remember.

Shortly before Christmas, Vivian Chaudry had an automobile accident: she who by her husband's account never drove a car any longer, had deliberately allowed her license to expire, went out with their daughter in the station wagon, drove too fast on pavement slick with ice, and crashed into a barrier. The front of the station wagon was crushed like an accordion but Mrs. Chaudry and the child were only banged up a little, as Scott called it; thank God there'd been no serious injuries, just the shock, the terrible shock of the experience. A few days later Scott Chaudry moved out of his home to take up temporary residence in a motel.

He telephoned Lydia and told her. He asked her to come to him so they could talk.

He would not speak of his wife these days but he spoke of his children—obsessively. He loved them, he said. He did not want to hurt them, he said. He loved Lydia, and he loved his children. *He did not want to hurt anyone.*

He was drinking, and Lydia drank too. She saw that her lover was a middle-aged man. He looked in fact a decade older than his age: eyes ringed with exhaustion, graying whiskers on his jaws. He had developed a nervous tic in one eye, and his old easy affable smile had become a sort of tic too. It frightened Lydia that the relationship between them seemed to have changed as if by a malevolent magic. She thought, I don't know this person. There is some mistake.

Scott Chaudry loved his children, but in the end it seemed he loved Lydia Freeman more. Or maybe his children were sick of him, had been turned against him by their mother. But, no: he loved Lydia more. His girl, his darling, his life. You won't leave me? he was begging. You won't leave me?

She would not leave him, she wasn't that kind of person. And of course she loved him.

She comforted him in the old inevitable ways.

He was working with a local carpenter, intent upon renovating the farmhouse out in Merced Township.

Lydia lived alone now. Meredith had moved out quietly. He was thirty-one years old and suddenly an adult. Though losing his hair, susceptible to stomach upsets and fits of coughing, embarrassingly vain about his standing amid the pack of other Ph.D. candidates in economics, he had acquired a new steeliness: a new manhood.

He and Lydia spoke frequently over the phone, since they had a good deal to discuss. And, now, almost calmly. Like brother and sister who have aired every grievance and secret mean thing, they now could speak of pragmatic matters, business. Against his family's counsel Meredith was filing for a divorce; he'd already seen a lawyer. He knew what he wanted and how to get it. Lydia admired him. The trajectory of his life without her was shrewdly plotted: his Ph.D. would be wrapped up within a few months, the divorce too, everything local settled so that he could move east without encumbrances. Such challenges were translatable into mere units of time: weeks, months. An economist specializing in statistics, Meredith Freeman did not doubt his capacity for navigating such finitude.

And how mature he'd become: adult enough, even, to apologize.

Adult enough to remark, once, unexpectedly, "You know, Lydia, of the two of us, I wouldn't have thought it would be you who would . . ."

Their minds worked sometimes in the same ways, along the same grooves. Lydia said, "Who would transgress?"

"Yes," Meredith said. " 'Transgress.' " He must have liked the taste of the word, its biblical solemnity; he repeated it: " 'Transgress.' "

They were speaking over the telephone. Lydia had to imagine her husband's expression: his faint perplexed smile, the familiar sheen of his forehead, which looked both bony and unprotected.

Repairs on the farmhouse were not proceeding so smoothly as Scott had hoped. But by mid-March there were at least windows both downstairs and up, and insulation, and a wood-burning stove for the kitchen, even a working toilet. So one weekend they drove out to Merced, through the snowy countryside, with groceries, beer, sleeping bags. An impromptu sort of thing, for the fun of it. Lydia had hesitated at first but quickly came around to looking forward to it, like a small child. It was a holiday of a sort, a small adventure.

And how beautiful, the drive into the hills: the snow-covered fields; the tall leafless trees, many-branched and -veined like bodies in X ray; the farmhouse down in the little hollow. Scott had to do some shoveling, Lydia had to rock the car back and forth to get it free where it was stuck, but eventually they got where they were going. Lydia said, "The world is perfect if you don't set yourself in opposition to it!"

At dusk they lit a kerosene lamp, ate their meal, drank beer from cans, settled in for the night. The wood-burning stove glowed with a rich interior heat that radiated grudgingly, to encompass a space of perhaps five feet in diameter. They laid their sleeping bags side by side in front of it.

Both were tired, and groggy from beer, but they made love, their new kind of love, Lydia thought it: slow, calm, domesticated, patient. These past several weeks, their desperation had lifted. Lydia, who had failed to complete her course work for the previous semester, had decided not to register for the spring semester; she'd given up her fellowship. All that, that part of her life, she would deal with in time. Now she took each day as it came. That seemed the best strategy, for now.

Scott continued with his teaching, of course, in the face of scandal. He was grim, he was stubborn, brazening it out in the community, meeting his classes as if nothing were wrong; perhaps nothing *was*. Things fell into place with a semblance of inevitability: his wife would keep the house for the time being; he could see the older children virtually at will; indeed, there might be less hurt, less heartbreak, than he'd feared. Repeatedly he assured Lydia, who felt such guilt, that none of this was her fault even remotely—he should have moved out months, years ago: "There was no love remaining in my marriage." Lydia said, "I should never have married Meredith. I did wrong, to marry him."

The more frequently these words were uttered, the more convincing they were.

A dozen times a day they said, "I love you." "I love *you*."

They whispered often, as with an old habit of conspiracy.

Lying in Lydia's arms in front of the wood-burning stove, still inside her, stunned with pleasure, Scott said, "*This* is where we belong." Lydia murmured, "Oh, yes."

Scott zipped himself up in his sleeping bag and slept, a heavy sleep, his breath rasping like a fine-notched saw. Lydia, alone, slept less readily. She was exhausted but something seemed to be beating between her eyes. She was damp too and sticky from lovemaking but loath to crawl out of her warm sleeping bag and grope her way to the bathroom, where the air was freezing. Gradually she dropped off to sleep, wakened intermittently by Scott's snoring and by the eerie silence of the country. She had forgotten the strange deep silence of the country in winter.

She woke before dawn, her knuckles jammed against her mouth.

Quietly she wriggled out of the sleeping bag, her limbs aching, a sharp pain in the small of her back. The fire in the stove was a dull mass of embers, giving no heat; Scott had intended to wake to put more wood inside but had forgotten. Lydia's breath steamed in anxious little puffs.

Her companion, slack-jawed, unshaven, sallow-skinned in the ashy light, slept and snored undisturbed. There was a strangeness about him, in the sleeping bag that was like a body bag, positioned on the newspaper-covered floorboards in front of the stove.

Lydia walked quietly, not wanting to wake him. She stood shivering at a window. If it had been a clear morning she would have seen a vista of fields and hills, the skeletal corncrib off to one side, but this morning there was fog, a damp opalescent mist, pressing up against the glass like a mouth. It was the first morning of her new life.

William Kotzwinkle

JEWEL OF THE MOON

She and Mother watched through the curtains as the handsome stranger and Father discussed her marriage. The stranger offered money, which Father said was too little. Then they smoked and Father grew poetic, calling her Jewel of the Moon, and she was afraid the bargaining would never finish. She desperately hoped it would, for the stranger was fine-looking and the frog-faced rug-seller of the village was also seeking her hand. Take me away, whispered her heart, and perhaps the stranger felt its delicate beat, for he suddenly doubled his offer of gold and Father agreed.

On the day of their marriage a celebration was held in the village. The drums spoke their hollow song, she danced, the sun was bright. Then as afternoon grew late, he took her away, onto the country road, toward his own village.

Confused, frightened, delighted, mad with anxiety, a virgin, she did not know what to say to him, though her thighs spoke silken words through her gown as she walked along the dirt road, aflame.

The setting sun cast her husband's face in deep red. His eyes burned through her and she too grew red, her stomach flip-flopping, young and silly, but her breasts were moving sweetly as she walked, her hips were full and swayed and how pretty were her bare painted toes. Her ears dangled with earrings and through their jingling she heard the sound of a distant flute.

"That is the musician of my village, welcoming you," said her husband.

She fell into sadness. To strange music, into a strange town, with childhood gone, Jewel of the Moon is letting herself be led. But circling, dancing in the air, the song enticed her, set her dreaming. Soon she would let her black hair down.

Ahead she saw the trees and rooftops of his village, and doubt ruined her again. Afraid to look at him now, she pulled her veil over her head, to hide, to die. How cruel of Father to abandon her, to trade Jewel of the Moon for two bags of gold to this stranger.

"Here we are," he said, turning onto a narrow dirt path.

At the end of the path she saw a small house. Slowly she walked toward it, numb with fear. Still she kept dignity, which Mother had taught her to maintain always, whatever the situation. She did not slouch, tremble, or faint crossing the strange threshold to the cool gloom of the living room. Out of the corner of her eye, through a small doorway, she saw the rattan foot of a bed.

Her husband pointed toward that room and she walked to the doorway, heart thundering.

A purple lamp hung there, and her skin turned to pale moon shades as she walked through the opening. My husband is an exotic, she thought, inspecting the ornate shade of the lamp, on which a thousand-armed God was embracing his naked purple-skinned wife. Will I be sophisticated or will I scream? In the purple den of love, she turned to face him.

He unwrapped the white marriage turban from his head and dark hair fell to his shoulders. Tenderness? Or will he ravish me with bloody sword? Her body played possibilities as he lit incense on the tiny altar by the bed.

She looked down at her toes, wanting to conceal the rest of herself from him, wanting also to reveal what he hadn't seen, wanting this and wanting that, frozen flame in a purple place. The window was near and she could escape, but she longed to surprise him with the fullness of her thighs.

"Sit down," he said. She sat on the edge of the bed, dropping her hips into the soft embrace of the mattress. I am ready.

He knelt before her, looked into her eyes. This is the moment.

"I'll sleep down here," he said, stretching himself out on the floor at her feet.

I must awake, she thought, trying to escape the silly dream.

"Perhaps you would like a glass of milk with a piece of toast?" he asked, raising himself on one elbow.

She looked dumbly at the far wall of the bedroom, as her husband hustled off to the kitchen. Nervously, she opened the ribbon on her hair and let her long black head-cloak fall, scented and shimmering. I am Jewel of the Moon. Why does he talk of milk and toast?

"Here I am," he said, coming toward her on his knees, holding the milk and toast.

She took the plate. He turned back down at her feet. "Just kick me if you want anything else."

I have married a madman. Jewel of the Moon peered over the edge of the bed.

Her husband's eyes quickly opened. "Anything else, Perfect One?"

Unable to speak, she shook her head, and though she was not hungry she ate the toast. Then she stretched out on the wedding bed and stared at the ceiling. I must escape. She waited until she was sure he was asleep, but as soon as her foot touched the floor, he was up, like a watchdog, watching her.

Frightened, she lay back down. She would look for another chance, but sleep overtook her, and she spent the night dreaming of a powerful horse who galloped her to freedom.

"Here is your breakfast, Daughter of the Sun," said her ridiculous husband in the morning, coming toward her on his knees with a silver tray of food.

She ate and he sat at her feet, watching the window, heedless of her morning beauty, as if his fearful bargaining for her had never been. She was truly miserable, for it was real, had been no dream, she'd married an imbecile. That is what he looks like, sitting there. He looks like an incredible idiot and I hate him.

"Here," she said, contemptuously, "I'm done."

"At once." Taking away her cup and plate, he scurried off to the kitchen. She watched him return, to the doorway only, where he lay down, and she covered her tearful eyes. Peeking through her fingers she saw him lying there, doglike, eyes on her, bright, stupid. She wanted to wave her tail at him, give him something to growl about.

"I'm going for a walk," she said, defiantly stepping over the crumpled man on the floor. Perhaps he will bite me, seek to hold me somehow.

"I'll just walk a few paces behind you," he said. "If you want anything, just spit on me."

They walked through the streets of his strange village. She knew no one there, except the shadowy dog at her heels. He lapped along behind her to the well. Women were fetching water and they gave her inquiring looks, as her husband curled up at her feet in the sand. They know I've been tricked by a weak-kneed fiend. Looking down she wanted to spit on him, but the women would love that too much.

She left the well and walked on through the village, curling her toes in the hot sand as the men of this new village eyed her bare feet and a bit more, perhaps, for her hips were expressing themselves, too enthusiastically for a married woman, but her so-called husband was licking along at the ground. I'll give him one more chance this afternoon.

She sat upon the bed, brushing her long hair over her heart. Her ankles were smooth and bare and she wriggled her toes as he entered the room, bathed in the gold of afternoon. But there came no spicy kiss upon her toes, only curried peas, served on a tray which he placed on her thighs.

Night. Beneath purple light he gave her milk and toast and curled down again on the floor. The milk and toast made her brain sleepy, but her pale thighs wanted something indescribably nice, and it wasn't milk toast.

She tossed on her pillow, recalling the passages from the Holy Sutra on Love. I studied the book faithfully, yet here I am, perspiring on an empty bed. She rose up and with her bare foot gave her husband a kick.

He rolled over, looking up from the floor like a whipped mongrel.

"Stop snoring," she said, angrily.

"I will stop breathing," he said, and wrapped a strip of linen around his nose.

The moon crossed her pillow. Slowly her passion subsided, like a body fallen away, and she moved in dreams, a queen with many servants, all of them her idiot husband.

As the wedding month went by, she grew tense. Her husband was silent, devoted, treated her like a queen, and she loathed him and his entire line of ancestors. She thrust her foot out, so that he might remove her sandals, which he did, handling her foot as carefully as a dish of precious rice, except that he did not taste or swallow the delight and it soon grew cold.

She raised her feet on the barren marriage bed, drawing her knees up to her breasts. I am so young. There are other men. They would not treat me like this. They would torture me with glances, drive me mad with their eyes. I will die soon of dullness. Neglect can end woman's life, so says the Holy Sutra.

She felt the end of the mattress suddenly sink down with unusual force. "What are you doing?" she cried, for the impudent servant was sitting on the foot of the bed.

"If you want anything," he said, curling up at her feet, "just kick me in the face."

She pulled herself into a fetal ball, wishing she could be reborn in some hidden world. The night bird blew his flute, she lay in purple moon-robe, and dreams of mating came to her. A shining man held her, ghostly thin he was, and she stretched herself out beneath him, at the same time touching with her toe accidentally the face of the vile sleeper at her feet.

"Yes, Tower of Grace," said her husband, sitting up quickly, "have you bad dreams? I will make a cup of tea which relaxes the mind."

He left and returned with a silver tray, surrounded by steam. He poured the tea and she let the sheet fall away from her, moonlight coming on her breasts, bare behind her thin midnight gown.

"This will help," he said, handing her a cup of the tea, not even glancing at the pale cups she had so immodestly revealed. She drew the sheet around herself again, hating him, and drank the tea, a gentle herb, which soon brought the charm of sleep.

Each night, following milk and toast, he slipped onto the foot of the bed, like a dog trained to warm the feet of his mistress. Silently, while he slept, she felt over his face lightly with her toe. The second month of their marriage passed this way, with her body inflamed by his nearness. Though his canine countenance expressed no more than a stupid smile, his simple animal nature inspired her, and in dreams she attacked him. *It has grown hot in this lagoon. I shall swim with him. She slipped into the warm water, where his silver face shined. Into his heat she swam.*

She woke, feverish. Her husband's hot breath was on her feet. Unable to resist, she tiptoed on the warm waves from his tongue, dancing there.

In the third month, the dog became a tortoise, crawling slowly up the mattress toward her. Each night she felt his shell coming closer. When she looked in the dark purple toward him, he seemed wrinkled as an ancient. His faithful dog-eye was gone and in its place was a wiser, if somewhat frightening beak, and two gleaming eyes, accustomed to the night sea.

She wanted to hide inside the pillow, to shrink into nothingness, to keep herself apart from his breathing on her knees, and from his devious turtle-eyes coldly haunting her.

Daytime brought her release from the illusion. She went to the temple and begged Kali to advise her. The beautiful altar goddess danced on the head of a slave. *If only I could be fierce as you, Goddess.* The statue was mute. The distraught girl rose and left the temple. Her husband was kneeling in the sand of the temple garden, the sun upon his dark curling hair. If he weren't so shifty, he might almost be good-looking, she thought, walking slowly toward him.

That night he came slowly toward her, to her thighs with his head. What fiendish ticklement is this, she wondered in a moment of clarity, before the warm cream of his breath poured over her thighs. She pressed them together to stop the sensation and it grew more intense. She spread them apart trying to cool them and her soft leg-flesh touched his nose.

"Yes, Queen," he said in a whisper.

"Please," she said, softly.

"What would you have me do?" asked the turtle.

Could she tell him her thighs were milk? She raised her hips just a little.

"Is there a lump in the mattress, Gracious Saint?"

"Oh, the dog!" she cried and turned quickly away, but her gown rose up so that perhaps he could see the soft underness of her thighs. What an immodesty, she thought, quickly pulling down her gown.

The fourth month of marriage brought the face of her husband directly in line with her secret. His breath upon her toes had been inflaming; his breathing on her rose was driving her insane. Streams of air reached between her thighs, gently handling her flower. She tried always to sleep on her stomach, so she would not be subjected to warm southern winds, but in dreams she soon rolled over again, into the tropic breeze from his nose, which played over the hot little island between her thighs.

Later, when they walked outside, she went head down, deep in confusion. Caught in the rain, she made no attempt to take cover. The cloudburst ran along her hot flesh and her husband stood with her in the rain, and the village women no doubt thought them mad.

At five months, his face lay by her stomach. His breath blew her gown lightly; she touched him with her belly, upon his hooked nose.

His eagle-eye saw through her gown, to the soul in her rolling ocean of jelly, to the eye in her navel. Into that canyon of time went his nose, filling it with warmth. She lay perspiring like a holy woman on a bed of coals, though she did not feel holy, in fact, quite the opposite.

When six months ended, the wandering slave in her bed had lodged at her breasts. His eyes gleamed in the dark like an idol's. The purple light played on his face. She tried to cover her breasts, to hide them from his dark look, but they are so tender, they hurt me, let him look if he dares to. His breath touched her lightly on her soft little island tops, her red-peaked nipples. Excited as if she were dancing in the village, her breasts heaved and touched him. In the crevice of dreams where her heart lay concealed, she enclosed his nose.

It tickled ridiculously. That was its strange power. She was ten-thousand-times-over afraid of it, yet somehow withstood the invasion. Encircle his nose again, my breasts, smother him with your sweetness, drive him mad too.

He remained calm. Yet in the seventh month he was stretched out entirely beside her. Kinglike he slept, lightly, staring sometimes at the ceiling for long hours. Around her body was an envelope of heat, as if she were afloat in a warm cloud. His breath seemed to have lingered all over her body, gathering around it like a mist. His elbow touched her. Quickly she drew her arm away. This bed is far too small for two people. She withdrew to the farthest corner. But in curling up she bumped him with her backside and he, amazingly, returned the bump.

This shocking demonstration was repeated on the following night and on many nights afterward. Like wandering taxis they bumped each other, bumper to bumper they lay pressed together in the street of feathers. It is mad play, but what pleasure. Later she rose up and looked at the impertinent fellow, naked to the waist in the moonlight.

"Yes, Lotus?" He woke and rose to her.

"I'm so thirsty," she said.

"At once," he said, and leapt out of the bed.

He returned with a cool drink of water. She drank it slowly and extended the glass back to him. As he retrieved it, his hand brushed light as a wing-tip across her breast. He put the glass down and crawled into bed beside her. Reaching for the thin sheet, the devil's finger touched her again. Her red breasts heaved to meet his hands, wanting that and wanting more.

On the following night, as he served her milk, she leaned in a most favorable angle and his palm touched underneath her breasts, in the softness, and lingered there.

Next night, she was seated on a cushion by the window. He came from the kitchen on his knees, bearing a tray on which a glass of red wine was balanced. He bowed. His black curling hair was like snakes in a dance. His hand came forward. All night he held the threads of her shoulder straps in his fingertips, and toward dawn he let them drop and, half awake, half dreaming, she watched her left moon appear, naked, round, full.

Earlier, in the fashion of the slave girls, she had made herself up, reddening the nipple, tanning the round globe, even underneath, where the sun never came. Now she dared not move, the silence was all around them. He stared at her breast like a devotee at a statue and she accepted his stare.

For days he stared at it, through the passing light of morning, afternoon, and evening. He pondered it from every angle, looking all around it and underneath it, like a monkey with a problem. She did not know what to do. Her thoughts were jumbled, her head was spinning, for they spent so much time in bed these days. Slowly his hand came forward. Was it an age or an instant that passed, she'd lost touch with time. Suddenly he was touching her on the left breast and fondling it.

So she spent the ninth month, one breast out. Each time she tried to tie her gown up, he untied it again. She felt so odd sitting eating dinner with one breast bare. Shortly after dinner he began stroking the other one, and each night it was the same, until the tenth month came and he slipped the knot on her right shoulder, rendering both breasts bare.

She sat, naked to the waist. All night he sat looking at her, and she at him. She nodded off to sleep finally, and her dreams were filled with insanity. She'd lost sight of father, mother, dignity, the world, except for two moons in the air. She felt a cloudy field all around her and she ran through a ghostly mist, awaking to his lips upon the tiny crater of her right moon.

Then he revolved both moons in his hands, until she was thrashing back and forth on the bed, most indecorously. She begged him to stop revolving them but he laughed and went on revolving them.

That morning she rose early and since she was in the kitchen before him, she prepared her own breakfast, and as an afterthought, prepared his too, and served it to him.

She knelt by the bed and slipped the tray over the covers. He opened his eyes and she lowered her own. He ate quietly and the sunlight came, turning the bed to a gold palanquin on which he seemed to float, looking down on her. She had covered her bosom to serve him. With a gesture of perfect sovereignty, he slipped the knots of her gown and bared her breasts again. He digested his breakfast, fondling them.

About noontime, after five hours of feeling her breasts, he began sucking them, first one, then the other, alternating on the hour. At dinnertime she could not help but scream, so tender had they grown from his feasting. This incredibly idiotic child is draining my soul, sucking it into himself, but she welcomed him nonetheless and in fact offered up to him with her hands the twin fruits.

By night he continued lowering her gown. Inch by inch he pulled it, a little each evening, until her stomach heaved up into the moonlight. Like a vast continent it came into view, but she did not feel continent, in fact, just the opposite, ravished as she was by feverish grindings in her stomach. He squeezed her moons and licked across the land of her belly, his moustache trailing in her navel.

Finally the gown was down to the edge of her secret. In a dream she was taken down the night to an ancient forest altar, a cave in which a priestess dwelled. It was a shimmering red crack in the mountain and she entered. The shining man was sitting on a throne, deep inside the cave.

She woke, moved her legs, felt suddenly free; her gown was gone. He was looking at her dark scented place, which sparkled as if with dewdrops. She felt older, parting her legs, then demurely closed them, feeling childish. He stared at it all night, and continued to stare at it throughout the morning, as the sun rose upon her little tangled grove. He ate lunch looking at it and spent the evening with his nose practically next to it. She felt herself burning alive.

She had to leave the bed. She ran naked through the house. He caught her in the kitchen, in a most peculiar position, putting his hand directly into her forest. She sank to her knees and bowed her head, worshipping him as he ran his finger all along the crack in the forest floor.

For the entire eleventh month he investigated that mysterious forest. He parted the underbrush so that the altar was plainly visible, and then like a blind man feeling letters, he ran his fingers along the sacred tabernacle, reading every wrinkle and fold. The altar streamed with the precious nectar. His finger slipped just the slightest bit inside it and remained there, all day, every day, for a month. She screamed, beating him about the head with her hands.

Silently, day by day, he worked like a hermit drawing with his finger on a cave wall. Then, by night, he brought his head to the cave and spoke a wordless whisper. She pressed her forest lips to his in silent answer and they kissed softly. All night, hour after hour, he kissed her there, while she squirmed, kicking her legs, beating her hands upon the mattress. For a month she writhed, groaning, in and out of delightful anguish.

From the devil he had learned to take in his lips the tiny turned-out root that hung from the mouth of her sacred cave. Known to no one, guarded and carefully hidden by her through all her years, it was now in the man's lips and he was humming on it. The tune was crazy, mad bees swarmed through her, but each time, just as she felt herself about to turn into sweetest honey, he stopped, leaving her hovering, dying, frantic.

They did not go out any longer. When he tried to lift his head away to bring food, she held him by the ears. The food grew cold and she grew hotter, running her fingers through his curly hair.

By day she followed him around the house, served him on her knees, washed his body, made his bed. He had enslaved her with his tongue. Her will was gone, sucked out in the night. Standing by the kitchen doorway, she moved aside to let him pass. His sleeping gown was loose and some devil played it open and she saw the outline of his manhood. He brushed past her and the hot organ touched her thigh.

Later in the day, as she bent over to pick up his slippers, he pressed it against her backside. Day after day then, she encountered it, and in her dreams she saw it standing on the throne inside the altar, shining, one-eyed, on fire.

Unable to resist any longer, she touched it, thinking he was asleep. He was not. He opened his eyes, fully awake.

"Please," she said. It was the twelfth month and she stretched out on the bed and spread her legs like a courtesan. Her forest stream was flowing, she was made of liquid, her body was undone, the veils of her passion unknotted.

"Please," she said, taking his member in her hand. He rose and knelt between her legs. Then he braced himself over her and slowly, like a man falling in a dream, lowered himself.

The night fell upon her. His thighs rested on hers and against her altar she felt the hot hard pressing, not of a fist or a finger, but of a finer thing, a more distinguished tool, of shape divine, like the shining thing in her dreams, and she longed to take it into herself. She pressed her forest crack against the fleshy head, feeling its wet eyedrop. She nibbled with her clumsy forest lips, dumbly trying to swallow the burning Godhead.

Each night for a week it played at her melting doorway, and just when she thought she could stand its presence, it entered the buttery folds and she gasped with amazement for she could not stand it, so painful and terrible was it, at last. She gave her hips just the slightest move, to appreciate her agony better.

"Don't move," he said in a dark voice beside her ear, and she didn't.

They lay that way each night for a week, like trees fallen together in a storm. Her legs entangled his, locking at the ankles, and her tiny cave-root was engaged.

Pressing deeper each night, he soon reached the tiny red curtain across her virgin altar. He pressed harder, but the way was small, the pressure unbearable. The space is too tight, she thought, weeping. I can never fit this thing into me, it is unendurable, it . . . seems to be going in a little farther.

No longer a virgin, she howled, for the jewel of the moon was red with blood. The veil is burning, the veil is gone. God's body slipped slowly into her.

Wheels of flame revolved in her brain and in the forest cave the

Godhead reigned, solemn, still, supreme, and she felt the beat of his burning heart-shape.

All night they lay that way, he did not allow her to move, but surreptitiously she managed to, flexing the tiny muscles of her secret mouth. Each time she did lights appeared to her and her warm tears flowed. The dreams of mating danced round her, encircling her, and she was their center and her hair was entwined with his. There was a beat, it is slow, this coming of beauty, and their locked bodies brought it nearer, so that by dawn it had almost arrived.

The need for nourishment finally overtook them and that afternoon he withdrew the Godhead from her and her cave closed shut. This is reality, she thought, stumbling naked toward the kitchen. She fried them lunch, a festival of grains, and naked they ate, lightly.

At sundown she lay down again and parted her legs. We are on the mountain of pleasure. It goes into me again. I am reassured of its constancy. I am . . . quite full, dearest, come closer.

When it was fully lodged in her, she spread her legs into a wide V, and raising them into the air, kicked them about, laughing madly, with elephants dancing, serpents too, and she walked in her brain, room by room, through waking dreams, down the road of joy, tossing, turning, coming closer to the mysterious presence. Panting, sweating, she held his buttocks, tried to make him move, to take them closer.

Not until the thirteenth month did he move, but that movement was definitive, marking a farther outpost of bliss. To feel his tool run in and out of me, that is the deep truth. Could there be more? She suspected another door.

Each night he stroked her once, so slowly, the entire night was needed for the length of his thousand-armed shaft to move in and out. At times she thought it was not moving at all, but it was, and in the extremities of slowness she saw concealed worlds.

Time changed; in a single second she saw great lengths of his organ. Breathless, afire, stupefied, she too learned to move slowly. Here the moment opens. In it are contained like tiny seeds a million more divisions. And she grew smaller.

It was the end of the thirteenth month. She loved him but wanted to reach their plateau, the resting spot. I am so hot. He is boiling me.

Still they went more slowly. She fell through enormous canyons of time, down the deep pocket of pleasure, swooning ever more slowly into the depths of delight. She heard dragons roaring, such a slow grinding noise, such a slow turning.

They ate only liquids, some ethereal force seeming to sustain them now, for they lost no weight, but grew light as lamps. His countenance became magical. In his face she saw blue God-masks, jewels, crowns. The sound, the sound of their divine grinding surrounded them. No longer human, they lived outside of time.

The beautiful presence came, as he touched her in the womb, and like spring burst forth. I am creation. From her came the universe, that was the roar. From her came worlds, she was their door. Spread across the galaxies, she moved her body slowly, coming everywhere, at once, very wise.

In the beat of moons, not seconds, he stroked her, so say the Scriptures.

Ward Just

THE COSTA BRAVA, 1959

Ted had been terribly sick in Saulieu, a combination of too much wine and a poisonous fish soup, and no one to blame but himself. He had chosen the night in Saulieu to be difficult about money, explaining to Bettina that a room and dinner for two plus wine at the glorious Côte d'Or was an extravagance they could not afford. It was only their third day in France, and he was not yet comfortable in francs. Gasoline was expensive, and it was necessary to keep a reserve for contingencies. The travel agent had said that Spain would be cheap, but she had also said that it would be warm in Europe; and when they had landed at Orly it was cold, forty degrees, and raining. And the room at the Continental had been very expensive, though he had wisely prepaid in Chicago.

They had driven hesitantly into the parking lot at the Côte d'Or, their little rented Renault conspicuous between two black Citröen sedans. The Côte d'Or had the appearance of an elegant country house. A bushy cat lay dozing on the doormat, and the trees in the courtyard were changing in a blaze of red and

165

gold. Bettina read the specialties from the Guide Michelin: *terrine royale, timbale de quenelles de brochet éminence, poularde de Bresse belle-aurore.* Two stars, twenty-three rooms. She rolled down the window and smiled slowly, arching her eyebrows. They could smell the kitchen.

He asked if she minded, and she said she didn't.

"It's so damn expensive," he said.

She said, "I'm so tired."

Ted said, "We'll take a nap before dinner."

They booked into the shabby hotel down the street, and Ted took a stroll around town while she slept. In the Basilique St.-Andoche he sat a moment in meditation, and then in prayer—her good health, his good health, their future together. Then he lit a taper and stood watching it burn; the air was chilly and damp inside the church. Later, they had an apéritif in a café and returned to the hotel to dine at a table by the front window. From the window they could see the Côte d'Or through the trees, a little privet hedge in front and a rosy glow within. It had begun to rain, and the hotel dining room was drafty and cold. Ted ordered the fish soup and roast chicken and knew right away that he had made a terrible mistake. Bettina ordered a plain omelet, and they ate in silence, looking out the window through the rain at the alluring Côte d'Or. He knew he had been very stupid; it was one of the best restaurants in France. To kill the taste of the soup, he drank two bottles of wine. Bettina, exhausted, went to bed immediately after dinner. Ted walked across the street alone to have a cognac at the tiny bar off the dining room of the Côte d'Or. There were two large parties still at table, and much laughter; they were talking back and forth. Ted's French was not good enough to eavesdrop seriously, but they seemed to be talking about American politics, John F. Kennedy, and the primary campaign, still months away. He heard "Weees-consin" and "Wes Virginia" and then a blast of laughter. He wondered who they were, to have such detailed knowledge of American elections. The room was very warm. Ted picked up a copy of *Le Monde,* but the text was impossible to read. Inside, however, was a piece on the Kennedy *stratégie.* It depressed him, not speaking French or reading it. It would be better in Spain, where he knew the language and admired the culture. His stomach was already sour, and he had three cognacs before returning to the hotel to be sick.

The weather improved as they drove south. They had a cheerful, lovely drive on secondary roads to Perpignan. They lunched on bread and cheese, choosing pretty places off the road to eat. And Bettina's strength returned. Her color improved, and she lost the preoccupied look she had had for three weeks, ever since the miscarriage. Five months pregnant, and it had seemed to Ted that she could get no larger. When she began to cramp early one evening, neither of them knew what it was, or what it meant; she was alarmed, but passed it off as an upset stomach. At midnight he had rushed her to the hospital, and in two hours knew that she had lost the babies, a boy and a girl. She had been pregnant with twins, and that was such a surprise because there were no twins on either side of the family. Of course there was no chance of saving either one, they were so tiny and undeveloped. The doctor said that Bettina was perfectly healthy, it was just something that had happened; she would have other children. Ted listened to all this in a stunned state. He did not know the mechanics of it, and when the doctor explained, he listened carefully but did not know the right questions to ask. There were certain obvious questions, but he did not want to seem a fool. Bettina had been wonderfully brave that evening, and later in the car rushing to the hospital, displaying a dignity and serenity that he had not known she possessed. It was the first crisis for either of them, and she had been great. To Ted, the doctor said that the twins were a shock to her system. She was a perfectly normal, healthy girl, but this was her first pregnancy and twins after all, what a surprise; it was simply too much. All this in the corridor outside Bettina's room, the two of them whispering together as if it were a conspiracy. The doctor had taken him out of earshot, but the door was open and Ted could see Bettina in her bed, and he knew she was watching them even though she was supposed to be asleep. Dr. McNab put his hand on Ted's shoulder and spoke confidentially, man to man. Ted gathered that this was information best kept to himself, the "shock to her system." He was flattered that the doctor would confide in him; the night before, the nurses had been brusque. He had sat in the waiting room for two hours with no word from anyone, and no idea what was happening except that it was precarious. The truth was, he had not had time to become accustomed to the idea of being a father; and now he wouldn't be one, at least not this year. But he accepted without question the doctor's explanation (such as it was) and cheerful prognosis. Of course they would have other children.

Bettina was not communicative, lying in her bed, the stack of books unread, staring out the window or at the ceiling. She cried only once, the next morning, when he arrived in her room with a dozen roses. No, she said, there was no pain; there had been, the night before. Now she was—uncomfortable. She wondered if, really, she was not the slightest bit relieved. She looked at him and frowned. Wrong word. Not *relieved,* exactly. But they had been married only a year and hardly knew each other, and children were a responsibility. Wasn't that what her mischievous friend Evie had said? Didn't everyone say that children would change their life together, and not absolutely for the better: diapers, three A.M. feedings, colic, tantrums, unreliable baby-sitters? She had quoted an Englishman to him: *The pram in the hallway is the enemy of art.* Ted was not amused. So she had reassured him, of course, that that was no argument for not having children; children were adorable and everyone wanted a family, but still. As the doctor said, they were both young. And they were happy on the practical surface of things: their house, their friends, Ted's job. And Ted was preoccupied, too; as it happened, he was working with the senior partner on his first big case. The senior partner was a legend on La Salle Street, and he seemed to look on Ted as a protégé. Ted described the case in detail to her as she lay in the narrow hospital bed; and as if to confirm his estimate of his excellent prospects with Estabrook, Mozart, they were interrupted by the nurse bearing an aspidistra with a get well card signed by the man himself in his muscular scrawl, E. L. Mozart.

Bettina was home in four days. She went immediately to her desk in the bedroom to look at the poem she had been writing. She had been very excited about it, but now the poem seemed—frivolous. About one inch deep, she said to Ted that night at dinner. And derivative, and the odd part was that it was derivative of a poet she did not admire:

e. e. cummings, with his erratic syntax and masculine sensibility. She had not seen that when she was working on the poem, nor had it seemed to her one inch deep. As she spoke, she knew that her life was changed in some unfathomable way. It was not simply the miscarriage, it was something more; the miscarriage had released hidden emotions. How strange a word it was, "miscarriage," as in miscarriage of justice. And the form that Ted had been given to sign did not use the word at all; the word on the form was "abortion."

That night he got the idea of a vacation.

Europe, he blurted. It was entirely spur of the moment, and she doubted it would ever happen. What about Mozart and the big case? The trip would have to wait until the case was settled—as, miraculously, it was, the following week, a fine out-of-court settlement for the client. This was an omen, and Ted was elated. He had never been to Europe or even out of America. Bettina had been two years before, the summer of her senior year in college. Ted was courting her then and wrote her every day from Chicago, where he was in his final year at law school. She had given him an itinerary, carefully typed by her father's secretary. Ted had sent her three or four long letters to every city on the itinerary, places he knew only from an atlas: London, Amsterdam, Paris, Lausanne, Venice, Florence, Rome. The letters were his way of holding her. Ted was terrified that she would meet someone sexy in Europe and would have a love affair that would change her forever. And then she would be lost to him. Later, he learned that the letters were the cause of much hilarity, some of it forced. Bettina was traveling with her roommates, the three of them determined to have an adventure before settling down and marrying someone. The letters were somehow inhibiting, and irritating in their wordy insistence and blunt postmark, CHICAGO.

All those damn letters, Evie St. John said later. *God,* Ted. It was like being followed by your family, *watched.* Just once we wanted to arrive at the hotel and find nothing at the desk. It was as if you were on the trip with us, and it was supposed to be girls-only. Or maybe Peggy and I were jealous. The only letters we got were from our mothers, asking us about the weather and reminding us to wash our underwear. But *really,* it was a bit much, don't you think? Bettina couldn't get away from you, even when we found those boys in Florence, *especially* when we found those boys in Florence. The cutest one was after Bettina. But there were four letters of yours at the hotel in Florence and it just made her sick with—it wasn't guilt.

What was it? he had asked.

I don't know, Evie replied. Disloyalty, perhaps.

Well, he said. What happened in Florence?

Laughing: I'll never tell.

They arrived at last on the Costa Brava. Spain was everything he imagined. They chose a pretty whitewashed town with a small bullring, a lovely fourteenth-century church, and two plain hotels. The hotel they chose was near the church, perched on a cliff overlooking the sea. The room was primitive, but they would use it only for sleeping. It was late afternoon, and they changed immediately and went to the beach. Bettina smiled happily; it was a great relief being out of the car.

The path to the beach wound through a stand of sweet-smelling pines. They spread their towels on the rough sand, side by side. Bettina was carrying a thick poetry miscellany. She murmured, "Isn't this nice," and at once lay down and went to sleep. She didn't say another word. Her forehead was beaded with sweat. She was lying on her side, her thighs up against her stomach, her cheek dead against her small fists. Her brown hair fell lifeless and tangled in a fan over her forearm. She looked defenseless, fast asleep. Ted looked down at her, his shadow falling across her stomach. He thought she needed a new bathing suit, something Bardot might favor, black or red, snug against the skin. The one she had on was heavy and loose, made in America. In her Lake Forest bathing suit she looked complacent and matronly, though she was obviously worn out from the drive, all day long in their small car on narrow roads, dodging diesel trucks and ox carts and every fifty kilometers a three-man patrol, the *Guardia Civil,* Franco's men, sinister in their black tricorns and green capes and carbines, though they looked scarcely older than boys, nodding impassively when Bettina waved. She thought they looked more droll than sinister; as Americans, she and Ted had nothing to fear from the *Guardia Civil.* He stepped back and looked at Bettina again. From her rolled-up position on the towel, she might have been at home in bed on the North Shore instead of on a sunny Mediterranean beach. Her skin was very white in the fading sun.

Ted turned and walked to the water's edge. There were no waves. The water seemed to slide up the sand, pause, and die. He looked left and right. The beach was wide, crescent-shaped and cozy. There were two other couples nearby, middle-aged people reading under beach umbrellas. Down the beach a girl stood staring out to sea. Presently a man joined her and they stood together. They were very tan, and Ted was conscious of his own white skin and frayed madras trunks. The girl wore a white bikini, and the man had a black towel around his waist. The girl stood with her legs apart, her arm around the man's dark shoulders; they were both wearing sunglasses. Ted looked back at Bettina. She was faced in his direction, but she had not moved. He turned back to the water, thinking how different it was from the shore at Lake Michigan—the fragrance of the beach, pine mixed with sea and sand, and the swollen bulk of two great rocks a hundred feet offshore. This coast was complicated and diverse, a place to begin or continue a love affair *sin vergüenza*. It was nothing at all like mediocre Lake Michigan; it was as different from Lake Michigan as he was from his American self. He walked into the water, chilly around his ankles. The woman in the bikini and the man in the towel were walking up the beach in the direction of the hotel, holding hands.

Ted began to swim in a slow crawl, feeling the water under his fingernails. He wished Bettina were with him at his side. The water slid around his thighs, slippery, a sexual sensation. He imagined them swimming together nude, unfettered in the Mediterranean. He swam steadily, kicking slowly, hot and knotted inside, his throat dusty and the sun warm on his back. Bettina would never swim nude but now and again he could coax her out of her bra and she would swim around and around in circles; this was always late at night in the deserted pool of the country club, after a party, illicit summer adventures before they were married. He slowed a little, lost in the sentimental memory of them together. The sensation mounted, a thick giddiness, incomplete. Ahead were the great rocks rising from the water ten feet apart. From his perspective they looked like skyscrapers, and beyond them nothing but the serene blue-gray Mediterranean and the milky sky overhead.

He wanted to climb the nearest rock to the summit and sit in the last of the afternoon sun. But above the waterline the rock was smooth, no handholds anywhere. The stone was warm to his touch and smooth as skin. When he tried to climb, his hands kept slipping, and at last he gave up and floated, the curve of the brown rocks always on the edges of his vision. Then on impulse he took a deep breath and dove, kicking and corkscrewing through the murky water. He could not see the bottom. Almost immediately the water chilled, offering resistance. He did not fight it, saving strength and breath. He struggled deeper, hanging in the heavy water, darkness all around him, the bottom out of sight. Something nudged his arm, and he felt a moment of panic. Lost, he had the sensation of rising in an elevator. The elevator was crowded with old men, their faces grim. Mozart was in front of him, lecturing in his flat prairie accent. There was a ringing in his ears, and he tried to push forward to get out through the heavy doors, away from the old men. He was dazzled by a profusion of winking red lights, a multitude of floors, all forbidden. Mozart would not yield, and the elevator came slowly to a halt, the atmosphere morbid and unspeakably oppressive. He recognized the faces of those around him, friends, colleagues, clients. Then his hand struck stone and the hallucination vanished. He had arched his back like a high-diver in midair, hanging upside down, watching afternoon light play on the flat surface of the water. Losing breath, he thought of the girl in the white bikini, so trim and self-possessed, and provocative as she stared out to sea. He wondered if she had had many lovers. Certainly a few, more than he had had; and more than Bettina, though they would all be about the same age. It was hard to know exactly how old she was, she could be eighteen or twenty-five; but a hard-muscled and knowing eighteen or twenty-five, having grown up in Europe. If the three of them met, what would they have to say to each other? He could describe for her the ins and outs of an Illinois land trust and the genius of E. L. Mozart. Bettina could talk to her about pregnancy or e. e. cummings. Well, there would be no common experience. And Bettina was so shy and he so green. She looked like a girl who would know her own mind, where she had been and where she was going. The cavalier with her looked as if he knew his own mind, too. She moved beautifully, like a dancer or an athlete. He thought of embracing her in the darkness and silence of the deep water.

When he broke the surface, gasping, he heard his name and turned to see Bettina on the beach, calling. The people under the umbrellas had put their books down and were rising, curious. Bettina saw him and dropped her hands, in an abrupt gesture of irritation and relief. She stood quietly a moment, shaking her head, then walked slowly back to the towel. The bells of the church began to toll, the dull sounds reaching him clearly across the water. He smiled, never having heard churchbells on a beach. He shook his head to clear his ears of water. The bells stopped, and there was no echo; the girl and her escort had disappeared down the beach. Ted remained a moment, treading water, looking closely at the rocks and knowing there was a way up somehow. There was always a way up. Perhaps on the far side; he could look on it as the north face of the Eiger, an incentive for tomorrow's swim. He pushed off and began a slow crawl back to the shore, where Bettina was already gathering their things.

They went directly to their room and made love, quickly and wordlessly; a model of efficiency, she thought but did not say. Ted had been ardent and a little rough, and now they lay together in the semidarkness, smoking and listening to two workmen gossip outside their window. Ted lay staring at the ceiling, blowing smoke rings. She was looking into an oval mirror atop their dresser beyond the foot of the bed. She was nearsighted and could not see her features clearly, but she knew how drained she looked, her sallow complexion, dead eyes, and oily hair, the pits. She hadn't washed her hair in a week, since they left Chicago. She touched it with her fingertips, then worked it into a single braid and brought it over her shoulder and smelled it—sweat, fish, and seaweed, ugh. It had to be washed, but she had no energy for that or for anything; no energy, or taste for food, drink, or sex. She had loved listening to the bells, though. The truth was, she looked the way she felt. Her looks were a mirror of her state of mind as surely as the mirror on her dresser reflected her looks, and there was no disguise she could wear. What should she do, put on a party hat? Pop a Miltown? No chance of that; she distrusted tranquilizers and had not filled the prescription the doctor gave her. She disliked suburban life as it was —how much more would she dislike it tranquilized? She felt as if half of her was empty. She was a fraction, half empty. She thought that something had been stolen from her, some valuable part of herself, and it was more than a fetus; but she did not know what it was or who had taken it. She felt so alone. She inhabited a country of which she was the only citizen; one citizen, speaking to herself in a personal tongue. Sometimes in her poetry she could hear a multitude of voices, a vivifying rialto in the dead suburban city. On the beach she had felt abandoned; and when she looked across the water and did not see him, she didn't know what to do; he had been there a moment before, looking at that girl. So she had gone to the water's edge and called, in a joky way; then she was filled with a sudden dread and called again, yelled really, just as he broke the surface, spraying water every which way, his arm straight up—and looked at her so shamefacedly, as if he had been caught red-handed. Then the bells began to toll and she listened, startled at first; they were so mournful and exact, churchbells from the Middle Ages, tolling an unrecognizable dirge. The church would have been built around the time of the beginning of the Inquisition, and she imagined the altar and the simulacrum behind it, an emaciated, bloody, mortified Christ, wearing a crown of thorns sharp and deadly as razor blades, the thorns resembling birds' talons. And for a long moment, within hearing of the bells, everything stopped, a kind of ecstatic suspension of all sound and motion. She turned away, fighting a desire to cry; she wanted tears, evidence of life.

She felt a movement next to her, Ted extinguishing his cigarette, sighing, and closing his eyes. Smoke from the Spanish tobacco hung in layers in the air, its odor pungent and unfamiliar. She stubbed out her own Chesterfield. He murmured, "Forty winks before dinner, Bee." She absently put her hand on his chest, his skin slick with sweat though the room was no longer warm—watching herself do this in the mirror, her hand rising slowly from her stomach, making its arc, and then falling, and he covering her hand with his own. He had nice hands, dry and light, uncallused. She felt his heart flutter, and the tension still inside him; she wondered if he could feel her tension as she felt his.

Probably not; she was so emotionally dense sometimes, and he was not
that kind of man.

It was almost dark now. The workmen had gone and she could
hear gentler voices, hotel guests moving along the path to the terrace.

She said, "Teddy?"

He made a sound and squeezed her hand.

"Nothing," she said.

He said, "No, what?" in a muddy voice.

She said, "Go back to sleep, Teddy." He stirred and did not reply.
It was quiet outside. She said quietly, "It's silly." She looked at the
ceiling, there was a ghost of a shadow from the light outside. "Are you
still sexy?"

He laughed softly. "A little."

She said, "Me, too."

He rolled over on his side, facing her.

She smiled at him, wrinkling her nose in a way that he liked; this
was a sign of absolution. "Did you know that?"

He grunted ambiguously and kissed her stomach. Then he reached
over her shoulder and took one of the Chesterfields from the pack on
the bedside table, lit it, and offered it to her. She shook her head,
watching all this dimly in the mirror; she had to crane her neck to see
over him when he reached for the cigarette. Then the flare of the match
in the glass.

She turned to look at him squarely. "I'll bet you didn't."

He said, "Did too."

She shook her head. "Unh-unh."

"I know all about you, Bettina."

Dense, she thought; an underbrush. Her poetry was dense, too, but
she liked it that way.

He began to make jokes about the various ways he knew all about
her, "Bettina through the ages." He always knew what she was thinking,
as she was an open book; she wore her heart on her sleeve, more or
less. Then he began to talk about himself, his disappointment with his
white skin and college-boy bathing suit, as obvious as a fingerprint or
a sore thumb. He said he wanted to lose his nationality, and she should

lose hers, too. They would become inconspicuous in Europe, part of the continent's mass. Perhaps he would become an international lawyer with offices in Lisbon and Madrid, master of half a dozen languages, a cosmopolitan. They would have a little villa on the Costa Brava within sight of the sea, a weekend place. He knew they would love the Costa Brava. He described swimming alone to the rocks, thinking of her, then diving, the water cold and heavy below the surface, and the hallucination that had transported him to La Salle Street, an elevator crowded with old men, red lights everywhere and no exit, a morbid oppression. The stone was slippery and warm to the touch, unfamiliar, the rocks sheer as Alps, no inhibitions on the Costa Brava—though what that had to do with it, with *her,* he couldn't say. At any event, he didn't.

She said, "Thinking about me? And then a real hallucination?"

He said, "Yes."

She said, "Nuts. You were watching that femme fatale in the bikini. The one with the flat stomach."

"No," he said. "It was you. You're my favorite."

She lay quietly, holding her breath; she had a moment of déjà vu, come and gone in an instant. She tried to recapture it, but the memory feathered away. Distracted, she said, "I'll never have a flat stomach, ever again." She prodded her soft belly. It was as if there were an empty place in her stomach, an empty room, a VACANCY. There was no spring or bounce to her; her muscles were loose. Almost a month, and she had not returned to normal; depressed, always tired, petulant, negative, frequently near tears. But what was normal? She was an anomaly. She had a young mother's flabby body, but she was not a young mother. "And I need a new bathing suit." She looked at the coral-colored Jantzen lying crumpled in the corner; ardent Teddy, he couldn't wait. He couldn't get it off fast enough. What a surprising boy he was in Europe, so curious about things, a young *husband.* At home he was reserved, wanting so to fit in. They both looked at the bathing suit. There were bones in the bra and she didn't need bones. She didn't need bones any more than the femme fatale did, except now she might, now that she looked like a young mother. Was her body changed forever? She looked at him in the darkness and then turned away, blinking back tears. She wanted him to touch her and say that he loved her body, would love it always, that it was a beautiful young body even in the coral-colored Jantzen, Marshall Field chic. His cigarette flared and he blew a smoke ring. She sighed; there would be no tears after all. And he would not tell her that she had a beautiful young body, even if he believed it. Tomorrow she would buy a new bathing suit, a bathing suit à la mode. No bikinis, though. Bikinis were unforgiving. She said, "He was much too old for her."

"Who was?" Teddy rose and stepped to the window, peeking out through the blind.

"That man she was with. That señorito in the black towel."

"So," he said. "You were watching him."

"Why not?" she said. "Jesus, he was a handsome man."

She took her time bathing and dressing, selecting a white skirt and a blue silk shirt and the pearls Teddy had given her at their wedding. She washed her hair, and took care making up her eyes. It was nine before they presented themselves on the terrace. Lanterns here and there threw a soft light. Each table had a single candle and a tiny vase of flowers and a jar of wine. The tables were set for two or four; they were round tables with heavy ladder-back chairs. One of the waiters looked up, smiling, and indicated they could sit anywhere. It was an informal seating. The terrace was not crowded, and conversation was subdued in the balmy night. The handsome señorito and his girl were at a table on the edge of the terrace, overlooking the sea. They were holding hands and talking earnestly. Bettina led the way to an empty table nearby, also on the edge.

The moon was full and brilliant. The sea spread out before them, steely in the moonlight, seeming to go on forever. The drop to the sea was sheer, and although it was a hundred feet or more, Ted felt he could lean over the iron railing and touch the water. The rocks were off to their left, dark masses in the water. From the terrace the rocks did not look as large as skyscrapers. A way out to sea there was a single light, a freighter bound for Barcelona. Ted looked at Bettina, but she was lost in some private thought, absently twisting her pearls around her index finger, her eyes in shadows. She did it whenever she was nervous or distracted, and he wondered what she was thinking about now, so withdrawn; probably the handsome couple at the table nearby. She had seated herself so that she could look at them, and perhaps guess their provenance. She loved inventing exotic histories for strangers.

The waiter arrived and took their order. Conversation on the terrace rose and fell in a low murmur. There was laughter and a patter of French behind him. Bettina looked up, raising her chin to look over his shoulder, her fingers working at the pearls. Ted sat uncomfortably a moment, then poured wine into both their glasses. Bettina touched hers with her fingernails, *click,* and smiled thanks. She was still looking past him, concentrating as if committing something to memory.

"Isn't it pretty?"

She said, "Another world."

"Did you imagine it like this? I didn't."

She said, "I didn't know what to expect."

He said, "You're twisting your pearls."

"You gave them to me." She took a sip of wine. "I have a right to twist them if I want to." She said after a moment, "I wish I had brought my poem with me, the one I was working on. It was the one that began as one thing and then when I got out of the hospital it was another thing, the one I told you about after, that night. There's one part of it that I can't remember. Isn't it a riot? I wrote it and now I can't remember it."

"Begin another," Ted said. "That's the great thing about writing poetry: all you need is a pencil and a piece of paper." And a memory, he thought but did not say.

"No, there's this one part. I have to know what it is because I want to revise it. I want to revise it here. It means a lot to me, and I know I'll remember if I try."

"Is it the beginning or the end?"

"The middle," she said.

"Good," he said and laughed.

She looked at him, confused.

"I figured the poem was about me. Or us. Us together."

"No," she said. "It wasn't."

"What was it about, Bee?"

She looked away, across the water, her chin in her hands. The

breeze, freshening, moved her hair, and she tilted her chin and shook
her head lightly, evidently enjoying the sensation. "Me, the baby, that's
what the poem was about." She smiled without irony or guile. "What
happens when things are pregnant." She took a sip of wine, holding
the glass by its stem in front of her eyes. She said, "I'll never be able
to think of them separately, as distinct and different personalities, a
brother and a sister. It'll always be just 'the baby.'"

"You were extremely brave," he said.

She gestured impatiently. "No," she said. "That isn't it."

"Still," he began, then didn't finish the sentence. Why was she so
reluctant to take the credit that was hers? If you couldn't take the credit
you deserved, you couldn't take the blame either and you ended up
with nothing, always in debt to someone else. But he did not want to
argue, so he said, "I didn't know what was going on."

"Like the other night in Saulieu."

"What night was that? You mean when I got so sick?"

"Teddy," she said. "Sometimes, you know, you could just *ask.*"

"All right then," he said. "I'm asking."

She looked at him innocently, the beginnings of a smile. "I thought
a lawyer never asked a question without knowing the answer to it."
When he reacted, she said, "Please, don't be angry. This is so pretty,
and I'm happy to be here. I feel like a human being for the first time
in ages, and I feel that it's *possible,* right here. This country is so old,
and it's gone through so much." She glanced over his shoulder and
smiled; he heard a flurry of laughter. "You know, we're not so dumb.
We don't know everything. Probably we don't know as much as those
two, but we can learn. I feel." She leaned toward him across the table,
sliding her hand forward like a gambler wagering a stack of chips. "I
feel we don't try for the best there is. We're surrounded by nonentities,
like you in your elevator, all those organization men. What did you
call it? You called it morbid, that atmosphere."

He nodded, touched by her sincerity. But what they didn't know
would fill an encyclopedia. And he didn't like her reference to organization men, and he didn't know what she meant about the night in
Saulieu; then he got it. "It was just a restaurant, Bee. I didn't have the
money straight and didn't know how expensive things were. And how

lousy that hotel would be. I thought it was important to keep a reserve for emergencies."

She nodded: Sure.

"See?"

She looked at him across the table, wondering if she could make clear what it was that she felt. She wanted him to listen—and here, this terrace, this table, the Mediterranean, this was the place. She had been stupid to mention Saulieu, off the subject. She took another sip of wine. "But there are times when you shouldn't leave me. The night in Saulieu was one of the times, and the night in the hospital another. You and McNab in the corridor, talking about *me.* You wouldn't look at me while you were talking to him, and I didn't know what it was that was so secret. If it was secret, it couldn't be anything good, isn't that right? So I thought something was being kept from me, and I felt excluded, you two men in the corridor and me in bed."

He said, "I didn't know. I thought you were asleep. It's what McNab wanted. I didn't know what he was talking about, and I was too dumb to ask the right questions." He looked around him, embarrassed; their voices were sharp in the subdued ambience of the terrace.

"It's that you have to stand up for what's yours, Teddy." She filled his wineglass and her own. She looked at both glasses, full, and smiled. She watched him closely, wondering if he had really listened, and if he understood. Probably he had; he looked bothered. In the candlelight she thought him good-looking, a good-looking American; he only needed a few years. The Costa Brava became him. And her, too. Spain gave her courage. She gave a bright laugh. "I was brave, was I?"

"Yes."

"Tell me how brave."

He said, "Brave as can be." Her eyes were sparkling, brilliant in the soft light.

"Oh," she said suddenly, lowering her voice. "Oh, Teddy. Turn around."

He did as she directed. The handsome señorito and the girl were embracing. She had her bare arms around his neck. Her head was thrown back as she leaned into him, on tiptoe. Against the light and motion of the moon and the sea, it was an exalted moment. Bettina whispered, "I know who they are." She commenced a dreamy narrative, a vivid sketch of him, a romantic poet and playwright like García Lorca, close to the Spanish people. There was definitely something literary and slightly dangerous about him. As for her, she was a political, a young *Pasionaria,* a woman of character and resolve. They had been in love for ages, exiled together, now returned to Catalonia incognito . . .

Bettina took his hand and held it. She described the poem she had been working on, reciting a few of the lines, the ones she could remember. She was going to write another poem, and McNab would be a character in it. She was going to write it tomorrow on the beach while he climbed to the summit of the largest rock. What better place to write? The Costa Brava was a tonic. In time she would be as healthy and resolute as the girl in the bikini, and he would be as lean and dangerous as the man in the towel.

Ted opened his mouth to make a comment, then thought better of it. He looked out to sea and it occurred to him suddenly that they were sitting literally on the edge of Europe, the precipice at their feet a boundary as clear and present as the Urals or the Atlantic. He had never considered the Mediterranean a European sea, and Spain herself was always on the margins of modern history. A puff of wind caused the candles to flicker and dance. Ted imagined the air originating in North Africa, bringing the scent and languor of the Sahara or the casbah. There were two lights now on the horizon. What a distance it was, from their stronghold in the heart of America to the rim of Europe! Was it true that everything was possible in Europe? Ted thought of the Spanish war and the twenty years of peace, the *veinte años de paz,* that had followed. Franco's hard-faced *paz.* He had read all the books but could not imagine what it had been like in Catalonia. He had thought he knew but now, actually in the country, face to face with the people and the terrain, he had no idea at all.

Grace Paley

An INTEREST IN LIFE

My husband gave me a broom one Christmas. This wasn't right. No one can tell me it was meant kindly.

"I don't want you not to have anything for Christmas while I'm away in the Army," he said. "Virginia, please look at it. It comes with this fancy dustpan. It hangs off a stick. Look at it, will you? Are you blind or cross-eyed?"

"Thanks, chum," I said. I had always wanted a dustpan hooked up that way. It was a good one. My husband doesn't shop in bargain basements or January sales.

Still and all, in spite of the quality, it was a mean present to give a woman you planned on never seeing again, a person you had children with and got onto all the time, drunk or sober, even when everybody had to get up early in the morning.

I asked him if he could wait and join the Army in a half hour, as I had to get the groceries. I don't like to leave kids alone in a three-room apartment full of gas and electricity. Fire may break out from a nasty remark. Or the oldest decides to get even with the youngest.

"Just this once," he said. "But you better figure out how to get along without me."

"You're a handicapped person mentally," I said. "You should've been institutionalized years ago." I slammed the door. I didn't want to see him pack his underwear and ironed shirts.

I never got further than the front stoop, though, because there was Mrs. Raftery, wringing her hands, tears in her eyes as though she had a monopoly on all the good news.

"Mrs. Raftery!" I said, putting my arm around her. "Don't cry." She leaned on me because I am such a horsy build. "Don't cry, Mrs. Raftery, please!" I said.

"That's like you, Virginia. Always looking at the ugly side of things. 'Take in the wash. It's rainin'!' That's you. You're the first one knows it when the dumbwaiter breaks."

"Oh, come on now, that's not so. It just isn't so," I said. "I'm the exact opposite."

"Did you see Mrs. Cullen yet?" she asked, paying no attention. "Where?"

"Virginia!" she said, shocked. "She's passed away. The whole house knows it. They've got her in white like a bride and you never saw a beautiful creature like that. She must be eighty. Her husband's proud."

"She was never more than an acquaintance; she didn't have any children," I said.

"Well, I don't care about that. Now, Virginia, you do what I say now, you go downstairs and you say like this—listen to me—say, 'I hear, Mr. Cullen, your wife's passed away. I'm sorry.' Then ask him how he is. Then you ought to go around the corner and see her. She's in Witson & Wayde. Then you ought to go over to the church when they carry her over."

"It's not my church," I said.

"That's no reason, Virginia. You go up like this," she said, parting from me to do a prancy dance. "Up the big front steps, into the church you go. It's beautiful in there. You can't help kneeling only for a minute. Then round to the right. Then up the other stairway. Then you come

to a great oak door that's arched above you, then," she said, seizing a
deep, deep breath, for all the good it would do her, "and then turn the
knob slo-owly and open the door and see for yourself: Our Blessed
Mother is in charge. Beautiful. Beautiful. Beautiful."

I sighed in and I groaned out, so as to melt a certain pain around
my heart. A steel ring like arthritis, at my age.

"You are a groaner," Mrs. Raftery said, gawking into my mouth.

"I am not," I said. I got a whiff of her, a terrible cheap-wine lush.

My husband threw a penny at the door from the inside to take my
notice from Mrs. Raftery. He rattled the glass door to make sure I
looked at him. He had a fat duffel bag on each shoulder. Where did
he acquire so much worldly possession? What was in them? My grand-
ma's goose feathers from across the ocean? Or all the diaper-service
diapers? To this day the truth is shrouded in mystery.

"What the hell are you doing, Virginia?" he said, dumping them
at my feet. "Standing out here on your hind legs telling everybody your
business? The Army gives you a certain time, for God's sakes, they're
not kidding." Then he said, "I beg your pardon," to Mrs. Raftery. He
took hold of me with his two arms as though in love and pressed his
body hard against mine so that I could feel him for the last time and
suffer my loss. Then he kissed me in a mean way to nearly split my
lip. Then he winked and said, "That's all for now," and skipped off
into the future, duffel bags full of rags.

He left me in an embarrassing situation, nearly fainting, in front
of that old widow, who can't even remember the half of it. "He's a
crock," said Mrs. Raftery. "Is he leaving for good or just temporarily,
Virginia?"

"Oh, he's probably deserting me," I said, and sat down on the stoop,
pulling my big knees up to my chin.

"If that's the case, tell the Welfare right away," she said. "He's a
bum, leaving you just before Christmas. Tell the cops," she said. "They'll
provide the toys for the little kids gladly. And don't forget to let the
grocer in on it. He won't be so hard on you expecting payment."

She saw that sadness was stretched world-wide across my face. Mrs.
Raftery isn't the worst person. She said, "Look around for comfort,
dear." With a nervous finger she pointed to the truckers eating lunch

on their haunches across the street, leaning on the loading platforms. She waved her hand to include all the men marching up and down in search of a decent luncheonette. She didn't leave out the six longshoremen loafing under the fish-market marquee. "If their lungs and stomachs ain't crushed by overwork, they disappear somewhere in the world. Don't be disappointed, Virginia. I don't know a man living'd last you a lifetime."

Ten days later Girard asked, "Where's Daddy?"

"Ask me no questions, I'll tell you no lies." I didn't want the children to know the facts. Present or past, a child should have a father.

"Where *is* Daddy?" Girard asked the week after that.

"He joined the Army," I said.

"He made my bunk bed," said Phillip.

"The truth shall make ye free," I said.

Then I sat down with pencil and pad to get in control of my resources. The facts, when I added and subtracted them, were that my husband had left me with fourteen dollars, and the rent unpaid, in an emergency state. He'd claimed he was sorry to do this, but my opinion is, out of sight, out of mind. "The city won't let you starve," he'd said. "After all, you're half the population. You're keeping up the good work. Without you the race would die out. Who'd pay the taxes? Who'd keep the streets clean? There wouldn't be no Army. A man like me wouldn't have no place to go."

I sent Girard right down to Mrs. Raftery with a request about the whereabouts of Welfare. She responded RSVP with an extra comment in left-handed script: "Poor Girard . . . he's never the boy my John was!"

Who asked her?

I called on Welfare right after the new year. In no time I discovered that they're rigged up to deal with liars, and if you're truthful it's disappointing to them. They may even refuse to handle your case if you're too truthful.

They asked sensible questions at first. They asked where my husband had enlisted. I didn't know. They put some letter writers and agents after him. "He's not in the United States Army," they said. "Try the Brazilian Army," I suggested.

They have no sense of kidding around. They're not the least bit lighthearted and they tried. "Oh no," they said. "That was incorrect. He is not in the Brazilian Army."

"No?" I said. "How strange! He must be in the Mexican Navy."

By law, they had to hound his brothers. They wrote to his brother who has a first-class card in the Teamsters and owns an apartment house in California. They asked his two brothers in Jersey to help me. They have large families. Rightfully they laughed. Then they wrote to Thomas, the oldest, the smart one (the one they all worked so hard for years to keep him in college until his brains could pay off). He was the one who sent ten dollars immediately, saying, "What a bastard! I'll send something time to time, Ginny, but whatever you do, don't tell the authorities." Of course I never did. Soon they began to guess they were better people than me, that I was in trouble because I deserved it, and then they liked me better.

But they never fixed my refrigerator. Every time I called I said patiently, "The milk is sour . . ." I said, "Corn beef went bad." Sitting in that beer-stinking phone booth in Felan's for the sixth time (sixty cents) with the baby on my lap and Barbie tapping at the glass door with an American flag, I cried into the secretary's hardhearted ear, "I bought real butter for the holiday, and it's rancid . . ." They said, "You'll have to get a better bid on the repair job."

While I waited indoors for a man to bid, Girard took to swinging back and forth on top of the bathroom door, just to soothe himself, giving me the laugh, dreamy, nibbling calcimine off the ceiling. On first sight Mrs. Raftery said, "Whack the monkey, he'd be better off on arsenic."

But Girard is my son and I'm the judge. It means a terrible thing for the future, though I don't know what to call it.

It was from constantly thinking of my foreknowledge on this and other subjects, it was from observing, when I put my lipstick on daily, how my face was just curling up to die, that John Raftery came from Jersey to rescue me.

On Thursdays, anyway, John Raftery took the tubes in to visit his mother. The whole house knew it. She was cheerful even before breakfast. She sang out loud in a girlish brogue that only came to tongue for grand occasions. Hanging out the wash, she blushed to recall what a remarkable boy her John had been. "Ask the sisters around the corner," she said to the open kitchen windows. "They'll never forget John."

That particular night after supper Mrs. Raftery said to her son, "John, how come you don't say hello to your old friend Virginia? She's had hard luck and she's gloomy."

"Is that so, Mother?" he said, and immediately climbed two flights to knock at my door.

"Oh, John," I said at the sight of him, hat in hand in a white shirt and blue-striped tie, spick-and-span, a Sunday-school man. "Hello!"

"Welcome, John!" I said. "Sit down. Come right in. How are you? You look awfully good. You do. Tell me, how've you been all this time, John?"

"How've I been?" he asked thoughtfully. To answer within reason, he described his life with Margaret, marriage, work, and children up to the present day.

I had nothing good to report. Now that he had put the subject around before my very eyes, every burnt-up day of my life smoked in shame, and I couldn't even get a clear view of the good half hours.

"Of course," he said, "you do have lovely children. Noticeable-looking, Virginia. Good looks is always something to be thankful for."

"Thankful?" I said. "I don't have to thank anything but my own foolishness for four children when I'm twenty-six years old, deserted, and poverty-struck, regardless of looks. A man can't help it, but I could have behaved better."

"Don't be so cruel on yourself, Ginny," he said. "Children come from God."

"You're still great on holy subjects, aren't you? You know damn well where children come from."

He did know. His red face reddened further. John Raftery has had that color coming out on him boy and man from keeping his rages so inward.

Still he made more sense in his conversation after that, and I poured fresh tea to tell him how my husband used to like me because I was a passionate person. That was until he took a look around and saw how

in the long run this life only meant more of the same thing. He tried
to turn away from me once he came to this understanding, and make
me hate him. His face changed. He gave up his brand of cigarettes,
which we had in common. He threw out the two pairs of socks I knitted
by hand. "If there's anything I hate in this world, it's navy blue," he
said. Oh, I could have dyed them. I would have done anything for him,
if he were only not too sorry to ask me.

"You were a nice kid in those days," said John, referring to certain
Saturday nights. "A wild, nice kid."

"Aaah," I said, disgusted. Whatever I was then was on the way to
where I am now. "I was fresh. If I had a kid like me, I'd slap her
cross-eyed."

The very next Thursday John gave me a beautiful radio with a
record player. "Enjoy yourself," he said. That really made Welfare
speechless. We didn't own any records, but the investigator saw my
burden was lightened and he scribbled a dozen pages about it in his
notebook.

On the third Thursday he brought a walking doll (twenty-four
inches) for Linda and Barbie with a card inscribed, "A baby doll for a
couple of dolls." He had also had a couple of drinks at his mother's,
and this made him want to dance. "La-la-la," he sang, a ramrod swaying
in my kitchen chair. "La-la-la, let yourself go . . ."

"You gotta give a little," he sang, "live a little . . ." He said, "Virginia,
may I have this dance?"

"Sssh, we finally got them asleep. Please, turn the radio down. Quiet.
Deathly silence, John Raftery."

"Let me do your dishes, Virginia."

"Don't be silly, you're a guest in my house," I said. "I still regard
you as a guest."

"I want to do something for you, Virginia."

"Tell me I'm the most gorgeous thing," I said, dipping my arm to
the funny bone in dish soup.

He didn't answer. "I'm having a lot of trouble at work," was all
he said. Then I heard him push the chair back. He came up behind
me, put his arms around my waistline, and kissed my cheek. He whirled

me around and took my hands. He said, "An old friend is better than rubies." He looked me in the eye. He held my attention by trying to be honest. And he kissed me a short sweet kiss on my mouth.

"Please sit down, Virginia," he said. He kneeled before me and put his head in my lap. I was stirred by so much activity. Then he looked up at me and, as though proposing marriage for life, he offered—because he was drunk—to place his immortal soul in peril to comfort me.

First I said, "Thank you." Then I said, "No."

I was sorry for him, but he's devout, a leader of the Fathers' Club at his church, active in all the lay groups for charities, orphans, etc. I knew that if he stayed late to love with me, he would not do it lightly but would in the end pay terrible penance and ruin his long life. The responsibility would be on me.

So I said no.

And Barbie is such a light sleeper. All she has to do, I thought, is wake up and wander in and see her mother and her new friend John with his pants around his knees, wrestling on the kitchen table. A vision like that could affect a kid for life.

I said no.

Everyone in this building is so goddamn nosy. That evening I had to say no.

But John came to visit, anyway, on the fourth Thursday. This time he brought the discarded dresses of Margaret's daughters, organdy party dresses and glazed cotton for every day. He gently admired Barbara and Linda, his blue eyes rolling to back up a couple of dozen oohs and ahs.

Even Phillip, who thinks God gave him just a certain number of hellos and he better save them for the final judgment, Phillip leaned on John and said, "Why don't you bring your boy to play with me? I don't have nobody who to play with." (Phillip's a liar. There must be at least seventy-one children in this house, pale pink to medium brown, English-talking and gibbering in Spanish, rough-and-tough boys, the Lone Ranger's bloody pals, or the exact picture of Supermouse. If a boy wanted a friend, he could pick the very one out of his neighbors.)

Also, Girard is a cold fish. He was in a lonesome despair. Sometimes he looked in the mirror and said, "How come I have such an ugly face? My nose is funny. Mostly people don't like me." He was a liar too. Girard has a face like his father's. His eyes are the color of those little blue plums in August. He looks like an advertisement in a magazine. He could be a child model and make a lot of money. He is my first child, and if he thinks he is ugly, I think I am ugly.

John said, "I can't stand to see a boy mope like that. . . . What do the sisters say in school?"

"He doesn't pay attention is all they say. You can't get much out of them."

"My middle boy was like that," said John. "Couldn't take an interest. Aaah, I wish I didn't have all that headache on the job. I'd grab Girard by the collar and make him take notice of the world. I wish I could ask him out to Jersey to play in all that space."

"Why not?" I said.

"Why, Virginia, I'm surprised you don't know why not. You know I can't take your children out to meet my children."

I felt a lot of strong arthritis in my ribs.

"My mother's the funny one, Virginia." He felt he had to continue with the subject matter. "I don't know. I guess she likes the idea of bugging Margaret. She says, 'You goin' up, John?' 'Yes, Mother,' I say. 'Behave yourself, John,' she says. 'That husband might come home and hack-saw you into hell. You're a Catholic man, John,' she says. But I figured it out. She likes to know I'm in the building. I swear, Virginia, she wishes me the best of luck."

"I do too, John," I said. We drank a last glass of beer to make sure of a peaceful sleep. "Good night, Virginia," he said, looping his muffler neatly under his chin. "Don't worry. I'll be thinking of what to do about Girard."

I got into the big bed that I share with the girls in the little room. For once I had no trouble falling asleep. I only had to worry about Linda and Barbara and Phillip. It was a great relief to me that John had taken over the thinking about Girard.

John was sincere. That's true. He paid a lot of attention to Girard, smoking out all his sneaky sorrows. He registered him into a wild pack of cub scouts that went up to the Bronx once a week to let off steam.

He gave him a Junior Erector Set. And sometimes when his family wasn't listening he prayed at great length for him.

One Sunday, Sister Veronica said in her sweet voice from another life, "He's not worse. He might even be a little better. How are *you, Virginia?*" putting her hand on mine. Everybody around here acts like they know everything.

"Just fine," I said.

"We ought to start on Phillip," John said, "if it's true Girard's improving."

"You should've been a social worker, John."

"A lot of people have noticed that about me," said John.

"Your mother was always acting so crazy about you, how come she didn't knock herself out a little to see you in college? Like we did for Thomas?"

"Now, Virginia, be fair. She's a poor old woman. My father was a weak earner. She had to have my wages, and I'll tell you, Virginia, I'm not sorry. Look at Thomas. He's still in school. Drop him in this jungle and he'd be devoured. He hasn't had a touch of real life. And here I am with a good chunk of a family, a home of my own, a name in the building trades. One thing I have to tell you, the poor old woman is sorry. I said one day (oh, in passing—years ago) that I might marry you. She stuck a knife in herself. It's a fact. Not more than an eighth of an inch. You never saw such a gory Sunday. One thing—you would have been a better daughter-in-law to her than Margaret."

"Marry me?" I said.

"Well, yes. . . . Aaah—I always liked you, then . . . Why do you think I'd sit in the shade of this kitchen every Thursday night? For God's sakes, the only warm thing around here is this teacup. Yes, sir, I did want to marry you, Virginia."

"No kidding, John? Really?" It was nice to know. Better late than never, to learn you were desired in youth.

I didn't tell John, but the truth is, I would never have married him. Once I met my husband with his winking looks, he was my only interest. Wild as I had been with John and others, I turned all my wildness over to him and then there was no question in my mind.

Still, face facts, if my husband didn't budge on in life, it was my fault. On me, as they say, be it. I greeted the morn with a song. I had a hello for everyone but the landlord. Ask the people on the block, come or go—even the Spanish ones, with their sad dark faces—they have to smile when they see me.

But for his own comfort, he should have done better lifewise and moneywise. I was happy, but I am now in possession of knowledge that this is wrong. Happiness isn't so bad for a woman. She gets fatter, she gets older, she could lie down, nuzzling a regiment of men and little kids, she could just die of the pleasure. But men are different, they have to own money, or they have to be famous, or everybody on the block has to look up to them from the cellar stairs.

A woman counts her children and acts snotty, like she invented life, but men *must* do well in the world. I know that men are not fooled by being happy.

"A funny guy," said John, guessing where my thoughts had gone. "What stopped him up? He was nobody's fool. He had a funny thing about him, Virginia, if you don't mind my saying so. He wasn't much distance up, but he was all set and ready to be looking down on us all."

"He was very smart, John. You don't realize that. His hobby was crossword puzzles, and I said to him real often, as did others around here, that he ought to go out on the '$64 Question.' Why not? But he laughed. You know what he said? He said, 'That proves how dumb you are if you think I'm smart.' "

"A funny guy," said John. "Get it all off your chest," he said. "Talk it out, Virginia; it's the only way to kill the pain."

By and large, I was happy to oblige. Still I could not carry through about certain cruel remarks. It was like trying to move back into the dry mouth of a nightmare to remember that the last day I was happy was the middle of a week in March, when I told my husband I was going to have Linda. Barbara was five months old to the hour. The boys were three and four. I had to tell him. It was the last day with anything happy about it.

Later on he said, "Oh, you make me so sick, you're so goddamn big and fat, you look like a goddamn brownstone, the way you're squared off in front."

"Well, where are you going tonight?" I asked.

"How should I know?" he said. "Your big ass takes up the whole goddamn bed," he said. "There's no room for me." He bought a sleeping bag and slept on the floor.

I couldn't believe it. I would start every morning fresh. I couldn't believe that he would turn against me so, while I was still young and even his friends still liked me.

But he did, he turned absolutely against me and became no friend of mine. "All you ever think about is making babies. This place stinks like the men's room in the BMT. It's a fucking *pissoir*." He was strong on truth all through the year. "That kid eats more than the five of us put together," he said. "Stop stuffing your face, you fat dumbbell," he said to Phillip.

Then he worked on the neighbors. "Get that nosy old bag out of here," he said. "If she comes on once more with 'my son in the building trades' I'll squash her for the cat."

Then he turned on Spielvogel, the checker, his oldest friend, who only visited on holidays and never spoke to me (shy, the way some bachelors are). "That sonofabitch, don't hand me that friendship crap, all he's after is your ass. That's what I need—a little shitmaker of his using up the air in this flat."

And then there was no one else to dispose of. We were left alone fair and square, facing each other.

"Now, Virginia," he said, "I come to the end of my rope. I see a black wall ahead of me. What the hell am I supposed to do? I only got one life. Should I lie down and die? I don't know what to do any more. I'll give it to you straight, Virginia, if I stick around, you can't help it, you'll hate me . . ."

"I hate you right now," I said. "So do whatever you like."

"This place drives me nuts," he mumbled. "I don't know what to do around here. I want to get you a present. Something."

"I told you, do whatever you like. Buy me a rattrap for rats."

That's when he went down to the House Appliance Store, and he brought back a new broom and a classy dustpan.

"A new broom sweeps clean," he said. "I got to get out of here," he said. "I'm going nuts." Then he began to stuff the duffel bags, and

I went to the grocery store but was stopped by Mrs. Raftery, who had to tell me what she considered so beautiful—death—then he kissed me and went to join some army somewhere.

I didn't tell John any of this, because I think it makes a woman look too bad to tell on how another man has treated her. He begins to see her through the other man's eyes, a sitting duck, a skinful of flaws. After all, I had come to depend on John. All my husband's friends were strangers now, though I had always said to them, "Feel welcome."

And the family men in the building looked too cunning, as though they had all personally deserted me. If they met me on the stairs, they carried the heaviest groceries up and helped bring Linda's stroller down, but they never asked me a question worth answering at all.

Besides that, Girard and Phillip taught the girls the days of the week: Monday, Tuesday, Wednesday, Johnday, Friday. They waited for him once a week, under the hallway lamp, half asleep like bugs in the sun, sitting in their little chairs with their names on in gold, a birth present from my mother-in-law. At fifteen after eight he punctually came, to read a story, pass out some kisses, and tuck them into bed.

But one night, after a long Johnday of them squealing my eardrum split, after a rainy afternoon with brother constantly raising up his hand against brother, with the girls near ready to go to court over the proper ownership of Melinda Lee, the twenty-four-inch walking doll, the doorbell rang three times. Not any of those times did John's face greet me.

I was too ashamed to call down to Mrs. Raftery, and she was too mean to knock on my door and explain.

He didn't come the following Thursday either. Girard said sadly, "He must've run away, John."

I had to give him up after two weeks' absence and no word. I didn't know how to tell the children: something about right and wrong, goodness and meanness, men and women. I had it all at my finger tips, ready to hand over. But I didn't think I ought to take mistakes and truth away from them. Who knows? They might make a truer friend in this world somewhere than I have ever made. So I just put them to bed and sat in the kitchen and cried.

In the middle of my third beer, searching in my mind for the next step, I found the decision to go on "Strike It Rich." I scrounged some paper and pencil from the toy box and I listed all my troubles, which must be done in order to qualify. The list when complete could have brought tears to the eye of God if He had a minute. At the sight of it my bitterness began to improve. All that is really necessary for survival of the fittest, it seems, is an interest in life, good, bad, or peculiar.

As always happens in these cases where you have begun to help yourself with plans, news comes from an opposite direction. The doorbell rang, two short and two long—meaning John.

My first thought was to wake the children and make them happy. "No! No!" he said. "Please don't put yourself to that trouble. Virginia, I'm dog-tired," he said. "Dog-tired. My job is a damn headache. It's too much. It's all day and it scuttles my mind at night, and in the end who does the credit go to?

"Virginia," he said, "I don't know if I can come any more. I've been wanting to tell you. I just don't know. What's it all about? Could you answer me if I asked you? I can't figure this whole thing out at all."

I started the tea steeping because his fingers when I touched them were cold. I didn't speak. I tried looking at it from his man point of view, and I thought he had to take a bus, the tubes, and a subway to see me; and then the subway, the tubes, and a bus to go back home at 1 A.M. It wouldn't be any trouble at all for him to part with us forever. I thought about my life, and I gave strongest consideration to my children. If given the choice, I decided to choose not to live without him.

"What's that?" he asked, pointing to my careful list of troubles. "Writing a letter?"

"Oh no," I said, "it's for 'Strike It Rich.' I hope to go on the program."

"Virginia, for goodness' sakes," he said, giving it a glance, "you don't have a ghost. They'd laugh you out of the studio. Those people really suffer."

"Are you sure, John?" I asked.

"No question in my mind at all," said John. "Have you ever seen that program? I mean, in addition to all of this—the little disturbances of man"—he waved a scornful hand at my list—"they *suffer*. They live in the forefront of tornadoes, their lives are washed off by floods—catastrophes of God. Oh, Virginia."

"Are you sure, John?"

"For goodness' sake . . ."

Sadly I put my list away. Still, if things got worse, I could always make use of it.

Once that was settled, I acted on an earlier decision. I pushed his cup of scalding tea aside. I wedged myself onto his lap between his hard belt buckle and the table. I put my arms around his neck and said, "How come you're so cold, John?" He has a kind face and he knew how to look astonished. He said, "Why, Virginia, I'm getting warmer." We laughed.

John became a lover to me that night.

Mrs. Raftery is sometimes silly and sick from her private source of cheap wine. She expects John often. "Honor your mother, what's the matter with you, John?" she complains. "Honor. Honor."

"Virginia dear," she says. "You never would've taken John away to Jersey like Margaret. I wish he'd've married you."

"You didn't like me much in those days."

"That's a lie," she says. I know she's a hypocrite, but no more than the rest of the world.

What is remarkable to me is that it doesn't seem to conscience John as I thought it might. It is still hard to believe that a man who sends out the Ten Commandments every year for a Christmas card can be so easy buttoning and unbuttoning.

Of course we must be very careful not to wake the children or disturb the neighbors, who will enjoy another person's excitement just so far, and then the pleasure enrages them. We must be very careful for ourselves too, for when my husband comes back, realizing the babies are in school and everything easier, he won't forgive me if I've started it all up again—noisy signs of life that are so much trouble to a man.

We haven't seen him in two and a half years. Although people have suggested it, I do not want the police or Intelligence or a private eye or anyone to go after him to bring him back. I know that if he expected to stay away forever he would have written and said so. As it is, I just don't know what evening, any time, he may appear. Sometimes, stumbling over a blockbuster of a dream at midnight, I wake up to vision his soft arrival.

He comes in the door with his old key. He gives me a strict look and says, "Well, you look older, Virginia." "So do you," I say, although he hasn't changed a bit.

He settles in the kitchen because the children are asleep all over the rest of the house. I unknot his tie and offer him a cold sandwich. He raps my backside, paying attention to the bounce. I walk around him as though he were a Maypole, kissing as I go.

"I didn't like the Army much," he says. "Next time I think I might go join the Merchant Marine."

"What army?" I say.

"It's pretty much the same everywhere," he says.

"I wouldn't be a bit surprised," I say.

"I lost my cuff link, goddamnit," he says, and drops to the floor to look for it. I go down too on my knees, but I know he never had a cuff link in his life. Still I would do a lot for him.

"Got you off your feet that time," he says, laughing. "Oh yes, I did." And before I can even make myself half comfortable on that polka-dotted linoleum, he got onto me right where we were, and the truth is, we were so happy, we forgot the precautions.

David Leavitt

Houses

When I arrived at my office that morning—the morning after Susan took me back—an old man and woman wearing wide-brimmed hats and sweatpants were peering at the little snapshots of houses pinned up in the window, discussing their prices in loud voices. There was nothing surprising in this, except that it was still spring, and the costume and demeanor of the couple emphatically suggested summer vacations. It was very early in the day as well as the season—not yet eight and not yet April. They had the look of people who never slept, people who propelled themselves through life on sheer adrenaline, and they also had the look of kindness and good intention gone awry which so often seems to motivate people like that.

I lingered for a few moments outside the office door before going in, so that I could hear their conversation. I had taken a lot of the snapshots myself, and written the descriptive tags underneath them, and I was curious which houses would pique their interest. At first, of course, they looked at the mansions—one of them, oceanfront with ten bathrooms and two pools, was listed for $10.5 million. "Can you imagine?" the wife said. "Mostly it's corporations that buy those," the husband answered. Then their attentions shifted to some more moderately priced, but still expensive, contemporaries. "I don't know, it's like living on the starship *Enterprise,* if you ask me," the wife said. "Personally, I never would get used to a house like that." The husband chuckled. Then the wife's mouth opened and she said, "Will you look at this, Ed? Just look!" and pointed to a snapshot of a small, cedar-shingled house which I happened to know stood not five hundred feet from the office—$165,000, price negotiable. "It's adorable!" the wife said. "It's just like the house in my dream!"

I wanted to tell her it was my dream house too, my dream house first, to beg her not to buy it. But I held back. I reminded myself I already had a house. I reminded myself I had a wife, a dog.

Ed took off his glasses and peered skeptically at the picture. "It doesn't look too bad," he said. "Still, something must be wrong with it. The price is just too low."

"It's the house in my dream, Ed! The one I dreamed about! I swear it is!"

"I told you, Grace-Anne, the last thing I need is a handyman's special. These are my retirement years."

"But how can you know it needs work? We haven't even seen it! Can't we just look at it? Please?"

"Let's have breakfast and talk it over."

"Okay, okay. No point in getting overeager, right?" They headed toward the coffee shop across the street, and I leaned back against the window.

It was just an ordinary house, the plainest of houses. And yet, as I unlocked the office door to let myself in, I found myself swearing I'd burn it down before I'd let that couple take possession of it. Love can push you to all sorts of unlikely threats.

What had happened was this: The night before, I had gone back to my wife after three months of living with a man. I was thirty-two years old, and more than anything in the world, I wanted things to slow, slow down.

It was a quiet morning. We live year-round in a resort town, and except for the summer months, not a whole lot goes on here. Next week things would start gearing up for the Memorial Day closings—my wife Susan's law firm was already frantic with work—but for the moment I was in a lull. It was still early—not even the receptionist had come in yet—so I sat at my desk, and looked at the one picture I kept there, of Susan running on the beach with our golden retriever, Charlotte. Susan held out a tennis ball in the picture, toward which Charlotte, barely out of puppyhood, was inclining her head. And of course I remembered that even now Susan didn't know the extent to which Charlotte was wound up in all of it.

Around nine forty-five I called Ted at the Elegant Canine. I was halfway through dialing before I realized that it was probably improper for me to be doing this, now that I'd officially gone back to Susan, that Susan, if she knew I was calling him, would more than likely have sent me packing—our reconciliation was that fragile. One of her conditions for taking me back was that I not see, not even speak to Ted, and in my shame I'd agreed. Nonetheless, here I was, listening as the phone rang. His boss, Patricia, answered. In the background was the usual cacophony of yelps and barks.

"I don't have much time," Ted said, when he picked up a few seconds later. "I have Mrs. Morrison's poodle to blow-dry."

"I didn't mean to bother you," I said. "I just wondered how you were doing."

"Fine," Ted said. "How are you doing?"

"Oh, okay."

"How did things go with Susan last night?"

"Okay."

"Just okay?"

"Well—it felt so good to be home again—in my own bed, with Susan and Charlotte—" I closed my eyes and pressed the bridge of my nose with my fingers. "Anyway," I said, "it's not fair of me to impose all of this on you. Not fair at all. I mean, here I am, back with Susan, leaving you—"

"Don't worry about it."

"I do worry about it. I do."

There was a barely muffled canine scream in the background, and then I could hear Patricia calling for Ted.

"I have to go, Paul—"

"I guess I just wanted to say I miss you. There, I've said it. There's nothing to do about it, but I wanted to say it, because it's what I feel."

"I miss you too, Paul, but listen, I have to go—"

"Wait, wait. There's something I have to tell you."

"What?"

"There was a couple today. Outside the office. They were looking at our house."

"Paul—"

"I don't know what I'd do if they bought it."

"Paul," Ted said, "it's not our house. It never was."

"No, I guess it wasn't." Again I squeezed the bridge of my nose. I could hear the barking in the background grow louder, but this time Ted didn't tell me he had to go.

"Ted?"

"What?"

"Would you mind if I called you tomorrow?"

"You can call me whenever you want."

"Thanks," I said, and then he said a quick good-bye, and all the dogs were gone.

Three months before, things had been simpler. There was Susan, and me, and Charlotte. Charlotte was starting to smell, and the monthly ordeal of bathing her was getting to be too much for both of us, and anyway, Susan reasoned, now that she'd finally paid off the last of her law school loans, we really did have the right to hire someone to bathe our dog. (We were both raised in penny-pinching families; even in relative affluence, we had no cleaning woman, no gardener. I mowed our lawn.) And so, on a drab Wednesday morning before work, I bundled Charlotte into the car and drove her over to the Elegant Canine. There, among the fake emerald collars, the squeaky toys in the shape of mice and hamburgers, the rawhide bones and shoes and pizzas, was Ted. He had wheat-colored hair and green eyes, and he smiled at me in a frank and unwavering way I found difficult to turn away from. I smiled back, left Charlotte in his capable-seeming hands and headed off to work. The morning proceeded lazily. At noon I drove back to fetch Charlotte, and found her looking golden and glorious, leashed to a small post in a waiting area just to the side of the main desk. Through the door behind the desk I saw a very wet Pekingese being shampooed in a tub and a West Highland white terrier sitting alertly on a metal table, a chain around its neck. I rang a bell, and Ted emerged, waving to me with an arm around which a large bloody bandage had been carefully wrapped.

"My God," I said. "Was it—"

"I'm afraid so," Ted said. "You say she's never been to a groomer's?"

"I assure you, never in her entire life—we've left her alone with small children—our friends joke that she could be a babysitter—" I turned to Charlotte, who looked up at me, panting in that retriever way. "What got into you?" I said, rather hesitantly. And even more hesitantly: "Bad, bad dog—"

"Don't worry about it," Ted said, laughing. "It's happened before and it'll happen again."

"I am so sorry. I am just so—sorry. I had no idea, really."

"Look, it's an occupational hazard. Anyway we're great at first aid around here." He smiled again, and, calmed for the moment, I smiled back. "I just can't imagine what got into her. She's supposed to go to the vet next week, so I'll ask him what he thinks."

"Well, Charlotte's a sweetheart," Ted said. "After our initial hostilities, we got to be great friends, right, Charlotte?" He ruffled the top of her head, and she looked up at him adoringly. We were both looking at Charlotte. Then we were looking at each other. Ted raised his eyebrows. I flushed. The look went on just a beat too long, before I turned away, and he was totaling the bill.

Afterwards, at home, I told Susan about it, and she got into a state. "What if he sues?" she said, running her left hand nervously through her hair. She had taken her shoes off; the heels of her panty hose were black with the dye from her shoes.

"Susan, he's not going to sue. He's a very nice kid, very friendly."

I put my arms around her, but she pushed me away. "Was he the boss?" she said. "You said someone else was the boss."

"Yes, a woman."

"Oh, great. Women are much more vicious than men, Paul, believe me. Especially professional women. He's perfectly friendly and wants to forget it, but for all we know she's been dreaming about going on *People's Court* her whole life." She hit the palm of her hand against her forehead.

"Susan," I said, "I really don't think—"

"Did you give him anything?"

"Give him anything?"

"You know, a tip. Something."

"No."

"Jesus, hasn't being married to a lawyer all these years taught you anything?" She sat down and stood up again. "All right, all right, here's what we're going to do. I want you to have a bottle of champagne sent over to the guy. With an apology, a note. Marcia Grossman did that after she hit that tree, and it worked wonders." She blew out breath. "I don't see what else we *can* do at this point, except wait, and hope—"

"Susan, I really think you're making too much of all this. This isn't New York City, after all, and really, he didn't seem to mind at all—"

"Paul, honey, please trust me. You've always been very naive about these things. Just send the champagne, all right?"

Her voice had reached an unendurable pitch of annoyance. I stood up. She looked at me guardedly. It was the beginning of a familiar fight between us—in her anxiety, she'd say something to imply, not so subtly, how much more she understood about the world than I did, and in response I would stalk off, insulted and pouty. But this time I did not stalk off—I just stood there—and Susan, closing her eyes in a manner which suggested profound regret at having acted rashly, said in a very soft voice, "I don't mean to yell. It's just that you know how insecure I get about things like this, and really, it'll make me feel so much better to know we've done something. So send the champagne for my sake, okay?" Suddenly she was small and vulnerable, a little girl victimized by her own anxieties. It was a transformation she made easily, and often used to explain her entire life.

"Okay," I said, as I always said, and that was the end of it.

The next day I sent the champagne. The note read (according to Susan's instructions): "Dear Ted: Please accept this little gift as a token of thanks for your professionalism and good humor. Sincerely, Paul Hoover and Charlotte." I should add that at this point I believed I was leaving Susan's name off only because she hadn't been there.

The phone at my office rang the next morning at nine-thirty. "Listen," Ted said, "thanks for the champagne! That was so thoughtful of you."

"Oh, it was nothing."

"No, but it means a lot that you cared enough to send it." He was quiet for a moment. "So few clients do, you know. Care."

"Oh, well," I said. "My pleasure."

Then Ted asked me if I wanted to have dinner with him sometime during the week.

"Dinner? Um—well—"

"I know, you're probably thinking this is sudden and rash of me, but— Well, you seemed like such a nice guy, and—I don't know—I don't meet many people I can really even stand to be around—men, that is—so what's the point of pussyfooting around?"

"No, no, I understand," I said. "That sounds great. Dinner, that is—sounds great."

Ted made noises of relief. "Terrific, terrific. What night would be good for you?"

"Oh, I don't know. Thursday?" Thursday Susan was going to New York to sell her mother's apartment.

"Thursday's terrific," Ted said. "Do you like Dunes?"

"Sure." Dunes was a gay bar and restaurant I'd never been to.

"So I'll make a reservation. Eight o'clock? We'll meet there?"

"That's fine."

"I'm so glad," Ted said. "I'm really looking forward to it."

It may be hard to believe, but even then I still told myself I was doing it to make sure he didn't sue us.

Now, I should point out that not *all* of this was a new experience for me. It's true I'd never been to Dunes, but in my town, late at night, there is a beach, and not too far down the highway, a parking area. Those nights Susan and I fought, it was usually at one of these places that I ended up.

Still, nothing I'd done in the dark prepared me for Dunes, when I got there Thursday night. Not that it was so different from any other restaurant I'd gone to—it was your basic scrubbed-oak, piano-bar sort of place. Only everyone was a man. The maître d', white-bearded and red-cheeked, a displaced Santa Claus, smiled at me and said, "Meeting someone?"

"Yes, in fact." I scanned the row of young and youngish men sitting at the bar, looking for Ted. "He doesn't seem to be here yet."

"Ted Potter, right?"

I didn't know Ted's last name. "Yes, I think so."

"The dog groomer?"

"Right."

The maître d', I thought, smirked. "Well, I can seat you now, or you can wait at the bar."

"Oh, I think I'll just wait here, thanks, if that's okay."

"Whatever you want," the maître d' said. He drifted off toward a large, familial-looking group of young men who'd just walked in the door. Guardedly I surveyed the restaurant for a familiar face, which, thankfully, never materialized. I had two or three co-workers who I suspected ate here regularly.

I had to go to the bathroom, which was across the room. As far as I could tell, there was no ladies' room at all. As for the men's room, it was small and cramped, with a long trough reminiscent of junior high school summer camp instead of urinals. Above the trough a mirror had been strategically tilted at a downward angle.

By the time I'd finished, and emerged once again into the restaurant, Ted had arrived. He looked breathless and a little worried and was consulting busily with the maître d'. I waved; he waved back with his bandaged hand, said a few more words to the maître d' and strode up briskly to greet me. "Hello," he said, clasping my hand with his unbandaged one. It was a large hand, cool and powdery. "Gosh, I'm sorry I'm late. I have to say, when I got here, and didn't see you, I was worried you might have left. Joey—that's the owner—said you'd been standing there one minute and the next you were gone."

"I was just in the bathroom."

"I'm glad you didn't leave." He exhaled what seemed an enormous quantity of breath. "Wow, it's great to see you! You look great!"

"Thanks," I said. "So do you." He did. He was wearing a white oxford shirt with the first couple of buttons unbuttoned, and a blazer the color of the beach.

"There you are," said Joey—the maître d'. "We were wondering where you'd run off to. Well, your table's ready." He escorted us to the middle of the hubbub. "Let's order some wine," Ted said as we sat down. "What kind do you like?"

I wasn't a big wine expert—Susan had always done the ordering for us—so I deferred to Ted, who, after conferring for a few moments with Joey, mentioned something that sounded Italian. Then he leaned back and cracked his knuckles, bewildered, apparently, to be suddenly without tasks.

"So," he said.

"So," I said.

"I'm glad to see you."

"I'm glad to see you too."

We both blushed. "You're a real estate broker, right? At least, that's what I figured from your business card."

"That's right."

"How long have you been doing that?"

I dug back. "Oh, eight years or so."

"That's great. Have you been out here the whole time?"

"No, no, we moved out here six years ago."

"We?"

"Uh—Charlotte and I."

"Oh." Again Ted smiled. "So do you like it, living year-round in a resort town?"

"Sure. How about you?"

"I ended up out here by accident and just sort of stayed. A lot of people I've met have the same story. They'd like to leave, but you know—the climate is nice, life's not too difficult. It's hard to pull yourself away."

I nodded nervously.

"Is that your story too?"

"Oh—well, sort of," I said. "I was born in Queens, and then—I was living in Manhattan for a while—and then we decided to move out here—Charlotte and I—because I'd always loved the beach, and wanted to have a house, and here you could sell real estate and live all year round." I looked at Ted: Had I caught myself up in a lie or a contradiction? What I was telling him, essentially, was my history, but without Susan—and that was ridiculous, since my history was bound up with Susan's every step of the way. We'd started dating in high school, gone to the same college. The truth was I'd lived in Manhattan only while she was in law school, and had started selling real estate to help pay her tuition. No wonder the story sounded so strangely motiveless as I told it. I'd left out the reason for everything. Susan was the reason for everything.

A waiter—a youngish blond man with a mustache so pale you could barely see it—gave us menus. He was wearing a white T-shirt and had a corkscrew outlined in the pocket of his jeans.

"Hello, Teddy," he said to Ted. Then he looked at me and said very fast, as if it were one sentence, "I'm Bobby and I'll be your waiter for the evening would you like something from the bar?"

"We've already ordered some wine," Ted said. "You want anything else, Paul?"

"I'm fine."

"Okay, would you like to hear the specials now?"

We both nodded, and Bobby rattled off a list of complex-sounding dishes. It was hard for me to separate one from the other. I had no appetite. He handed us our menus and moved on to another table.

I opened the menu. Everything I read sounded like it would make me sick.

"So do you like selling houses?" Ted asked.

"Oh yes, I love it—I love houses." I looked up, suddenly nervous that I was talking too much about myself. Shouldn't I ask him something about himself? I hadn't been on a date for fifteen years, after all, and

even then the only girl I dated was Susan, whom I'd known forever.
What was the etiquette in a situation like this? Probably I should ask
Ted something about his life, but what kind of question would be
appropriate?

Another waiter arrived with our bottle of wine, which Ted poured.

"How long have you been a dog groomer?" I asked rather tentatively.

"A couple of years. Of course I never intended to be a professional
dog groomer. It was just something I did to make money. What I really
wanted to be, just like about a million and a half other people, was an
actor. Then I took a job out here for the summer, and like I said, I
just stayed. I actually love the work. I love animals. When I was growing
up my mom kept saying I should have been a veterinarian. She still
says that to me sometimes, tells me it's not too late. I don't know.
Frankly, I don't think I have what it takes to be a vet, and anyway, I
don't want to be one. It's important work, but let's face it, I'm not for
it and it's not for me. So I'm content to be a dog groomer." He picked
up his wineglass and shook it, so that the wine lapped the rim in little
waves.

"I know what you mean," I said, and I did. For years Susan had
been complaining that I should have been an architect, insisting that I
would have been happier, when the truth was she was just the tiniest
bit ashamed of being married to a real estate broker. In her fantasies,
"My husband is an architect" sounded so much better.

"My mother always wanted me to be an architect," I said now. "But
it was just so she could tell her friends. For some reason people think
real estate is a slightly shameful profession, like prostitution or something. They just assume on some level you make your living ripping
people off. There's no way around it. An occupational hazard, I guess."

"Like dog bites," said Ted. He poured more wine.

"Oh, about that—" But Bobby was back to take our orders. He
was pulling a green pad from the pocket on the back of his apron when
another waiter came up to him from behind and whispered something
in his ear. Suddenly they were both giggling wildly.

"You going to fill us in?" Ted asked, after the second waiter had
left.

"I'm really sorry about this," Bobby said, still giggling. "It's just—" He bent down close to us, and in a confiding voice said, "Jill over at the bar brought in some like really good Vanna, just before work, and like, everything seems really hysterical to me? You know, like it's five years ago and I'm this boy from Emporia, Kansas?" He cast his eyes to the ceiling. "God, I'm like a complete retard tonight. Anyway, what did you say you wanted?"

Ted ordered grilled paillard of chicken with shiitake mushrooms in a papaya vinaigrette; I ordered a cheeseburger.

"Who's Jill?" I asked after Bobby had left.

"Everyone's Jill," Ted said. "They're all Jill."

"And Vanna?"

"Vanna White. It's what they call cocaine here." He leaned closer. "I'll bet you're thinking this place is really ridiculous, and you're right. The truth is, I kind of hate it. Only can you name me someplace else where two men can go on a date? I like the fact that you can act datish here, if you know what I mean." He smiled. Under the table our hands interlocked. We were acting very datish indeed.

It was all very unreal. I thought of Susan, in Queens, with her mother. She'd probably called the house two or three times already, was worrying where I was. It occurred to me, dimly and distantly, like something in another life, that Ted knew nothing about Susan. I wondered if I should tell him.

But I did not tell him. We finished dinner, and went to Ted's apartment. He lived in the attic of a rambling old house near the center of town.

We never drank more than a sip or two each of the cups of tea he made for us.

It was funny—when we began making love that first time, Ted and I, what I was thinking was that, like most sex between men, this was really a matter of exorcism, the expulsion of bedeviling lusts. Or exercise, if you will. Or horniness—a word that always makes me think of demons. So why was it, when we finished, there were tears in my eyes, and I was turning, putting my mouth against his hair, preparing to whisper something—who knows what?

Ted looked upset. "What's wrong?" he asked. "Did I hurt you?"

"No," I said. "No. You didn't hurt me."

"Then what is it?"

"I guess I'm just not used to— I didn't expect— I never expected—" Again I was crying.

"It's okay," he said. "I feel it too."

"I have a wife," I said.

At first he didn't answer.

I've always loved houses. Most people I know in real estate don't love houses; they love making money, or making deals, or making sales pitches. But Susan and I, from when we first knew each other, from when we were very young, we loved houses better than anything else. Perhaps this was because we'd both been raised by divorced parents in stuffy apartments in Queens—I can't be sure. All I know is that as early as senior year in high school we shared a desire to get as far out of that city we'd grown up in as we could; we wanted a green lawn, and a mailbox, and a garage. And that passion, as it turned out, was so strong in us that it determined everything. I needn't say more about myself, and as for Susan—well, name me one other first-in-her-class in law school who's chosen—*chosen*—basically to do house closings for a living.

Susan wishes I was an architect. It is her not-so-secret dream to be married to an architect. Truthfully, she wanted me to have a profession she wouldn't have to think was below her own. But the fact is, I never could have been a decent architect because I have no patience for the engineering, the inner workings, the slow layering of concrete slab and wood and Sheetrock. Real estate is a business of surfaces, of first impressions; you have to brush past the water stain in the bathroom, put a Kleenex box over the gouge in the Formica, stretch the life expectancy of the heater from three to six years. Tear off the tile and the paint, the crumbly wallboard and the crackly blanket of insulation, and you'll see what flimsy scarecrows our houses really are, stripped down to their bare beams. I hate the sight of houses in the midst of renovation, naked and exposed like that. But give me a finished house, a polished floor, a sunny day; then I will show you what I'm made of.

The house I loved best, however, the house where, in those mad months, I imagined I might actually live with Ted, was the sort that most brokers shrink from—pretty enough, but drab, undistinguished. No dishwasher, no cathedral ceilings. It would sell, if it sold at all, to a young couple short on cash, or a retiring widow. So don't ask me why I loved this house. My passion for it was inexplicable, yet intense. Somehow I was utterly convinced that this, much more than the sleek suburban one-story Susan and I shared, with its Garland stove and Sub-Zero fridge—this was the house of love.

The day I told Susan I was leaving her, she threw the Cuisinart at me. It bounced against the wall with a thud, and that vicious little blade, dislodged, rolled along the floor like a revolving saw, until it gouged the wall. I stared at it, held fast and suspended above the ground. "How can you just come home from work and tell me this?" Susan screamed. "No preparation, no warning—"

"I thought you'd be relieved," I said.

"Relieved!"

She threw the blender next. It hit me in the chest, then fell on my foot. Instantly I dove to the floor, buried my head in my knees and was weeping as hoarsely and furiously as a child.

"Stop throwing things!" I shouted weakly.

"I can't believe you," Susan said. "You tell me you're leaving me for a man and then you want me to mother you, take care of you? Is that all I've ever been to you? Fuck that! You're not a baby!"

I heard footsteps next, a car starting, Charlotte barking. I opened my eyes. Broken glass, destroyed machinery, all over the tiles.

I got in my car and followed her. All the way to the beach. "Leave me alone!" she shouted, pulling off her shoes and running out onto the sand. "Leave me the fuck alone!" Charlotte romped after her, barking.

"Susan!" I screamed. "Susan!" I chased her. She picked up a big piece of driftwood and hit me with it. I stopped, dropped once again to my knees. Susan kept running. Eventually she stopped. I saw her a few hundred feet up the beach, staring at the waves.

Charlotte kept running between us, licking our faces, in a panic of barks and wails.

Susan started walking back toward me. I saw her getting larger and larger as she strode down the beach. She strode right past me.

"Charlotte!" Susan called from the parking lot. "Charlotte!" But Charlotte stayed.

Susan got back in her car and drove away.

At first I stayed at Ted's house. But Susan—we were seeing each other again, taking walks on the beach, negotiating—said that was too much, so I moved into the Dutch Boy Motel. Still, every day, I went to see the house, either to eat my lunch or just stand in the yard, feeling the sun come down through the branches of the trees there. I was learning a lot about the house. It had been built in 1934 by Josiah Applegate, a local contractor, as a wedding present for his daughter, Julia, and her husband, Spencer Bledsoe. The Bledsoes occupied the house for six years before the birth of their fourth child forced them to move, at which point it was sold to another couple, Mr. and Mrs. Hubert White. They, in turn, sold the house to Mr. and Mrs. Salvatore Rinaldi, who sold it to Mrs. Barbara Adams, a widow, who died. The estate of Mrs. Adams then sold the house to Arthur and Penelope Hilliard, who lived in it until their deaths just last year at the ages of eighty-six and eighty-two. Mrs. Hilliard was the first to go, in her sleep; according to her niece, Mr. Hilliard then wasted away, eventually having to be transferred to Shady Manor Nursing Home, where a few months later a heart attack took him. They had no children. Mr. Hilliard was a retired postman. Mrs. Hilliard did not work, but was an active member of the Ladies' Village Improvement Society. She was famous for her apple cakes, which she sold every year at bake sales. Apparently she went through periods when she would write letters to the local paper every week, long diatribes about the insensitivity of the new houses and new people. I never met her. She had a reputation for being crotchety but maternal. Her husband was regarded as docile and wicked at poker.

The house had three bedrooms—one pitifully small—and two and a half baths. The kitchen cabinets were made of knotty, dark wood which had grown sticky from fifty years of grease, and the ancient yellow Formica countertops were scarred with burns and knife scratches. The wallpaper was red roses in the kitchen, leafy green leaves in the living room, and was yellowing and peeling at the edges. The yard contained a dogwood, a cherry tree and a clump of gladiolas. Overgrown privet hedges fenced the front door, which was white with a beaten brass knocker. In the living room was a dusty pair of sofas, and dark wood shelves lined with Reader's Digest Condensed Books, and a big television from the early seventies. The shag carpeting—coffee brown—appeared to be a recent addition.

The quilts on the beds, the Hilliards' niece told me, were handmade, and might be for sale. They were old-fashioned patchwork quilts, no doubt stitched together over several winters in front of the television. "Of course," the niece said, "if the price was right, we might throw the quilts in—you know, as an extra."

I was a man with the keys to fifty houses in my pockets. Just that morning I had toured the ten bathrooms of the $10.5-million ocean-front. And I was smiling. I was smiling like someone in love.

I took Ted to see the house about a week after I left Susan. It was a strange time for both of us. I was promising him my undying love, but I was also waking up in the middle of every night crying for Susan and Charlotte. We walked from room to room, just as I'd imagined, and just as I'd planned, in the doorway to the master bedroom, I turned him around to face me, bent his head down (he was considerably taller than me) and kissed him. It was meant to be a moment of sealing, of confirmation, a moment that would make radiantly, abundantly clear the extent to which this house was meant for us, and we for it. But instead the kiss felt rehearsed, dispassionate. And Ted looked nervous. "It's a cute house, Paul," he said. "But God knows I don't have any money. And you already own a house. How can we just *buy* it?"

"As soon as the divorce is settled, I'll get my equity."

"You haven't even filed for divorce yet. And once you do, it could take years."

"Probably not *years*."

"So when *are* you filing for divorce?"

He had his hands in his pockets. He was leaning against a window draped with white flounces of cotton and powderpuffs.

"I need to take things slow," I said. "This is all new for me."

"It seems to me," Ted said, "that you need to take things slow and take things fast at the same time."

"Oh, Ted!" I said. "Why do you have to complicate everything? I just love this house, that's all. I feel like this is where I—where we—where we're meant to live. Our dream house, Ted. Our love nest. Our cottage."

Ted was looking at his feet. "Do you really think you'll be able to leave Susan? For good?"

"Well, of course, I— Of course."

"I don't believe you. Soon enough she's going to make an ultimatum. Come back, give up Ted, or that's it. And you know what you're going to do? You're going to go back to her."

"I'm not," I said. "I wouldn't."

"Mark my words," Ted said.

I lunged toward him, trying to pull him down on the sofa, but he pushed me away.

"I love you," I said.

"And Susan?"

I faltered. "Of course, I love Susan too."

"You can't love two people, Paul. It doesn't work that way."

"Susan said the same thing, last week."

"She's right."

"Why?"

"Because it isn't fair."

I considered this. I considered Ted, considered Susan. I had known Susan since Mrs. Polanski's homeroom in fourth grade. We played *Star Trek* on the playground together, and roamed the back streets of Bayside. We were children in love, and we sought out every movie or book we could find about children in love.

Ted I'd known only a few months, but we'd made love with a passion I'd never imagined possible, and the sight of him unbuttoning his shirt made my heart race.

It was at that moment that I realized that while it is possible to love two people at the same time, in different ways, in the heart, it is not possible to do so in the world.

I had to choose, so of course, I chose Susan.

That day—the day of Ed and Grace-Anne, the day that threatened to end with the loss of my beloved house—Susan did not call me at work.

The morning progressed slowly. I was waiting for Ed and Grace-Anne to reappear at the window and walk in the office doors, and sure enough, around eleven-thirty, they did. The receptionist led them to my desk.

"I'm Ed Cavallaro," Ed said across my desk, as I stood to shake his hand. "This is my wife."

"How do you do?" Grace-Anne said. She smelled of some sort of fruity perfume or lipstick, the kind teenaged girls wear. We sat down.

"Well, I'll tell you, Mr. Hoover," Ed said, "we've been summering around here for years, and I've just retired—I worked over at Grumman, upisland?"

"Congratulations," I said.

"Ed was there thirty-seven years," Grace-Anne said. "They gave him a party like you wouldn't believe."

"So, you enjoying retired life?"

"Just between you and me, I'm climbing the walls."

"We're active people," Grace-Anne said.

"Anyway, we've always dreamed about having a house near the beach."

"Ed, let *me* tell about the dream."

"I didn't mean *that* dream."

"I had a dream," Grace-Anne said. "I saw the house we were meant to retire in, clear as day. And then, just this morning, walking down the street, we look in your window, and what do we see? The very same house! The house from my dream!"

"How amazing," I said. "Which house was it?"

"That cute little one for one sixty-five," Grace-Anne said. "You know, with the cedar shingles?"

"I'm not sure."

"Oh, I'll show you."

We stood up and walked outside, to the window. "Oh, that house!" I said. "Sure, sure. Been on the market almost a year now. Not much interest in it, I'm afraid."

"Now why is that?" Ed asked, and I shrugged.

"It's a pleasant enough house. But it does have some problems. It'll require a lot of TLC."

"TLC we've got plenty of," Grace-Anne said.

"Grace-Anne, I told you," Ed said, "the last thing I want to do is waste my retirement fixing up."

"But it's my dream house!" Grace-Anne fingered the buttons of her blouse. "Anyway, what harm can it do to look at it?"

"I have a number of other houses in roughly the same price range which you might want to look at—"

"Fine, fine, but first, couldn't we look at that house? I'd be so grateful if you could arrange it."

I shrugged my shoulders. "It's not occupied. Why not?"

And Grace-Anne smiled.

Even though the house was only a few hundred feet away, we drove. One of the rules of real estate is: Drive the clients everywhere. This means your car has to be both commodious and spotlessly clean. I spent a lot—too much—of my life cleaning my car—especially difficult, considering Charlotte.

And so we piled in—Grace-Anne and I in front, Ed in back—and drove the block or so to Maple Street. I hadn't been by the house for a few weeks, and I was happy to see that the spring seemed to have treated it well. The rich greens of the grass and the big maple trees framed it, I thought, rather lushly.

I unlocked the door, and we headed into that musty interior odor which, I think, may well be the very essence of stagnation, cryogenics and bliss.

"Just like I dreamed," Grace-Anne said, and I could understand why. Probably the Hilliards had been very much like the Cavallaros.

"The kitchen's in bad shape," Ed said. "How's the boiler?"

"Old, but functional." We headed down into the spidery basement. Ed kicked things.

Grace-Anne was rapturously fingering the quilts. "Ed, I love this house," she said. "I love it."

Ed sighed laboriously.

"Now, there are several other nice homes you might want to see—"

"None of them was in my dream."

But Ed sounded hopeful. "Grace-Anne, it can't hurt to look. You said it yourself."

"But what if someone else snatches it from under us?" Grace-Anne asked, suddenly horrified.

"I tend to doubt that's going to happen," I said in as comforting a tone as I could muster. "As I mentioned earlier, the house has been on the market for over a year."

"All right," Grace-Anne said reluctantly, "I suppose we could look—*look*—at a few others."

"I'm sure you won't regret it."

"Yes, well."

I turned from them, breathing evenly.

Of course she had no idea I would sooner make sure the house burned down than see a contract for its purchase signed with her husband's name.

I fingered some matches in my pocket. I felt terrified. Terrified and powerful.

When I got home from work that afternoon, Susan's car was in the driveway and Charlotte, from her usual position of territorial inspection on the front stoop, was smiling up at me in her doggy way. I patted her head and went inside, but when I got there, there was a palpable silence which was far from ordinary, and soon enough I saw that its source was Susan, leaning over the kitchen counter in her sleek lawyer's suit, one leg tucked under, like a flamingo.

"Hi," I said.

I tried to kiss her, and she turned away.

"This isn't going to work, Paul," she said.

I was quiet a moment. "Why?" I asked.

"You sound relieved, grateful. You do. I knew you would."

"I'm neither of those things. Just tell me why you've changed your mind since last night."

"You tell me you're in love with a man, you up and leave for three months, then out of the blue you come back. I just don't know what you expect—do you want me to jump for joy and welcome you back like nothing's happened?"

"Susan, yesterday you said—"

"Yesterday," Susan said, "I hadn't thought about it enough. Yesterday I was confused, and grateful, and— God, I was so relieved. But now—now I just don't know. I mean, what the hell has this been for you, anyway?"

"Susan, honey," I said, "I love you. I've loved you my whole life. Remember what your mother used to say, when we were kids, and we'd come back from playing on Saturdays? 'You two are joined at the hip,' she'd say. And we still are."

"Have you ever loved me sexually?" Susan asked, suddenly turning to face me.

"Susan," I said.

"Have you?"

"Of course."

"I don't believe you. I think it's all been cuddling and hugging. Kid stuff. I think the sex only mattered to me. How do I know you weren't thinking about men all those times?"

"Susan, of course not—"

"What a mistake," Susan said. "If only I'd known back then, when I was a kid—"

"Doesn't it matter to you that I'm back?"

"It's not like you never left, for Christ's sake!" She put her hands on my cheeks. "You *left*," she said quietly. "For three months you *left*. And I don't know, maybe love *can* be killed."

She let go. I didn't say anything.

"I think you should leave for a while," Susan said. "I think I need some time alone—some time alone knowing you're alone too."

I looked at the floor. "Okay," I said. And I suppose I said it too eagerly, because Susan said, "If you go back to Ted, that's it. We're finished for good."

"I won't go back to Ted," I said.

We were both quiet for a few seconds.

"Should I go now?"

Susan nodded.

"Well, then, good-bye," I said. And I went.

. . .

This brings me to where I am now, which is, precisely, nowhere. I waited three hours in front of Ted's house that night, but when, at twelve-thirty, his car finally pulled into the driveway, someone else got out with him. It has been two weeks since that night. Each day I sit at my desk, and wait for one of them, or a lawyer, to call. I suppose I am homeless, although I think it is probably inaccurate to say that a man with fifty keys in his pocket is ever homeless. Say, then, that I am a man with no home, but many houses.

Of course I am careful. I never spend the night in the same house twice. I bring my own sheets, and in the morning I always remake the bed I've slept in as impeccably as I can. The fact that I'm an early riser helps as well—that way, if another broker arrives, or a cleaning woman, I can say I'm just checking the place out. And if the owners are coming back, I'm always the first one to be notified.

The other night I slept at the $10.5-million oceanfront. I used all the bathrooms; I swam in both the pools.

As for the Hilliards' house—well, so far I've allowed myself to stay there only once a week. Not because it's inconvenient—God knows, no one ever shows the place—but because to sleep there more frequently would bring me closer to a dream of unbearable pleasure than I feel I can safely go.

The Cavallaros, by the way, ended up buying a contemporary in the woods for a hundred and seventy-five, the superb kitchen of which turned out to be more persuasive than Grace-Anne's dream. The Hilliards' house remains empty, unsold. Their niece just lowered the price to one fifty—quilts included.

Funny: Even with all my other luxurious possibilities, I look forward to those nights I spend at the Hilliards' with greater anticipation than anything else in my life. When the key clicks, and the door opens onto that living room with its rows of Reader's Digest Condensed Books, a rare sense of relief runs through me. I feel as if I've come home.

One thing about the Hilliards' house is that the lighting is terrible. It seems there isn't a bulb in the house over twenty-five watts. And perhaps this isn't surprising—they were old people, after all, by no means readers. They spent their lives in front of the television. So when

I arrive at night, I have to go around the house, turning on light after light, like ancient oil lamps. Not much to read by, but dim light, I've noticed, has a kind of warmth which bright light lacks. It casts a glow against the woodwork which is exactly, just exactly, like the reflection of raging fire.

Maria Thomas

COME TO AFRICA AND SAVE YOUR MARRIAGE

Things in the tropics have different proportions, like the vegetation, intense and overgrown. Like Rashak, his eyes deep set with long, dark lashes, his nose thin, arched, aristocratic, a bird of prey. High cheekbones and deep olive skin, and his lush hair, copper in the sun, curled below his ears. If I had been Lewis Rashak's wife—me, Marlene—and someone else as well, someone on the outside looking in, I might have seen the humor in it all. Lewis liked to stage our lives— producer, director, playwright—our little, in-the-kitchen one-acts with no audience, but the players, me and the kids, and then, finally, Marie D'Avignon.

Lewis fell in love with Marie. He told me, rather "had to tell me," as soon as they became lovers, a confession made all the more dramatic by the understated way we played it, seeing who was more mature.

I said, "Well, it's okay, it happens, but aren't you ratting on Marie, my best friend?"

"She isn't happy about that part of it," he said.

She was outside, in fact, waiting while he told me, sitting on her motorcycle staring into her helmet the

223

way she did. I went to her and said, "It's okay, Marie. Don't feel bad for me or anything. I mean it." I even hugged her, but she didn't look convinced. She was almost crying. She knew, of course, the way things were with Rashak and me.

Rashak was standing in the kitchen door with his back to us. A chair had blocked the entrance. Behind him you could see the filthy stove, the piled dishes, the soot from the charcoal we sometimes cooked on to save on the electric bill. When he heard us come in, he kicked over the chair and went into the kitchen. Marie followed him and I stepped away from them, down into the living room. I did the only thing I could, tidied aimlessly, but there was so much junk—the furniture had become obsolete, turned into storage space. In the corner was my "workshop," four orange crates, a coffee cup, the buckets of dried clay, the broken pots, and the headless dancer modeled from Hanna, my older daughter.

Hanna broke the silence. "Mommy! Daddy!" rushing toward the door shouting about a snake in the neighbors' yard. Jenny, the younger one, was hopping barefoot behind her over the stones.

"It was a co-brass," she shouted. "And its head went uuuup like this!"

"And its tongue went like thiiiiis." Hanna dashed—I saw it coming, but too late—her hand right through the screen.

"Goddamn it!" Rashak yelled from the kitchen. "I just taped that fucking screen. Christ, there are flies all over the place in here. We're lucky we don't all have cholera."

"What about the three windows that have fallen out upstairs?" Me, nagging from the other room. "Why don't you bother to fix those if you don't like flies?"

Marie had slipped to the dining room, so quietly I barely noticed. She sat at the table there. She drew Jenny to her lap. There were crayons and papers around, spread out from another time, so the two of them started to make pictures. Lewis grabbed a cup from the table and went back to the kitchen.

"Would you like some *instant,* Marie? Marlene, you? We only have *instant.*" This was sarcasm; he hated instant coffee. "One more cup of this stuff and I'll puke," he said. He tipped the cup, dribbling the residue over the floor. "Isn't there ever anything else to drink in this place?"

"There's tea," I told him. He hated tea.

225

COME TO
AFRICA
AND SAVE
YOUR
MARRIAGE

Living with Lewis Rashak was never a joke. His mother had been in show biz, a comedienne on the Catskill circuit. She had been a friend of Lenny Bruce. From her, Lewis picked up the habit of keeping oddballs around the house. At that time it was Ramji Gupta, an Indian mathematician and poet, his wife, Ingrid, who was Swedish and made documentary films, and their huge baby, whose name I can't remember. The University of Dar es Salaam had terminated Gupta's contract some seven months early for no reason and had put them out of their house. They had no place to go and were camping, to protest the broken contract, on the front lawn of their former house under canopies of faded cloths. Ingrid filmed their struggle and Ramji had written a long, satiric narrative poem about it which he jokingly compared to the *Ramayana*. But Gupta was far too skinny to clown around and no one ever laughed at his jokes.

When it had started to rain, Lewis took pity on them and invited them to fold up their tents and come stay at our place. They camped in our living room and the only compensation was Gupta's vegetarian food.

I hated it in Africa when we first came. We had no money, were already threadbare, and Lewis's salary as an instructor in the English department was an African salary, meant for people who can live on nothing. Everything had to be makeshift, permanently temporary. I couldn't do my pottery. I couldn't buy bricks for a kiln, or wood to fire it. I couldn't afford glazes. There was plenty of clay in the river and I tried to build a kiln of sun-dried brick. First I made the bricks and then I dug the foundation. Then the rains came. The bricks dissolved. Nothing remained. It was the first thing I learned about the tropics. The few pots I made went unfired, piled in the living room— the so-called living room—so brittle they were turning to dust: red dust on the books, on Rashak's desk, on the torn seat covers, the bare floor, the dying house plants. But in the end, I was glad I came, because I fell in love, too, though I hadn't told Lewis. When I did tell him, I wanted to be ready to stand back and watch the scene, outside myself, so I could laugh.

What I told him first was that I wanted out. "Move Marie over here and I'll live at her place." I knew he couldn't afford it. There were the kids and no way for me to get a job, an alien with no working papers.

He turned around and told Ingrid, "Marlene wants to split. She blames me for holding her back. She resents my work. All that shit."

Ingrid said, "Vomen need her independence." Her baby crawled out from under the table with Jenny's Fisher-Price truck.

"Was it Lewis's work that I had to hire out for odd jobs so his kids could eat while he played around for years writing some useless Ph.D. on African Literature, for God's sake? So he could get ahead? Ahead, my ass. What about *my* work, Rashak?"

"Oh, yes," he said, "those desiccating lumps of clay. She calls that dust in there 'her work.'"

Jenny was screaming, "*It's my truck!*" She had started to pummel the baby. There was so much yelling at times it hurt, physical pain, as though you'd been hit, across your back, across your chest.

"The Masai tribe make successes in marriage," Ingrid said, "by having absolutely nothing to do with each other but sex." She was serious. Her round red face, bright yellow hair, chapped and peeling lips, seemed suspended in the room like a Cheshire cat. The baby was quiet now, climbing the table, trying to stand up on it.

You should have seen how he came coaxing later; Rashak's style, an arrangement. "Look, Marlene, can't we just go on the way we were? Stay friends. We're mature adults, after all."

"So are you going to sleep with the two of us tag-team style?"

"Shit, Marlene," he said, "you know I can't do that. I'm a one-woman man." He meant one woman at a time, and of course that was Marie. We were all too close. *She* must have insisted.

"What am I supposed to do in the meantime?" I moved my hips to show him what.

"Take a lover," he said. I wanted to tell him right then, "I have a lover." But I was waiting.

The next Saturday night Ramji made his specialty for dinner, curried eggs, dhal, chapattis, green mango pickle, coconut chutney. Rashak had produced a bottle of red wine somehow and Marie brought brandy for after. The table was cleared and set, a miracle. There were even napkins and candles. Lewis was all prim in ironed jeans and a crisp blue shirt. I smelled his aftershave lotion. In the candlelight the place had a new look, as though new people had moved in. It lightened Rashak, who could flit around like an insect.

227

COME TO

AFRICA

AND SAVE

YOUR

MARRIAGE

But new people had not moved in. Gupta's baby, who didn't wear diapers, had climbed onto the table and managed to shit in one of the plates. Ingrid, laughing and talking Swedish, hauled him off. It was something I couldn't resist, giggling, carrying the plate, offering it to Lewis as an hors d'oeuvre. He didn't think it was funny, reeled with disgust, and grabbed the plate. For a minute I thought he would throw it at me, but he resisted, storming away from us. Marie flushed and followed him. She carried him a beer. His lover.

The food was good, the ambiance at the meal not so good. A paper plate thrown by Hanna landed in the egg curry and Jenny's braid caught fire as she leaned across a candle to grab a chapatti. She tried the mango pickle after Lewis warned her not to and then spit most of it into his plate.

"Why must we always have the *kids?*" he wanted to know.

Ingrid and Ramji talked steadily about how the United States was using wheat-crop politics to enslave the world, holding entire continents hostage to famine. Ingrid had read somewhere that the earth's poles were shifting and there would be drastic changes in the weather by the year two thousand. By an ironic twist of nature, only Canada, the United States, and Australia would be able to produce enough grain. They would try to suppress the world. But nature, Ingrid explained, was more than shifting winds and currents. Masses of starving dark people would rise up and take everything. They were out there right now, she warned, having more and more babies despite America's attempt to impose genocidal policies of population control. As a statement, Ingrid, herself, was planning to have ten children.

Later they were surprised when I said, "I'm going out for a walk."

"But is it safe?" Gupta asked.

"I'm coming with you," Rashak announced. Marie rose with him.

"Hey, I want to be alone. Understand?" They let me go, but I heard Lewis whisper to the others as I closed the screen door, "Marlene's taking it hard."

Truth was that I went to meet John Mwema, as we had planned, down behind the Danish couple's, at the bridge, just below where I tried to build my kiln, so that if they had looked from our living-room window, Rashak and the others, they would have seen me run to him and all the joy of it, lifting there, racing, laughing, and taking the hill, down to where we went. Mwema was one of Rashak's English students. A gifted poet. Rashak always talked him up—Mwema this, Mwema that—and had him to our house so much it just grew until there were no surprises in the end except how good it felt. So good it made me wonder what had ever gone on between me and Rashak that I had thought was love.

Mwema wasn't experienced with women—his marriage had been arranged; his wife, a stranger who stayed in a village far away—and he knew nothing about the world I came from. It made him seem shy when he wasn't, made him seem dull when he wasn't. But as I watched him discover the ability to write, I learned the truth about him. Rashak couldn't coach him, couldn't direct him; it was all there, ready-made, as if he had been born to feel everything and reflect it. Seeing a soul uncover itself that way was, for me, like finding a new fruit. Taste it. Taste it—like that—all you wanted to do. And we were luscious, we were sweet and juicy, even as it rained that first time, there on the beach, covered with sand, rolling in the storm. The bricks dissolved. Nothing remained. And it stayed like this for us all the times we were together.

When I got home that night, everything was dark and the doors were locked. I figured it was Lewis's revenge, so I climbed the grillwork behind the kitchen to the bathroom window. When I tried to open it, the flimsy frame broke and the damn thing clattered to the ground. The Gupta kid cried out somewhere downstairs and a knife or fork fell. I was able to get in, and sat on the can trying to fix the curtain so it would stop the mosquitoes. When I finally wandered into bed, Rashak wasn't there.

229

COME TO

AFRICA

AND SAVE

YOUR

MARRIAGE

Next morning, Ingrid and Ramji, as usual, were sprawled under their cloths on the floor. Their baby had crawled up to his favorite place on the table and gone to sleep with his head in a greasy plate. Our tiny house couldn't take it. The bathroom looked like the facility at the train station in Naples; the kitchen like a war zone. Ingrid woke up and we sat drinking instant coffee in what was left of the cool air from the night before. Maybe it was my guilt: I wanted to make excuses. I bitched about Rashak, telling the old story, because I wanted to tell everyone again and again. How I had worked at a dumb job while Lewis went to school, gave up everything. How Lewis made it seem as though it was for *us,* even bringing us to Africa, an attempt to save the marriage, a once-in-a-lifetime adventure, a chance to experience, to start over.

Ingrid gave her usual advice: "Marlene, you look too much to Lewis. Look to yourself."

Then Jenny came awake, found no one in our bed, and panicked, screaming. Before I could get there, Hanna had clobbered her, shouting, "She *woked* me up!" over and over again, as Jenny howled. The racket woke up Ingrid's baby and the whole place crumbled with noise. Lewis, arriving on Marie's bike, made it worse, shouting that I had abandoned the kids. He pounded on the table, said I was deliberately ruining his life. He couldn't think, couldn't work. I wanted him to fail. And it was all so cheap.

"Where were you last night?" he asked. "You saw her." He grabbed at Ingrid, wanting to drag her into the fight. "She just walked out of here for no reason. Where did she go?"

"I spent the night in my own bed," I answered. "I didn't see you there."

"You're jealous," he said. "I won't put up with that jealous shit."

When he finally stopped, it was as though someone had stopped air-hammering the sidewalk next door—the noise, and the effort, the work just tolerating the sound and then the blessed quiet, the dust and the rubble of blasted cement.

Some of Rashak's students threw a party at a house they had rented in Mikorosheni village. Down there, people fried things all night. There was no electricity and their charcoal fires and kerosene lanterns were the only lights, gathered under makeshift stalls, the midnight snackbars of the tropics. We collected goodies as we went, piled in Joe Ithana's car. There wasn't a road, only random open spaces between mud houses and battered palm trees. There was no moon that night and, black on their black verandas, people were all but invisible. Eyes, and the flash of pale cloths. A white T-shirt. I knew Mwema would be there and had decided that this was it, I was going to leave with him, or stay with him, whatever I had to do to make it clear. I thought, if I could stand outside myself and watch this, how it would make me laugh.

If I could see myself, even now—cozy with John Mwema in a corner near a candle. Something that sounds like a band starts and stops in another room, out of which tumble four or five radical sisters in battle fatigues. Ezekiel Mzizi is asking me about black theater in the States. He thinks that, since he's a good actor, he ought to go to New York. All night there are attempts at music but these fail and at two o'clock or so the party starts to droop around the edges. If I could see it, even now, as a pantomime: me, bleary, propped by Mwema on one elbow and a bookcase on the other. Lewis is in front of us, touching my hand, smiling, lips moving. He takes my shoulders and kisses me on the mouth, a brotherly little thing, but I say something that makes him stiffen. Mwema shrugs. Lewis speaks again, raises his hand. I think he's going to hit me but instead he spreads his fingers through his hair, talking and talking. I'm just laughing there, shaking my head.

And if I were going to do the dialogue for the scene, we'd hear Lewis say, "Time to go now, Marlene." The brotherly kiss now, me balancing against a bookcase, teetering away.

I say, "Well, I think I'll stay here with Mwema tonight." A little drunk. Lewis is stymied, staring so you think he's missed everything.

He says, "Marlene, I want you to leave this place with me. After that you can do what you want."

"I'm going to do what I want right now." At which point he raises his hand, reconsiders, fans open his fingers, combs his hair. There's no chance for his script in this theater, not with this audience, and not with the cast of characters he's got to work with—the tall, handsome African, the white wife, the cuckold husband.

Lewis didn't speak to me when I got home the next day. He'd gone on a house-cleaning binge. Ingrid, in a panic that he would kick them out, had folded her bedding and put the cushions back on the couch. I could see Ramji meditating in the yard. Jennifer, who had been prompted to play the neglected child, hurled herself at me, weeping, "Mommy! Mommy! Daddy said you were lost!"

"Did you? Did you tell her that, you bastard? Daddy knows I wasn't lost, Jenny. Daddy knows where I was." Rashak didn't respond. The silent treatment. He sulked at his desk, fixed his own food, and talked to Ingrid at long intervals and in whispers. But I knew that Lewis Rashak couldn't keep silent for long.

That night we ended up in the same bed. Lewis stripped completely and sat on the edge of it to smoke a cigarette. My back was toward him.

"At first Marie and I only kissed," he said. "For a long time. Just kissed. Because she was being true to *you!*" He laughed. "But it grew in intensity. I felt her tongue tentatively on my lips. She was shy; she told me there had only been two others. So I licked her tongue gently with my own. She was frightened, but she wanted more. She stopped wearing a bra, did you notice, so I could . . ."

I covered my ears with a pillow. "Jealous shit!" he shouted. His voice seemed to have changed. I didn't recognize it. "You listen to me!" He grabbed me hard by the neck and threw the pillow on the floor.

"You pervert!" I was crying now and afraid of him. I had never been afraid of him before.

"Sometimes if she wore a blouse," he went on, "or that red print dress with the buttons, she would let me unfasten it. She has beautiful breasts. But I had to move slowly with her. She was like a virgin . . ."

I tried not to hear it but his words beat into my ears, how he touched Marie, kissed her breasts, stroked her until she came, how she would moan, touch him, but she wouldn't let him screw her until one day, in a display of lust, he took her, weeping. They were both weeping. I thought: For God's sake, he raped her, raped her and is proud.

When he finished his story, he was breathing hard and I was scared he would want sex with me. I kept still, my back toward him. "Now you tell me." He pulled my arm, twisting me to look at him, his eyes so deep in their sockets they seemed to have disappeared. "Start by telling me how long you and the African have been cheating on me." I didn't move. I stayed there curled like a fetus. "Marlene, we can never get anywhere if you don't tell me." He touched me gently then. "Listen, you have humiliated me. When I said to take a lover, I did not mean one of my students. I did not mean an African."

I could hear him fumbling with some paper, rolling a joint. The smell of the match, the sulfur, the sharp perfume of the grass. He shook me, offering to share it. I rolled up, hunched over my knees. "Marlene, Marlene, when I visualize you two together, it revolts me." I sucked in the smoke, held my breath. "Marlene, I forbid you to continue this affair. You probably have a disease."

The grass was strong. Three pulls and the front of my brain opened up. I could see three hundred and sixty degrees through the round window of my skull. Lewis, garish, hair bright red, two dimensional, a cutout, pasted on the slick front of a rock album. Lewis then, like an animated drawing, pulling the straps of my nightgown, pressing down on me, pressing flat; and out the top of my head, a disk rimmed with eyes, I saw the walls, peeling paint, torn curtains, piles of books, dirty coffee mugs, black sky, and faded art prints over a bureau heaped with clothes. A broken lamp in the corner. A rectangle of light marking the bathroom door.

Next morning I woke up alone. I could hear Marie's motorcycle. I could hear voices talking below, a drone, tones only, no words. My husband came up to me with coffee, and I bargained with him for our last thousand dollars on the grounds that I had bought his Ph.D. Rashak wanted to throw the kids into the deal. "If you get the money," he argued, "you get the kids. I can't raise them on nothing." Rashak's fortune.

Meanwhile, downstairs Ramji was announcing that Jennifer and Hanna had lice. He could see tiny white eggs nestled in the hair that lined the base of their skulls. Ingrid yelled up at us in case we hadn't heard. It riled Lewis. He shouted, blaming me, dragging me down to look at the kids, charging me with gross child neglect. Marie came behind him trying to calm his panic, but he raged on. Sanitary conditions in the house, he shouted, were such that his guts were ravaged by parasites. All my fault.

He came from the kitchen and hurled a carton of milk at me. "Why is this stinking sour milk always put back in the refrigerator? I have to throw out most of my coffee." Jenny was standing in the door screaming. Marie had moved into the living room, crying, staring out the window. Ramji beat a hasty retreat to the garden for a quick meditation. And Ingrid, a head taller and a foot wider, advanced on Rashak. She hefted the little prick off the floor and slapped his face. I watched it all as though it had nothing to do with me. They were like cartoon characters: Lewis off the ground, trying to smash the big Viking, but she just grabbed his wrist.

"You and that fakir can get the hell out of here," he yelled. "Go to a fucking hotel. Go to hell. Just get out of here." Ramji was like an ivory carving placed in the garden, his head bowed, his hands folded.

Three days later Marie left for Paris. I could only attribute it to second thoughts about Lewis. Sooner or later everyone has second thoughts about Lewis. But he went into agony when she left. He began questioning me constantly about Mwema, insisting that the affair was shameful, a laughingstock. Mwema was married: he left his wife in some foul village rotting away with their kids while he fucked white women in town. "Where do you go?" he harped. He continued to want details, which I couldn't give. He badgered me, followed me around with threats. Finally, when he couldn't stand it anymore (he said), he took half our money and bought himself a round-trip ticket to France.

"I have to get away from you and that coon," he said. "You're driving me insane with your behavior."

"You bastard"—I was furious—"it was supposed to be my money."

And his incredible answer: "I divided it. In any divorce, the property gets divided in half."

"Give me half the Ph.D. then." I felt like someone who had just lost a bet, who didn't know she had been gambling.

I could easily have taken the rest of the money, or even used my return ticket to go with him and then home with the kids, but it never crossed my mind. I must have wanted to stay even though I felt deserted

233

COME TO

AFRICA

AND SAVE

YOUR

MARRIAGE

when he left. The last part of being held up is watching your assailant get away, how you want to shout, *"Come back!"* with your arm raised, your mouth opened, stunned to your bones. My mirror told me he'd left me shabbier than ever, threadbare, like a garment that's been washed for the last time.

Jenny begged me, "Mommy, please, get up," because she sensed I'd been in bed too long. And I knew I had, too. She was pulling my arm, weeping.

I remembered how Ingrid kept saying, "Look to yourself, Marlene. You look too much to Lewis." When I did look to myself, I saw there had to be some point to my coming to Africa, because it hadn't saved my marriage. More than just the memory I would have of John Mwema, I wanted to take something back, and it had to be something real that I could touch—an object—the way that people travel halfway around the world to places like Iran so they can bring back carpets, or to China for vases. And vases made me think of pots, and pots made me think of my pots, and maybe it was a silly thing, but I wanted to succeed in what I had tried to do when we first got here, to make something from the clay I dug so happily in the riverbed. A pot, like the beautiful pots that African women made, from start to finish, fired in my own kiln. And, for once, it didn't defeat me to look at the dust in the crisis of my living room, or the dried lumps of clay, or the kiln out there on the hillside, the shambles.

I wasn't sure when Lewis would come back from Paris, so I moved fast. I took the rest of the money. I bought real fire bricks. I built a real kiln. I watered and softened and worked my clay, kneading it, resting it, the cycles of getting it ready. I saw myself, a figure rounded to a task, shoulders and arms, as determined as earth. Mwema helped me. He helped me build the kiln and clean my house, repair the broken screens and furniture. The Danish couple knew about a small potter's wheel for sale that once had belonged to their ambassador's wife. I bought it and moved it to my living room, a real studio now, facing the window, the hill that fell away to dark ferns in the riverbed where lilies that looked like candy grew.

Lewis stayed in Paris a month.

235

COME TO

AFRICA

AND SAVE

YOUR

MARRIAGE

"Everything changed," he told me when he came back. He didn't want to talk about it. It must have flopped with Marie and it was hard on him. He was thinner than ever and his skin seemed shriveled. There were lines near his eyes and mouth that hadn't been there before. It amazed me that I felt sorry for him, even as I saw him try to manipulate—oh, he was so pleased to see I finally had my shit together, was working at last—trying to make it seem that he was part of it, but I wasn't the old Marlene anymore and he shouldn't have bothered.

"None of it matters much, Lewis," I told him. Perhaps I sounded dreamy. I think he thought I meant to forgive him and in ways I could do that, looking down, looking all around as he came close, because I was so much larger than he was, his hand on my neck, his lips, though he agreed, yes, he could wait, would wait until I was ready again, until the whole terrible year had been forgotten.

You learn to be fatalistic in the tropics. Or maybe it's just that you learn to be fatalistic when you're far away because there's nothing you control, not even the language. A language you don't understand reminds you how vulnerable you are. I knew that when Lewis's contract was up, the university wouldn't renew it and our visas would expire and then we would have to leave. That was a certain destiny. Even now, I can't say what it meant to Mwema and me to live that way, the feeling of a marked-out time. I think of tropical flowers with petals that burn and bleed, and I think of breaking things. But this isn't meant to be about him, or about how we managed to say good-bye.

The day we left, the Danish couple received a shipment of cheese from home and we sat with them and several other expatriates to share it. Paper-thin slices and aromatic chunks circulated. We sipped at the wine. No one in the room had even looked at a piece of cheese in months, but a decorum of self-restraint operated at the table. What held us back, mouths watering, when all we wanted to do was grab?

Lewis was too nervous to eat anything. He stood aside going through the standard motions of an air traveler, studying his ticket, his passport, his health card, fearing they might contain some hitch he hadn't seen, a detail that would abort the journey. Our winter coats were draped on a chair, portents, crumbled and faded as curtains in an old derelict theater, closing on some final scene. The room smelled of their storage—mildew and mothballs.

"Will there be snow?" Hanna asked.

"Snow snow snow!" Jenny was singing.

"Is it winter there now?" one of the Danes asked. They all smiled. "So easy to forget," he said.

My suitcase was nearest to the door and next to it was the pot I had chosen from the ones I made to carry back, so big it was ridiculous and I'd have to keep it on my lap like a baby. I still have it, a classic African beer pot, wide bellied, with a small mouth and a curving rim. Even now, when I see my pots on display in shows and shops, pressed into wild shapes from dreams and memories, when I see how much my work has changed, I like that simple, strong vessel the best and often wonder how I made it. The walls are too thin to hold the curve or to have survived the fire, and the symmetry is perfect despite the poor clay I used.

We flew home through two days and a night, Lewis and I, talking and talking because I knew we couldn't stay together and he didn't know. The children played and slept. And each time the plane landed in West Africa, looking out on tarmac and the fringe of palms, lights that lifted jungles from the dark, the kids asked, "Are we out of Africa yet?"

And each time, I told them, no.

Alice Walker

ᴛHE LOVER

Her husband had wanted a child and so she gave him one as a gift, because she liked her husband and admired him greatly. Still, it had taken a lot out of her, especially in the area of sexual response. She had never been particularly passionate with him, not even during the early years of their marriage; it was more a matter of being sexually comfortable. After the birth of the child she simply never thought of him sexually at all. She supposed their marriage was better than most, even so. He was a teacher at a university near their home in the Midwest and cared about his students— which endeared him to her, who had had so many uncaring teachers; and toward her own work, which was poetry (that she set very successfully to jazz), he showed the utmost understanding and respect.

She was away for two months at an artists' colony in New England and that is where she met Ellis, whom she immediately dubbed, once she had got over thinking he resembled (with his top lip slightly raised over his right eyetooth when he smiled) a wolf, "The Lover." They met one evening before dinner as she

237

was busy ignoring the pompous bullshit of a fellow black poet, a man many years older than she who had no concept of other people's impatience. He had been rambling on about himself for over an hour and she had at first respectfully listened because she was the kind of person whose adult behavior—in a situation like this—reflected her childhood instruction; and she was instructed as a child to be polite.

She was always getting herself stuck in one-sided conversations of this sort because she was—the people who talked to her seemed to think—an excellent listener. She was, up to a point. She was genuinely interested in older artists in particular and would sit, entranced, as they spun out their tales of art and lust (the gossip, though old, was delicious!) of forty years ago.

But there had been only a few of these artists whose tales she had listened to until the end. For as soon as a note of bragging entered into the conversation—a famous name dropped here, an expensive Paris restaurant's menu dropped there, and especially the names of the old artist's neglected books and on what occasion the wretched creature had insulted this or that weasel of a white person—her mind began to turn about upon itself until it rolled out some of her own thoughts to take the place of the trash that was coming in.

And so it was on that evening before dinner. The old poet—whose work was exceedingly mediocre, and whose only attractions, as far as she was concerned, were his age and his rather bitter wit—fastened his black, bloodshot eyes (in which she read desperation and a prayer of unstrenuous seduction) upon her and held her to a close attention to his words. Except that she had perfected the trick—as had many of her contemporaries who hated to be rude and who, also, had a strong sense of self-preservation (because the old poet, though, she thought, approaching senility, was yet a powerful figure in black literary circles and thought nothing of using his considerable influence to thwart the careers of younger talents)—of keeping her face quite animated and turned full onto the speaker, while inside her head she could be trying out the shades of paint with which to improve the lighting of her house. In fact, so intense did her concentration appear, it seemed she read the speaker's lips.

Ellis, who would be her lover, had come into the room and sat

down on a chair by the fire. For although it was the middle of summer,
a fire was needed against the chilly New England evenings.

"Have you been waiting long?" he asked.

And it suddenly occurred to her that indeed she had.

"But of course," she answered absently, noting the crooked smile
that reminded her of a snarling, though not disagreeable, wolf—and
turned back just as the old poet jealously reached out his hand to draw
her attention to the, for him, hilarious ending of his story. She laughed
and slapped her knee, a gesture of such fraudulent folksiness that she
was soon laughing in earnest. Catching Ellis's eye as she thus amused
herself, she noticed therein a particular gleam that she instantly recognized.

"My lover," she thought, noticing for the first time his head of blue-
black curls, his eyes as brown as the Mississippi, his skin that was not
as successfully tanned as it might have been but which would definitely
do. He was thin and tall, with practically no hips in the beige twill
jeans he wore.

At dinner they sat together, looking out at the blue New England
mountains in the distance, as the sun left tracings of orange and pink
against the pale blue sky. He had heard she'd won some sort of prize
—a prestigious one—for her "jazzed-up" poetry, and the way he said
it made her glance critically at his long fingers wrapped around his
wine glass. She wondered if they would be as sensitive on her skin as
they looked. She had never heard of him, though she did not say so,
probably because he had already said it for her. He talked a good
deal—easily and early—about himself, and she was quite relaxed—
even entertained—in her listener's role.

He wondered what, *if anything,* younger poets like herself had to
say, since he was of the opinion that not much was learned about life
until the middle years. He was in his forties. Of course he didn't look
it, but he was much older than she, he said, and the reason that he was
not better known was because he could not find a publisher for his two
novels (still, by the way, unpublished—in case she knew publishers) or
for his poetry, which an acquaintance of his had compared to something
or other by Montaigne.

"You're lovely," he said into the brief silence.

"And you seem bright," she automatically replied.

She had blocked him out since his mention of the two unpublished novels. By the time he began complaining about the preferential treatment publishers now gave minorities and women she was on the point of yawning or gazing idly about the room. But she did not do either for a very simple reason: when she had first seen him she had thought—after the wolf thing—"my lover," and had liked, deep down inside, the illicit sound of it. She had never had a lover; he would be her first. Afterwards, she would be truly a woman of her time. She also responded to his curly hair and slim, almost nonexistent hips, in a surprisingly passionate way.

She was a woman who, after many tribulations in her life, few of which she ever discussed even with close friends, had reached the point of being generally pleased with herself. This self-acceptance was expressed in her eyes, which were large, dark and clear and which, more often than not, seemed predisposed to smile. Though she was not tall, her carriage gave the illusion of height, as did her carefully selected tall sandals and her naturally tall hair, which stood in an elegant black afro with exactly seven strands of silver hair—of which she was very proud (she was just thirty-one)—shining across the top. She wore long richly colored skirts that—when she walked—parted without warning along the side, and exposed a flash of her creamy brown thigh, and legs that were curvaceous and strong. If she came late to the dining room and stood in the doorway a moment longer than necessary—looking about for a place to sit after she had her tray—for that moment the noise from the cutlery already in use was still.

What others minded at the Colony—whether too many frogs in the frog pond (which was used for swimming) or not enough wine with the veal (there was talk of cutting out wine with meals altogether, and thereby ending a fine old Colony tradition!)—she did not seem to mind. She seemed open, bright, occasionally preoccupied, but always ready with an appreciative ear, or at times a humorous, if outdated, joke of her own (which she nevertheless told with gusto and found funny herself, because she would laugh and laugh at it, regardless of what her listeners did). She seemed never to strain over her work, and literally never complained about its progress—or lack thereof. It was as if she worked only for herself, for her own enjoyment (or salvation), and was—whether working or simply thinking of working—calm about it.

Even the distraction caused by the birth of her child was a price she was, ultimately, prepared to pay. She did not intend to have a second one, after all—that would be too stupid—and this one would, before she knew it, be grown up enough for boarding school.

Relishing her short freedom during the summer as much as she contemplated enjoyment of her longer future one, she threw herself headlong into the interim relationship with Ellis, a professional lover of mainly older women artists who came to the Colony every year to work and play.

A New York Jew of considerable charm, intellectual pettiness, and so vast and uncritical a love of all things European it struck one as an illness (and who hated Brooklyn—where he had grown up—his parents, Jewish culture, and all he had observed of black behavior in New York City), Ellis found the listening silence of "the dark woman," as he euphemistically called her, restorative—after his endless evenings with talkative women who wrote for *Esquire* and the *New York Times.* Such women made it possible for him to be included in the proper tennis sets and swimming parties at the Colony—in which he hoped to meet contacts who would help his career along—but they were also driven to examine each and every one of their own thoughts aloud. His must be the attentive ear, since they had already "made it" and were comfortable exposing their own charming foibles to him, while he, not having made it yet, could afford to expose nothing that might discourage their assistance in his behalf.

It amused and thrilled him to almost hear the "click" when his eyes met those of the jazz poet. "Sex," he thought. And, "rest."

Of course he mistook her intensity.

After sitting before her piano for hours, setting one of her poems to music, she would fling open her cabin door and wave to him as he walked by on his way to or from the lake. He was writing a novella about his former wife and composed it in longhand down at the lake ("So if I get fed up with it I can toss myself in," he joked) and then took it back to his studio with him to type. She would call to him, her hair and clothing very loose, and entice him into her cabin with promises of sympathy and half her lunch.

When they made love she was disappointed. He did not appear to believe in unhurried pleasure, and thought the things she suggested he might do to please her very awkward at the least. But it hardly mattered, since what mattered was the fact of having a lover. She liked snuggling up to him, liked kissing him along the sides of his face—his cheeks were just beginning to be a trifle flabby but would still be good for several years—and loved to write him silly letters—scorching with passion and promises of abandon—that made her seem head over heels in love. She enjoyed writing the letters because she enjoyed feeling to her full capacity and for as long as possible the excitement having a lover brought. It was the kind of excitement she'd felt years ago, in high school and perhaps twice in college (once when she'd fallen for a student and once when she was seduced—with her help and consent —by a teacher), and she recognized it as a feeling to be enjoyed for all it was worth. Her body felt on fire, her heart jumped in her breast, her pulse raced—she was aware, for the first time in years, of actually *needing* to make love.

He began to think he must fight her off, at least a little bit. She was too intense, he said. He did not have time for intense relationships, that's why he had finally accepted a divorce from his wife. He was also writing a great poem which he had begun in 1950 and which—now that he was at the Colony—he hoped to finish. She should concentrate on her own work if she expected to win any more prizes. She *wanted* to win more, didn't she?

She laughed at him, but would not tell him why. Instead she tried, very gently (while sitting on his lap with her bosom maternally opposite his face), to tell him he misunderstood. That she wanted nothing from him beyond the sensation of being in love itself. (His stare was at first blank, then cynical, at this.) As for her work, she did not do hers the way he apparently did his. Hers did not mean to her what he seemed to think it meant. It did not get in the way of her living, for example, and if it ever did, she felt sure she would remove it. Prizes were nice —especially if they brought one money (which one might then use to explore Barbados! China! Mozambique!)—but they were not rewards she could count on. Her life, on the other hand, *was* a reward she could count on. (He became impatient with this explanation and a little angry.)

It was their first quarrel.

When he saw her again she had spent the weekend (which had been coming up) in nearby Boston. She looked cheerful, happy and relaxed. From her letters to him—which he had thought embarrassingly self-revealing and erotic, though flattering, of course, to him—he had assumed she was on the point of declaring her undying love and of wanting to run away with him. Instead, she had gone off for two days, without mentioning it to him. And she had gone, so she said, by herself!

She soothed him as best she could. Lied, which she hated more than anything, about her work. "It was going so *poorly,*" she complained (and the words rang metallic in her mouth); "I just couldn't bear staying here doing nothing where working conditions are so *idyllic!*" He appeared somewhat mollified. Actually, her work was going fine and she had sent off to her publishers a completed book of poems and jazz arrangements—which was what she had come to the Colony to do. "Your work was going swimmingly down at the lake." She giggled. "I didn't wish to disturb you."

And yet it was clear he was disturbed.

So she did not tell him she had flown all the way home.

He was always questioning her now about her town, her house, her child, her husband. She found herself describing her husband as if to a prospective bride. She lingered over the wiry bronze of his hair, the evenness of his teeth, his black, black eyes, the thrilling timbre of his deep voice. It *was* an exceptionally fine voice, it seemed to her now, listening to Ellis's rather whining one. Though, on second thought, it was perhaps nothing special.

At night, after a rousing but unsatisfactory evening with Ellis, she dreamed of her husband making love to her on the kitchen floor at home, where the sunlight collected in a pool beneath the window, and lay in bed next day dreaming of all the faraway countries, daring adventures, passionate lovers still to be found.

Nadine Gordimer

*S*AFE HOUSES

He's one of those dark-haired men whose beards grow out rusty-red. He could have dyed his hair to match—more or less—but a beard is the first thing they'd expect to find you behind. He's lived like this several times before; the only difference is that this time he came back into the country legally, came home—so much for the indemnity promised to exiles, so much for the changed era there, now bans on his kind of politics were supposed to be a thing of the past, he was supposed to be—free? He knows how their minds work—not much imagination, reliance on an Identikit compilation of how political subversives look and behave Underground. Underground: this time, as at other times, he's aware of how unsuitably abstract a term that is. To hide away, you have to be out in the open of life; too soon and easily run to ground, holed up somewhere. Best safety lies in crowds. Selective crowds; he goes to football matches with beer in a knapsack, and a cap with a plastic eyeshade over his sunglasses, but not to pop concerts, where the police keep an eye on young leftists whose democratic recreation this is. He goes to the movies but not to concerts although he longs for the company of strings and brass; someone among his intellectual buddies from long ago would be bound to gaze at him, reaching back for recognition. Small gatherings where everyone can be trusted are traps; glowing with the distinction of the secret encounter with a real revolutionary, someone will not be able to resist boasting to another, in strictest confidence, and that other will pass on the luminous dusting of danger.

The good friends who provide a bed sometimes offer the use of a car as well, but driving alone is another sure way to be traced and picked up. He walks, and takes buses among ordinary workers and students. He's a little too forty-five-ish, thickened around the jowl and diaphragm, to pass as a student, but with his cravat of tangled black hair showing in the neck of a sweat shirt and his observance of the uniform jogging shoes with soles cushioned like tires, he could be anyone among the passengers—the white artisans, railway and post office employees, even policemen. Reading a newspaper with its daily account of the proceedings at the group trial where he is a missing accused, worrying about these comrades in arms, he tries not to feel self-congratulatory at his escape of arrest, a form of complacency dangerous to one in his position, sitting there in a bus among people he knows would be glad to hand him over to the law; but he can't suppress a little thrill, a sort of inner giggle. Perhaps *this* is freedom? Something secret, internal, after all? But philosophizing is another danger, in his situation, undermining the concept of freedom for which he has risked discovery and imprisonment yet again.

One afternoon in the city he was gazing inattentively out of the window waiting for the bus to set off when he became aware of the presence just seating itself beside him. Aware like an animal: scenting something different in the bus's familiar sun-fug of sweat and deodorants, fruit-skins and feet. Perfume. Real perfume, at the price of a month's wages of the other passengers. And a sound, a sound of silk as a leg crossed the knee of another leg. He straightened away from the window, looked ahead for a decent interval and then slowly turned, as if merely fidgeting because the bus was taking too long to leave.

A woman, of course—he'd scented that. Gray silk pants or some

sort of fashionable skirt divided like pants, with an arched instep showing in a pastel sandal. Below the neckline of a loose blouse, silk slopes
shining—breasts rising and falling. Out of breath. Or exasperated. He
moved a little to give her more room. She nodded in acknowledgment
without looking at him; she didn't see him, she was going through
some sort of dialogue or more likely monologue in her head, annoyance,
exasperation twitched her lips.

Schoolgirls tramped onto the bus with their adolescent female odors
and the pop of gum blown between their lips like the text balloons in
comics. An old woman opened a bag of vinegary chips. The bus filled
but the driver was absent.

This misplaced person, this woman, this pampered almost-beauty
(he saw as she turned, throwing back her long, tiger-streaked hair cut
in a parrot-poll over the forehead, and smiling on perfectly conformed
teeth) had now accepted where she found herself. She indicated the
driver's seat. —What d'you think's happened to him?—

Taking a leak. —Having a cup of coffee, I suppose.— They shared
the polite moment of tolerance.

—I thought they had a strict timetable. Oh well. D'you know if
this takes us along Sylvia Pass?—

—Pretty near the top of the Pass.—

She pulled a face and blinked her thick-lashed eyes in resigned
dismay. Secretive, glossy eyes, knowing how to please, and folding at
the outer corners an attractive, experienced fan of faint lines.

—Where do you want to get off?—

—That's the problem—at the bottom of the Pass. I suppose I should
have taken some other bus . . . I don't know *why* taxis don't cruise in
this town as they do in any other civilized place! I've been looking for
one for half an hour, traipsing . . . —

—There should have been taxis for tourists at any hotel.—

—No, no, I live here, but this just isn't my day . . . my car's stuck
in a parking garage. Underground. Infuriating. Battery dead or something. I couldn't find a telephone booth where the receiver hadn't been
torn out . . . this town! I had to ask a shopkeeper to let me phone for
a mechanic . . . anyway, I couldn't wait any longer, I've left the keys
with the attendant.—

She felt better now that she had told someone, anyone. He was anyone.

When the driver appeared and fares were to be paid, of course she had neither season card nor change for a ticket. While she scrabbled in her bag, gold chains on her wrists sliding, he gave the conductor two tickets.

—Oh you are kind . . . — She was suddenly embarrassed by her privileged life, by her inability to cope with what for all the people surrounding her on the bus was daily routine. In their ignoring of her she felt a reproach that she had never traveled on the bus before, perhaps not this bus or any bus, at least since she was a schoolchild. He was no longer *anyone;* somehow an ally, although from his appearance he probably could ill afford to waste a bus ticket on a stranger. Yet there was something in his self-assurance, the amusement in his regard, that suggested he was not merely one of the other passengers. Unsure of this, in a habit of patronage—she was the kind who would treat her servants generously but send her children to segregated schools—she chattered to him to show she considered him an equal. —You make the journey every day? Isn't it always bliss to get home, out of this town?—

—Every day, no. But what's wrong with the city?— Too full of blacks for you, now, lady, blacks selling fruit and cheap jewelry and knitted caps, dirtying the streets, too full of men without work for whom you see your bracelets and that swish Italian suede bag as something to be taken from you.

She shifted to safe generalization. —Oh I'm no city girl. Not anywhere.—

—But you live in one?—

—Well, you'd hardly know it was there, from my house. Luckily. It's an old suburb . . . the trees—that's one thing about Johannesburg, isn't it, you can hide yourself in trees, just the highways humming, well out of sight!—

—Really?— He suddenly gave way in a great, open smile like the yawn of a predator.

She had the instinct to withdraw. —You don't live here?—

—Oh yes, I'm living here.—

She suppressed her casual curiosity as unwise encouragement. — Could you tell me when to get off? The nearest stop to Sylvia Pass.—

She did not know if she imagined a pause.

—I'll be getting off there.—

He stood behind her as she stepped down from the bus. They began to descend the steep and winding road. There was no distance between them but an aura which established they were not together, merely taking the same route. —Thank God it's down and not up. My heels are not exactly appropriate for this.—

—Take them off. It's safer. The surface is very smooth.—

—But it's hot! I'll burn my feet.—

She clattered along awkwardly, amused at her own manner of progress. —Isn't it typical? I've been jogging around here every morning for years and I've never come down the Pass before.—

—It would be up the Pass, wouldn't it—if you live at the bottom. Quite a strenuous jog.— An observation rather than a correction. And then: —Typical of what?—

None of his business! Who was he to quiz a manner of speaking, as if to find out if it had some significance in her life.

Yet she attempted an answer. —Oh . . . habit, I suppose . . . doing what you've become used to, not noticing . . . where you really are—

And wondering, now, no doubt, whether it was possible that this man off the bus really could be living in the suburb of large houses hidden by trees where she lived, or whether he had left the bus to follow her, and was to be feared, although he was white, in this city where so much was to be feared. It was true that he had picked one of his maze of trails about the city and suburbs in order to walk with her—an impulse like any of the impulses with which he had to fill in the days of his disconnection from consecutive action. The unexpected was his means of survival. To be Underground is to have a go at living without consequences. The corrupt little wriggle of freedom—there it was again. Shameful but enjoyable.

—Here's my corner.— She bent to pull the slipped strap of her sandal back over her heel and looked up ingratiatingly to soften dismissal.

—Goodbye then.— Again, that greedy warrior's smile, contra-
dicting the humble appearance.

As he turned his back she suddenly called as she might have remembered an instruction for some tradesman. —Have you far to go
—that was such a hot trek—would you like to come in for something
cool to drink?—

This time she was not mistaken; there was a pause, still with his
back to her. —I know I'm dying of thirst and you must be!—

So she drew him round, and murmuring casual thanks, he joined
her. Now they were walking together. At one of the pillared entrances
in white battlements topped with black iron spikes she pressed the
button of an intercom panel and spoke. The flats of a stage set, the
wide polished wooden gates slid back electronically. Trees, her trees,
led up to and overflowed the roof of the spread wings of the house.
Small dogs jumped about her. Sprinklers arched rainbows over lawns.
She called out in the joyous soprano used to summon faithful servants,
and ice and fruit juice were brought onto a shaded terrace. Behind him
the colors of Persian carpets, paintings and bowls of flowers blurred in
the deep perspective of one of those huge rooms used for parties.

—You have a lovely home.— He said what was blandly expected
of him as he drank juice in return for a bus ticket.

She came back with what was expected of her. —But too big. My
sons are at boarding school. For two people . . . too much.—

—But the garden, the privacy.—

She was embarrassed to think how he must be envying her. —Oh
yes. But most of the time I don't use the rest of the place (a gesture to
the room behind), I have my own little quarters on the other side of
the house. My husband's away such a lot on business—Japan, at the
moment. That's why I couldn't even get anyone to come and fetch me
from that wretched garage . . . his secretary's such an idiot, she's let
his driver go. I always tell him, he's drained her of all initiative, she's
so used to being ordered about. I can't stand subservient people, can
you—I mean, I want to shake them and get them to *stand up*—

—I don't think I know any.—

—Ah, that shows you move in the right circles!— They both
laughed. —But what do you do? Your profession, your work, I

mean.— Careful to show that "work" might be just as worthy as a profession.

Without realizing he could think so quickly, he began inventing
one—a profession combined with "work"—that would fit his appearance, he began telling it like a fairy tale, a bedtime story, it flowed
from him taking turns and details as if it could be true, as if he were
making an alternative life for himself. —I'm in construction. Construction engineer—that's where I was today, on some sites. Things go
wrong. . . . when you're talking about stress in a twenty-story building—

—Oh if it were to fall! I often look up and marvel how such piles
hold together, in fact I don't have much faith they will, I never walk
under those pavement shelters you people erect for pedestrians while
you're building, I always walk in the street, I'd rather get run over,
any time—

—Standards are pretty high, here; safety margins. You don't have
to worry. In some of the countries I've worked, it's rather different.
And one has always to think of how a construction will behave in an
earthquake, how do you build over a fault in the earth, Mexico City,
San Francisco—

—So you travel around, too. But not selling; building.—

—Sometimes pulling down. Preparing to rebuild. Destroying old
structures.— No—he must resist the devilry of amusing himself by
planting, in his fairy tale, symbols from his real life. As in all fairy tales,
there were enough improbabilities his listener would have to pass over
if not swallow. It surely must occur to her that a construction engineer
would be unlikely not to utilize his own car, even if his working garb
was appropriate to inspection of building sites. —Have you traveled
much with your husband? Go along with him?— Best to know where
she had been before elaborating on projects in Sri Lanka, Thailand,
North Africa. No, she liked to go to Europe, but hot places, crowded
places, dirty places—no.

So he was free to transform his experience of guerrilla training
camps in Tanzania and Libya, his presence in the offices of an exiled
High Command in cities deadened by northern snows or tropical heat,
to provide exotic backdrops for his skyscrapers. Anecdotes of bar en-
counters in such places—he merely changed the subjects discussed, not

the characters—entertained her. He was at ease in his invented persona; what would a woman know about engineering? She said it was time for a real drink; ice was brought again, a trolley was wheeled out in which bottles were slotted, a manservant appeared with a dish of snacks decorated with radish roses.

—I don't allow myself to drink on my own.—

—Why not?— He accepted the glass of whiskey and ice she had prepared for him.

At first she seemed not to hear the personal question, busying herself at the trolley. She sat down on a swinging sofa, holding her drink, and let the sandals drop from her feet. —Afraid.—

—Of being alone?—

—No. Of carrying on with it. Yes, of being alone. Isn't that why people drink—I mean really drink. But I suppose you're often alone.—

—What makes you think that?—

But now it was he who need not be afraid: she had no inkling of anything real behind his fairy tales. —Well, the nature of your work —always moving around, no time for roots.—

—No trees.— He lifted his shoulders, culpable.

—What about family . . . —

Should he have a family? —Dispersed. I don't have what you'd call a family, really.—

—Your wife? No children?—

—I had one once—a wife. I have a grown-up daughter—in Canada. A doctor, a pediatrician, bright girl.—

That was a mistake. —Oh where? I have a brother who emigrated to Canada, he's a doctor too, also a pediatrician, in Toronto.—

—Vancouver. She's the other side of the country.—

—They might have met at some conference. Doctors are always holding conferences. What's her name— She held out her hand to take his glass for a refill, gesturing him to be at ease. —Good lord, I haven't asked you yours—I'm, well, I'm Sylvie, Sylvie—

—That's enough. I'm Harry.—

—Well, maybe you're right—that's enough.— For someone met

on a bus, when you haven't traveled on a bus for, say, thirty years; she
laughed with the acknowledgment to herself.

—I'll leave you my card if you wish.— (His card!) They were both
laughing.

—I'm unlikely to need the services of a construction engineer.—

—Your husband might.— He was enjoying his recklessness, teasing
himself.

She put down her drink, crossed her arms and began to swing, like
a child wanting to go higher and higher. The couch squeaked and she
frowned sideways, comically. The whiskey made her lips fuller and
polished her eyes. —And how would I explain I got to know you, may
I ask.—

Re-establishing reserve, almost prim, he ended the repartee. When
he had emptied his glass he rose to leave. —I've imposed upon you too
long . . . —

—No . . . no . . . — She stood up, hands dangling at her sides,
bracelets slipping. —I hope you're refreshed . . . I certainly am.— She
pressed the button that opened her fortress and saw him to the gates.
—Maybe—I don't know, if you're not too busy—maybe you'd like to
come round sometime. Lunch, or a swim. I could ring you—

—Thank you.—

—When my husband is back.—

She gazed straight at him; as if he were an inferior reminded of
his manners, he produced a thank you, once more.

—Where can I reach you? Your phone—

He, who could pass a police station without crossing to the other
side of the street, tingled all the way up from his feet. Caught. —Well,
it's awkward . . . messages . . . I'm hardly ever in—

Her gaze changed; now she was the one who was put in her place.
—Oh. Well, drop by sometime. Anyway, it was nice meeting you. You
might as well take my number—

He could not refuse. He found a ballpoint in his trouser pocket but
no paper. He turned his left hand palm up and wrote the seven digits
across the veins showing on the vulnerable inner side of his wrist.

.   .   .

The number was a frivolous travesty of the brand concentration-camp survivors keep of their persecution; he noticed that when he got back to the house that was sheltering him at the time. He washed off her identification; it required the use of his hosts' nailbrush. The Movement wanted him to slip out of the country but he resisted the pressures that reached him. He had been in exile too long to go back to that state of being, once he had come home. Home? Yes, even sleeping on the floor in somebody's kitchen (his standard of shelter was extremely varied), going to football matches, banal movies, wandering the streets among the people to whom he knew he belonged, unrecognized, unacknowledged—that was home. He read every newspaper and had the rare events of carefully arranged clandestine meetings with people in the Movement, but these were too risky for both himself and them for this to happen often. He thought of writing something; he actually had been an academic once, long ago, another life, teaching the laws that he despised. But it was unwise to have bits of paper around you, anything written down was evidence of your existence, and his whole strategy was not to exist, for the time being, in any persona of his past or present. For the first time in his life he was bored. He ate peanuts, biscuits, biltong, buying these small sealed packets and tearing them open, tossing the contents from his palm into his mouth before he'd even left the shop, as he had done when he was an overweight schoolboy. Although he walked the streets, he had thickened, rounding into that mound under the diaphragm. Whatever he thought of to fill the days and nights, he stopped short of doing; either it would involve people who would be afraid to associate with him, or would endanger those who would risk it. Oddly, after more than a week the phone number came back to him at the sight of his own inner wrist as he fastened his watchstrap. Sylvie—what was her name? Sylvie. Just that. Sylvie, Sylvia Pass. Perhaps the name was also the invention of the moment, out of caution, self-protection, as his "Harry" had been. *May I speak to Sylvie? Who? I'm afraid you've got the wrong number*—it would be the husband's voice. And so she never had done anything stupid like picking up a man on a bus.

But from the point of view of his situation, if anyone was safe this

"Sylvie" was. He went to the telephone in the silent empty house, his present precarious shelter, from which everyone else had gone to work for the day. She herself answered. She did not sound surprised; he asked if he might take up her offer of a swim. —But of course. After work?— Of course—after he'd left the dust and heat of the building sites.

She was dressed to swim, the strap of a two-piece suit showing above the neck of some loose-flowing robe, and the ridge of the bikini pants outlined under the cloth somewhere below where her navel must be. But she did not swim; she sat smiling, with the thigh-high split in the robe tucked closed round her leg, and watched him as he emerged from the chintzy rustic change-room (my god, what luxury compared with his present sleeping quarters) and stalked down to the pool holding in his belly and conscious that this effort—with that diaphragm bulge—made him strut like a randy pigeon. She gave encouraging cries when he dived, he felt she was counting the lengths he did, backstroke, butterfly, crawl. He was irritated and broke water right at her bare feet with his greedy grin of a man snatching life on the run. He must not let that grin escape him too often. She wiggled her toes as water flew from him, his dripping pelt of chest hair, the runnels off his strong legs, spattering her feet. A towel big as a sheet provided a toga for him; wrapped in his chair, he was modestly protected as she was, whether or not she had sized him up like a haunch in a butcher's shop.

The whiskey and ice were wheeled out. The kitchen was forewarned this time; there were olives and salami, linen napkins. —Am I going to meet your husband before I go?— The man surely would be driving up any minute. It would be best for "Harry" to get out of the towel and into his clothes in order to seem the stranger he was. He wanted to ask how she had decided to explain his presence, since she must, indeed, have so decided. The question was in his face although he didn't come out with it. It suddenly seemed impatiently simple to him. Why not just say they'd met in a bus, what was there to hide—or were the circumstances of the casual acquaintance indeed too proletarian for the gentleman, beneath his wife's dignity! If only they'd met in the Members' Pavilion at the races, now!

—Not here.— It was brusque. —It was necessary to go to Hong Kong after Japan. Apparently opportunities are opening up there . . . I don't know what it's all about. And then to Australia.—

—Quite a trip.—

—So long as he's back by the time the boys come home for the holidays at the end of next month. They expect to do things together with him. Fishing trips. Things I'm no good at. You've got a daughter—lucky. I go along, but just for the ride.—

—Well, I'm sorry—

—Another time. But you're not going . . . you'll stay for dinner. Just something light, out here, such a lovely evening.—

—But haven't you other plans I'd be disturbing, friends coming? — Harry cannot attend dinner parties, thank you.

—Nothing. Not-a-thing. I'm planning an early night, I've been gadding too much. You know how friends imagine, when you're alone, you can't be left to yourself for a single evening. I'm sick of them.—

—Then I should push off and leave you in peace.—

—No, just a salad, whatever they've got—you'll share pot luck—

Sick of them. A cure for boredom: hers. The paradox, rather than her company, was his enjoyment. He accepted the role so wide of his range; he opened the bottles of white wine—dry with the fish mousse, a Sauternes with the strawberries—in place of the man of the house.

Her fascination with their encounter rose to the surface in the ease over food and drink. —How many years is it since you met anyone you were not introduced to—can you remember? I certainly can't. It's a chain, isn't it, it's like Auld Lang Syne all the year, every year, it just goes on and on, a hand on this side taken by a hand on that side . . . it's never broken into, always friends of friends, acquaintances of acquaintances, whether they're from Japan or Taiwan or London, down the road or god knows where.—

—Good friends. They're necessary.— He was careful.

—But don't you find that? Particularly for people like you and him—my husband—I mean, the circle of people who have particular business interests, a profession. Round and round . . . But I suppose it's natural for us because we have things in common. I thought, that other day—when my car broke down, you know—I never walk around the streets like this, what have all these people to do with me—

It was coming now, of course, the guilt of her class in a wail of self-accusation of uselessness, of not belonging to real life. Hadn't she shown a hint of it in the bus? But he was wrong, and in his turn, fascinated by the overturning of his kind of conventional assumption.

—They're unreal to me. I don't just mean because most of them are black. That's obvious, that we have nothing in common. I wish them well, they ought to have a better life . . . conditions . . . I suppose it's good that things are changing for them . . . but I'm not involved, how could I be, we give money for their schools and housing and so on—my husband's firm does, like everybody else . . . I suppose you too . . . I don't know what your views are—

—I'm no armchair politician.—

—I thought not. But the others—what have I in common with those whites, either . . . I don't count in their life, and they don't count in mine. And the few who might—who're hidden away in the crowd in those streets (why is this town so ugly and dirty), it's unlikely I'd recognize them.— She really was quite attractive, unaware of a crumb at the side of her mouth. —Even sitting next to me in a bus.—

They laughed and she made the move to clink glasses.

A black man in white uniform and cotton gloves hung about wearily; her guest was conscious of this witness to everything that went on in whites' houses, but for once felt that his own whiteness guaranteed anonymity. She told the servant he could leave the table and clear it in the morning. Frog bassoons and fluting crickets filled comfortable silences. —I must go.— He spoke, not moving.

—What about a quick dip first? One for the road.— Although he had dressed, she had eaten dinner in her robe.

He was not eager to get into water again but it was a way of rounding off the evening and he felt there was a need for doing this definitively, for himself. There were too few safe subjects between them—she was more right than she knew—they had too little in common, the acquaintance had come to the end of its possibilities. He went to the change-room again.

The water crept like a cool hand over his genitals; she was already swimming. She doubled up and went under with a porpoise flip, and the light from the terrace streamed off her firm backside and thighs. She kept her distance in the water, they circled one another. Hitching herself out on long arms, she sat on the side of the pool and, again, he was aware of her watching him. He surfaced below where she sat, and suddenly, for a moment only, closed his hand on her wrist before leaving the pool, shaking himself like a dog, scrubbing at his arms and chest with the big towel. —Cold, cold.—

She repeated with a mock shiver: —Cold, cold.—

They stood up, in accord to get dressed.

The ring of water in his ears jinglingly mingled with the sound of the frogs. He put his arms round her and in a rush of heat, as if all the blood in his chilled body had retreated to engorge there, pressed his genitals tightly against her. He felt an enormous thrill and a fiercely crashing desire, all the abstinence of a planned nonexistence imploded like the destruction of one of his imaginary twenty-stories that she feared might fall on her head. She held him as he held her. There was no kiss. She broke away neatly and ran indoors. He dressed, raged against by his roused body, among the chintz drapings in the change-room. When he came out the water in the pool was black, with the reflection of stars thrown there like dying matches. She had turned off the terrace lights and was standing in the dark.

—Good night. I apologize.—

—I hope your car hasn't been pinched. Should have brought it into the drive.—

—There is no car.—

He was too tired and dispirited to lie. Yet he must summon some slapdash resource of protection. —Friends were coming this way, they dropped me. I said I'd call a taxi to take me back.—

The dark and the cover of chanting frogs hid whatever she might be thinking.

—Stay.— She turned, and he followed her into the house, that he had not before entered.

.   .   .

They began again, the right way, with kisses and caresses. A woman his own age, who knew how to make love, who both responded and initiated, knowing what they wanted; in common. On this territory between them, there was even a kind of unexpected bluntness. Gently pinching his nipples before the second intercourse, she said —You're not AIDS positive, are you?—

He put a hand over the delight of her fingers on him.

—A bit late to ask . . . Not so far as I know. And I've no reason to believe otherwise.—

—But you've no wife.—

—Yes, but I'm rather a constant character—despite my nomadic profession.—

—How will you explain you didn't come home?—

He laughed. —Who to?—

—The first day you were here . . . "awkward," you said, for me to phone you.—

—There's no one. There's no woman I'm accountable to at present.—

—You understand, it's none of my business. But we don't want to make things difficult for either of us.—

The husband. —Of course, I understand, don't worry. You're a lovely—preposterous!—woman.— And he began to kiss her as if he were a cannibal tasting flesh.

She was a practical woman, too. Sometime in the early hours he stirred with a grunt and found a strange woman standing over him in dawn shadows—oh yes, "Sylvie." So that's where, waking often in unfamiliar rooms, he was this time. He had learnt to be quick to adjust his sense of place.

—Come. There's another bed.— He wandered behind her down a passage. She had made up a big bed in a guest-room; he stumbled into it and slept again.

In the morning at breakfast on her terrace she gaily greeted the black man who served them. —Mr. Harry is a friend of the master. I asked him to stay the night with us.—

So she, too, had the skills of vigilance, making it safe for herself.

Harry went back every night that week. Harry really existed, now, out of the nonexistence of himself. Harry the construction engineer, a successful, highly-paid, professionally well-regarded man of the world, with a passing fancy, a mistress not young but beautiful, a creature lavished by the perfumed unguents of care, from the poll of curly tendrils he would lift to expose her forehead, to the painted nails of her pedicured toes. Like him, she had her erratic moments of anguish, caused by conflict with the assertion of reality—her reality—rising within her to spoil an episode outside her life, a state without consequences. These moments found their expression as non sequitur remarks or more often as gestures, the inner scuffle breaking through in some odd physical manifestation. One night she squatted naked on the bed with her arms round her knees, clasping her curled feet tight in either hand. He was disturbed, and suppressed the reason that was sending a sucker from the root of his life: after interrogation in detention he had sat on the floor of his cell holding his feet like that, still rigid with his resistance against pain. A sear of resentment: *she*—she was only interrogating herself. Yet of course he had feeling for her—hadn't he just made love to her, and she to him, as she did so generously—he should not let himself dismiss the relative sufferings of people like her as entirely trivial because it was on behalf of nothing larger than themselves.

—A long phone call from Australia . . . and all I could think about while we were talking was how when we're alone in here at night he never closes the bathroom door while he pees. I hear him, like a horse letting go in the street. Never closes the door. And sometimes there's a loud fart as well. He never stops to think that I can hear, that I'm lying here. And that's all I could think about while he's talking to me, that's all.—

He smiled at her almost fondly. —Well, we're pretty crude, we men . . . but oh come on, you're not squeamish—you're a very physical lady—

—About lovemaking, yes . . . you think, because of the things I do, with you. But that's different, that's lovemaking, it's got nothing to do with what I'm talking about.—

—If sex doesn't disgust you as a function of the body, then why so fastidious about its other functions? You accept a lover's body or you don't.—

—Would you still accept your lover's body if she had, say, a breast off?—

He lay down beside her with a hand on the dune of her curved smooth back. —How do I know? What woman? When? It would depend on many things, wouldn't it? I can say now, *yes,* just to say the right thing, if you want—

—That's it! That's what's good! You don't say the right thing, like other people.—

—Oh I do, I do. I'm very careful, I have a wary nature, I assure you.—

—Well, I don't know you.— She let go of her feet and pulled the bow of her body back, under his palm. Restlessly she swiveled round to him, pushing the fingers of her two hands up through the poll on her forehead, holding the hair dragged away. —Why do I let that bloody pansy hairdresser do this to me? . . . I look common. Cheap, common.—

He murmured intimately. —I didn't think so.—

On the bus, yes. —Maybe you wouldn't have got off if I hadn't looked like this. Where were you really going, I wonder.— But it was not a question; she was satisfied she wouldn't get an answer, he wouldn't come out with the right thing. She was not asking, just as she never questioned that he appeared as out of nowhere, every night, apparently dropped by taxi somewhere out of sight of the house. And he did not ask when the husband would come home; there would be a sign he would read for himself. Stretched out, she quietly took the hand that had been on her back and placed it between her thighs.

There was no sign, but at the end of that week he knew he would not go back again. Enough. It was time. He left as he had followed her, without explanation. Using the same trail for more than a week, he might have made a path for himself by which he could be followed. He moved from where he had been staying, to be taken in at another house. This was the family of a plumber, a friend of the Movement, not quite white, but too ambiguous of pigment for classification, so that the itinerant lodger could pass for a lighter relative. One of the young-sters gave up his bed; the lodger shared the room with three other children. Every day of the trial, new evidence brought by the Prose-cutor's state witnesses involved his name. It claimed him from every newspaper, citing several aliases under which he had been active. But not "Harry."

He was making his way back to the plumber's house one afternoon when the youngster, on roller skates, zigzagged up the street. The boy staggered to a halt, almost knocking him down, and he struck out playfully at him. But the boy was panting. —My dad says don't come. I been waiting to tell you and my brother's there at the other end of the street in case you take that way. Dad send us. They come this morning and went all over the house, only Auntie was there, Ma was also at work already. Looking for you. With dogs and everything. He say don't worry for your things, he's going to bring them where you can pick them up—he didn't tell me nothing, not where, but that you know—

A cold jump of fear under his pectorals. He let it pass, and con-centrated on getting out of the area. He took a bus, and another bus. He went into a cinema and sat through some film about three men bringing up a baby. When he came out of the cinema's eternal dusk, the street was dark. Somewhere to go for the night: he had to have that, to decide where to go tomorrow, which hide on the list in his mind it was possible to use again. Likely that the list was not in his mind alone; nothing on it was left that could be counted on as safe, now.

He got out of the taxi a block away. He pressed the intercom button at the wide teak gates. There was the manservant's accented voice on the other end.

—It's Mr. Harry.—

—Just push, Mr. Harry.— There was a buzz.

Her trees, the swimming pool; he stood in the large room that was always waiting for a party to fill it. On low tables were the toys such people give each other: metal balls that (as he set them in motion with a flick) click together in illustration of some mathematical or physical

principle, god knows what . . . Click-clack; a metronome of trivial time.
She was there, in the doorway, in rumpled white trousers, barefoot, a
woman who expected no one or perhaps was about to choose what she
would wear for an evening out. —Hul-*lo.*— Raised eyebrows.

—I had to go away unexpectedly—trouble with the foundations
on one of our sites in Natal. I meant to phone—

—But phoning's awkward.— She recalled, but quite serenely, only
half-wishing to score against him.

—I'm not disturbing you . . . —

—No, no. I've just been tidying up . . . some cupboards . . . I get
very careless—

When alone: so the husband wasn't back yet. —Could I ask for a
drink—I've had a heavy day.—

She opened her palms, away from her body: as if he need ask; and,
indeed, the servant appeared with the trolley. —I put it outside,
madam?—

Quite like coming home; the two of them settled back on the terrace,
as before. —I thought it would be so nice to see you.—

She had dropped ice in his drink and was handing it to him. —It
is nice.—

He closed his fingers round hers, on the glass.

After they had eaten, she asked —Are you going to stay? Just for
tonight.—

They were silent a few moments, to the accompaniment of those
same frogs. —I feel I'd like to very much.— It was sincere, strangely;
he was aware of a tender desire for her, pushing out of mind fear that
this, too, was an old trail that might be followed, and awareness that
his presence was just a pause in which tomorrow's decision must be
made. —And what about you?—

—Yes, I'd like you to. D'you want to swim?—

—Not much.—

—Well, it's maybe a bit chilly.—

When the servant came to clear the table she gave an order. —Ask
Leah please to make up the bed in the first guest-room, will you. For
Mr. Harry.—

Lying side by side on long chairs in the dark, he stroked her arm and drew back her hair from her shoulder to kiss her neck. She stood up and, taking his hand, led him indeed to that room and not her own. So that was how it was to be; he said nothing, kissed her on the forehead in acceptance that this was the appropriate way for him to be dismissed with a polite good night. But after he had got naked into bed she came in, naked, drew back the curtains and opened the windows so that the fresh night blew in upon them, and lay down beside him. Their flesh crept deliciously under the double contact of the breeze and each other's warmth. There was great tenderness, which perhaps prompted her to remark, with languid frankness, on a contrast: —You know you were awful, that first day, the way you just thrust yourself against me. Not a touch, not a kiss.— Now between a sudden change to wild kisses he challenged her knowingly. —And you, you, you didn't mind, ay, you showed no objection . . . You were not insulted! But was I really so crude—did I really . . . ?—

—You certainly did. And no other man I know—

—And any other woman would have pushed me into the swimming pool.—

They embraced joyously again and again; she could feel that he had not been with "any other woman," wherever it was he had disappeared to after last week. In the middle of the night, each knew the other had wakened and was looking at the blur of sinking stars through the open windows. He was sure, for no logical reason, that he was safe, this night, that no one would know, ever, that he was here. She suddenly raised herself on one elbow, turning to him although she certainly could not read his face in the faint powdering of light from the sky. —Who are you?—

But he wasn't found out, he wasn't run to ground. It wasn't suspicion founded on any knowledge relevant to his real identity; she knew nothing of the clandestine world of revolution; when she walked in the streets of the dirty city among the angry, the poor and the unemployed they had "nothing to do" with her—she'd said it. Who he was didn't exist for her; he was safe. She could seek only to place him intriguingly within the alternatives she knew of—was there some financial scandal behind his anonymity, was there a marriage he was running away from—these were the calamities of her orbit. Never in her wildest

imagination could she divine what he was doing, there in her bed.

And then it struck him that this was not her bed: this time she had not taken him into the bed she shared with the husband. Not in those sheets; ah, he understood this was the sign he knew *he* would divine, when the time came. Clean sheets on that bed, not to be violated. The husband was coming home tomorrow. *Just for tonight.*

He left early. She did not urge him to stay for breakfast on the terrace. He must get back to bathe and change . . . She nodded as if she knew what was coming. —Before getting to the site.— She waved to him as to a friend, down there at the gates, for the eyes of the manservant and a gardener, who was singing a hymn while mowing the lawn. He had made a decision, in the respite she granted him. He would take a chance of leaving the city and going to a small town where there was an old contact, dropped out of activity long ago, who might be prevailed upon to revive old loyalties and take him in.

It was perhaps a mistake; who knows. Best safety lies in crowds. The town was too small to get lost in. After three days, when the old contact reluctantly kept him in an outhouse in the company of a discarded sewing machine, stained mattresses and mouse droppings, he went out for air one early morning in his host's jogging outfit looking exactly like all the other overweight men toiling along the streets, and was soon aware that a car was following. There was nothing to do but keep jogging; at a traffic light the car drew up beside him and two plainclothesmen ordered him to come to the police station with them. He had a fake document with him, which he presented with the indignation of a good citizen, but at the station they had a dossier that established his identity. He was taken into custody and escorted back to Johannesburg, where he was detained in prison. He was produced at the trial for which he had been the missing accused and the press published photographs of him from their files. With and without a beard; close-cropped and curly-headed; the voracious, confident smile was the constant in these personae. His successful evasion of the police for many months made a sensational story certain to bring grudging admiration even from his enemies.

In his cell, he wondered—an aside from his preoccupation with the

trial, and the exhilaration, after all, of being once again with his comrades, the fellow accused—he wondered whether she had recognized
him. But it was unlikely she would follow reports of political trials.
Come to think of it, there were no newspapers to be seen around her
house, that house where she thought herself safe among trees, safe from
the threat of him and his kind, safe from the present.

Laurie Colwin

FRANK AND BILLY

At a perfectly ordinary cocktail party given by the *Journal of American Economic Thought* for its staff and contributors, Francis Clemens was introduced to the author of some articles he had admired on the subject of medieval capitalism. Her name was Josephine Delielle (nicknamed Billy) and although it slipped right by him at the time, he fell in love with her at once.

She had lank brown hair, gray-blue eyes, and a deadpan mug. Her expression ranged from a frown to a somewhat grudging grin.

"Oh, how nice to meet you," Billy said. "You had an article in last month's issue. Aren't you the guy who writes about economics and architecture?"

Francis noticed that her bottom teeth were slightly crooked, and asked her what she had thought about this article.

"I thought it was a little goofy," she said. Francis surveyed her further and saw that her shirttail was hanging out on the side.

"Oh, yes?" Francis said. "Which parts did you find especially goofy?"

In the ensuing conversation, it was made clear to Francis that she found all or most of his article goofy. She explained why she felt this way, and then she said: "Don't you think this is the most boring thing you've ever been to?"

"Not by a long shot," Francis said. "But then I'm considerably older than you."

Billy gave him a hard stare—the look of an appraiser at a diamond. This clear, naked child-gaze of hers made it difficult for Francis to guess how old she was. These days it was hard for Francis to tell how old most women were, and Billy could have been anywhere from twenty-five to thirty-nine. She looked older than his oldest son's girl-friend, who was twenty-six, but younger than his wife Vera's partner in her interior design business, who was forty-two.

Billy was speaking, but Francis's attention had wandered. He felt a kind of inward lurch, as if he were having a dream about falling off a ledge. The air in his chest felt sweet as it does after a long laugh or when a headache has finally gone away. He felt as if he and Billy were standing in thick hazy sunshine. He heard the word "husband." Her husband, Grey Delielle, was at a conference in Switzerland—he was the economic adviser to a small foundation. Francis had heard of this foundation and his head cleared further. Vera was in San Diego redoing a beach house. It occurred to him that Billy might be lonely for company at dinner. He suggested they leave the party and go off to a restaurant.

"Swell," she said, and they went to get their coats.

At dinner Francis discovered that Billy taught two classes a week at the business school, and Billy discovered that Francis had resigned from his banking firm several years ago and now consulted to clients on the telephone. He was also writing a book on the relationship of architectural and financial trends. Billy revealed that she was working on her dissertation, the subject of which was the effect of the medieval wool trade on a Cotswold village. A long conversation about English architecture ensued.

Francis spoke a little about his wife, Vera—Billy must meet her—and his two grown sons, Quentin and Aaron. Billy said that Grey, her husband, was sort of a genius but she did not say that Francis must meet him.

It was a lovely night in early May. Francis walked Billy home. She and Grey lived on two floors of a brownstone, into which Billy invited Francis for a drink or a cup of tea. He asked for tea and it was several months before he realized that he had chosen it over the drink he really wanted because its preparation might keep him with Billy for a few minutes more. He also realized that one of the reasons he had found her living room so ugly was that it is perfectly normal for the lover to hate his or her beloved's place of legal and habitual residence.

Francis did not know that he was embarking on a love affair. He went home and slept peacefully, after making himself a strong, bracing drink. In the morning he remembered Billy's saying that she had been looking for a certain book, a book he owned. He dispatched it to her at once, and she responded by sending him an article *he* had mentioned which she happened to have in her files. They met, not entirely by chance, at the *Journal* office. It was just around lunchtime and so they went around the corner for a sandwich. A week later Francis just happened to be near the business school and he just happened to bump into Billy after her class.

After several months of meetings and luncheons, Francis became familiar with Billy's uninspired wardrobe and her array of faded sweatshirts, shapeless turtlenecks, and worn corduroy skirts and frayed boys' shirts.

One day he said, looking at her brother's old sweater and a skirt that might once have been olive green: "You're the one girl, Billy, whom you dread to hear say: I'm going to slip into something more comfortable."

It was clearly provocative, and not at all the sort of thing Francis was used to saying. Billy did not bat an eyelash. She put down her pastrami sandwich, wiped her lips with a paper napkin, and said: "No one my age ever says anything like that. We just take our clothes off."

A long while later she revealed that she had said this to hurt him, and he did not think it wise to tell her how effective she had been.

It was months before he kissed her, and by that time the idea of kissing her had turned into an overwhelming desire he was tired of fending off. Reluctantly he came to the conclusion that he was simply looking for an opportunity.

One evening, after taking Vera to the airport on another of her trips to San Diego, a terrible restlessness took possession of him. The idea of going to a movie or going home to his empty house made him more restless than ever. It could have been said that he was looking for action, but that phrase was not in his working vocabulary. He drove into Manhattan in an agitated state until it occurred to him that he might very well pay a call on that charming young couple Billy and Grey Delielle. They were doubtless at home—Francis had heard Billy say many times that there was no hell more hellish than the hell of social life. She did not like to go out, and she did not like to entertain, either. It was not very late. Francis could easily just stop by, although just stopping by was not the sort of thing he generally did.

On the other hand, the Delielles might be ready for bed. They might in fact *be* in bed—a terrible thought. As he neared their neighborhood he wondered what he would do if in fact they were out. He felt it was possible that he might have a fit.

He found a parking space directly in front of their brownstone, bounded up the stairs, and rang the bell.

Billy answered the door, wearing blue jeans and a pair of tasseled loafers that had seen so many, many better days that they were kept together with a variety of duct and electrical tapes. She did not seem surprised to see him. Rather a kind of impish smirk overtook her usually expressionless features. It was almost plain to see that she was repressing a smile.

"I was right around the corner," Francis lied. "At a very boring dinner party. I don't generally drop by, but I was right in the neighborhood."

"Oh," said Billy.

"I hope I'm not dropping by at a bad time. I mean, you and Grey might have already turned in." Francis felt his scalp begin to prickle.

"Grey's in Chicago," said Billy. "I was working. Come in and I'll give you a drink."

But she did not go toward the kitchen. Absentmindedly she wandered up the stairs toward her study. Francis followed her. His heart was beating wildly. The bedroom and the guest room were also upstairs, he knew. Where was she taking him?

He had forgotten how these things are accomplished. Did one grab the girl by the arm, or tackle her by the ankle? Did one pluck at the sleeve of her turtleneck, tap her on the back? Ask? Beg?

Of course Francis had forgotten that in the case of true love, things simply happen—almost the only circumstances under which they do. People just look at each other in a certain way, and the signal is as unmistakable as the mating behavior of Atwater's prairie chicken.

What happened was that Billy got to the door of her study and then turned around, clearly confused. Only later did Francis realize that she had no idea of what she was doing. She looked at him with a puzzled, unfocused aspect that was totally out of character for her.

"What am I doing up here?" she said. "I was supposed to make you a drink."

She looked up at him, and he looked down at her. The realization that he had fallen in love caused his heart first to shrink and then to expand.

Billy took a step toward the stair, which only moved her a step closer to Francis. His chin, he saw, would graze her head. One more step in either direction—she toward him, or he toward her—and they were in each other's arms. Francis felt impelled to move: he felt in the grip of a great many involuntary actions. His hand was on her shoulder. It was on her back. His other arm encircled her. He pulled her close. Some other hand—it had to have been his right or left—entangled its fingers in her hair and tipped her head back. Francis felt her arms slowly creep up his sides and around his neck in a gesture that was either tender or grudging. To his amazement he saw that Billy's eyes were closed. She looked soft and dreamy—quite unlike her usual exasperated self. He was about to kiss her when she opened her eyes. These eyes, generally a hard, unavailing, unsentimental blue-gray, the sort of eyes that see right through a thing, had turned, it seemed to him, one shade darker. Francis felt very like a swimmer about to jump into a deep pool of cold water. It was now or never. He pulled her close again. Their lips met.

Hers were soft, and tasted of raspberries. Her hair smelled of baby shampoo.

Of course, first kisses tell it all. They reveal, as it were, the inner man. Billy's first responses were tentative and noncommittal—as noncommittal as you can be wrapped up in someone else's arms. She *was* grudging, and Francis knew that she would always be. But when she really kissed him back, he learned that she felt about him as he felt about her, although he knew it would be rather like breaking rocks ever to get her to say it. He would never hear a whispered endearment from her lips, he was certain. As for Francis, even he knew what he was broadcasting. Relief, guilt, and liberation made him passionate. He was hers entirely, after a manner of speaking.

Their first actual kiss was a one-celled organism which, after they had been standing on the stairway kissing for some time, evolved into something rather grander—a bird of paradise, for example. Francis was afraid to stop kissing her. He feared that she might vanish as smoke, or throw herself against the wall and accuse him of being a cad, or she might sob out Grey's name and fling herself down the stairs. But he longed to look at her to see what effect, if any, all this kissing had on her. He took her very firmly by the arms so that she could not vanish or fling, but he was unable to read her expression because she was staring at the floor. This made him angry and he shook her ever so slightly. When she did look up, there was so much on her face he hardly knew where to begin. She looked confused, enraptured, upset, and stunned. He saw desire, despair, elation, surprise, mistrust, and longing. So that was what her determined expressionlessness concealed!

She looked up and uttered two words.

"Oh, more," she said, and this time she put her arms around him. Francis's heart melted with gratitude. It was one thing to be in love. It was quite another to be loved back. Francis kissed her and kissed her. They kissed with their eyes closed, like teenagers. Finally Billy pushed herself away. She looked disarranged and upset. Any fool, after all, knows that two adults cannot stand around kissing endlessly. Decisions of one sort or another usually present themselves for immediate attention.

"Enough of this nonsense," Billy said in an unsteady voice.

"I wish you'd stop staring at the floor," said Francis. "It's very disconcerting."

"I can't look at you," Billy said. "It's too dangerous."

At this a smile overtook him—a smile of triumph. He pulled her close again.

"This doesn't have to happen ever again," Francis said, lying through his teeth.

"Interesting," said Billy, "if true." With this she slid against him as easily as people slide against each other in a swimming pool and in a very few minutes the decision was made to repair to Billy's unattractive little study, where, on her threadbare and faded couch, they discovered how ardently and secretly they had waited for one another.

The first kiss is a snap. It is the aftermath of the first real connection that produces such a mire of unwanted feelings. Billy sat up. The faded quilt she had pulled over them to keep off the chill slipped away. Francis noticed that without her clothes she looked quite chic, unlike most people, who look more stylish when dressed. Perhaps, he thought, it was the contrast between her nice body and her awful clothes.

Billy stared at the wall, then pushed the hair out of her eyes and scowled her exasperated frown. It was a gesture which by now Francis had seen dozens of times.

"Gee, I feel awful," she said.

"Oh, do you?" said Francis fiercely. He pulled her down, and quickly established that she did not feel quite so awful as she said. Their hunger for one another was quite startling—a subject Francis felt would never be discussed.

Francis did not know what to expect in the way of an aftermath. He had never had a real love affair before. He had had romances; he had gotten married; and from time to time he had found himself in bed with some old friend or other—nothing serious at all: it wasn't romance so much as social service or cheering someone up. Next to him Billy lay with her arms crossed on her chest, looking at the ceiling like a child filled with some secret, inner amusement.

"In bed with Frank and Billy," she began. "Chapter One. Frank and Billy have just gone to bed. They have been in bed for who can say how long. Doubtless they will go to bed again, and the funny thing is, they're both married, and to other people! What a situation. How long, they might ask, has this been going on? Who will ask first?"

"How long has this been going on?" Francis said.

"That wasn't necessarily a cue," Billy said, and silence fell between them.

Instead, Francis watched his beloved begin to get dressed. As she slipped her clothes over her head, he realized how considerably less gorgeous she was making herself. When she pulled on her tatty corduroys, he saw before him the old recognizable Billy, who like the strange, unclothed Billy was also his.

When she put on her shoes Francis felt it was time for him to get dressed, too. He looked at the clock. "Good Lord," he said. "We've been on this couch for two and a half hours."

Billy gave him a look he could not interpret. Did it mean that two and a half hours was a very long time, or not a very long time by her lights?

As he put his shirt on, he noticed that some of her mild, sweet smell seemed to have rubbed off on him. He was terribly happy—as happy as it is possible to be under these circumstances, which bring the kind of happiness that is devoid of any contentment.

It was quite amazing, he thought, that such a welter of complex feeling can arise from the simplest things—the sight of a shirttail hanging out. He had wanted to kiss that deadpan mug's face the instant he had seen it, he now admitted.

Billy folded up the quilt. The couch looked as if no one had ever so much as sat upon it. Reality set in, cold as a fog. Vera would have landed in San Diego by now and would be calling in if she had not already done so. How lovely it would be to live in a movie in which lovers have only time, not the telephone calls of absent spouses to worry

about. But what about Billy? Did she expect him to stay? Oh, how
complicated these things were!

"Do you want a cup of tea before you leave?" Billy said, standing
at the door.

"Are you so anxious to get rid of me?" asked Francis. He was
relieved and sad. The fact that he would soon leave set him free.

"You weren't thinking of sleeping over, were you?" said Billy,
shocked. She looked about fifteen years old.

Downstairs Francis sat on a stool in Billy's kitchen while she boiled the
water for tea. In novels, Francis reflected, lovers indulge in some form
of afterglow: they beam at one another or smile radiant smiles. It was
very clear that only the remotest afterglow was going to envelop him
and Billy, but as he watched her set out the cups, his heart began to
ache. She looked small in her big serious-looking kitchen, and he knew
because she had told him how much she hated to cook. He wondered
where she truly belonged. And where did he belong? How torn he felt
by his own joy at where he was sitting and the terrible strangeness of
sitting there!

No one, he reflected sadly, ever possesses anyone else. The act of
love can be performed by complete strangers, but it is quite another
thing to have access to what someone else actually *thinks*. Even though
they were officially lovers, Francis felt himself tongue-tied and confused.
He grabbed her by the arm as she walked by him. He spun her around
hard and pressed her to him.

"I'm in love with you," he said.

"I know," Billy said.

"Well, what about you?" said Francis. "Or do you always sleep
with people when Grey is out of town?"

"Geez," Billy said. "What's wrong with you, anyway?"

"You told me you young people just take your clothes off."

Billy gave him a baleful look.

"I guess I'm a desperate man," Francis said.

"Oh, pish," Billy said. "Why don't you just ask me instead of filling
the air with innuendo?"

"All right," Francis said. "Are you in love with me?"

"Sure," said Billy. After a long pause, she said, "Watch out. The water's boiling right behind you."

With these words was Francis's heart set at ease.

Francis was a thoroughly married man, and had been for many years. He thought like a married person and therefore the aftermath of his evening with Billy filled him with guilt and glee. He did not know what he felt worse about—the guilt or the glee. They existed in equal measure, along with a number of other things he had not felt in quite a long time: he was as excited, hopeful, and confused as a teenaged boy. He was also extremely tired. He made himself a drink and thought he might take a bath, but instead he crawled into bed quite aware of the fact that he did not want to wash the evening off himself so quickly.

Francis had not slept alone very much in his adult life, but now that Vera traveled for her work, he found that he rather liked being in bed by himself. The bed they shared was enormous—and was covered, due to Vera's domestic genius and connections in the world of decoration, with a blue and white coverlet of early American design homespun by a weaver in Vermont who specialized in reproductions. It was possibly the largest blue and white coverlet of its kind in the world.

He sipped his drink and tried to make his mind a perfect blank, but the image of Billy in many guises darted through his tired brain. He looked over at Vera's side of the bed and imagined Billy in it. Vera wore linen shifts to bed and piled her hair on top of her head to sleep. She slept like a kitten and smelled of Rose Bleue. Billy, he imagined, slept in a rotten-looking flannel nightgown. How he wished she were next to him!

He dozed off, calculating that he had five days until Vera returned, and five hours until he could call up his grouchy girlfriend and hear her voice again.

That had been in the spring. It was now October. On a sultry, hazy day, Francis drove to Billy's. She said she thought they ought to have a serious talk. Two blocks from her house, he was confronted by the sight of his beloved mistress struggling under a load of men's suits in plastic bags—Grey's suits which she was fetching from the cleaners. It was hot and Billy looked sweaty and cross. These were doubtless Grey's fall and winter suits coming out of storage in time for Grey's trip to Switzerland. This trip was of consuming interest to Francis as Vera was due to go to Honolulu at the same time, and it was his single-minded desire to take Billy away with him somewhere for a few days to find out what, if anything, she wore in bed.

It occurred to him to stop the car and help her, but this seemed to him an ambiguous gesture, and so he drove on. Did Grey, that swine, expect Billy to run these errands for him? Or did she do it out of love? He gave her time to get home, and when he drove up her street he found her again, this time with a bundle of laundry. She was taking Grey's shirts and the sheets to be laundered. This time she saw him and hopped into the car. Why, he wondered, did he always have to see her carrying such intimate bundles?

Francis drove her to the laundry and then followed her into her living room where, he supposed, this serious talk was about to begin. But he was wrong. The sky darkened and lightning flashed directly overhead. It began to pour. Billy sprang up. "I left the windows open," she said, and dashed up the stairs.

Francis followed. She banged down the windows in her study and then went into the bedroom. Francis had looked into this room many times but he had never actually been in it.

Of course, the lover's nuptial couch is an object of horrible fascination. The lover is drawn to it, drawn to lie down upon it, and drawn to say what a miserable bed it is.

Francis sat down. The bed was a four-poster, high off the ground and not, Francis noted, very wide. It was covered by a pink quilt, which was the nicest thing he had yet seen of Billy's possessions. He stretched out, in a tentative way.

"Jesus," he said. "This is a very hard mattress. Or maybe it isn't a mattress. Maybe it's a plank of wood."

"I have a plank of wood, you have a football field," Billy said, referring to Francis's enormous cot, which she had been shown during a tour of his house. She thought his house was frightful, and said so often. She referred to it as "your charming little snuggery." Francis's house was usually considered to be quite beautiful. Billy said it made her feel as if she was imprisoned inside a tea cozy.

It was amazing how many things prevented Billy and Francis from having their serious conversation. It was put off dozens of times, during which Francis went forward to achieve his heart's desire: he wanted to take Billy on a little trip and sleep the whole night through with her next to him. He saw an ad for a cottage in Vermont and rented it on the spot for five days when Vera and Grey would be away at the same time. This happened very infrequently and not for this long—a whole week. Francis felt this should be taken advantage of. Billy, of course, was mute.

The Sunday before he and Billy were due to leave, Francis put Vera on her plane and began his restless way back into Manhattan. He thought he might take a little drive past Billy's just to see if she was visible. She might be sitting on her front steps, or walking down the street with the Sunday paper.

She was walking down the street, but not with the Sunday papers. She was walking with her very husband, Grey. They were holding hands and laughing. It was not jealousy that lashed against Francis's heart, but anger: she never *told* him that she held Grey's hand or that they ever laughed. His vision of their marriage was a still photo of two people at opposite ends of the table who are silent because they have absolutely nothing whatsoever to say to one another. Francis had always assumed that she and Grey had nothing—nothing in common. It was amazing how exotic they looked to Francis, who was so used to the sight of Billy with him that he could not get over the sight of her with her lawful husband. Of course it was not unknown for Francis to hold Vera's hand, or for them to laugh at the same jokes, but that was quite another thing entirely.

One night in the bedroom of the rented love nest in Vermont, Francis turned to Billy. She was wearing his T-shirt and reading a book. The bed they were lying in was a little smaller than the bed Billy and Grey shared, and it was necessary for Francis and Billy to sleep like bunnies, or spoons or vines.

"Is that what you normally wear to bed?" Francis said.

"Normally I don't wear *your* T-shirt to bed," said Billy.

"Isn't that the one I wore today?" said Francis.

"Uh-huh," Billy said. "I like 'em broken in."

Francis was in a partial swoon. The cottage was drafty and the television didn't work. Now they lay in bed with their separate books. The idea that he was actually in bed with Billy and reading—or pretending to read—made his heart a little wild.

"Sex is a funny thing," he began in a fatherly tone.

"Yes, hilarious," said Billy. "Listen to this." She held up her book. It was entitled *Green Demons,* by someone called Ardith Chase Lamondt. "He drew her to him with a quick intake of breath. The delicate ribs along her spine quivered slightly."

"Yours never do," Francis said.

"You never draw me to you with a quick intake of breath," Billy said. "I tell you, sex in this book is a pretty funny thing. What's your book?" She leaned over and turned his book toward her. "Oh, yick," she said. "I got my book off the shelf in the living room. You actually *packed* yours. I didn't see any books by Important Thinkers in this house. I think it's hilarious that you actually brought a book along to our illicit love nest."

"I wish you wouldn't talk that way," Francis said.

"Oh, come on," Billy said. "Isn't that book the most boring thing you've ever read?"

"This man is very important, miss. If you weren't so smug, you'd read him, too. Besides, a man needs to keep up with his times."

"Huh," said Billy. "Well, I made up an all-purpose Important Title for you in the car. I was thinking about your bookshelves and I synthesized all the titles into one Very Important Title. You can use it when people ask you what you're reading and you aren't actually reading anything."

"What's that?" said Francis.

"It's *Towards a Scarcity of Needs,*" she said. "I'm ever so proud of it. It has a nice, official sound and it means absolutely nothing at all. It's the right title for a man who goes on an illicit trip and brings a book along, to say nothing of constantly listening to the news on the radio."

Towards a Scarcity of Needs! No one in the world except Francis and Billy would ever know what this meant. If he ever mentioned it in passing, no one would have the slightest idea what he was talking about.

Having a love affair, Francis reflected, was not unlike being the co-governor of a tiny, private kingdom in some remote country with only two inhabitants—you and the other co-governor. This kingdom had flora and fauna, a national bird, language, reference, conceit, a national anthem (*Towards a Scarcity of Needs*), cheers, songs, and gestures. It also had national censorship—the taboo subjects are taboo. The idea that one of the co-governors has a life outside the kingdom always brings pain. For example, the afternoon Francis's eye fell on a thick air letter in an elderly hand. When pressed, Billy turned red and explained that for many years she had been having a correspondence with a retired schoolteacher in the town of Northleach whom she had met during one of her research periods in the Cotswolds. He sent her hand-knitted mittens of local wool. She sent him new mystery books. They wrote a letter each month. This information left Francis speechless, like a blow to the stomach with a flat object. The moment he stepped out of her house her life without him began. Of course, the same could be said of him.

What richness! what privacy! what sadness!

Suddenly, Francis was exhausted. It had been a long two days: a tiring drive to Vermont, the strangeness of having Billy all to himself with no curfew, their odd and scarce hours of sleep. He leaned against the insufficient pillows. At home he slept with two pillows filled amply with European goosedown.

Life was really very simple. What he wanted to know was this: did Billy love him more than she loved her husband, Grey? On the other hand, life was very complicated. He did not want to know any of the possible answers to this question. His eyelids were heavy but he thought he might rouse himself and ask Billy some burning question such as: what *are* we doing together?

He turned and there was Billy wearing his T-shirt. Her hair fell into her eyes, and she brushed it off her face with a drowsy hand. She was fast asleep, her head full of alien, unknowable dreams.

John Updike

LOVE SONG, FOR A MOOG SYNTHESIZER

She was good in bed. She went to church. Her I.Q. was 145. She repeated herself. Nothing fit; it frightened him. Yet Tod wanted to hang on, to hang on to the bits and pieces, which perhaps were not truly pieces but islands, which a little lowering of sea level would reveal to be rises on a sunken continent, peaks of a subaqueous range, secretly one, a world.

He called her Pumpkin, or Princess. She had been a parody of a respectable housewife—active in all causes, tireless in all aspects of housekeeping from fumigation to floor-waxing, an ardent practitioner of the minor arts of the Halloween costumer and the Cub Scout den mother, a beaming, posing, conveniently shaped ornament to her husband at cocktail parties, beach parties, dinner parties, fund-raising parties. Always prim, groomed, proper, perfect.

But there was a clue, which he picked up: she never listened. Her eyebrows arched politely, her upper lip lifted alertly; nevertheless she brushed her gaze past the faces of her conversational partners in a terrible icy hurry, and repeated herself so much that he wondered if she was sane.

Her heart wasn't in this.

She took to jabbing him at parties, jabbing so hard it hurt. This piece of herself, transferred to his ribs, his kidneys, as pain, lingered there, asked to be recognized as love.

His brain—that impatient organ, which deals, with the speed of light, in essences and abstractions—opted to love her perhaps too early, before his heart—that plodder, that problem-learner—had had time to collect quirks and spiritual snapshots, to survey those faults and ledges of the not-quite-expected where affection can silt and accumulate. He needed a body. Instead there was something skeletal, spacy.

But then the shivering. That was lovable. As they left a fine restaurant in an elegant, shadowy district of the city, Princess complained (her talk was unexpectedly direct) that her underpants kept riding up. Drunk, his drunkenness glazing the bricks of the recently restored pavement beneath them, the marquee of the cunningly renovated restaurant behind them, the other pedestrians scattered around them as sketchily as figures in an architectural drawing, and the artificially antique street lamp above them, its wan light laced by the twigs of a newly planted tree that had also something of an architect's stylization about it, Tod knelt down and reached up into her skirt with both hands and pulled down her underpants, so adroitly she shivered. She shivered, involuntarily, expressing—what? Something that came upon her like a breeze. Then, recovering poise, with an adroitness the equal of his, she stepped out of her underpants. Her black high heels, shiny as Shirley Temple dancing pumps, stepped from the two silken circles on the bricks—one, two, primly, quickly, as she glanced over her shoulder, to see if they had been seen. She was wearing a black dress, severe, with long sleeves, that he had last seen her wear to a mutual friend's funeral. Tod stood and crumpled his handful of gossamer into his coat pocket. They walked on, her arm in his. He seemed taller, she softer. The stagy light webbed them, made her appear all circles. She said she could feel the wind on her cunt.

He had loved that shiver, that spasm she could not control; for love must attach to what we cannot help—the involuntary, the telltale, the fatal. Otherwise, the reasonableness and the mercy that would make our lives decent and orderly would overpower love, crush it, root it out, tumble it away like a striped tent pegged in sand.

Time passed. By sunlight, by a window, he suddenly saw a web, a radiating system, of wrinkles spread out from the corners of her eyes when she smiled. From her lips another set of creases, so delicate only the sun could trace them, spread upward; the two systems commingled on her cheeks. Time was interconnecting her features, which had been isolated in the spaces of her face by a certain absentminded perfection. She was growing old within their love, within their suffering. He examined a snapshot he had taken a year ago. A smooth, staring, unlistening face. Baby fat.

Tod liked her ageing, felt warmed by it, for it too was involuntary. It had happened to her with him, yet was not his fault. He wanted nothing to be his fault. This made her load double.

As mistress, she adapted well to the harrowing hours, the phone conversations that never end, the posing for indecent photographs, the heavy restaurant meals. She mainly missed of her former, decent, orderly life the minor blessings, such as shopping in the A & P without fear of being snubbed by a fellow-parishioner, or of encountering Tod's outraged wife across a pyramid of dog food.

Their spouses' fixed fury seemed rooted in a kind of professional incredulity; it was as if they had each been specialists (a repairer of Cyrillic typewriters, or a gerbil currier) whose specialty was so narrow there had been no need to do it very well.

But how he loved dancing with Pumpkin! She was so solid on her feet, her weight never on him, however close he held her. She tried to teach him to waltz; her husband having been a dashing, long-legged waltzer. But Tod could not learn: the wrong foot, the foot that had just received his weight, would dart out again, as if permanently appointed Chief Foot, at the start of the new trio of steps; he was a binary computer trying to learn left-handedness from a mirror.

So Tod too had his gaps, his spaces. He could not learn to repeat himself. He could do everything only once.

On a hotel bed, for variety, he sat astride her chest and masturbated her, idly at first, then urgingly, the four fingers of his right hand vying in massage of her electric fur, until her hips began to rock and she came, shivering. He understood that shivering better now. He was the conduit, the open window, by which, on rare occasions, she felt the *ventus Dei.* In the center of her sensuality, she was God's plaything.

And then, in another sort of wind, she would rage, lifted above reason; she would rage in spirals of indignation and frenzy fed from within, her voice high, a hurled stone frozen at the zenith of its arc, a mask of petulance clamped so hard upon her face that the skin around the lips went quite white. Strange little obstructions set her off, details in her arrangements with her husband; it was a fault, a failure, Tod felt, in himself, not to afford her an excuse for such passion. She would stare beyond him, exhausted in the end as if biologically, by the satisfaction of a cycle. It fairly frightened him, such a whirlwind; it blew, and blew itself out, in a region of her where he had never lived. An island, but in a desert. Her lips and eye-whites would look parched afterwards.

Sometimes it occurred to him that not everyone could love this woman. This did not frighten him. It made him feel like a child still young enough to be proud that he has been given a special assignment.

And yet he felt great rest with her. Her body beside his, he would fall in the spaces of her, sink, relax, one of her cool hands held at his chest, and the other, by a physical miracle he never troubled to analyze, lightly clasped above his head, by the hand of his of which the arm was crooked beneath his head as a pillow. How her arm put her hand there, he never could see, for his back was turned, his buttocks nestled in her lap. Sleep would sweep them away simultaneously, like mingled heaps of detritus.

Though in college a Soc. Sci. major, and in adult life a do-gooder, she ceased to read a newspaper. When her husband left, the subscription lapsed. Whereas Tod, sleeping with her, his consciousness diffused among the vast sacred spaces of her oblivion, dreamt of statesmen, of Gerald Ford and Giscard d'Estaing, of the great: John Lennon had a comradely arm about him, and Richard Burton, murmuring with his resonant actor's accent, was seeking marital advice.

Sometimes her storms of anger and her repetitions threatened to drive him away, as the blows in his ribs had offered to do. (Was that why he held her hands, sleeping—a protective clinch?) And he thought of organizing a retreat from sexuality, a concession of indefensible territory: Kutuzov after Borodino, Thieu before Danang. A magnificent simplification.

But then, a hideous emptiness. "O Pumpkin," he would moan in the dark, "never leave me. Never: promise." And the child within him would cringe with a terror for which, when daylight dawned bleak on the scattered realities of their situation, he would silently blame her, and hope to make her pay.

They became superb at being tired with one another. They competed in exhaustion. "Oh, God, Princess, how long can this go on?" Their conversations were so boring. Them. Us. Us and them others. The neighbors, the children, the children's teachers, the lawyers' wives' investment brokers' children's piano teachers. "It's killing me," she cheerfully admitted. Away from her, he would phone when she was asleep. She would phone in turn when he was napping. Together at last, they would run to the bed, hardened invalids fighting for the fat pillow, for the side by the window, with its light and air. They lay on their rumpled white plinth, surrounded by ashtrays and books, subjects of a cosmic quarantine.

First thing in the morning, Pumpkin would light a cigarette. Next thing, Tod would scold. She wanted to kill herself, to die. He took this as a personal insult. She was killing herself to make him look bad. She told him not to be silly, and inhaled. She had her habits, her limits. She had her abilities and her disabilities. She could not pronounce the word "realtor." She could spread her toes to make a tense little monkey's foot, a foot trying to become a star. He would ask her to do this.

Grimacing pridefully, she would oblige, first the right foot, then the left, holding them high off the sheets, the toe tendons white with the effort, her toenails round and bridal as confetti bits. He would laugh, and love, and laugh again. He would ask her to say the word "realtor."

She would refuse. This tiny refusal stunned him. A blow to the heart. They must be perfect, must. He would beg. He had wagered his whole life, his happiness and the happiness of the world around him, on this, this little monkey's stunt she would not do. Just one word. "Realtor."

Still she refused, primly, princesslike; her eyes brushed by his in a terrible icy hurry. He could pronounce "realtor" if he wanted, she chose not to.

She had her severe limitations.

And yet, and yet. One forenoon, unforeseen, he felt her beside him and she was of a piece, his. They were standing somewhere, in a run-down section of the city, themselves tired, looking at nothing, and her presence beside him was like the earth's beneath his feet, continuous, extensive and dry, there by its own rights, unthinkingly assumed to be there. She had become his wife.

Edna O'Brien

ΤHE LOVE OBJECT

He simply said my name. He said "Martha," and once again I could feel it happening. My legs trembled under the big white cloth and my head became fuzzy, though I was not drunk. It's how I fall in love. He sat opposite. The love object. Elderly. Blue eyes. Khaki hair. The hair was graying on the outside and he had spread the outer gray ribs across the width of his head as if to disguise the khaki, the way some men disguise a patch of baldness. He had what I call a very religious smile. An inner smile that came on and off, governed as it were by his private joy in what he heard or saw: a remark I made, the waiter removing the cold dinner plates that served as ornament and bringing warmed ones of a different design, the nylon curtain blowing inward and brushing my bare, summer-ripened arm. It was the end of a warm London summer.

"I'm not mad about them, either," he said. We were engaged in a bit of backbiting. Discussing a famous couple we both knew. He kept his hands joined all the time as if they were being put to prayer. There were no barriers between us. We were strangers. I am a television announcer; we had met to do a job, and out of courtesy he asked me to dinner. He told me about his wife— who was thirty like me—and how he knew he would marry her the very first moment he set eyes on her. (She was his third wife.) I made no inquiries as to what she looked like. I still don't know. The only memory I have of her is of her arms sheathed in big, mauve, crocheted sleeves; the image runs away with me and I see his pink, praying hands vanishing into those sleeves and the two of them waltzing in some large, grim room, smiling rapturously at their good fortune in being together. But that came much later.

We had a pleasant supper and figs for afters. The first figs I'd ever tasted. He tested them gently with his fingers, then put three on my side plate. I kept staring down at their purple-black skins, because with the shaking I could not trust myself to peel them. He took my mind off my nervousness by telling me a little story about a girl who was being interviewed on the radio and admitted to owning thirty-seven pairs of shoes and buying a new dress every Saturday, which she later endeavored to sell to friends or family. Somehow I knew that it was a story he had specially selected for me and also that he would not risk telling it to many people. He was in his way a serious man, and famous, though that is hardly of interest when one is telling about a love affair. Or is it? Anyhow, without peeling it, I bit into one of the figs.

How do you describe a taste? They were a new food and he was a new man and that night in my bed he was both stranger and lover, which I used to think was the ideal bed partner.

In the morning he was quite formal but unashamed; he even asked for a clothes brush because there was a smudge of powder on his jacket where we had embraced in the taxi coming home. At the time I had no idea whether or not we would sleep together, but on the whole I felt that we would not. I have never owned a clothes brush. I own books and records and various bottles of scent and beautiful clothes, but I never buy cleaning stuffs or aids for prolonging property. I expect it is improvident, but I just throw things away. Anyhow, he dabbed the powder smear with his handkerchief and it came off quite easily. The other thing he needed was a piece of sticking plaster because a new shoe had cut his heel. I looked but there was none left in the tin.

My children had cleared it out during the long summer holidays. In fact, for a moment I saw my two sons throughout those summer days, slouched on chairs, reading comics, riding bicycles, wrestling, incurring cuts which they promptly covered with Elastoplast, and afterward, when the plasters fell, flaunting the brown-rimmed marks as proof of their valor. I missed them badly and longed to hold them in my arms— another reason why I welcomed his company. "There's no plaster left," I said, not without shame. I thought how he would think me neglectful. I wondered if I ought to explain why my sons were at boarding school when they were still so young. They were eight and ten. But I didn't. I had ceased to want to tell people the tale of how my marriage had ended and my husband, unable to care for two young boys, insisted on boarding school in order to give them, as he put it, a stabilizing influence. I believed it was done in order to deprive me of the pleasure of their company. I couldn't.

We had breakfast outdoors. The start of another warm day. The dull haze that precedes heat hung from the sky, and in the garden next door the sprinklers were already on. My neighbors are fanatic gardeners. He ate three pieces of toast and some bacon. I ate also, just to put him at his ease, though normally I skip breakfast. "I'll stock up with plaster, clothes brush, and cleaning fluids," I said. My way of saying, "You'll come again?" He saw through it straightaway. Hurrying down the mouthful of toast, he put one of his prayer hands over mine and told me solemnly and nicely that he would not have a mean and squalid little affair with me, but that we would meet in a month or so and he hoped we would become friends. I hadn't thought of us as friends, but it was an interesting possibility. I remembered the earlier part of our evening's conversation and his referring to his earlier wives and his older grown-up children, and I thought how honest and unnostalgic he was. I was really sick of sorrows and people multiplying them even to themselves. Another thing he did that endeared him was to fold back the green silk bedspread, a thing I never do myself.

When he left I felt quite buoyant and in a way relieved. It had been nice and there were no nasty aftereffects. My face was pink from kissing and my hair tossed from our exertions. I looked a little wanton. Feeling tired from such a broken night's sleep, I drew the curtains and got back into bed. I had a nightmare. The usual one, where I am being put to death by a man. People tell me that a nightmare is healthy and from that experience I believe it. I wakened calmer than I had been for months and passed the remainder of the day happily.

Two mornings later he rang and asked was there a chance of our meeting that night. I said yes, because I was not doing anything and it seemed appropriate to have supper and seal our secret decently. But we started recharging.

"We did have a very good time," he said. I could feel myself making little petrified moves denoting love, shyness; opening my eyes wide to look at him, exuding trust. This time he peeled the figs for both of us. We positioned our legs so that they touched and withdrew them shortly afterward, confident that our desires were flowing. He brought me home. I noticed when we were in bed that he had put cologne on his shoulder and I thought that he must have set out to dinner with the hope if not the intention of sleeping with me. I liked the taste of his skin better than the foul chemical and I had to tell him so. He just laughed. Never had I been so at ease with a man. For the record, I had slept with four other men, but there always seemed to be a distance between us, conversation-wise. I mused for a moment on their various smells as I inhaled his, which reminded me of some herb. It was not parsley, not thyme, not mint, but some nonexistent herb compounded of these three smells. On this second occasion our lovemaking was more relaxed.

"What will you do if you make an avaricious woman out of me?" I asked.

"I will pass you on to someone very dear and suitable," he said. We coiled together, and with my head on his shoulder I thought of pigeons under the railway bridge nearby, who passed their nights nestled together, heads folded into mauve breasts. In his sleep we kissed and murmured. I did not sleep. I never do when I am overhappy, over-unhappy, or in bed with a strange man.

Neither of us said, "Well, here we are, having a mean and squalid little affair." We just started to meet. Regularly. We stopped going to restaurants because of his being famous. He would come to my house for dinner. I'll never forget the flurry of those preparations—putting flowers in vases, changing the sheets, thumping knots out of pillows, trying to cook, putting on makeup, and keeping a hairbrush nearby in case he arrived early. The agony of it! It was with difficulty that I answered the doorbell when it finally rang.

"You don't know what an oasis this is," he would say. And then in the hallway he would put his hands on my shoulders and squeeze them through my thin dress and say, "Let me look at you," and I would hang my head, both because I was overwhelmed and because I wanted to be. We would kiss, often for a full five minutes. He kissed the inside of my nostrils. Then we would move to the sitting room and sit on the chaise longue still speechless. He would touch the bone of my knee and say what beautiful knees I had. He saw and admired parts of me that no other man had ever bothered with. Soon after supper we went to bed.

Once, he came unexpectedly in the late afternoon when I was dressed to go out. I was going to the theater with another man.

"How I wish I were taking you," he said.

"We'll go to the theater one night?" He bowed his head. We would. It was the first time his eyes looked sad. We did not make love because I was made up and had my false eyelashes on and it seemed impractical. He said, "Has any man ever told you that to see a woman you desire when you cannot do a thing about it leaves you with an ache?"

The ache conveyed itself to me and stayed all through the theater. I felt angry for not having gone to bed with him, and later I regretted it even more, because from that evening onward our meetings were fewer. His wife, who had been in France with their children, returned. I knew this when he arrived one evening in a motorcar and in the course of conversation mentioned that his small daughter had that day peed over an important document. I can tell you now that he was a lawyer.

From then on it was seldom possible to meet at night. He made afternoon dates and at very short notice. Any night he did stay, he arrived with a travel bag containing toothbrush, clothes brush, and a few things a man might need for an overnight, loveless stay in a provincial hotel. I expect she packed it. I thought, How ridiculous. I felt no pity for her. In fact, the mention of her name—it was Helen—

made me angry. He said it very harmlessly. He said they'd been burgled in the middle of the night and he'd gone down in his pajamas while his wife telephoned the police from the extension upstairs.

"They only burgle the rich," I said hurriedly, to change the conversation. It was reassuring to find that he wore pajamas with her, when he didn't with me. My jealousy of her was extreme, and of course grossly unfair. Still, I would be giving the wrong impression if I said her existence blighted our relationship at that point. Because it didn't. He took great care to speak like a single man, and he allowed time after our lovemaking to stay for an hour or so and depart at his leisure. In fact, it is one of those after-love sessions that I consider the cream of our affair. We were sitting on the bed, naked, eating smoked-salmon sandwiches. I had lighted the gas fire because it was well into autumn and the afternoons got chilly. The fire made a steady, purring noise. It was the only light in the room. It was the first time he noticed the shape of my face, because he said that up to then my coloring had drawn all of his admiration. His face and the mahogany chest and the pictures also looked better. Not rosy, because the gas fire did not have that kind of glow, but resplendent with a whitish light. The goatskin rug underneath the window had a special luxurious softness. I remarked on it. He happened to say that he had a slight trace of masochism, and that often, unable to sleep at night in a bed, he would go to some other room and lie on the floor with a coat over him and fall fast asleep. A thing he'd done as a boy. The image of the little boy sleeping on the floor moved me to enormous compassion, and without a word from him, I led him across to the goatskin and laid him down. It was the only time our roles were reversed. He was not my father. I became his mother. Soft and totally fearless. Even my nipples, about which I am squeamish, did not shrink from his rabid demands. I wanted to do everything and anything for him. As often happens with lovers, my ardor and inventiveness stimulated his. We stopped at nothing. Afterward, remarking on our achievement—a thing he always did—he reckoned it was the most intimate of all our intimate moments. I was inclined to agree. As we stood up to get dressed, he wiped his armpits with the white blouse I had been wearing and asked which of my lovely dresses I would wear to dinner that night. He chose my black one for

me. He said it gave him great pleasure to know that although I was
to dine with others my mind would ruminate on what he and I had
done. A wife, work, the world, might separate us, but in our thoughts
we were betrothed.

"I'll think of you," I said.

"And I, of you."

We were not even sad at parting.

It was after that I had what I can only describe as a dream within
a dream. I was coming out of sleep, forcing myself awake, wiping my
saliva on the pillow slip, when something pulled me, an enormous
weight dragged me down into the bed, and I thought: I have become
infirm. I have lost the use of my limbs and this accounts for my list-
lessness for several months when I've wanted to do nothing except drink
tea and stare out the window. I am a cripple. All over. Even my mouth
won't move. Only my brain is ticking away. My brain tells me that a
woman downstairs doing the ironing is the only one who could locate
me, but she might not come upstairs for days, she might think I'm in
bed with a man, committing a sin. From time to time I sleep with a
man, but normally I sleep alone. She'll leave the ironed clothes on the
kitchen table, and the iron itself upright on the floor so that it won't
set fire to anything. Blouses will be on hangers, their frilled collars
white and fluid like foam. She's the sort of woman who even irons the
toes and heels of nylon stockings. She'll slip away, until Thursday, her
next day in. I feel something at my back or, strictly speaking, tugging
at my bedcovers, which I have mounted right up the length of my back
to cover my head. For shelter. And I know now that it's not infirmity
that's dragging me down, but a man. How did he get in there? He's
on the inside, near the wall. I know what he's going to do to me, and
the woman downstairs won't ever come to rescue me, she'd be too
ashamed or she might not think I want to be rescued. I don't know
which of the men it is, whether it's the big tall bruiser that's at the
door every time I open it innocently, expecting it's the laundry boy and
find it's Him, with an old black carving knife, its edge glittering because
he's just sharpened it on a step. Before I can scream, my tongue isn't
mine anymore. Or it might be the Other One. Tall too, he gets me by
my bracelet as I slip between the banisters of the stairs. I've forgotten

that I am not a little girl anymore and that I don't slip easily between banisters. If the bracelet snapped in two I would have made my escape, leaving him with one half of a gold bracelet in his hand, but my goddamn provident mother had a safety chain put on it because it was nine-carat. Anyhow, he's in the bed. It will go on forever, the thing he wants. I daren't turn around to look at him. Then something gentle about the way the sheet is pulled down suggests that he might be the New One. The man I met a few weeks ago. Not my type at all, tiny broken veins on his cheeks, and red, actually red, hair. We were on a goatskin. But it was raised off the ground, high as a bed. I had been doing most of the loving; breasts, hands, mouth, all yearned to minister to him. I felt so sure, never have I felt so sure of the rightness of what I was doing. Then he started kissing me down there and I came to his lapping tongue and his head was under my buttocks and it was like I was bearing him, only there was pleasure instead of pain. He trusted me. We were two people, I mean, he wasn't someone on me, smothering me, doing something I couldn't see. I could see. I could have shat on his red hair if I wanted. He trusted me. He stretched the come to the very last. And all the things that I loved up to then, like glass or lies, mirrors and feathers, and pearl buttons, and silk, and willow trees, became secondary compared with what he'd done. He was lying so that I could see it: so delicate, so thin, with a bunch of worried blue veins along its sides. Talking to it was like talking to a little child. The light in the room was a white glow. He'd made me very soft and wet, so I put it in. It was quick and hard and forceful, and he said, "I'm not considering you now, I think we've considered you," and I said that was perfectly true and that I liked him roughing away. I said it. I was no longer a hypocrite, no longer a liar. Before that he had often remonstrated with me, he had said, "There are words we are not going to use to each other, words such as 'Sorry' and 'Are you angry?'" I had used these words a lot. So I think from the gentle shuffle of the bedcovers—like a request really—that it might be him, and if it is I want to sink down and down into the warm, dark, sleepy pit of the bed and stay in it forever, coming with him. But I am afraid to look in case it is not Him but One of the Others.

When I finally woke up I was in a panic and I had a dreadful urge to telephone him, but though he never actually forbade it, I knew he would have been most displeased.

When something has been perfect, as our last encounter in the gaslight had been, there is a tendency to try hard to repeat it. Unfortunately, the next occasion was clouded. He came in the afternoon and brought a suitcase containing all the paraphernalia for a dress dinner which he was attending that night. When he arrived he asked if he could hang up his tails, as otherwise they would be very creased. He hooked the hanger on the outer rim of the wardrobe, and I remember being impressed by the row of war medals along the top pocket. Our time in bed was pleasant but hasty. He worried about getting dressed. I just sat and watched him. I wanted to ask about his medals and how he had merited them, and if he remembered the war, and if he'd missed his then wife, and if he'd killed people, and if he still dreamed about it. But I asked nothing. I sat there as if I were paralyzed.

"No braces," he said as he held the wide black trousers around his middle. His other trousers must have been supported by a belt.

"I'll go to Woolworth's for some," I said. But that was impractical because he was already in danger of being late. I got a safety pin and fastened the trousers from the back. It was a difficult operation because the pin was not really sturdy enough.

"You'll bring it back?" I said. I am superstitious about giving people pins. He took some time to reply because he was muttering "Damn" under his breath. Not to me. But to the stiff, inhuman, starched collar, which would not yield to the little gold studs he had wanted to pierce through. I tried. He tried. Each time when one of us failed the other became impatient. He said if we went on, the collar would be grubby from our hands. And that seemed a worse alternative. I thought he must be dining with very critical people, but of course I did not give my thoughts on the matter. In the end we each managed to get a stud through and he had a small sip of whiskey as a celebration. The bow tie was another ordeal. He couldn't do it. I daren't try.

"Haven't you done it before?" I said. I expect his wives—in succession—had done it for him. I felt such a fool. Then a lump of hatred. I thought how ugly and pink his legs were, how repellent the shape of his body, which did not have anything in the way of a waist, how deceitful his eyes, which congratulated him in the mirror when he succeeded in making a clumsy bow. As he put on the coat the sound of the medals tinkling enabled me to remark on their music. There was so little I could say. Lastly he donned a white silk scarf that came below his middle. He looked like someone I did not know. He left hurriedly. I ran with him down the road to help get a taxi, and trying to keep up with him and chatter was not easy. All I can remember is the ghostly sight of the very white scarf swinging back and forth as we rushed. His shoes, which were patent, creaked unsuitably.

"Is it all-male?" I asked.

"No. Mixed," he replied.

So that was why we hurried. To meet his wife at some appointed place. The hatred began to grow.

He did bring back the safety pin, but my superstition remained, because four straight pins with black rounded tops that had come off his new shirt were on my window ledge. He refused to take them. *He* was not superstitious.

Bad moments, like good ones, tend to be grouped together, and when I think of the dress occasion, I also think of the other time when we were not in utter harmony. It was on a street; we were searching for a restaurant. We had to leave my house because a friend had come to stay and we would have been obliged to tolerate her company. Going along the street—it was October and very windy—I felt that he was angry with me for having drawn us out into the cold where we could not embrace. My heels were very high and I was ashamed of the hollow sound they made. In a way I felt we were enemies. He looked in the windows of restaurants to see if any acquaintances of his were there. Two restaurants he decided against, for reasons best known to himself. One looked to be very attractive. It had orange bulbs inset in the walls and the light came through small squares of iron grating. We crossed the road to look at places on the opposite side. I saw a group of rowdies coming toward us, and for something to say—what with my aggressive heels, the wind, traffic going by, the ugly unromantic street, we had run out of agreeable conversation—I asked if he ever felt apprehensive about encountering noisy groups like that, late at night. He said that in fact a few nights before he had been walking home very late and

saw such a group coming toward him, and before he even registered
fear, he found that he had splayed his bunch of keys between his fingers
and had his hand, armed with the sharp points of the keys, ready to
pull out of his pocket should they have threatened him. I suppose he
did it again while we were walking along. Curiously enough, I did not
feel he was my protector. I only felt that he and I were two people,
that there was in the world trouble, violence, sickness, catastrophe, that
he faced it in one way and that I faced it—or to be exact, that I shrank
from it—in another. We would always be outside one another. In the
course of that melancholy thought the group went by, and my conjecture
about violence was all for nothing. We found a nice restaurant and
drank a lot of wine.

Later our lovemaking, as usual, was perfect. He stayed all night. I
used to feel specially privileged on the nights he stayed, and the only
little thing that lessened my joy was spasms of anxiety in case he should
have told his wife he was at such and such a hotel and her telephoning
there and not finding him. More than once I raced into an imaginary
narrative where she came and discovered us and I acted silent and
ladylike and he told her very crisply to wait outside until he was ready.
I felt no pity for her. Sometimes I wondered if we would ever meet or
if in fact we had already met on an escalator at some point. Though
that was unlikely, because we lived at opposite ends of London.

Then to my great surprise the opportunity came. I was invited to
a Thanksgiving party given by an American magazine. He saw the
card on my mantelpiece and said, "You're going to that, too?" and I
smiled and said maybe. Was he? "Yes," he said. He tried to make me
reach a decision there and then but I was too canny. Of course I would
go. I was curious to see his wife. I would meet him in public. It shocked
me to think that we had never met in the company of any other person.
It was like being shut off . . . a little animal locked away. I thought
very distinctly of a ferret that a forester used to keep in a wooden box
with a sliding top, when I was a child, and of another ferret being
brought to mate with it once. The thought made me shiver. I mean, I
got it confused; I thought of white ferrets with their little pink nostrils
in the same breath as I thought of him sliding a door back and slipping
into my box from time to time. His skin had a lot of pink in it.

"I haven't decided," I said, but when the day came I went. I took a lot of trouble with my appearance, had my hair set, and wore virginal attire. Black and white. The party was held in a large room with paneled walls of brown wood; blown-up magazine covers were along the panels. The bar was at one end, under a balcony. The effect was of shrunken barmen in white, lost underneath the cliff of the balcony, which seemed in danger of collapsing on them. A more unlikely room for a party I have never seen. There were women going around with trays, but I had to go to the bar because there was champagne on the trays and I have a preference for whiskey. A man I knew conducted me there, and en route another man placed a kiss on my back. I hoped that he witnessed this, but it was such a large room with hundreds of people around that I had no idea where he was. I noticed a dress I quite admired, a mauve dress with very wide crocheted sleeves. Looking up the length of the sleeves, I saw its owner's eyes directed on me. Perhaps she was admiring my outfit. People with the same tastes often do. I have no idea what her face looked like, but later when I asked a girlfriend which was his wife, she pointed to this woman with the crocheted sleeves. The second time I saw her in profile. I still don't know what she looked like, nor do those eyes into which I looked speak to my memory with anything special, except, perhaps, slight covetousness.

Finally, I searched him out. I had a mutual friend walk across with me and apparently introduce me. He was unwelcoming. He looked strange, the flush on his cheekbones vivid and unnatural. He spoke to the mutual friend and virtually ignored me. Possibly to make amends he asked, at length, if I was enjoying myself.

"It's a chilly room," I said. I was referring of course to his manner. Had I wanted to describe the room I would have used "grim," or some such adjective.

"I don't know about you being chilly but I'm certainly not," he said with aggression. Then a very drunk woman in a sack dress came and took his hand and began to slobber over him. I excused myself and went off. He said most pointedly that he hoped he would see me again sometime.

I caught his eye just as I left the party, and I felt both sorry for him and angry with him. He looked stunned, as if important news had just been delivered to him. He saw me leave with a group of people and I stared at him without the whimper of a smile. Yes, I was sorry for him. I was also piqued. The very next day when we met and I brought it up, he did not even remember that a mutual friend had introduced us.

"Clement Hastings!" he said, repeating the man's name. Which goes to show how nervous he must have been.

It is impossible to insist that bad news delivered in a certain manner and at a certain time will have a less awful effect. But I feel that I got my walking papers from him at the wrong moment. For one thing, it was morning. The clock went off and I sat up wondering when he had set it. Being on the outside of the bed, he was already attending to the push button.

"I'm sorry, darling," he said.

"Did you set it?" I said, indignant. There was an element of betrayal here, as if he'd wanted to sneak away without saying goodbye.

"I must have," he said. He put his arm around me and we lay back again. It was dark outside and there was a feeling—though this may be memory feeling—of frost.

"Congratulations, you're getting your prize today," he whispered. I was being given an award for my announcing.

"Thank you," I said. I was ashamed of it. It reminded me of being back at school and always coming first in everything and being guilty about this but not disciplined enough to deliberately hold back.

"It's beautiful that you stayed all night," I said. I was stroking him all over. My hands were never still in bed. Awake or asleep, I constantly caressed him. Not to excite him, simply to reassure and comfort him and perhaps to consolidate my ownership. There is something about holding on to things that I find therapeutic. For hours I hold smooth stones in the palm of my hand or I grip the sides of an armchair and feel the better for it. He kissed me. He said he had never known anyone so sweet or so attentive. Encouraged, I began to do something very intimate. I heard his sighs of pleasure, the "oy, oy" of delight when he was both indulging it and telling himself that he mustn't. At first I was unaware of his speaking voice.

"Hey," he said jocularly, just like that. "This can't go on, you know." I thought he was referring to our activity at that moment, because of course it was late and he would have to get up shortly. Then I raised my head from its sunken position between his legs and I looked at him through my hair, which had fallen over my face. I saw that he was serious.

"It just occurred to me that possibly you love me," he said. I nodded and pushed my hair back so that he would read it, my testimony, clear and clean upon my face. He put me lying down so that our heads were side by side and he began:

"I adore you, but I'm not in love with you; with my commitments I don't think I could be in love with anyone; it all started gay and lighthearted . . ." Those last few words offended me. It was not how I saw it or how I remembered it: the numerous telegrams he sent me saying, "I long to see you," or "May the sun shine on you," the first few moments each time when we met and were overcome with passion, shyness, and the shock of being so disturbed by each other's presence. We had even searched in our dictionaries for words to convey the specialness of our regard for each other. He came up with "cense," which meant to adore or cover with the perfume of love. It was a most appropriate word, and we used it over and over again. Now he was negating all this. He was talking about weaving me into his life, his family life . . . becoming a friend. He said it, though, without conviction. I could not think of a single thing to say. I knew that if I spoke I would be pathetic, so I remained silent. When he'd finished I stared straight ahead at the split between the curtains, and looking at the beam of raw light coming through, I said, "I think there's frost outside," and he said that possibly there was, because winter was upon us. We got up, and as usual he took the bulb out of the bedside lamp and plugged in his razor. I went off to get breakfast. That was the only morning I forgot about squeezing orange juice for him and I often wonder if he took it as an insult. He left just before nine.

The sitting room held the traces of his visit. Or, to be precise, the remains of his cigars. In one of the blue, saucer-shaped ashtrays there were thick turds of dark-gray cigar ash. There were also stubs, but it was the ash I kept looking at, thinking that its thickness resembled the thickness of his unlovely legs. And once again I experienced hatred for him. I was about to tip the contents of the ashtray into the fire grate when something stopped me, and what did I do but get an empty lozenge box and with the aid of a sheet of paper lift the clumps of ash in there and carry the tin upstairs. With the movement the turds lost their shape, and whereas they had reminded me of his legs, they were now an even mass of dark-gray ash, probably like the ashes of the dead. I put the tin in a drawer underneath some clothes.

Later in the day I was given my award—a very big silver medallion with my name on it. At the party afterward I got drunk. My friends tell me that I did not actually disgrace myself, but I have a humiliating recollection of beginning a story and not being able to go ahead with it, not because the contents eluded me, but because the words became too difficult to pronounce. A man brought me home, and after I'd made him a cup of tea, I said good night over-properly; then when he was gone I staggered to my bed. When I drink heavily I sleep badly. It was still dark outside when I woke up and straightaway I remembered the previous morning and the suggestion of frost outside, and his cold warning words. I had to agree. Although our meetings were perfect, I had a sense of doom impending, of a chasm opening up between us, of someone telling his wife, of souring love, of destruction. And still we hadn't gone as far as we should have gone. There were peaks of joy and of its opposite that we should have climbed to, but the time was not left to us. He had of course said, "You still have a great physical hold over me," and that in its way I found degrading. To have gone on making love when he had discarded me would have been repellent. It had come to an end. The thing I kept thinking of was a violet in a wood and how a time comes for it to drop off and die. The frost may have had something to do with my thinking, or rather, with my musing. I got up and put on a dressing gown. My head hurt from the hangover, but I knew that I must write to him while I had some resolution. I know my own failings, and I knew that before the day was out I would want to see him again, sit with him, coax him back with sweetness and my overwhelming helplessness.

I wrote the note and left out the bit about the violet. It is not a thing you can put down on paper without seeming fanciful. I said if he didn't think it prudent to see me, then not to see me. I said it had been a nice interlude and that we must entertain good memories of it. It was a remarkably controlled letter. He wrote back promptly. My decision came as a shock, he said. Still, he admitted that I was right. In the middle of the letter he said he must penetrate my composure and to do so he must admit that above and beyond everything he loved me and would always do so. That of course was the word I had been snooping around for, for months. It set me off. I wrote a long letter back to him. I lost my head. I oversaid everything. I testified to loving him, to sitting on the edge of madness in the intervening days, to my hoping for a miracle.

It is just as well that I did not write out the miracle in detail, because possibly it is, or was, rather inhuman. It concerned his family.

He was returning from the funeral of his wife and children, wearing black tails. He also wore the white silk scarf I had seen him with, and there was a black mourning tulip in his buttonhole. When he came toward me I snatched the black tulip and replaced it with a white narcissus, and he in turn put the scarf around my neck and drew me toward him by holding its fringed ends. I kept moving my neck back and forth within the embrace of the scarf. Then we danced divinely on a wooden floor that was white and slippery. At times I thought we would fall, but he said, "You don't have to worry, I'm with you." The dance floor was also a road and we were going somewhere beautiful.

For weeks I waited for a reply to my letter, but there was none. More than once I had my hand on the telephone, but something cautionary—a new sensation for me—in the back of my mind bade me to wait. To give him time. To let regret take charge of his heart. To let him come of his own accord. And then I panicked. I thought that perhaps the letter had gone astray or had fallen into other hands. I'd posted it, of course, to the office in Lincoln's Inn where he worked. I wrote another. This time it was a formal note, and with it I enclosed a postcard with the words YES and NO. I asked if he had received my previous letter to kindly let me know by simply crossing out the word which did not apply on my card, and send it back to me. It came back with the NO crossed out. Nothing else. So he had received my letter. I think I looked at the card for hours. I could not stop shaking, and to calm myself I took several drinks. There was something so brutal about the card, but then you could say that I had asked for it by approaching the situation in that way. I took out the box with his ash in it and wept over it, and wanted both to toss it out of the window and to preserve it forevermore.

In general I behaved very strangely. I rang someone who knew him and asked for no reason at all what she thought his hobbies might be. She said he played the harmonium, which I found unbearable news altogether. Then I entered a black patch, and on the third day I lost control.

Well, from not sleeping and taking pep pills and whiskey, I got very odd. I was shaking all over and breathing very quickly, the way one might after witnessing an accident. I stood at my bedroom window, which is on the second floor, and looked at the concrete underneath. The only flowers left in bloom were the hydrangeas, and they had faded to a soft russet, which was much more fetching than the harsh pink they were all summer. In the garden next door there were frost hats over the fuchsias. Looking first at the hydrangeas, then at the fuchsias, I tried to estimate the consequences of my jumping. I wondered if the drop was great enough. Being physically awkward, I could only conceive of injuring myself fatally, which would be worse, because I would then be confined to my bed and imprisoned with the very thoughts that were driving me to desperation. I opened the window and leaned out, but quickly drew back. I had a better idea. There was a plumber downstairs installing central heating—an enterprise I had embarked upon when my lover began to come regularly and we liked walking around naked eating sandwiches and playing records. I decided to gas myself and to seek the help of the plumber in order to do it efficiently. I am aware —someone must have told me—that there comes a point in the middle of the operation when the doer regrets it and tries to withdraw but cannot. That seemed like an extra note of tragedy that I had no wish to experience. So I decided to go downstairs to this man and explain to him that I *wanted* to die, and that I was not telling him simply for him to prevent me, or console me, that I was not looking for pity— there comes a time when pity is of no help—and that I simply wanted his assistance. He could show me what to do, settle me down, and—

303

THE

LOVE

OBJECT

this is absurd—be around to take care of the telephone and the doorbell for the next few hours. Also to dispose of me with dignity. Above all, I wanted that. I even decided what I would wear: a long dress, which in fact was the same color as the hydrangeas in their russet phase and which I've never worn except for a photograph or on television. Before going downstairs, I wrote a note which said simply: "I am committing suicide through lack of intelligence, and through not knowing, not learning to know, how to live."

You will think I am callous not to have taken the existence of my children into account. But, in fact, I did. Long before the affair began, I had reached the conclusion that they had been parted from me irrevocably by being sent to boarding school. If you like, I felt I had let them down years before. I thought—it was an unhysterical admission—that my being alive or my being dead made little difference to the course of their lives. I ought to say that I had not seen them for a month, and it is a shocking fact that although absence does not make love less, it cools down our physical need for the ones we love. They were due home for their mid-term holiday that very day, but since it was their father's turn to have them, I knew that I would only see them for a few hours one afternoon. And in my despondent state that seemed worse than not seeing them at all.

Well, of course, when I went downstairs the plumber took one look at me and said, "You could do with a cup of tea." He actually had tea made. So I took it and stood there warming my child-sized hands around the barrel of the brown mug. Suddenly, swiftly, I remembered my lover measuring our hands when we were lying in bed and saying that mine were no bigger than his daughter's. And then I had another and less edifying memory about hands. It was the time we met when he was visibly distressed because he'd caught those same daughter's hands in a motorcar door. The fingers had not been broken but were badly bruised, and he felt awful about it and hoped his daughter would forgive him. Upon being told the story, I bolted off into an anecdote about almost losing *my* fingers in the door of someone's Jaguar. It was pointless, although a listener might infer from it that I was a boastful and heartless girl. I would have been sorry for any child whose fingers were caught in a motorcar door, but at that moment I was trying to recall him to the hidden world of him and me. Perhaps it was one of the things that made him like me less. Perhaps it was then he resolved to end the affair. I was about to say this to the plumber, to warn him about so-called love often hardening the heart, but like the violets, it is something that can miss awfully, and when it does two people are mortally embarrassed. He'd put sugar in my tea and I found it sickly.

"I want you to help me," I said.

"Anything," he said. I ought to know that. We were friends. He would do the pipes tastefully. The pipes would be little works of art and the radiators painted to match the walls.

"You may think I will paint these white, but in fact they will be light ivory," he said. The whitewash on the kitchen walls had yellowed a bit.

"I want to do myself in," I said hurriedly.

"Good God," he said, and then burst out laughing. He always knew I was dramatic. Then he looked at me, and obviously my face was a revelation. For one thing I could not control my breathing. He put his arm around me and led me into the sitting room and we had a drink. I knew he liked drink and thought, It's an ill wind that doesn't blow some good. The maddening thing was that I kept thinking a live person's thoughts. He said I had so much to live for. "A young girl like you— people wanting your autograph, a lovely new car," he said.

"It's all . . ." I groped for the word. I had meant to say "meaningless," but "cruel" was the word that came out.

"And your boys," he said. "What about your boys?" He had seen photographs of them, and once I'd read him a letter from one of them. The word "cruel" seemed to be blazing in my head. It screamed at me from every corner of the room. To avoid his glance, I looked down at the sleeve of my angora jersey and methodically began picking off pieces of fluff and rolling them into a little ball.

There was a moment's pause.

"This is an unlucky road. You're the third," he said.

"The third what?" I said, industriously piling the black fluff into my palm.

"A woman farther up; her husband was a bandleader, used to be out late. One night she went to the dance hall and saw him with another girl; she came home and did it straightaway."

"Gas?" I asked, genuinely curious.

"No, sedation," he said, and was off on another story, about a girl who'd gassed herself and was found by him because he was in the house treating dry rot at the time. "Naked, except for a jersey," he said, and speculated on why she should be attired like that. His manner changed considerably as he recalled how he went into the house, smelled gas, and searched it out.

I looked at him. His face was grave. He had scaled eyelids. I had never looked at him so closely before. "Poor Michael," I said. A feeble apology. I was thinking that if he had abetted my suicide he would then have been committed to the memory of it.

"A lovely young girl," he said, wistful.

"Poor girl," I said, mustering up pity.

There seemed to be nothing else to say. He had shamed me out of it. I stood up and made an effort at normality—I took some glasses off a side table and moved in the direction of the kitchen. If dirty glasses are any proof of drinking, then quite a lot of it had been done by me over the past few days.

"Well," he said, and rose and sighed. He admitted to feeling pleased with himself.

As it happened, there would have been a secondary crisis that day. Although my children were due to return to their father, he rang to say that the older boy had a temperature, and since—though he did not say this—he could not take care of a sick child, he would be obliged to bring them to my house. They arrived in the afternoon. I was waiting inside the door, with my face heavily made up to disguise my distress. The sick boy had a blanket draped over his tweed coat and one of his father's scarves around his face. When I embraced him, he began to cry. The younger boy went around the house to make sure that everything was as he had last seen it. Normally I had presents for them on their return home, but I had neglected it on this occasion, and consequently they were a little downcast.

"Tomorrow," I said.

"Why are there tears in your eyes?" the sick boy asked as I undressed him.

"Because you are sick," I said, telling a half-truth.

"Oh, Mamsies," he said, calling me by a name he had used for years. He put his arms around me and we both began to cry. I felt he was crying for the numerous unguessed afflictions that the circumstances of a broken home would impose upon him. It was strange and unsatisfying to hold him in my arms, when over the months I had got used to my lover's size—the width of his shoulders, the exact height of his body, which obliged me to stand on tiptoe so that our limbs could correspond perfectly. Holding my son, I was conscious only of how small he was and how tenaciously he clung.

The younger boy and I sat in the bedroom and played a game which entailed reading out questions such as "A river?" "A famous footballer?" and then spinning a disk until it steadied down at one letter and using that letter as the first initial of the river or the famous footballer or whatever the question called for. I was quite slow at it, and so was the sick boy. His brother won easily, although I had asked him to let the invalid win. Children are callous.

We all jumped when the heating came on, because the boiler, from the basement just underneath, gave an almighty churning noise and made the kind of sudden erupting move I had wanted to make that morning when I stood at the bedroom window and tried to pitch myself out. As a special surprise and to cheer me up, the plumber had called in two of his mates, and among them they got the job finished. To make us warm and happy, as he put it when he came to the bedroom to tell me. It was an awkward moment. I'd avoided him since our morning's drama. At teatime I'd even left his tea on a tray out on the landing. Would he tell other people how I had asked him to be my murderer? Would he have recognized it as that? I gave him and his friends a drink, and they stood uncomfortably in the children's bedroom and looked at the little boy's flushed face and said he would soon be better. What else could they say!

For the remainder of the evening, the boys and I played the quiz game over and over again, and just before they went to sleep I read them an adventure story. In the morning they both had temperatures.

I was busy nursing them for the next couple of weeks. I made beef tea a lot and broke bread into it and coaxed them to swallow those sops of savory bread. They were constantly asking to be entertained. The only thing I could think of in the way of facts were particles of nature lore I had gleaned from one of my colleagues in the television canteen. Even with embellishing, it took not more than two minutes to tell my children: of a storm of butterflies in Venezuela, of animals called sloths that are so lazy they hang from trees and become covered with moss, and of how the sparrows in England sing different from the sparrows in Paris.

"More," they would say. "More, more." Then we would have to play that silly game again or embark upon another adventure story.

At these times I did not allow my mind to wander, but in the evenings, when their father came, I used to withdraw to the sitting room and have a drink. Well, that was disastrous. The leisure enabled me to brood; also, I have very weak bulbs in the lamps and the dimness gives the room a quality that induces reminiscence. I would be transported back. I enacted various kinds of reunion with my lover, but my favorite one was an unexpected meeting in one of those tiled, inhuman, pedestrian subways and running toward each other and finding ourselves at a stairway which said (one in London actually does say), TO CENTRAL ISLAND ONLY, and laughing as we leaped up those stairs propelled by miraculous wings. In less indulgent phases, I regretted that we hadn't seen more sunsets, or cigarette advertisements, or something, because in memory our numerous meetings became one long uninterrupted state of lovemaking without the ordinariness of things in between to fasten those peaks. The days, the nights with him, seemed to have been sandwiched into a long, beautiful, but single night, instead of being stretched to the seventeen occasions it actually was. Ah, vanished peaks. Once I was so sure that he had come into the room that I tore off a segment of an orange I had just peeled, and handed it to him.

But from the other room I heard the low, assured voice of the children's father delivering information with the self-importance of a man delivering dogmas, and I shuddered at the degree of poison that lay between us when we'd once professed to love. Plagued love. Then, some of the feeling I had for my husband transferred itself to my lover, and I reasoned with myself that the letter in which he had professed to love me was sham, that he had merely written it when he thought he was free of me, but finding himself saddled once again, he withdrew and let me have the postcard. I was a stranger to myself. Hate was welling up. I wished multitudes of humiliation on him. I even plotted a dinner party that I would attend, having made sure that he was invited, and snubbing him throughout. My thoughts teetered between hate and the hope of something final between us, so that I would be certain of his feelings toward me. Even as I sat in a bus, an advertisement which caught my eye was immediately related to him. It said, DON'T PANIC. WE MEND, WE ADAPT, WE REMODEL. It was an advertisement for pearl stringing. I would mend and with vengeance.

I cannot say when it first began to happen, because that would be too drastic, and anyhow, I do not know. But the children were back at school, and we'd got over Christmas, and he and I had not exchanged cards. But I began to think less harshly of him. They were silly thoughts, really. I hoped he was having little pleasures like eating in restaurants, and clean socks, and red wine the temperature he liked it, and even— yes, even ecstasies in bed with his wife. These thoughts made me smile to myself inwardly, the new kind of smile I had discovered. I shuddered at the risk he'd run by seeing me at all. Of course, the earlier injured thoughts battled with these new ones. It was like carrying a taper along a corridor where the drafts are fierce and the chances of it staying alight pretty meager. I thought of him and my children in the same instant, their little foibles became his: my children telling me elaborate lies about their sporting feats, his slight puffing when we climbed steps and his trying to conceal it. The age difference between us must have saddened him. It was then I think that I really fell in love with him. His courtship of me, his telegrams, his eventual departure, even our lovemaking, were nothing compared with this new sensation. It rose like sap within me, it often made me cry, the fact that he could not benefit from it! The temptation to ring him had passed away.

His phone call came quite out of the blue. It was one of those times when I debated about answering it or not, because mostly I let it ring. He asked if we could meet, if, and he said this so gently, my nerves were steady enough. I said my nerves were never better. That was a liberty I had to take. We met in a café for tea. Toast again. Just like the beginning. He asked how I was. Remarked on my good complexion. Neither of us mentioned the incident of the postcard. Nor did he say what impulse had moved him to telephone. It may not have been impulse at all. He talked about his work and how busy he'd been, and then relayed a little story about taking an elderly aunt for a drive and driving so slowly that she asked him to please hurry up because she would have walked there quicker.

"You've recovered," he said then, suddenly. I looked at his face. I could see it was on his mind.

"I'm over it," I said, and dipped my finger into the sugar bowl and let him lick the white crystals off the tip of my finger. Poor man. I could not have told him anything else, he would not have understood. In a way it was like being with someone else. He was not the one who had folded back the bedspread and sucked me dry and left his cigar ash for preserving. He was the representative of that one.

"We'll meet from time to time," he said.

"Of course." I must have looked dubious.

"Perhaps you don't want to?"

"Whenever you feel you would like to." I neither welcomed nor dreaded the thought. It would not make any difference to how I felt. That was the first time it occurred to me that all my life I had feared imprisonment, the nun's cell, the hospital bed, the places where one faced the self without distraction, without the crutches of other people—but sitting there feeding him white sugar, I thought, I now have entered a cell, and this man cannot know what it is for me to love him the way I do, and I cannot weigh him down with it, because he is in another cell, confronted with other difficulties.

The cell reminded me of a convent, and for something to say, I mentioned my sister the nun.

"I went to see my sister."

"How is she?" he asked. He had often inquired about her. He used to take an interest in her and ask what she looked like. I even got the impression that he had a fantasy about seducing her.

"She's fine," I said. "We were walking down a corridor and she asked me to look around and make sure that there weren't any other sisters looking, and then she hoisted her skirts up and slid down the banister."

"Dear girl," he said. He liked that story. The smallest things gave him such pleasure.

I enjoyed our tea. It was one of the least fruitless afternoons I'd had in months, and coming out he gripped my arm and said how perfect it would be if we could get away for a few days. Perhaps he meant it.

In fact, we kept our promise. We do meet from time to time. You could say things are back to normal again. By normal I mean a state whereby I notice the moon, trees, fresh spit upon the pavement; I look at strangers and see in their expressions something of my own predicament; I am part of everyday life, I suppose. There is a lamp in my bedroom that gives out a dry crackle each time an electric train goes by, and at night I count those crackles because it is the time he comes back. I mean the real he: not the man who confronts me from time to time across a café table, but the man that dwells somewhere within me. He rises before my eyes—his praying hands, his tongue that liked to suck, his sly eyes, his smile, the veins on his cheeks, the calm voice speaking sense to me. I suppose you wonder why I torment myself like this with details of his presence, but I need it, I cannot let go of him now, because if I did, all our happiness and my subsequent pain—I cannot vouch for his—will all have been nothing, and nothing is a dreadful thing to hold on to.

Norman Rush

*I*NSTRUMENTS OF SEDUCTION

The name she was unable to remember was torturing her. She kept coming up with Bechamel, which was ridiculously wrong yet somehow close. It was important to her that she remember: a thing in a book by this man lay at the heart of her secret career as a seducer of men, three hundred and twelve of them. She was a seducer, not a seductress. The male form of the term was active. A seductress was merely someone who was seductive and who might or might not be awarded a victory. But a seducer was a professional, a worker, and somehow a record of success was embedded in the term. "Seducer" sounded like a credential. Game was afoot tonight. Remembering the name was part of the preparation. She had always prepared before tests.

Male or female, you couldn't be considered a seducer if you were below a certain age, had great natural beauty, or if you lacked a theory of what you were doing. Her body of theory began with a scene in the book she was feeling the impulse to reread. The book's title was lost in the mists of time. As she

313

remembered the scene, a doctor and perhaps the woman of the house are involved together in some emergency lifesaving operation. The woman has to assist. The setting is an apartment in Europe, in a city. The woman is not attractive. The doctor is. There has been shelling or an accident. The characters are disparate in every way and would never normally be appropriate for one another. The operation is described in upsetting detail. It's touch and go. When it's over, the doctor and the woman fall into one another's arms—to their own surprise. Some fierce tropism compels them. Afterward they part, never to follow up. The book was from the French. She removed the Atmos clock from the living room mantel and took it to the pantry to get it out of sight.

The scene had been like a flashbulb going off. She had realized that, in her seductions up to that point, she had been crudely and intuitively using the principle that the scene made explicit. Putting it bluntly, a certain atmosphere of allusion to death, death-fear, death threats, mystery pointing to death, was, in the right hands, erotic and could lead to a bingo. Of course, that was hardly all there was to it. The subject of what conditions conduce—that was her word for it— to achieving a bingo was immense. For example, should you strew your conversation with a few petals of French? The answer was not always yes, and depended on age and educational level. For some older types, France meant looseness and Pigalle. But for some it meant you were parading your education or your travel opportunities. One thing, it was never safe to roll your *R*s. She thought, Everything counts: chiaroscuro, no giant clocks in evidence and no wristwatches either, music or its absence, what they can assume about privacy and *le futur*. That was critical. You had to help them intuit you were acting from appetite, like a man, and that when it was over you would be yourself and not transformed before their eyes into a love-leech, a limbless tube of long- ing. You had to convince them that what was to come was, no question about it, a transgression, but that for you it was about at the level of eating between meals.

She was almost fifty. For a woman, she was old to be a seducer. The truth was that she had been on the verge of closing up shop. The corner of Bergen County they had lived in was scorched earth, pretty much. Then Frank had been offered a contract to advise African governments on dental care systems. They had come to Africa for two years.

In Botswana, where they were based, everything was unbelievably conducive. Frank was off in the bush or advising as far away as Lusaka or Gwelo for days and sometimes weeks at a time. So there was space. She could select. Gaborone was comfortable enough. And it was full of transient men: consultants, contractors, travelers of all kinds, seekers. Embassy men were assigned for two-year tours and knew they were going to be rotated away from the scene of the crime sooner rather than later. Wives were often absent. Either they were slow to arrive or they were incessantly away on rest and recreation in the United States or the Republic of South Africa. For expatriate men, the local women were a question mark. Venereal disease was pandemic, and local attitudes toward birth control came close to being surreal. She had abstained from Batswana men. She knew why. The very attractive ones seemed hard to get at. There was a feeling of danger in the proposition, probably irrational. The surplus of more familiar white types was a simple fact. In any case, there was still time. This place had been designed with her in mind. The furniture the government provided even looked like it came from a bordello. And Botswana was unnerving in some overall way there was only one word for: conducive. The country depended on copper and diamonds. Copper prices were sinking. There were too many diamonds of the wrong kind. Development projects were going badly and making people look bad, which made them nervous and susceptible. What was there to do at night? There was only one movie house in town. The movies came via South Africa and were censored to a fare-thee-well—no nudity, no blue language. She suspected that for American men the kind of heavy-handed dummkopf censorship they sat through at the Capitol Cinema was in fact stimulating. Frank was getting United States Government money, which made them semiofficial. She had to admit there was fun in foiling the eyes and ears of the embassy network. She would hate to leave.

Only one thing was sad. There was no one she could tell about her life. She had managed to have a remarkable life. She was ethical. She never brought Frank up or implied that Frank was the cause in any way of what she chose to do. Nor would she ever seduce a man who could conceivably be a recurrent part of Frank's life or sphere. She assumed feminists would hate her life if they knew. She would like to talk to feminists about vocation, about goal-setting, about using one's mind, about nerve and strength. Frank's ignorance was one of her feats. How many women could do what she had done? She was modestly endowed and now she was even old. She was selective. Sometimes she felt she would like to tell Frank, when it was really over, and see what he said. She would sometimes let herself think he would be proud, in a way, or that he could be convinced he should be. There was no one she could tell. Their daughter was a cow and a Lutheran. Her gentleman was late. She went into the pantry to check the time.

For this evening's adventure she was conceivably a little too high-priestess, but the man she was expecting was not a subtle person. She was wearing a narrowly cut white silk caftan, a seed-pod necklace, and sandals. The symbolism was a little crude: silk, the ultracivilized material, over the primitive straight-off-the-bush necklace. Men liked to feel things through silk. But she wore silk as much for herself as for the gentlemen. Silk energized her. She loved the feeling of silk being slid up the backs of her legs. Her nape hairs rose a little as she thought about it. She had her hair up, in a loose, flat bun. She was ringless. She had put on and then taken off her scarab ring. Tonight she wanted the feeling that bare hands and bare feet would give. She would ease off her sandals at the right moment. She knew she was giving up a proven piece of business—idly taking off her ring when the occasion reached a certain centigrade. Men saw it subliminally as taking off a wedding ring and as the first act in undressing. She had worked hard on her feet. She had lined her armpits with tissue that would stay just until the doorbell rang. With medical gentlemen, hygiene was a fetish. She was expecting a doctor. Her breath was immaculate. She was proud of her teeth, but then she was married to a dentist. She thought about the Danish surgeon who brought his own boiled-water ice cubes to cocktail parties. She had some bottled water in the refrigerator, just in case it was indicated.

Her gentleman was due and overdue. Everything was optimal. There was a firm crossbreeze. The sight lines were nice. From where they would be sitting they would look out at a little pad of healthy lawn, the blank wall of the inner court, and the foliage of the tree whose blooms still looked to her like scrambled eggs. It would be self-evident that they would be private here. The blinds were drawn. Everything was secure and cool. Off the hall leading to the bathroom, the door to the bedroom stood open. The bedroom was clearly a working bedroom, not taboo, with a nightlight on and an oscillating fan performing on low. He would sit on leather; she would sit half-facing, where she could reach the bar trolley, on sheepskin, her feet on a jennet-skin kaross. He should sit in the leather chair because it was regal but uncomfortable. You would want to lie down. She would be in a slightly more reclining mode. Sunset was on. Where was her gentleman? The light was past its peak.

The doorbell rang. Be superb, she thought.

The doctor looked exhausted. He was gray-faced. Also, he was older than the image of him she had been entertaining. But he was all right. He had nice hair. He was fit. He might be part Indian, with those cheekbones and being from Vancouver. Flats were never a mistake. He was not tall. He was slim.

She led him in. He was wearing one of the cheaper safari suits, with the S-for-something embroidery on the left breast pocket. He had come straight from work, which was in her favor.

When she had him seated, she said, "Two slight catastrophes to report, doctor. One is that you're going to have to eat appetizers from my own hand. As the British say, my help are gone. My cook and my maid are sisters. Their aunt died. For the second time, actually. Tebogo is forgetful. In any case, they're in Mochudi for a few days and I'm alone. Frank won't be home until Sunday. *And* the Webers are off for tonight. They can't come. We're on our own. I hope we can cope."

He smiled weakly. The man was exhausted.

She said, "But a cool drink, quick, wouldn't you say? What would you like? I have everything."

He said it should be anything nonalcoholic, any kind of juice would be good. She could see work coming. He went to wash up.

He took his time in the bathroom, which was normally a good sign. He looked almost crisp when he came back, but something was the matter. She would have to extract it.

He accepted iced rooibos tea. She poured Bombay gin over crushed ice for herself. Men noticed what you drank. This man was not strong. She was going to have to underplay.

She presented the appetizers, which were genius. You could get through a week on her collations if you needed to, or you could have a few select tastes and go on to gorge elsewhere with no one the wiser. But you would remember every bite. She said, "You might like these. These chunks are bream fillet, poached, from Lake Ngami. No bones. Vinaigrette. They had just started getting these down here on a regular basis on ice about a year ago. AID had a lot of money in the Lake Ngami fishery project. Then the drought struck, and Lake Ngami, pouf, it's a damp spot in the desert. This is real Parma ham. I nearly had to kill someone to get it. The cashews are a little on the tangy side. That's the way they like them in Mozambique, apparently. They're good."

He ate a little, sticking to mainstream items like the gouda cheese cubes, she was sorry to see. Then he brought up the climate, which made her writhe. It was something to be curtailed. It led the mind homeward. It was one of the three deadly *W*s: weather, wife, and where to eat—in this country, where not to eat. She feigned sympathy. He was saying he was from British Columbia so it was to be expected that it would take some doing for him to adjust to the dry heat and the dust. He said he had to remind himself that he'd been here only four months and that ultimately his mucous membrane system was supposed to adapt. But he said he was finding it wearing. Lately he was dreaming about rain, a lot, he said.

Good! she thought. "Would you like to see my *tokoloshi?*" she asked, crossing her legs.

He stopped chewing. She warned herself not to be reckless.

"Dream animals!" she said. "Little effigies. I collect them. The Bushmen carve them out of softwood. They use them as symbols of evil in some ceremony they do. They're turning up along with all the other Bushman artifacts, the puberty aprons and so on, in the craft shops. Let me show you."

She got two *tokoloshi* from a cabinet.

"They call these the evil creatures who come to you at night in dreams. There are some interesting features. What you see when you look casually is this manlike figure with what looks like the head of a fox or rabbit or zebra at first glance. But look at the clothing. Doesn't this look like a clerical jacket? The collar shape? They're all like that. And look closely at the animal. It's actually a spotted jackal, the most despised animal there is because of its taste for carrion. Now look in front at this funny little tablet that looks like a huge belt buckle with these X shapes burned into it. My theory is that it's a Bushman version of the Union Jack. If you notice on this one, the being is wearing a funny belt. It looks like a cartridge belt to me. Some of the *tokoloshi* are smoking these removable pipes. White tourists buy these things and think they're cute. I think each one is a carved insult to the West. And we buy loads of them. I do. The black areas like the jacket are done by charring the wood with hot nails and things."

He handled the carvings dutifully and then gave them back to her. He murmured that they were interesting.

He took more tea. She stood the *tokoloshi* on an end table halfway across the room, facing them. He began contemplating them, sipping his tea minutely. Time was passing. She had various mottoes she used on herself. One was, Inside every suit and tie is a naked man trying to get out. She knew they were stupid, but they helped. He was still in the grip of whatever was bothering him.

"I have something that might interest you," she said. She went to the cabinet again and returned with a jackal-fur wallet, which she set down on the coffee table in front of him. "This is a fortune-telling kit the witch doctors use. It has odd things inside it." He merely looked at it.

"Look inside it," she said.

He picked it up reluctantly and held it in his hand, making a face. He was thinking it was unsanitary. She was in danger of becoming impatient. The wallet actually was slightly fetid, but so what: it was an organic thing. It was old.

She reached over and guided him to open and empty the wallet, touching his hands. He studied the array of bones and pebbles on the tabletop. Some of the pebbles were painted or stained. The bones were knucklebones, probably opossum, she told him, after· he showed no interest in trying to guess what they were. She had made it her business to learn a fair amount about Tswana divination practices, but he wasn't asking. He moved the objects around listlessly.

She lit a candle, though she felt it was technically premature. It would give him something else to stare at if he wanted to, and at least he would be staring in her direction, more or less.

The next segment was going to be taxing. The pace needed to be meditative. She was fighting impatience.

She said, "Africa is so strange. You haven't been here long, but you'll see. We come here as . . . bearers of science, the scientific attitude. Even the dependents do, always telling the help about nutrition and weaning and that kind of thing.

"Science so much defines us. One wants to be scientific, or at least not *un*scientific. Science is our religion, in a way. Or at least you begin to feel it is. I've been here nineteen months . . ."

He said something. Was she losing her hearing or was the man just unable to project? He had said something about noticing that the *tokoloshi* weren't carrying hypodermic needles. He was making the point, she guessed, that the Batswana didn't reject Western medicine. He said something further about their attachment to injections, how they felt you weren't actually treating them unless they could have an injection, how they seemed to love injections. She would have to adapt to a certain lag in this man's responses. I am tiring, she thought.

She tried again, edging her chair closer to his. "Of course, your world is different. You're more insulated at the Ministry, where everyone is a scientist of sorts. You're immersed in science. That world is . . . safer. Are you following me?"

He said that he wasn't sure that he was.

"What I guess I mean is that one gets to want to really *uphold* science. Because the culture here is so much the opposite. So relentlessly so. You resist. But then the first thing you know, very peculiar things start happening to you. Or you talk to some of the old-settler types, whites, educated people from the Protectorate days who decided to stay on as citizens, before the government made that such an obstacle course. The white settlers are worse than your everyday Batswana. They accept everything supernatural, almost. At first you dismiss it as a pose."

She knew it was strictly pro forma, but she offered him cigarettes from the caddy. He declined. There was no way she could smoke, then. Nothing tonight was going to be easy. Bechamel was right next door to the name she was trying to remember: Why couldn't she get it?

"But it isn't a pose," she said. "Their experiences have changed them utterly. There is so much witchcraft. It's called *muti*. It's so routine. It wasn't so long ago that if you were going to open a business you'd go to the witch doctor for good luck rites with human body parts as ingredients. A little something to tuck under the cornerstone of your bottle store. People are still being killed for their parts. It might be a windpipe or whatever. It's still going on. Sometimes they dump the body onto the railroad tracks after they've taken what they need, for the train to grind up and disguise. Recently they caught somebody that way. The killers threw this body on the track but the train was late. They try to keep it out of the paper, I know that for a fact. But it's still happening. An undertow."

She worked her feet out of her sandals. Normally she would do one and let an intriguing gap fall before doing the other. She scratched an instep on an ankle.

She said, "I know a girl who's teaching in the government secondary in Bobonong who tells me what a hard time the matron is having getting the girls to sleep with their heads out of the covers. It seems they're afraid of *bad women* who roam around at night, who'll scratch their faces. These are women called *baloi,* who go around naked, wearing only a little belt made out of human neckbones. Naturally, anyone would say what a fantasy this is. Childish.

"But I really did once see a naked woman dodging around near some rondavels late one night, out near Mosimane. It was only a glimpse. No doubt it was innocent. But she did have something white and shimmering around her waist. We were driving past. You begin to wonder."

She waited. He was silent.

"Something's bothering you," she said.

He denied it.

She said, "At any rate, don't you think it's interesting that there are no women members of the so-called traditional doctors' association? I know a member, what an oaf! I think it's a smoke-screen association. They want you to think they're just a benign bunch of herbalists trying out one thing or another, a lot of which ought to be in the regular pharmacopeia if only white medical people weren't so narrow-minded. They come to seminars all jolly and humble. But if you talk to the Batswana, you know that it's the women, the witches, who are the really potent ones."

Still he was silent.

"Something's happened, hasn't it? To upset you. If it's anything I've said, please tell me." A maternal tone could be death. She was flirting with failure.

He denied that she was responsible in any way. It seemed sincere. He was going inward again, right before her eyes. She had a code name for failures. She called them case studies. Her attitude was that every failure could be made to yield something of value for the future. And it was true. Some of her best material, anecdotes, references to things, aphrodisiana of all kinds, had come from case studies. The cave paintings at Gargas, in Spain, of mutilated hands . . . hand prints, not paintings . . . stencils of hundreds of hands with joints and fingers missing. Archaeologists were totally at odds as to what all that meant. One case study had yielded the story of fat women in Durban buying tainted meat from butchers so as to contract tapeworms for weight loss purposes. As a case study, if it came to that, tonight looked unpromising. But you could never tell. She had an image for case studies: a grave robber, weary, exhausted, reaching down into some charnel mass and pulling up a lovely ancient sword somehow miraculously still keen that had been overlooked. She could name case studies that were more precious to her than bingoes she could describe.

She had one quiver left. She meant arrow. She hated using it.

She could oppose her silence to his until he broke. It was difficult to get right. It ran counter to being a host, being a woman, and to her own nature. The silence had to be special, not wounded, receptive, with a spine to it, maternal, in fact.

She declared silence. Slow moments passed.

He stirred. His lips stirred. He got up and began pacing.

He said, "You're right." Then for a long time he said nothing, still pacing.

"You read my mind!" he said. "Last night I had an experience . . . I still . . . it's still upsetting. I shouldn't have come, I guess."

She felt sorry for him. He had just the slightest speech defect, which showed up in noticeable hesitations. This was sad.

"Please tell me about it," she said perfectly.

He paced more, then halted near the candle and stared at it.

"I hardly drink," he said. "Last night was an exception. Phoning home to Vancouver started it, domestic nonsense. I won't go into that. They don't understand. No point in going into it. I went out. I went drinking. One of the hotel bars, where Africans go. I began drinking. I was drinking and buying drinks for some of the locals. I drank quite a bit.

"All right. These fellows are clever. Bit by bit I am being taken over by one, this one fellow, George. I can't explain it. I didn't like him. He took me over. That is, I notice I'm paying for drinks but this fellow's passing them on to whomever he chooses, his friends. But I'm buying. But I have no say.

"We're in a corner booth. It's dark and loud, as usual. This fellow, his head was shaved, he was strong-looking. He spoke good English, though. Originally, I'd liked talking to him, I think. They flatter you. He was a combination of rough and smooth. Now he was working me. He was a refugee from South Africa, that always starts up your sympathy. Terrible breath, though. I was getting a feeling of something being off about the ratio between the number of drinks and what I was laying out. I think he was taking something in transit.

"I wanted to do the buying. I took exception. All right. Remember that they have me wedged in. That was stupid, but I was, I allowed it. Then I said I was going to stop buying. George didn't like it. This man had a following. I realized they were forming a cordon, blocking us in. Gradually it got nasty. Why wouldn't I keep buying drinks, didn't I have money, what was my job, didn't the Ministry pay expatriates enough to buy a few drinks?—so on ad nauseam."

His color was coming back. He picked up a cocktail napkin and touched at his forehead.

He was looking straight at her now. He said, "You don't know what the African bars are like. Pandemonium. I was sealed off. As I say, his friends were all around.

"Then it was all about apartheid. I said I was Canadian. Then it was about Canada the lackey of America the supporter of apartheid. I'm not political. I was scared. All right. When I tell him I'm really through buying drinks he asks me how much money have I got left, exactly. I tell him again that I'm through buying drinks. He says not to worry, he'll sell me something instead. All right. I knew I was down to about ten pula. And I had dug in on buying drinks, the way you will when you've had a few too many. No more buying drinks, that was decided. But he was determined to get my money, I could damned well see that.

"He said he would sell me something I'd be very glad to know. Information. All right. So then comes a long runaround on what kind of information. Remember that he's pretty well three sheets to the wind himself. It was information I would be glad to have as a doctor, he said.

"Well, the upshot here was that this is what I proposed, so as not to seem totally stupid and taken. I would put all my money down on the table in front of me. I took out my wallet and made sure he could see that what I put down was all of it, about ten pula, change and everything. All right. And I would keep the money under the palm of my hand. And he would whisper the information to me and if I thought it was a fair trade I would just lift my hand. Of course, this was all just face-saving on my part so as not to just hand over my money to a thug. And don't think I wasn't well aware it might be a good idea at this stage of things to be seen getting rid of any cash I had, just to avoid being knocked down on the way to my car."

"This is a wonderful story," she said spontaneously, immediately regretting it.

"It isn't a story," he said.

"You know what I mean," she said. "I mean, since I see you standing here safe and sound I can assume the ending isn't a tragedy. But please continue. Really."

"In any event. There we are. There was more back and forth over what kind of information this was. Finally he says it's not only something a doctor would be glad of. He is going to tell me the secret of how they are going to make the revolution in South Africa, a secret plan. An actual plan.

"God knows I have no brief for white South Africans. I know a few professionally, doctors. Medicine down there is basically about up to 1950, in my opinion, despite all this veneer of the heart transplants. But the doctors I know seem to be decent. Some of them hate the system and will say so.

"I go along. Empty my wallet, cover the money with my hand.

"Here's what he says. They had a sure way to drive out the whites. It was a new plan and was sure to succeed. It would succeed because they, meaning the blacks, could bring it about with only a handful of men. He said that the Boers had won for all time if the revolution meant waiting for small groups to grow into bands and then into units, battalions and so on, into armies that would fight the Boers. The Boers were too intelligent and had too much power. They had corrupted too many of the blacks. The blacks were divided. There were too many spies for the Boers among them. The plan he would tell me would take less than a hundred men.

"Then he asked me, if he could tell me such a plan would it be worth the ten pula. Would I agree that it would? I said yes."

"This is extraordinary!" she said. *Duhamel!* she thought, triumphant. The name had come back to her: *Georges Duhamel.* She could almost see the print. She was so grateful.

"Exciting!" she said, gratitude in her voice.

He was sweating. "Well, this is what he says. He leans over, whispers. The plan is simple. The plan is to assemble a shock force, he called it. Black people who are willing to give their lives. And this is all they do: *they kill doctors.* That's it! They start off with a large first wave, before the government can do anything to protect doctors. They simply kill doctors, as many as they can. They kill them at home, in their offices, in hospitals, in the street. You can get the name of every doctor in South Africa through the phone book. Whites need doctors, without doctors they think they are already dying, he says. Blacks in South Africa have no doctors to speak of anyway, especially in the homelands where they are all being herded to die in droves. Blacks are dying of the system every day regardless, he says. But whites would scream. They would rush like cattle to the airports, screaming. They would stream out of the country. The planes from Smuts would be jammed full. After the first strike, you would continue, taking them by ones and twos. The doctors would leave, the ones who were still alive. No new ones would come, not even Indians. He said it was like taking away water from people in a desert. The government would capitulate. That was the plan.

"I lifted my hand and let him take the money. He said I was paying the soldiery, and he thanked me in the name of the revolution. Then I was free to go."

He looked around dazedly for something, she wasn't clear what. Her glass was still one-third full. Remarkably, he picked it up and drained it, eating the remnants of ice.

She stood up. She was content. The story was a brilliant thing, a gem.

He was moving about. It was hard to say, but possibly he was leaving. He could go or stay.

They stood together in the living room archway. Without prelude, he reached for her, awkwardly pulled her side against his chest, kissed her absurdly on the eye, and with his free hand began squeezing her breasts.

Doris Lessing

THE HABIT OF LOVING

In 1947 George wrote again to Myra, saying that now the war was well over she should come home and marry him. She wrote back from Australia, where she had gone with her two children in 1943 because there were relations there, saying she felt they had drifted apart; she was no longer sure she wanted to marry George. He did not allow himself to collapse. He cabled her the air fare and asked her to come over and see him. She came, for two weeks, being unable to leave the children for longer. She said she liked Australia; she liked the climate; she did not like the English climate any longer; she thought England was, very probably, played out; and she had become used to missing London. Also, presumably, to missing George Talbot.

For George this was a very painful fortnight. He believed it was painful for Myra, too. They had met in 1938, had lived together for five years, and had exchanged for four years the letters of lovers separated by fate. Myra was certainly the love of his life. He had believed he was of hers until now. Myra, an attractive woman made beautiful by the suns and beaches of Australia, waved goodbye at the airport, and her eyes were filled with tears.

George's eyes, as he drove away from the airport, were dry. If one person has loved another truly and wholly, then it is more than love that collapses when one side of the indissoluble partnership turns away with a tearful goodbye. George dismissed the taxi early and walked through St. James's Park. Then it seemed too small for him, and he went to the Green Park. Then he walked into Hyde Park and through to Kensington Gardens. When the dark came and they closed the great gates of the park he took a taxi home. He lived in a block of flats near the Marble Arch. For five years Myra had lived with him there, and it was here he had expected to live with her again. Now he moved into a new flat near Covent Garden. Soon after that he wrote Myra a very painful letter. It occurred to him that he had often received such letters, but had never written one before. It occurred to him that he had entirely underestimated the amount of suffering he must have caused in his life. But Myra wrote him a sensible letter back, and George Talbot told himself that now he must finally stop thinking about Myra.

Therefore he became rather less of a dilettante in his work than he had been recently, and he agreed to produce a new play written by a friend of his. George Talbot was a man of the theatre. He had not acted in it for many years now; but he wrote articles, he sometimes produced a play, he made speeches on important occasions and was known by everyone. When he went into a restaurant people tried to catch his eye, and he often did not know who they were. During the four years since Myra had left, he had had a number of affairs with young women round and about the theatre, for he had been lonely. He had written quite frankly to Myra about these affairs, but she had never mentioned them in her letters. Now he was very busy for some months and was seldom at home; he earned quite a lot of money, and he had a few more affairs with women who were pleased to be seen in public with him. He thought about Myra a great deal, but he did not write to her again, nor she to him, although they had agreed they would always be great friends.

One evening in the foyer of a theatre he saw an old friend of his he had always admired, and he told the young woman he was with

that that man had been the most irresistible man of his generation—
no woman had been able to resist him. The young woman stared briefly
across the foyer and said, "Not really?"

When George Talbot got home that night he was alone, and he
looked at himself with honesty in the mirror. He was sixty, but he did
not look it. Whatever had attracted women to him in the past had
never been his looks, and he was not much changed: a stoutish man,
holding himself erect, grey-haired, carefully brushed, well-dressed. He
had not paid much attention to his face since those many years ago
when he had been an actor; but now he had an uncharacteristic fit of
vanity and remembered that Myra had admired his mouth, while his
wife had loved his eyes. He took to taking glances at himself in foyers
and restaurants where there were mirrors, and he saw himself as un-
changed. He was becoming conscious, though, of a discrepancy between
that suave exterior and what he felt. Beneath his ribs his heart had
become swollen and soft and painful, a monstrous area of sympathy
playing enemy to what he had been. When people made jokes he was
often unable to laugh; and his manner of talking, which was light and
allusive and dry, must have changed, because more than once old friends
asked him if he was depressed, and they no longer smiled appreciatively
as he told his stories. He gathered he was not being good company. He
understood he might be ill, and he went to the doctor. The doctor said
there was nothing wrong with his heart, he had thirty years of life in
him yet—luckily, he added respectfully, for the British theatre.

George came to understand that the word "heartache" meant that
a person could carry a heart that ached around with him day and night
for, in his case, months. Nearly a year now. He would wake in the
night, because of the pressure of pain in his chest; in the morning he
woke under a weight of grief. There seemed to be no end to it; and
this thought jolted him into two actions. First, he wrote to Myra a
tender, carefully phrased letter, recalling the years of their love. To this
he got, in due course, a tender and careful reply. Then he went to see
his wife. With her he was, and had been for many years, good friends.
They saw each other often, but not so often now the children were
grown up; perhaps once or twice a year, and they never quarreled.

His wife had married again after they divorced, and now she was a widow. Her second husband had been a member of Parliament, and she worked for the Labour Party, and she was on a Hospital Advisory Committee and on the Board of Directors of a progressive school. She was fifty, but did not look it. On this afternoon she was wearing a slim gray suit and gray shoes, and her gray hair had a wave of white across the front which made her look distinguished. She was animated, and very happy to see George; and she talked about some deadhead on her hospital committee who did not see eye to eye with the progressive minority about some reform or other. They had always had their politics in common, a position somewhere left of center in the Labour Party. She had sympathized with his being a pacifist in the First World War—he had been for a time in prison because of it; he had sympathized with her militant feminism. Both had helped the strikers in 1926. In the Thirties, after they were divorced, she had helped with money when he went on tour with a company acting Shakespeare to people on the dole, or hunger-marching.

Myra had not been at all interested in politics, only in her children. And in George, of course.

George asked his first wife to marry him again, and she was so startled that she let the sugar tongs drop and crack a saucer. She asked what had happened to Myra, and George said: "Well, dear, I think Myra forgot about me during those years in Australia. At any rate, she doesn't want me now." When he heard his voice saying this it sounded pathetic, and he was frightened, for he could not remember ever having to appeal to a woman. Except to Myra.

His wife examined him and said briskly: "You're lonely, George. Well, we're none of us getting any younger."

"You don't think you'd be less lonely if you had me around?"

She got up from her chair in order that she could attend to something with her back to him, and she said that she intended to marry again quite soon. She was marrying a man considerably younger than herself, a doctor who was in the progressive minority at her hospital. From her voice George understood that she was both proud and ashamed of this marriage, and that was why she was hiding her face from him. He congratulated her and asked her if there wasn't perhaps a chance for him yet? "After all, dear, we were happy together, weren't we? I've never really understood why that marriage ever broke up. It was you who wanted to break it up."

"I don't see any point in raking over that old business," she said, with finality, and returned to her seat opposite him. He envied her very much, looking young with her pink and scarcely lined face under that brave lock of deliberately whitened hair.

"But, dear, I wish you'd tell me. It doesn't do any harm now, does it? And I always wondered. . . . I've often thought about it and wondered." He could hear the pathetic note in his voice again, but he did not know how to alter it.

"You wondered," she said, "when you weren't occupied with Myra."

"But I didn't know Myra when we got divorced."

"You knew Phillipa and Georgina and Janet and Lord knows who else."

"But I didn't care about them."

She sat with her competent hands in her lap, and on her face was a look he remembered seeing when she told him she would divorce him. It was bitter and full of hurt. "You didn't care about me either," she said.

"But we were happy. Well, I was happy . . ." he trailed off, being pathetic against all his knowledge of women. For, as he sat there, his old rake's heart was telling him that if only he could find them, there must be the right words, the right tone. But whatever he said came out in this hopeless, old dog's voice, and he knew that this voice could never defeat the gallant and crusading young doctor. "And I did care about you. Sometimes I think you were the only woman in my life."

At this she laughed. "Oh, George, don't get maudlin now, please."

"Well, dear, there was Myra. But when you threw me over there was bound to be Myra, wasn't there? There were two women, you and then Myra. And I've never never understood why you broke it all up when we seemed to be so happy."

"You didn't care for me," she said again. "If you had, you would never have come home from Phillipa, Georgina, Janet, *et al.,* and said calmly, just as if it didn't matter to me in the least, that you had been with them in Brighton or wherever it was."

"But if I had cared about them I would never have told you."

She was regarding him incredulously, and her face was flushed. With what? Anger? George did not know.

"I remember being so proud," he said pathetically, "that we had solved this business of marriage and all that sort of thing. We had such a good marriage that it didn't matter, the little flirtations. And I always thought one should be able to tell the truth. I always told you the truth, didn't I?"

"Very romantic of you, dear George," she said dryly; and soon he got up, kissed her fondly on the cheek, and went away.

He walked for a long time through the parks, hands behind his erect back, and he could feel his heart swollen and painful in his side. When the gates shut, he walked through the lighted streets he had lived in for fifty years of his life, and he was remembering Myra and Molly, as if they were one woman, merging into each other, a shape of warm easy intimacy, a shape of happiness walking beside him. He went into a little restaurant he knew well, and there was a girl sitting there who knew him because she had heard him lecture once on the state of the British theatre. He tried hard to see Myra and Molly in her face, but he failed; and he paid for her coffee and his own and went home by himself. But his flat was unbearably empty, and he left it and walked down by the Embankment for a couple of hours to tire himself, and there must have been a colder wind blowing than he knew, for next day he woke with a pain in his chest, which he could not mistake for heartache.

He had flu and a bad cough, and he stayed in bed by himself and did not ring up the doctor until the fourth day, when he was getting light-headed. The doctor said it must be the hospital at once. But he would not go to the hospital. So the doctor said he must have day and night nurses. This he submitted to until the cheerful friendliness of the nurses saddened him beyond bearing, and he asked the doctor to ring up his wife, who would find someone to look after him who would be sympathetic. He was hoping that Molly would come herself to nurse him, but when she arrived he did not like to mention it, for she was busy with preparations for her new marriage. She promised to find him someone who would not wear a uniform and make jokes. They naturally had many friends in common; and she rang up an old flame of his in the theatre who said she knew of a girl who was looking for a secretary's job to tide her over a patch of not working, but who didn't really mind what she did for a few weeks.

So Bobby Tippett sent away the nurses and made up a bed for herself in his study. On the first day she sat by George's bed sewing. She wore a full dark skirt and a demure printed blouse with short frills at the wrist, and George watched her sewing and already felt much better. She was a small, thin, dark girl, probably Jewish, with sad black eyes. She had a way of letting her sewing lie loose in her lap, her hands limp over it; and her eyes fixed themselves, and a bloom of dark introspection came over them. She sat very still at these moments, like a small china figure of a girl sewing. When she was nursing George, or letting in his many visitors, she put on a manner of cool and even languid charm; it was the extreme good manners of heartlessness, and at first George was chilled: but then he saw through the pose; for whatever world Bobby Tippett had been born into he did not think it was the English class to which these manners belonged. She replied with a "yes," or a "no," to questions about herself; he gathered that her parents were dead, but there was a married sister she saw sometimes; and for the rest she had lived around and about London, mostly by herself, for ten or more years. When he asked her if she had not been lonely, so much by herself, she drawled, "Why, not at all, I don't mind being alone." But he saw her as a small, brave child, a waif against London, and was moved.

He did not want to be the big man of the theatre; he was afraid of evoking the impersonal admiration he was only too accustomed to; but soon he was asking her questions about her career, hoping that this might be the point of her enthusiasm. But she spoke lightly of small parts, odd jobs, scene-painting and understudying, in a jolly good-little-trouper's voice; and he could not see that he had come any closer to her at all. So at last he did what he had tried to avoid and, sitting up against his pillows like a judge or an impresario, he said: "Do something for me, dear. Let me see you." She went next door like an obedient child, and came back in tight black trousers, but still in her demure little blouse, and stood on the carpet before him, and went into a little song-and-dance act. It wasn't bad. He had seen a hundred worse. But he was very moved; he saw her now above all as the little urchin, the gamin, boy-girl and helpless. And utterly touching. "Actually," she said, "this is half of an act. I always have someone else."

There was a big mirror that nearly filled the end wall of the large, dark room. George saw himself in it, an elderly man sitting propped up on pillows watching the small doll-like figure standing before him on the carpet. He saw her turn her head towards her reflection in the darkened mirror, study it, and then she began to dance with her own reflection, dance against it, as it were. There were two small, light figures dancing in George's room; there was something uncanny in it. She began singing, a little broken song in stage cockney, and George felt that she was expecting the other figure in the mirror to sing with her; she was singing at the mirror as if she expected an answer.

"That's very good, dear," he broke in quickly, for he was upset, though he did not know why. "Very good indeed." He was relieved when she broke off and came away from the mirror, so that the uncanny shadow of her went away.

"Would you like me to speak to someone for you, dear? It might help. You know how things are in the theatre," he suggested apologetically.

"I don't maind if I dew," she said in the stage cockney of her act; and for a moment her face flashed into a mocking, reckless, gaminlike charm. "Perhaps I'd better change back into my skirt?" she suggested. "More natural-like for a nurse, ain't it?"

But he said he liked her in her tight black trousers, and now she always wore them, and her neat little shirts; and she moved about the flat as a charming feminine boy, chattering to him about the plays she had had small parts in and about the big actors and actresses and producers she had spoken to, who were, of course, George's friends or, at least, equals. George sat up against his pillows and listened and watched, and his heart ached. He remained in bed longer than there was need, because he did not want her to go. When he transferred himself to a big chair, he said: "You mustn't think you're bound to stay here, dear, if there's somewhere else you'd rather go." To which she replied, with a wide flash of her black eyes, "But I'm resting, darling, resting. I've nothing better to do with myself." And then: "Oh aren't I aw*ful,* the things wot I sy?"

"But you do like being here? You don't mind being here with me, dear?" he insisted.

There was the briefest pause. She said: "Yes, oddly enough I do like it." The "oddly enough" was accompanied by a quick, half-laughing, almost flirtatious glance; and for the first time in many months the pressure of loneliness eased around George's heart.

Now it was a happiness to him because when the distinguished ladies and gentlemen of the theatre or of letters came to see him, Bobby became a cool, silky little hostess; and the instant they had gone she relapsed into urchin charm. It was a proof of their intimacy. Sometimes he took her out to dinner or to the theatre. When she dressed up she wore bold, fashionable clothes and moved with the insolence of a mannequin; and George moved beside her, smiling fondly, waiting for the moment when the black, reckless, freebooting eyes would flash up out of the languid stare of the woman presenting herself for admiration, exchanging with him amusement at her posing, amusement at the world; promising him that soon, when they got back to the apartment, by themselves, she would again become the dear little girl or the gallant, charming waif.

Sometimes, sitting in the dim room at night, he would let his hand close over the thin point of her shoulder; sometimes, when they said goodnight, he bent to kiss her, and she lowered her head, so that his lips encountered her demure, willing forehead.

George told himself that she was unawakened. It was a phrase that had been the prelude to a dozen warm discoveries in the past. He told himself that she knew nothing of what she might be. She had been married, it seemed—she dropped this information once, in the course of an anecdote about the theatre; but George had known women in plenty who after years of marriage had been unawakened. George asked her to marry him; and she lifted her small sleek head with an animal's startled turn and said: "Why do you want to marry me?"

"Because I like being with you, dear. I love being with you."

"Well, I like being with you." It had a questioning sound. She was questioning herself? "Strainge," she said in cockney, laughing. "Strainge but trew."

The wedding was to be a small one, but there was a lot about it in the papers. Recently several men of George's generation had married young women. One of them had fathered a son at the age of seventy. George was flattered by the newspapers, and told Bobby a good deal about his life that had not come up before. He remarked, for instance, that he thought his generation had been altogether more successful about this business of love and sex than the modern generation. He said, "Take my son, for instance. At his age I had had a lot of affairs and knew about women; but there he is, nearly thirty, and when he stayed here once with a girl he was thinking of marrying, I know for a fact they shared the same bed for a week and nothing ever happened. She told me so. Very odd it all seems to me. But it didn't seem odd to her. And now he lives with another young man and listens to that long-playing record thing of his, and he's engaged to a girl he takes out twice a week, like a schoolboy. And there's my daughter: she came to me a year after she was married, and she was in an awful mess, really awful. . . . It seems to me your generation are very frightened of it all. I don't know why."

"Why my generation?" she asked, turning her head with that quick listening movement. "It's not my generation."

"But you're nothing but a child," he said fondly.

He could not decipher what lay behind the black, full stare of her sad eyes as she looked at him now; she was sitting cross-legged in her black glossy trousers before the fire, like a small doll. But a spring of alarm had been touched in him and he didn't dare say any more.

"At thirty-five, I'm the youngest child alive," she sang, with a swift sardonic glance at him over her shoulder. But it sounded gay.

He did not talk to her again about the achievements of his generation.

After the wedding he took her to a village in Normandy where he had been once, many years ago, with a girl called Eve. He did not tell her he had been there before.

It was spring, and the cherry trees were in flower. The first evening he walked with her in the last sunlight under the white-flowering branches, his arm around her thin waist, and it seemed to him that he was about to walk back through the gates of a lost happiness.

They had a large comfortable room with windows, which overlooked the cherry trees, and there was a double bed. Madame Cruchot, the farmer's wife, showed them the room with shrewd, non-commenting eyes, said she was always happy to shelter honeymoon couples, and wished them a good night.

George made love to Bobby, and she shut her eyes, and he found she was not at all awkward. When they had finished, he gathered her in his arms, and it was then that he returned simply, with an incredulous awed easing of the heart, to a happiness which—and now it seemed to him fantastically ungrateful that he could have done—he had taken for granted for so many years of his life. It was not possible, he thought, holding her compliant body in his arms, that he could have been by himself, alone, for so long. It had been intolerable. He held her silent breathing body, and he stroked her back and thighs, and his hands remembered the emotions of nearly fifty years of loving. He could feel the memoried emotions of his life flooding through his body, and his heart swelled with a joy it seemed to him he had never known, for it was a compound of a dozen loves.

He was about to take final possession of his memories when she turned sharply away, sat up, and said: "I want a fag. How about yew?"

"Why, yes, dear, if you want."

They smoked. The cigarettes finished, she lay down on her back, arms folded across her chest, and said, "I'm sleepy." She closed her eyes. When he was sure she was asleep, he lifted himself on his elbow and watched her. The light still burned, and the curve of her cheek was full and soft, like a child's. He touched it with the side of his palm, and she shrank away in her sleep, but clenched up, like a fist; and her hand, which was white and unformed, like a child's hand, was clenched in a fist on the pillow before her face.

George tried to gather her in his arms, and she turned away from him to the extreme edge of the bed. She was deeply asleep, and her sleep was unsharable. George could not endure it. He got out of bed and stood by the window in the cold spring night air, and saw the white cherry trees standing under the white moon, and thought of the cold girl asleep in her bed. He was there in the chill moonlight until the dawn came; in the morning he had a very bad cough and could not get up. Bobby was charming, devoted, and gay. "Just like old times, me nursing you," she commented, with a deliberate roll of her black eyes. She asked Madame Cruchot for another bed, which she placed in the corner of the room, and George thought it was quite reasonable she should not want to catch his cold; for he did not allow himself to remember the times in his past when quite serious illness had been no obstacle to the sharing of the dark; he decided to forget the sensualities of tiredness, or of fever, or of the extremes of sleeplessness. He was even beginning to feel ashamed.

For a fortnight the Frenchwoman brought up magnificent meals, twice a day, and George and Bobby drank a great deal of red wine and of calvados and made jokes with Madame Cruchot about getting ill on honeymoons. They returned from Normandy rather earlier than had been arranged. It would be better for George, Bobby said, at home, where his friends could drop in to see him. Besides, it was sad to be shut indoors in springtime, and they were both eating too much.

On the first night back in the flat, George waited to see if she would go into the study to sleep, but she came to the big bed in her pajamas, and for the second time he held her in his arms for the space of the act, and then she smoked, sitting up in bed and looking rather tired and small and, George thought, terribly young and pathetic. He did not sleep that night. He did not dare move out of bed for fear of disturbing her, and he was afraid to drop off to sleep for fear his limbs remembered the habits of a lifetime and searched for hers. In the morning she woke smiling, and he put his arms around her, but she kissed him with small gentle kisses and jumped out of bed.

That day she said she must go and see her sister. She saw her sister often during the next few weeks and kept suggesting that George should have his friends around more than he did. George asked why didn't the sister come to see her here, in the flat? So one afternoon she came to tea. George had seen her briefly at the wedding and disliked her, but now for the first time he had a spell of revulsion against the marriage itself. The sister was awful—a commonplace, middle-aged female from some suburb. She had a sharp, dark face that poked itself inquisitively

into the corners of the flat, pricing the furniture, and a thin acquisitive
nose bent to one side. She sat, on her best behavior, for two hours over
the teacups, in a mannish navy blue suit, a severe black hat, her brogued
feet set firmly side by side before her; and her thin nose seemed to be
carrying on a silent, satirical conversation with her sister about George.
Bobby was being cool and well-mannered, as it were, deliberately tired
of life, as she always was when guests were there, but George was sure
this was simply on his account. When the sister had gone, George was
rather querulous about her; but Bobby said, laughing, that of course
she had known George wouldn't like Rosa; she *was* rather ghastly; but
then who had suggested inviting her? So Rosa came no more, and
Bobby went out to meet her for a visit to the pictures, or for shopping.
Meanwhile, George sat alone and thought uneasily about Bobby, or
visited his old friends. A few months after they returned from Normandy, someone suggested to George that perhaps he was ill. This
made George think about it, and he realized he was not far from being
ill. It was because he could not sleep. Night after night he lay beside
Bobby, after her cheerfully affectionate submission to him; and he saw
the soft curve of her cheek on the pillow, the long dark lashes lying
close and flat. Never had anything in his life moved him so deeply as
that childish cheek, the shadow of those lashes. A small crease in one
cheek seemed to him the signature of emotion; and the lock of black
glossy hair falling across her forehead filled his throat with tears. His
nights were long vigils of locked tenderness.

Then one night she woke and saw him watching her.

"What's the matter?" she asked, startled. "Can't you sleep?"

"I'm only watching you, dear," he said hopelessly.

She lay curled up beside him, her fist beside her on the pillow,
between him and her. "Why aren't you happy?" she asked suddenly;
and as George laughed with a sudden bitter irony, she sat up, arms
around her knees, prepared to consider this problem practically.

"This isn't marriage; this isn't love," he announced. He sat up beside
her. He did not know that he had never used that tone to her before.
A portly man, his elderly face flushed with sorrow, he had forgotten
her for the moment, and he was speaking across her from his past,
resurrected in her, to his past. He was dignified with responsible ex-

perience and the warmth of a lifetime's responses. His eyes were heavy, satirical, and condemning. She rolled herself up against him and said with a small smile, "Then show me, George."

"Show you?" he said, almost stammering. "Show you?" But he held her, the obedient child, his cheek against hers, until she slept; then a too close pressure of his shoulder on hers caused her to shrink and recoil from him away to the edge of the bed.

In the morning she looked at him oddly, with an odd sad little respect, and said, "You know what, George? You've just got into the habit of loving."

"What do you mean, dear?"

She rolled out of bed and stood beside it, a waif in her white pajamas, her black hair ruffled. She slid her eyes at him and smiled. "You just want something in your arms, that's all. What do you do when you're alone? Wrap yourself around a pillow?"

He said nothing; he was cut to the heart.

"My husband was the same," she remarked gaily. "Funny thing is, he didn't care anything about me." She stood considering him, smiling mockingly. "Strainge, ain't it?" she commented and went off to the bathroom. That was the second time she had mentioned her husband.

That phrase, "the habit of loving," made a revolution in George. It was true, he thought. He was shocked out of himself, out of the instinctive response to the movement of skin against his, the pressure of a breast. It seemed to him that he was seeing Bobby quite newly. He had not really known her before. The delightful little girl had vanished, and he saw a young woman toughened and wary because of defeats and failures he had never stopped to think of. He saw that the sadness that lay behind the black eyes was not at all impersonal; he saw the first sheen of gray lying on her smooth hair; he saw that the full curve of her cheek was the beginning of the softening into middle age. He was appalled at his egotism. Now, he thought, he would really know her, and she would begin to love him in response to it.

Suddenly, George discovered in himself a boy whose existence he had totally forgotten. He had been returned to his adolescence. The accidental touch of her hand delighted him; the swing of her skirt could make him shut his eyes with happiness. He looked at her through the

jealous eyes of a boy and began questioning her about her past, feeling
that he was slowly taking possession of her. He waited for a hint of
emotion in the drop of her voice, or a confession in the wrinkling of
the skin by the full, dark, comradely eyes. At night, a boy again,
reverence shut him into ineptitude. The body of George's sensuality
had been killed stone dead. A month ago he had been a man vigorous
with the skilled harboring of memory; the long use of his body. Now
he lay awake beside this woman, not longing for the past, for that past
had dropped away from him, but dreaming of the future. And when
he questioned her, like a jealous boy, and she evaded him, he could see
it only as the locked virginity of the girl who would wake in answer
to the worshipping boy he had become.

But still she slept in a citadel, one fist before her face.

Then one night she woke again, roused by some movement of his.
"What's the matter *now,* George?" she asked, exasperated.

In the silence that followed, the resurrected boy in George died
painfully.

"Nothing," he said. "Nothing at all." He turned away from her,
defeated.

It was he who moved out of the big bed into the narrow bed in
the study. She said with a sharp, sad smile, "Fed up with me, George?
Well, I can't help it, you know. I didn't ever like sleeping beside someone
very much."

George, who had dropped out of his work lately, undertook to
produce another play, and was very busy again; and he became drama
critic for one of the big papers and was in the swim and at all the first
nights. Sometimes Bobby was with him, in her startling, smart clothes,
being amused with him at the whole business of being fashionable.
Sometimes she stayed at home. She had the capacity of being by herself
for hours, apparently doing nothing. George would come home from
some crowd of people, some party, and find her sitting cross-legged
before the fire in her tight trousers, chin in hand, gone off by herself
into some place where he was now afraid to try and follow. He could
not bear it again, putting himself in a position where he might hear
the cold, sharp words that showed she had never had an inkling of
what he felt, because it was not in her nature to feel it. He would come

in late, and she would make them both some tea; and they would sit hand in hand before the fire, his flesh and memories quiet. Dead, he thought. But his heart ached. He had become so used to the heavy load of loneliness in his chest that when, briefly, talking to an old friend, he became the George Talbot who had never known Bobby, and his heart lightened and his oppression went, he would look about him, startled, as if he had lost something. He felt almost light-headed without the pain of loneliness.

He asked Bobby if she wasn't bored, with so little to do, month after month after month, while he was so busy. She said no, she was quite happy doing nothing. She wouldn't like to take up her old work again.

"I wasn't ever much good, was I?" she said.

"If you'd enjoy it, dear, I could speak to someone for you."

She frowned at the fire but said nothing. Later he suggested it again, and she sparked up with a grin and: "Well, I don't maind if I dew. . . ."

So he spoke to an old friend, and Bobby returned to the theatre, to a small act in a little intimate revue. She had found somebody, she said, to be the other half of her act. George was very busy with a production of *Romeo and Juliet,* and did not have time to see her at rehearsal, but he was there on the night *The Offbeat Revue* opened. He was rather late and stood at the back of the gimcrack little theatre, packed tight with fragile little chairs. Everything was so small that the well-dressed audience looked too big, like oversize people crammed in a box. The tiny stage was left bare, with a few black-and-white posters stuck here and there, and there was one piano. The pianist was good, a young man with black hair falling limp over his face, playing as if he were bored with the whole thing. But he played very well. George, the man of the theatre, listened to the first number, so as to catch the mood, and thought, Oh Lord, not again. It was one of the songs from the First World War, and he could not stand the flood of easy emotion it aroused. He refused to feel. Then he realized that the emotion was, in any case, blocked: the piano was mocking the song; "There's a Long, Long Trail" was being played like a five-finger exercise; and "Keep the Home Fires Burning" and "Tipperary" followed, in the same style,

as if the piano were bored. People were beginning to chuckle; they had
caught the mood. A young blond man with a moustache and wearing
the uniform of 1914 came in and sang fragments of the songs, like a
corpse singing; and then George understood he was supposed to be one
of the dead of that war singing. George felt all his responses blocked,
first because he could not allow himself to feel any emotion from that
time at all—it was too painful; and then because of the five-finger
exercise style, which contradicted everything, all pain or protest, leaving
nothing, an emptiness. The show went on; through the Twenties, with
bits of popular songs from that time, a number about the General Strike,
which reduced the whole thing to the scale of marionettes without
passion, and then on to the Thirties. George saw it was a sort of potted
history, as it were—Noël Coward's falsely heroic view of his time
parodied. But it wasn't even that. There was no emotion, nothing.
George did not know what he was supposed to feel. He looked curiously
at the faces of the people around him and saw that the older people
looked puzzled, affronted, as if the show were an insult to them. But
the younger people were in the mood of the thing. But what mood? It
was the parody of a parody. When the Second World War was evoked
by "Run Rabbit Run," played like *Lohengrin,* while the soldiers in the
uniforms of the time mocked their own understated heroism from the
other side of death, then George could not stand it. He did not look
at the stage at all. He was waiting for Bobby to come on, so he could
say that he had seen her. Meanwhile he smoked and watched the face
of a very young man near him; it was a pale, heavy, flaccid face, but
it was responding, it seemed from a habit of rancor, to everything that
went on on the stage. Suddenly, the young face lit into sarcastic delight,
and George looked at the stage. On it were two urchins, identical, it
seemed, in tight black glossy trousers, tight crisp white shirts. Both had
short black hair, neat little feet placed side by side. They were standing
together, hands crossed loosely before them at the waist, waiting for
the music to start. The man at the piano, who had a cigarette in the
corner of his mouth, began playing something very sentimental. He
broke off and looked with sardonic enquiry at the urchins. They had
not moved. They shrugged and rolled their eyes at him. He played a
marching song, very loud and pompous. The urchins twisted a little

and stayed still. Then the piano broke fast and sudden into a rage of jazz. The two puppets on the stage began a furious movement, their limbs clashing with each other and with the music, until they fell into poses of helpless despair while the music grew louder and more desperate. They tried again, whirling themselves into a frenzied attempt to keep up with the music. Then, two waifs, they turned their two small white sad faces at each other, and, with a formal nod, each took a phrase of music from the fast flood of sound that had already swept by them, held it, and began to sing. Bobby sang her bad stage-cockney phrases, meaningless, jumbled up, flat, hopeless; the other urchin sang drawling languid phrases from the upper-class jargon of the moment. They looked at each other, offering the phrases, as it were, to see if they would be accepted. Meanwhile, the hard, cruel, hurtful music went on. Again the two went limp and helpless, unwanted, unaccepted. George, outraged and hurt, asked himself again: What am I feeling? What am I supposed to be feeling? For that insane nihilistic music demanded some opposition, some statement of affirmation, but the two urchins, half-boy, half-girl, as alike as twins (George had to watch Bobby carefully so as not to confuse her with "the other half of her act"), were not even trying to resist the music. Then, after a long, sad immobility, they changed roles. Bobby took the languid jaw-writhing part of a limp young man, and the other waif sang false-cockney phrases in a cruel copy of a woman's voice. It was the parody of a parody. George stood tense, waiting for a resolution. His nature demanded that now, and quickly, for the limp sadness of the turn was unbearable, the two false urchins should flash out in some sort of rebellion. But there was nothing. The jazz went on like hammers; the whole room shook—stage, walls, ceiling—and it seemed the people in the room jigged lightly and helplessly. The two children on the stage twisted their limbs into the wilful mockery of a stage convention, and finally stood side by side, hands hanging limp, heads lowered meekly, twitching a little while the music rose into a final crashing discord and the lights went out. George could not applaud. He saw that the damp-faced young man next to him was clapping wildly, while his lank hair fell all over his face. George saw that the older people were all, like himself, bewildered and insulted.

When the show was over, George went backstage to fetch Bobby. She was with "the other half of the act," a rather good-looking boy of about twenty, who was being deferential to the impressive husband of Bobby. George said to her: "You were very good, dear, very good indeed." She looked smilingly at him, half-mocking, but he did not know what it was she was mocking now. And she had been good. But he never wanted to see it again.

The revue was a success and ran for some months before it was moved to a bigger theatre. George finished his production of *Romeo and Juliet,* which, so the critics said, was the best London had seen for many years, and refused other offers of work. He did not need the money for the time being, and besides, he had not seen very much of Bobby lately.

But of course now she was working. She was at rehearsals several times a week, and away from the flat every evening. But George never went to her theatre. He did not want to see the sad, unresisting children twitching to the cruel music.

It seemed Bobby was happy. The various little parts she had played with him—the urchin, the cool hostess, the dear child—had all been absorbed into the hard-working female who cooked him his meals, looked after him, and went out to her theatre giving him a friendly kiss on the cheek. Their relationship was most pleasant and amiable. George lived beside this good friend, his wife Bobby, who was doing him so much credit in every way, and ached permanently with loneliness.

One day he was walking down the Charing Cross Road, looking into the windows of bookshops, when he saw Bobby strolling up the other side with Jackie, the other half of her act. She looked as he had never seen her: her dark face was alive with animation, and Jackie was looking into her face and laughing. George thought the boy very handsome. He had a warm gloss of youth on his hair and in his eyes; he had the lithe, quick look of a young animal.

George was not jealous at all. When Bobby came in at night, gay and vivacious, he knew he owed this to Jackie and did not mind. He was even grateful to him. The warmth Bobby had for "the other half of the act" overflowed toward him; and for some months Myra and his wife were present in his mind, he saw and felt them, two loving presences, young women who loved George, brought into being by the feeling between Jackie and Bobby. Whatever that feeling was.

The Offbeat Revue ran for nearly a year, and then it was coming off, and Bobby and Jackie were working out another act. George did not know what it was. He thought Bobby needed a rest, but he did not like to say so. She had been tired recently, and when she came in at night there was strain beneath her gaiety. Once, at night, he woke to see her beside his bed. "Hold me for a little, George," she asked. He opened his arms and she came into them. He lay holding her, quite still. He had opened his arms to the sad waif, but it was an unhappy woman lying in his arms. He could feel the movement of her lashes on his shoulder, and the wetness of tears.

He had not lain beside her for a long time—years, it seemed. She did not come to him again.

"You don't think you're working too hard, dear?" he asked once, looking at her strained face; but she said briskly, "No, I've got to have something to do, can't stand doing nothing."

One night it was raining hard, and Bobby had been feeling sick that day, and she did not come home at her usual time. George became worried and took a taxi to the theatre and asked the doorman if she was still there. It seemed she had left some time before. "She didn't look too well to me, sir," volunteered the doorman, and George sat for a time in the taxi, trying not to worry. Then he gave the driver Jackie's address; he meant to ask him if he knew where Bobby was. He sat limp in the back of the taxi, feeling the heaviness of his limbs, thinking of Bobby ill.

The place was in a mews, and he left the taxi and walked over rough cobbles to a door which had been the door of stables. He rang, and a young man he didn't know let him in, saying yes, Jackie Dickson was in. George climbed narrow, steep, wooden stairs slowly, feeling the weight of his body, while his heart pounded. He stood at the top of the stairs to get his breath, in a dark which smelled of canvas and oil and turpentine. There was a streak of light under a door; he went toward it, knocked, heard no answer, and opened it. The scene was a high, bare, studio sort of place, badly lighted, full of pictures, frames, junk of various kinds. Jackie, the dark, glistening youth, was seated cross-legged before the fire, grinning as he lifted his face to say something to Bobby, who sat in a chair, looking down at him. She was wearing a formal dark dress and jewelry, and her arms and neck were bare and white. She looked beautiful, George thought, glancing once, briefly, at her face, and then away; for he could see on it an emotion he did not want to recognize. The scene held for a moment before they realized he was there and turned their heads, with the same lithe movement of disturbed animals, to see him standing there in the doorway. Both faces froze. Bobby looked quickly at the young man, and it was in some kind of fear. Jackie looked sulky and angry.

"I've come to look for you, dear," said George to his wife. "It was raining and the doorman said you seemed ill."

"It's very sweet of you," she said and rose from the chair, giving her hand formally to Jackie, who nodded with bad grace at George.

The taxi stood in the dark, gleaming rain, and George and Bobby got into it and sat side by side, while it splashed off into the street.

"Was that the wrong thing to do, dear?" asked George, when she said nothing.

"No," she said.

"I really did think you might be ill."

She laughed. "Perhaps I am."

"What's the matter, my darling? What is it? He was angry, wasn't he? Because I came?"

"He thinks you're jealous," she said shortly.

"Well, perhaps I am rather," said George.

She did not speak.

"I'm sorry, dear, I really am. I didn't mean to spoil anything for you."

"Well, that's certainly *that,*" she remarked, and she sounded impersonally angry.

"Why? But why should it be?"

"He doesn't like—having things asked of him," she said, and he remained silent while they drove home.

Up in the warmed, comfortable old flat, she stood before the fire, while he brought her a drink. She smoked fast and angrily, looking into the fire.

"Please forgive me, dear," he said at last. "What is it? Do you love him? Do you want to leave me? If you do, of course you must. Young people should be together."

She turned and stared at him, a black strange stare he knew well.

"George," she said, "I'm nearly forty."

"But, darling, you're a child still. At least, to me."

"And he," she went on, "will be twenty-two next month. I'm old enough to be his mother." She laughed, painfully. "Very painful, maternal love . . . or so it seems . . . but then how should I know?" She held out her bare arm and looked at it. Then, with the fingers of one hand she creased down the skin of that bare arm toward the wrist, so that the aging skin lay in creases and folds. Then, setting down her glass, her cigarette held between tight, amused, angry lips, she wriggled her shoulders out of her dress, so that it slipped to her waist, and she looked down at her two small, limp, unused breasts. "Very painful, dear George," she said, and shrugged her dress up quickly, becoming again the formal woman dressed for the world. "He does not love me. He does not love me at all. Why should he?" She began singing:

"He does not love me
With a love that is trew. . . ."

Then she said, in stage cockney, "Repeat: I could 'ave bin 'is muvver, see?" And with the old rolling derisive black flash of her eyes she smiled at George.

George was thinking only that this girl, his darling, was suffering now what he had suffered, and he could not stand it. She had been going through this for how long now? But she had been working with that boy for nearly two years. She had been living beside him, George, and he had had no idea at all of her unhappiness. He went over to her, put his old arms around her, and she stood with her head on his shoulder and wept. For the first time, George thought, they were together. They sat by the fire a long time that night, drinking, smoking, and her head

was on his knee and he stroked it, and thought that now, at last, she
had been admitted into the world of emotion and they would learn to
be really together. He could feel his strength stirring along his limbs
for her. He was still a man, after all.

Next day she said she would not go on with the new show. She
would tell Jackie he must get another partner. And besides, the new
act wasn't really any good. "I've had one little act all my life," she said,
laughing. "And sometimes it's fitted in, and sometimes it hasn't."

"What was the new act? What's it about?" he asked her.

She did not look at him. "Oh, nothing very much. It was Jackie's
idea, really. . . ." Then she laughed. "It's quite good really, I
suppose. . . ."

"But what is it?"

"Well, you see . . ." Again he had the impression she did not want
to look at him. "It's a pair of lovers. We make fun . . . it's hard to
explain, without doing it."

"You make fun of love?" he asked.

"Well, you know, all the attitudes . . . the things people say. It's a
man and a woman—with music, of course. All the music you'd expect,
played offbeat. We wear the same costume as for the other act. And
then we go through all the motions. . . . It's rather funny, really. . . ."
She trailed off, breathless, seeing George's face. "Well," she said, suddenly very savage, "if it isn't all bloody funny, what is it?" She turned
away to take a cigarette.

"Perhaps you'd like to go on with it after all?" he asked ironically.

"No. I can't. I really can't stand it. I can't stand it any longer,
George," she said, and from her voice he understood she had nothing
to learn from him of pain.

He suggested they both needed a holiday, so they went to Italy.
They traveled from place to place, never stopping anywhere longer than
a day, for George knew she was running away from any place around
which emotion could gather. At night he made love to her, but she
closed her eyes and thought of the other half of the act; and George
knew it and did not care. But what he was feeling was too powerful
for his old body; he could feel a lifetime's emotions beating through
his limbs, making his brain throb.

Again they curtailed their holiday, to return to the comfortable old flat in London.

On the first morning after their return, she said: "George, you know you're getting too old for this sort of thing—it's not good for you; you look ghastly."

"But, darling, why? What else am I still alive for?"

"People'll say I'm killing you," she said, with a sharp, half-angry, half-amused, black glance.

"But, my darling, believe me . . ."

He could see them both in the mirror; he, an old pursy man, head lowered in sullen obstinacy; she . . . but he could not read her face.

"And perhaps *I'm* getting too old?" she remarked suddenly.

For a few days she was gay, mocking, then suddenly tender. She was provocative, teasing him with her eyes; then she would deliberately yawn and say, "I'm going to sleep. Goodnight George."

"Well of course, my darling, if you're tired."

One morning she announced she was going to have a birthday party; it would be her fortieth birthday soon. The way she said it made George feel uneasy.

On the morning of her birthday she came into his study, where he had been sleeping, carrying his breakfast tray. He raised himself on his elbow and gazed at her, appalled. For a moment he had imagined it must be another woman. She had put on a severe navy blue suit, cut like a man's; heavy black-laced shoes; and she had taken the wisps of black hair back off her face and pinned them into a sort of clumsy knot. She was suddenly a middle-aged woman.

"But, my darling," he said, "my darling, what have you done to yourself?"

"I'm forty," she said. "Time to grow up."

"But, my darling, I do so love you in your nice clothes. I do so love you being beautiful in your lovely clothes."

She laughed, and left the breakfast tray beside his bed, and went clumping out on her heavy shoes.

That morning she stood in the kitchen beside a very large cake, on which she was carefully placing forty small pink candles. But it seemed only the sister had been asked to the party, for that afternoon the three

of them sat around the cake and looked at one another. George looked
at Rosa, the sister, in her ugly, straight, thick suit, and at his darling
Bobby, all her grace and charm submerged into heavy tweed, her hair
dragged back, without makeup. They were two middle-aged women,
talking about food and buying.

George said nothing. His whole body throbbed with loss.

The dreadful Rosa was looking with her sharp eyes around the
expensive flat, and then at George and then at her sister.

"You've let yourself go, haven't you, Bobby?" she commented at
last. She sounded pleased about it.

Bobby glanced defiantly at George. "I haven't got time for all this
nonsense any more," she said. "I simply haven't got time. We're all
getting on now, aren't we?"

George saw the two women looking at him. He thought they had
the same black, hard, inquisitive stare over sharp-bladed noses. He could
not speak. His tongue was thick. The blood was beating through his
body. His heart seemed to be swelling and filling his whole body, an
enormous soft growth of pain. He could not hear for the tolling of the
blood through his ears. The blood was beating up into his eyes, but he
shut them so as not to see the two women.

Richard Bausch

*L*ETTER TO THE LADY OF THE HOUSE

It's exactly twenty minutes to midnight, on this the eve of my seventieth birthday, and I've decided to address you, for a change, in writing—odd as that might seem. I'm perfectly aware of how many years we've been together, even if I haven't been very good about remembering to commemorate certain dates, certain days of the year. I'm also perfectly aware of how you're going to take the fact that I'm doing this at all, so late at night, with everybody due to arrive tomorrow, and the house still unready. I haven't spent almost five decades with you without learning a few things about you that I can predict and describe with some accuracy, though I admit that, as you put it, lately we've been more like strangers than husband and wife. Well, so if we are like strangers, perhaps there are some things I can tell you that you won't have already figured out about the way I feel.

Tonight, we had another one of those long, silent evenings after an argument (remember?) over pepper. We had been bickering all day, really, but at dinner I put pepper on my potatoes and you said that about how I shouldn't have pepper because it always upsets my stomach. I bothered to remark that I used to eat chili peppers for breakfast and if I wanted to put plain old ordinary black pepper on my potatoes, as I had been doing for more than sixty years, that was my privilege. Writing this now, it sounds far more testy than I meant it, but that isn't really the point.

In any case, you chose to overlook my tone. You simply said, "John, you were up all night the last time you had pepper with your dinner."

I said, "I was up all night because I ate green peppers. Not black pepper, but green peppers."

"A pepper is a pepper, isn't it?" you said. And then I started in on you. I got, as you call it, legal with you—pointing out that green peppers are not black pepper—and from there we moved on to an evening of mutual disregard for each other that ended with your decision to go to bed early. The grandchildren will make you tired, and there's still the house to do; you had every reason to want to get some rest, and yet I felt that you were also making a point of getting yourself out of proximity with me, leaving me to my displeasure, with another ridiculous argument settling between us like a fog.

So, after you went to bed, I got out the whiskey and started pouring drinks, and I had every intention of putting myself into a stupor. It was almost my birthday, after all, and—forgive this, it's the way I felt at the time—you had nagged me into an argument and then gone off to bed; the day had ended as so many of our days end now, and I felt, well, entitled. I had a few drinks, without any appreciable effect (though you might well see this letter as firm evidence to the contrary), and then I decided to do something to shake you up. I would leave. I'd make a lot of noise going out the door; I'd take a walk around the neighborhood and make you wonder where I could be. Perhaps I'd go check into a motel for the night. The thought even crossed my mind that I might leave you altogether. I admit that I entertained the thought, Marie. I saw our life together now as the day-to-day round of petty quarreling and tension that it's mostly been over the past couple of years or so, and I wanted out as sincerely as I ever wanted anything.

My God, I wanted an end to it, and I got up from my seat in front of the television and walked back down the hall to the entrance of our room to look at you. I suppose I hoped you'd still be awake so I could tell you of this momentous decision I felt I'd reached. And maybe you were awake: one of our oldest areas of contention being the noise I make—the feather-thin membrane of your sleep that I am always disturbing with my restlessness in the nights. All right. Assuming you were asleep and don't know that I stood in the doorway of our room, I will say that I stood there for perhaps five minutes, looking at you in the half-dark, the shape of your body under the blanket—you really did look like one of the girls when they were little and I used to stand in the doorway of their rooms; your illness last year made you so small again—and, as I said, I thought I had decided to leave you, for your peace as well as mine. I know you have gone to sleep crying, Marie. I know you've felt sorry about things and wished we could find some way to stop irritating each other so much.

Well, of course I didn't go anywhere. I came back to this room and drank more of the whiskey and watched television. It was like all the other nights. The shows came on and ended, and the whiskey began to wear off. There was a little rain shower. I had a moment of the shock of knowing I was seventy. After the rain ended, I did go outside for a few minutes. I stood on the sidewalk and looked at the house. The kids, with their kids, were on the road somewhere between their homes and here. I walked up to the end of the block and back, and a pleasant breeze blew and shook the drops out of the trees. My stomach was bothering me some, and maybe it was the pepper I'd put on my potatoes. It could just as well have been the whiskey. Anyway, as I came back to the house, I began to have the eerie feeling that I had reached the last night of my life. There was this small discomfort in my stomach, and no other physical pang or pain, and I am used to the small ills and side effects of my way of eating and drinking; yet I felt the sense of the end of things more strongly than I can describe. When I stood in the entrance of our room and looked at you again, wondering if I would make it through to the morning, I suddenly found myself trying to think what I would say to you if indeed this *were* the last time I would ever be able to speak to you. And I began to know I would write you this letter.

At least words in a letter aren't blurred by tone of voice, by the old aggravating sound of me talking to you. I began with this and with the idea that, after months of thinking about it, I would at least try to say something to you that wasn't colored by our disaffections. What I have to tell you must be explained in a rather roundabout way.

I've been thinking about my cousin Louise and her husband. When he died and she stayed with us last summer, something brought back to me what is really only the memory of a moment; yet it reached me, that moment, across more than fifty years. As you know, Louise is nine years older than I, and more like an older sister than a cousin. I must have told you at one time or another that I spent some weeks with her, back in 1933, when she was first married. The memory I'm talking about comes from that time, and what I have decided I have to tell you comes from that memory.

Father had been dead four years. We were all used to the fact that times were hard and that there was no man in the house, though I suppose I filled that role in some titular way. In any case, when Mother became ill there was the problem of us, her children. Though I was the oldest, I wasn't old enough to stay in the house alone, or to nurse her, either. My grandfather came up with the solution—and everybody went along with it—that I would go to Louise's for a time, and the two girls would go to stay with Grandfather. You'll remember that people did pretty much what that old man wanted them to do.

So we closed up the house, and I got on a train to Virginia. I was a few weeks shy of fourteen years old. I remember that I was not able to believe that anything truly bad would come of Mother's pleurisy, and was consequently glad of the opportunity it afforded me to travel the hundred miles south to Charlottesville, where cousin Louise had moved with her new husband only a month earlier, after her wedding. Because *we* traveled so much at the beginning, you never got to really know Charles when he was young—in 1933 he was a very tall, imposing fellow, with bright red hair and a graceful way of moving that always made me think of athletics, contests of skill. He had worked at the Navy Yard in Washington, and had been laid off in the first months of Roosevelt's New Deal. Louise was teaching in a day school in Charlottesville so they could make ends meet, and Charles was spending most of his time looking for work and fixing up the house. I had only met Charles once or twice before the wedding, but already I admired him and wanted to emulate him. The prospect of spending time in his house, of perhaps going fishing with him in the small streams of central Virginia, was all I thought about on the way down. And I remember that we did go fishing one weekend, that I wound up spending a lot of time with Charles, helping to paint the house and to run water lines under it for indoor plumbing. Oh, I had time with Louise, too— listening to her read from the books she wanted me to be interested in, walking with her around Charlottesville in the evenings and looking at the city as it was then. Or sitting on her small porch and talking about the family, Mother's stubborn illness, the children Louise saw every day at school. But what I want to tell you has to do with the very first day I was there.

I know you think I use far too much energy thinking about and pining away for the past, and I therefore know that I'm taking a risk by talking about this ancient history, and by trying to make you see it. But this all has to do with you and me, my dear, and our late inability to find ourselves in the same room together without bitterness and pain.

That summer, 1933, was unusually warm in Virginia, and the heat, along with my impatience to arrive, made the train almost unbearable. I think it was just past noon when it pulled into the station at Charlottesville, with me hanging out one of the windows, looking for Louise or Charles. It was Charles who had come to meet me. He stood in a crisp-looking seersucker suit, with a straw boater cocked at just the angle you'd expect a young, newly married man to wear a straw boater, even in the middle of economic disaster. I waved at him and he waved back, and I might've jumped out the window if the train had slowed even a little more than it had before it stopped in the shade of the platform. I made my way out, carrying the cloth bag my grandfather had given me for the trip—Mother had said through her rheum that I looked like a carpetbagger—and when I stepped down to shake hands with Charles I noticed that what I thought was a new suit was tattered at the ends of the sleeves.

"Well," he said. "Young John."

I smiled at him. I was perceptive enough to see that his cheerfulness was not entirely effortless. He was a man out of work, after all, and so in spite of himself there was worry in his face, the slightest shadow in an otherwise glad and proud countenance. We walked through the station to the street, and on up the steep hill to the house, which was a small clapboard structure, a cottage, really, with a porch at the end of a short sidewalk lined with flowers—they were marigolds, I think —and here was Louise, coming out of the house, her arms already stretched wide to embrace me. "Lord," she said. "I swear you've grown since the wedding, John." Charles took my bag and went inside.

"Let me look at you, young man," Louise said.

I stood for inspection. And as she looked me over I saw that her hair was pulled back, that a few strands of it had come loose, that it was brilliantly auburn in the sun. I suppose I was a little in love with her. She was grown, and married now. She was a part of what seemed a great mystery to me, even as I was about to enter it, and of course you remember how that feels, Marie, when one is on the verge of things—nearly adult, nearly old enough to fall in love. I looked at Louise's happy, flushed face, and felt a deep ache as she ushered me into her house. I wanted so to be older.

Inside, Charles had poured lemonade for us and was sitting in the easy chair by the fireplace, already sipping his. Louise wanted to show me the house and the backyard—which she had tilled and turned into a small vegetable garden—but she must've sensed how thirsty I was, and so she asked me to sit down and have a cool drink before she showed me the upstairs. Now, of course, looking back on it, I remember that those rooms she was so anxious to show me were meager indeed. They were not much bigger than closets, really, and the paint was faded and dull; the furniture she'd arranged so artfully was coming apart; the pictures she'd put on the walls were prints she'd cut out—magazine covers, mostly—and the curtains over the windows were the same ones that had hung in her childhood bedroom for twenty years. ("Recognize these?" she said with a deprecating smile.) Of course, the quality of her pride had nothing to do with the fineness—or lack of it—in these things, but in the fact that they belonged to her, and that she was a married lady in her own house.

On this day in July, in 1933, she and Charles were waiting for the delivery of a fan they had scrounged enough money to buy from Sears, through the catalogue. There were things they would rather have been doing, especially in this heat, and especially with me there. Monticello wasn't far away, the university was within walking distance, and without too much expense one could ride a taxi to one of the lakes nearby. They had hoped that the fan would arrive before I did, but since it hadn't, and since neither Louise nor Charles was willing to leave the other alone while traipsing off with me that day, there wasn't anything to do but wait around for it. Louise had opened the windows and shut the shades, and we sat in her small living room and drank the lemonade, fanning ourselves with folded parts of Charles's morning newspaper. From time to time an anemic breath of air would move the shades slightly, but then everything grew still again. Louise sat on the arm of Charles's chair, and I sat on the sofa. We talked about pleurisy and, I think, about the fact that Thomas Jefferson had invented the dumbwaiter, how the plumbing at Monticello was at least a century ahead of its time. Charles remarked that it was the spirit of invention that would make a man's career in these days. "That's what I'm aiming for, to be inventive in a job. No matter what it winds up being."

When the lemonade ran out, Louise got up and went into the kitchen to make some more. Charles and I talked about taking a weekend to go fishing. He leaned back in his chair and put his hands behind his head, looking satisfied. In the kitchen, Louise was chipping ice for our glasses, and she began singing something low, for her own pleasure, a barely audible lilting, and Charles and I sat listening. It occurred to me that I was very happy. I had the sense that soon I would be embarked on my own life, as Charles was, and that an attractive woman like Louise would be there with me. Charles yawned and said, "God, listen to that. Doesn't Louise have the loveliest voice?"

And that's all I have from that day. I don't even know if the fan arrived later, and I have no clear memory of how we spent the rest of the afternoon and evening. I remember Louise singing a song, her husband leaning back in his chair, folding his hands behind his head, expressing his pleasure in his young wife's voice. I remember that I felt quite extraordinarily content just then. And that's all I remember.

But there are, of course, the things we both know: we know they moved to Colorado to be near Charles's parents; we know they never had any children; we know that Charles fell down a shaft at a construction site in the fall of 1957 and was hurt so badly that he never walked again. And I know that when she came to stay with us last summer she told me she'd learned to hate him, and not for what she'd had to help him do all those years. No, it started earlier and was deeper than that. She hadn't minded the care of him—the washing and feeding and all the numberless small tasks she had to perform each and every day, all day—she hadn't minded this. In fact, she thought there was something in her makeup that liked being needed so completely. The trouble was simply that whatever she had once loved in him she had stopped loving, and for many, many years before he died, she'd felt only suffocation when he was near enough to touch her, only irritation and anxiety when he spoke. She said all this, and then looked at me, her cousin, who had been fortunate enough to have children, and to be in love over time, and said, "John, how have you and Marie managed it?"

And what I wanted to tell you has to do with this fact—that while you and I had had one of our whispering arguments only moments before, I felt quite certain of the simple truth of the matter, which is that whatever our complications, we *have* managed to be in love over time.

"Louise," I said.

"People start out with such high hopes," she said, as if I wasn't there. She looked at me. "Don't they?"

"Yes," I said.

She seemed to consider this a moment. Then she said, "I wonder how it happens."

I said, "You ought to get some rest." Or something equally pointless and admonitory.

As she moved away from me, I had an image of Charles standing on the station platform in Charlottesville that summer, the straw boater set at its cocky angle. It was an image I would see most of the rest of that night, and on many another night since.

· · ·

I can almost hear your voice as you point out that once again I've managed to dwell too long on the memory of something that's past and gone. The difference is that I'm not grieving over the past now. I'm merely reporting a memory, so that you might understand what I'm about to say to you.

The fact is, we aren't the people we were even then, just a year ago. I know that. As I know things have been slowly eroding between us for a very long time; we are a little tired of each other, and there are annoyances and old scars that won't be obliterated with a letter—even a long one written in the middle of the night in desperate sincerity, under the influence, admittedly, of a considerable portion of bourbon whiskey, but nevertheless with the best intention and hope: that you may know how, over the course of this night, I came to the end of needing an explanation for our difficulty. We have reached this—place. Everything we say seems rather aggravatingly mindless and automatic, like something one stranger might say to another in any of the thousand circumstances where strangers are thrown together for a time, and the silence begins to grow heavy on their minds, and someone has to say something. Darling, we go so long these days without having anything at all to do with each other, and the children are arriving tomorrow, and once more we'll be in the position of making all the gestures that give them back their parents as they think their parents are, and what I wanted to say to you, what came to me as I thought about Louise and Charles on that day so long ago, when they were young and so obviously glad of each other, and I looked at them and knew it and was happy—what came to me was that even the harsh things that happened to them, even the years of anger and silence, even the disappointment and the bitterness and the wanting not to be in the same room anymore, even all that must have been worth it for such loveliness. At least I am here, at seventy years old, hoping so. Tonight, I went back to our room again and stood gazing at you asleep, dreaming whatever you were dreaming, and I had a moment of thinking how we were always friends, too. Because what I wanted finally to say was that I remember well our own sweet times, our own old loveliness, and I would like to think that even if at the very beginning of our lives together I had somehow been shown that we would end up here, with this longing to be away from each other, this feeling of being trapped together, of being tied to each other in a way that makes us wish for other times, some other place—I would have known enough to accept it all freely for the chance at that love. And if I could, I would do it all again, Marie. All of it, even the sorrow. My sweet, my dear adversary. For everything that I remember.

Biographical Notes

RACHEL INGALLS is the author of *Be My Guest*, two novellas, and *The End of Tragedy*, a short story collection, among other works of fiction.

STEVEN MILLHAUSER is the author of *Edwin Mullhouse*, *Portrait of a Romantic*, *In the Penny Arcade*, and *From the Realm of Morpheus*. He lives with his wife and two children in Saratoga Springs, New York, where he teaches at Skidmore College.

ANDRE DUBUS lives in Haverhill, Massachusetts. He has been a Marine Corps captain, a member of the Iowa Writer's Workshop, a Guggenheim Fellow, and a MacArthur fellow. Among his books are *Selected Stories* and *Charon's Wharf*, an essay collection.

CHARLES BUKOWSKI was born in Andernach, Germany, and raised in Los Angeles. He has published over forty books of poetry and prose, including *Ham on Rye*, *You Get So Alone at Times it Just Makes Sense*, *Hollywood*, and the original screenplay for *Barfly*.

HAROLD BRODKEY was born in 1930 in Staunton, Illinois, grew up in Missouri, and was graduated from Harvard College. He lives in New York City with his wife, novelist Ellen Schwamm. He is the author of two collections of short stories,

First Love and Other Sorrows and *Stories in an Almost Classical Mode*, and a novel, *The Runaway Soul*.

MARY GAITSKILL is the author of *Bad Behavior*, a collection of short stories, and *Two Girls, Fat and Thin*. She lives in northern California and New York City.

JOYCE CAROL OATES has won the National Book Award and the 1990 Rea Award for Achievement in the Short Story. Among her works of fiction are the novels *Black Water* and *Because it is Bitter, and Because it is My Heart*, and the short story collections *Morning and Other Stories* and *Where Is Here?* She lives in Princeton, New Jersey.

WILLIAM KOTZWINKLE is the author of *Fata Morgana*, *Doctor Rat*, *E. T. The Extra-Terrestrial*, *The Midnight Examiner*, *The Exile*, and the short story collections, *Jewel of the Moon* and *The Hot Jazz Trio*, among other works of fiction.

WARD JUST is the author of *21 Stories* and the novels *Jack Gance* and *The American Ambassador*, among several other works of fiction. He was previously a journalist. Originally from Indiana, he and his wife divide their time between Paris and Martha's Vineyard.

GRACE PALEY was born in New York City in 1922. A graduate of Hunter College, she has taught at Columbia University, Syracuse University, and Sarah Lawrence College. She is the author of three collections of short stories: *The Little Disturbances of Man*, *Later the Same Day*, and *Enormous Changes at the Last Minute*.

DAVID LEAVITT is the author of two collections of short stories, *Family Dancing* and *A Place I've Never Been*, and the novels *The Lost Language of Cranes* and *Equal Affections*. He is the recipient of a Guggenheim fellowship and was foreign writer-in-residence at the Institute of Catalan Letters in Barcelona. He lives in East Hampton, New York.

MARIA THOMAS is the author of the novel *Antonia Saw the Oryx First* and the short story collections *Come to Africa and Save Your Marriage* and *African Visa*, which was published posthumously. She lived in Africa for more than seventeen years, spending much of that time in Ethiopia. She died in a plane crash in the summer of 1989, while accompanying Congressman Mickey Leland on a relief mission to refugee camps on the border of Ethiopia and the Sudan.

ALICE WALKER was born in Eatonton, Georgia, and lives in northern California. Her novel, *The Color Purple*, won an American Book Award and a Pulitzer Prize. She is the author of the novel *Possessing the Secret of Joy*.

NADINE GORDIMER was born and lives in South Africa. She has written several novels, including *Burger's Daughter* and *July's People*, and several short story collections, including *Something Out There* and *Jump*. She has won the Booker Prize and was awarded the Nobel Prize for Literature in 1991.

LAURIE COLWIN was born in Chicago and raised in Philadelphia. She lives in New York City. She is the author of several novels and short story collections, including *Another Marvelous Thing*.

JOHN UPDIKE was born in Shillington, Pennsylvania, in 1932. He graduated from Harvard College in 1954 and spent a year in England on the Knox Fellowship, at the Ruskin School of Drawing and Fine Art in Oxford. Since 1957 he has lived in Massachusetts. He is the father of four children and the author of fifteen novels—among them *Rabbit at Rest* and *Memories of the Ford Administration*—numerous short story collections, several volumes of poetry, a memoir, and collected essays and criticism. His fiction has won the Pulitzer Prize, the National Book Award, the American Book Award, and the National Book Critics Circle Award.

EDNA O'BRIEN is the author of five short story collections and twelve novels, among them *The Country Girl*, *A Fanatic Heart*, *Lantern Slides*, and *Time and Tide*. She lives in London.

NORMAN RUSH was born and raised in the San Francisco Bay area. He graduated from Swarthmore College in 1956. He has been an antiquarian bookseller, a college instructor, and, with his wife Elsa, lived and worked in Africa for several years. He is the author of a short story collection, *Whites*, and a novel, *Mating*, which won the 1991 National Book Award.

DORIS LESSING was born of British parents in Persia in 1919. When she was five, her family moved to Southern Rhodesia where she grew up on a farm. She moved to England in 1949 and has lived there ever since. She has written over thirty books, among them *African Stories*, *The Golden Notebook*, and *The Fifth Child*.

RICHARD BAUSCH is the author of four novels, including *Mr. Field's Daughter* and *Violence*, and two story collections, including *The Fireman's Wife and Other Stories*. He lives in Virginia with his wife, Karen, and their five children.

Acknowledgments